THE BLOOD STRAND

Also by Chris Ould and Available from Titan Books

THE KILLING BAY
THE FIRE PIT (FEBRUARY 2018)

THE BLOOD STRAND

A FAROES NOVEL

CHRIS OULD

TITAN BOOKS

The Blood Strand
Mass-market edition ISBN: 9781785656002
Electronic edition ISBN: 9781783297054

Published by Titan Books
A division of Titan Publishing Group Ltd
144 Southwark St, London SE1 0UP

First mass-market edition: November 2017
2 4 6 8 10 9 7 5 3 1

A CIP catalogue record for this title is available from the British Library.

Printed and bound in the United States.

For Nathaniel – best boy

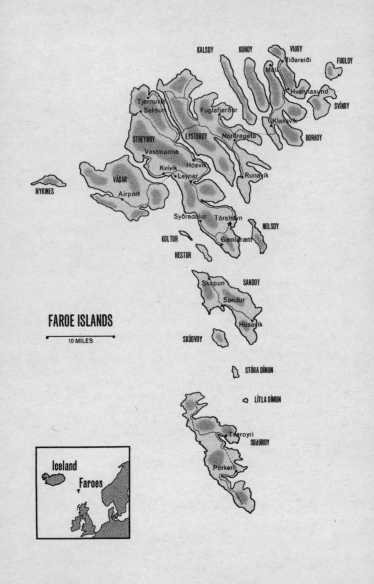

KALSOY   KUNOY   VIÐOY
                            Viðareiði   FUGLOY
                      Múli
                                         SVÍNOY
Tjørnuvík   •Hvannasund
Saksun   Fuglafjørður
                                  Klaksvík
STREYMOY   EYSTUROY   Norðragøta   BORÐOY
Vestmanna
         Kvívík Hósvík
VÁGAR   •Leynar
MYKINES   Runavík
      Airport

         Syðradalur   Tórshavn
                                 NOLSOY
KOLTUR   Gamlarætt

    HESTUR

                 Skopun   SANDOY
                      Sandur

FAROE ISLANDS
                      Húsavík
10 MILES   SKÚGVOY

                         STÓRA DÍMUN

                      • LÍTLA DÍMUN

                              •Tvøroyri
                                 SUÐUROY

                         Porkeri

Iceland

   Faroes

FAROESE PRONUNCIATION

THE FAROESE LANGUAGE IS RELATED TO OLD NORSE AND Icelandic and is spoken by fewer than eighty thousand people worldwide. Its grammar is complicated and many words are pronounced far differently to the way they appear to an English-speaker. As a general rule, ø is a "uh" sound, and the Ð or ð is usually silent, so Fríða would be pronounced "Free-a". *V* is generally pronounced as w; *j* as a y. Hjalti is pronounced "Yalti". In Faroese *harra* means "Mr" and *frú* is "Mrs".

PRELUDE

BY THE TIME HERI KALSØ HAD PAID FOR HIS COFFEE, ANNIKA Mortensen was already outside, leaning on the wing of the patrol car to smoke a cigarette. She sipped her tea between drags and kept her back turned. It could not have been plainer that she did not want or expect Heri to join her.

Watching her through the window of the filling-station shop, Heri Kalsø decided he would stay inside. It was a little after 7 a.m. and in another half an hour they could head back to Tórshavn – in silence, of course – and at last put an end to the shift. Nearly eight hours was a long time to sit in the freezer.

For want of anything better to do, he made a desultory survey of the postcards in a rack by the door: the ubiquitous puffins and sheep and brightly coloured houses against mountainous backdrops. He wondered if he should buy one and write something to Annika. Would she see it as a romantic and contrite gesture? Perhaps not in her current mood. Besides, he had no idea what he would write.

If he was honest, Heri still didn't really see what all

9

the fuss was about. It was only one photograph, after all. Annika looked good in it, and it wasn't like he'd been showing it round the entire station – only to Arne, although in retrospect that probably hadn't been wise. Still, a week should be enough time to get over it, surely.

Outside, Annika Mortensen was unperturbed by the blustery, damp wind, or by the fact that she knew Heri was still feeling unfairly done by. Good. Simply blanking him whenever they passed in the station was satisfying, but being partnered together for the Sunday–Monday night shift gave far more opportunity to make her feelings clear. After this she'd let it go on for a couple more days and then maybe – maybe – she'd reconsider.

"Unit 6, receiving?"

It was Tina, over the radio. Annika answered it before Heri could jump in. "Yes, Tina, we're here."

"Can you go to Tjørnuvík – to the lay-by next to the radio mast on the headland? We've had a 112 call from a Jacob Nybo concerning an unconscious man in a car there. An ambulance is on its way but it's coming from Leirvík, so you're closer."

"Is there a crime?"

"That's unknown at the moment."

Annika exhaled a final plume of smoke, then crushed out her cigarette. "Okay, we'll get there as soon as possible," she told Tina. "Leaving now."

As she discarded her cup in the bin, Heri was coming out of the shop. "I'll drive if you like," he called as he approached. "Give you a break?"

Annika shook her head but said nothing.

Heri gave an exasperated sigh. "*For helviti, Annika…*"

But by then Annika Mortensen was already getting into the driver's seat, leaving no room for discussion.

A little under ten minutes later they pulled in at the lay-by on the eastern headland of Tjørnuvík bay. It was high here – a forty-metre drop more or less straight down to the sea – and the hard-gusting wind rocked a rusty Toyota pickup parked on the gravel.

Annika stopped the patrol car behind the Toyota and saw that it was empty. However, when she and Heri got out of the car there was a shout from a man twenty metres away. He was standing beside the open door of a dark blue BMW 5 Series, parked part way down a slope beneath the level of the road.

What the man had shouted was lost on the stiff breeze, but his gesturing was clear enough and Annika and Heri headed towards him.

The first thing Annika noted was that although the glass from the driver's side window lay in cubes on the gravel, the BMW showed no sign of a collision or accident. The second thing she saw was a white-haired figure slumped, apparently lifeless, over the car's steering wheel.

"*Harra* Nybo? I'm Officer Mortensen, this is Officer Kalsø. Is this the casualty?"

"*Ja*," Nybo nodded vigorously. "I can't tell what's wrong with him. He's unconscious."

Nybo was in his early sixties, wearing work clothes and a woollen hat. Now that police officers had arrived he moved away from the car with some relief, Annika thought.

11

"I'll check him out," Heri said. He'd brought the first-aid kit, so Annika didn't object. She stepped aside with Jacob Nybo instead.

"Can you tell me how you found him?" she asked. "How long ago?"

"Twenty minutes, not much more," Nybo said. "I saw the car here as I came past and I thought it was strange – you know, for this time of the morning. So I stopped to see if it was a breakdown or something, and that's when I saw him. I thought he was asleep but when I banged on the window he still didn't move. I tried the door but it was locked."

"So you broke the window?"

Nybo nodded, slightly reluctant to make the admission. "I wasn't sure if I should, but I didn't know what else to do. I thought he might be dead."

The unconscious man was in his seventies, Heri estimated, with white stubble and slack skin around his jowls. There was a faint carotid pulse and under a suede jacket the man's shoulders moved almost imperceptibly with slow, shallow breaths. On his left temple there was a small graze over a discoloured lump, but nothing serious.

Heri shook the man's shoulder again, a bit more firmly this time, but still not too hard in case there was some injury. "Hello? Can you hear me? I'm a police officer."

Nothing.

By now Annika had approached. She examined the outside of the car for a moment, then bent down for a closer look inside.

"Has he any injuries?" she asked Heri, quickly surveying

the man's torso before her eye was caught by the polished walnut stock of a shotgun. It was propped against the passenger seat, barrels pointing down into the footwell.

"Looks like a bump on his head: nothing much," Heri said. "Why?"

Annika Mortensen stepped back to look at the driver's door again. "Because there's blood here," she said.

"Are you sure?"

Annika cast him a look then keyed her radio. "Control, from Unit 6, do we have anyone from CID free to attend at Tjørnuvík?"

After Haldarsvík the road climbed with the contours of the hillside and afforded Detective Hjalti Hentze a better view across the choppy waters in Sundini Sound. The wind was stronger up here and it broke up the clouds, letting shafts of sunlight race across the far landscape around Eiði and turn the sea a dirty turquoise where it touched.

Hentze was an unpolished man, at least in appearance. Beneath his parka he wore a thick traditional sweater, jeans and solid boots. His hair was cropped short, thinning a little on the crown, and his hands were square and stubby on the steering wheel. Hjalti Hentze had a stolidness and an unhurried temperament which suggested he was someone who would be most at home in a boat or a field, rather than dealing with the subtleties of police investigations.

But Hentze had been a police officer for the last twenty-one years, and in many ways the fact that he didn't look like one was his greatest asset. Many people didn't like talking to the police, but, if they had to, they often preferred speaking to someone like Hentze. Here was a man who wasn't so very different to them, at least on the surface; here was a man who would understand their sensibilities and proceed in a calm, straightforward manner, which – for the most part – Hjalti Hentze did.

Ahead he saw the radio mast and slowed his Volvo before letting it run on to the gravel and come to a halt behind the patrol car. Inside it he saw Annika Mortensen turn her head to look and when she recognised him she raised a hand in greeting and then spoke into her radio.

Hentze forced his door open against the breeze and got out of the car. The wind whistled and moaned discordantly through the rigging and spars of the radio mast, rattling the solar panel and whipping at his coat.

The wind also swirled Annika Mortensen's blonde hair back from her face as she left her own vehicle and came back to meet Hentze. She moved easily and with some grace, despite the bulk of her utility jacket and belt.

"Hey, Hjalti," she said, raising her voice over the wind.

"Hey," Hentze said. "How come you're on your own?"

Annika made a pained expression. "I told Heri to go in the ambulance with the victim. I didn't want him just sitting out here with a face like a cod."

Hentze chuckled. "Things are no better between you two then?"

"No. He's still an arsehole," Annika told him decidedly. She tugged a stray strand of hair from her mouth.

"You'll never change him."

"Who said I want to?"

Hentze laughed again, then turned to look round. "So, what have we got?"

"Over here," Annika said and gestured towards the BMW. "You know whose it is, right?" she asked.

Hentze nodded. "Signar Ravnsfjall. So Ári's very keen that we get the full picture."

Ári Niclasen, the inspector, was a decent guy, although not necessarily the bravest. And because old man Ravnsfjall wasn't without significance in the islands, Niclasen had been keen to impress on Hentze the importance of getting things just right. They needed to be discreet in case the situation turned out to be entirely beyond reproach, but at the same time they should demonstrate an appropriate level of concern in case it was not.

Annika and Hentze walked across to the BMW together as Annika explained how Jacob Nybo had found the car and its occupant and had broken the window with a rock. When she'd finished she waited as Hentze assessed the shattered window glass on the gravel chippings in front of them.

"The doors were locked?" he asked. "I mean, he did try them *before* he smashed the window?"

"So he said."

"Right," Hentze nodded. Then: "What about the blood?"

"Here," Annika said, stepping forward to indicate a pattern of smooth, reddish-brown splashes across the upper part of the door panel. Hentze moved in to look more closely, squatted down and squinted until he remembered his new reading glasses. He dug them out of his coat and perched them on his nose, then looked again.

The largest splash marks were near the top of the panel, but none of them was bigger than a one-króna coin. Lower down on the door the splashes were smaller, angled downwards towards the back of the car. Hentze was pretty sure the splashes *were* blood, though there was always a chance that it wasn't human.

For a moment he considered the car as it stood, then he asked, "Who identified the casualty as Signar Ravnsfjall?"

"I found a wallet in his pocket before the paramedics took him away," Annika said. "And I've checked the car registration. It's his."

"Did he have any injuries?"

"He has a graze on his head and also on a knee where his trousers are torn, but nothing that would have left blood splashes like that. The paramedics think he could have fallen out here, then had a stroke or maybe a heart attack once he got back in the car. He could have been here all night."

"Will he live, do they think?"

Annika shrugged. "Sounded as if it might be touch and go."

Hentze nodded, digesting that, then searched his pockets for latex gloves and pulled them on before moving to look inside the car.

Of course, the paramedics as well as Jacob Nybo had all been in contact with the interior and exterior of the car to varying degrees, but just the same Hentze was careful to disturb things as little as possible before he'd decided what they were dealing with.

He opened the driver's door and looked around, noting the fact that Signar Ravnsfjall kept the interior of his car spotlessly clean. The cream-leather driver's seat was stained by urine and faeces now, though, and the footwell was littered with cubes of broken window glass.

Changing position, Hentze reached for the ignition key and checked its position: off. He turned it to first position and the console lit up. The fuel warning sign was illuminated, too, and when he looked at the petrol gauge it was on empty.

"Was the ignition on or off when you got here?"

"On. Heri turned it off for safety, but there's no fuel. I thought maybe the engine had ticked over all night until it ran out."

"Or he pulled in here *because* he ran out of fuel," Hentze said, although he was inclined to think Annika's was the more likely scenario.

Extricating himself from the car, Hentze moved round to the passenger side and checked the glove box – mints, a packet of tissues – and then opened the back door to look at the shotgun which lay, broken open, on the seat. Two cartridges were still in place and when he looked more closely he saw the indentation of the firing pin in one of the brass caps but not the other.

"You said the gun was in the front when you got here?" he asked Annika.

"Yeah, in the passenger footwell. I made it safe and moved it into the back," she told him. "I used gloves."

"Good. We'll bag it up for Technical. Has anyone checked the boot?"

"Not that I know of."

Hentze moved round to the rear of the car, searched for the boot catch for a moment, then sprang the lid. Inside, the carpeted lining was as spotless as the rest of the car, the only contents a cheap, faux-leather attaché case with a plastic handle. Hentze drew it towards him, then flicked the catches open. When he lifted the lid he saw several neat bundles of thousand-krónur notes held together with paper bands. There were at least twenty of them.

By his shoulder Annika Mortensen let out a low whistle. "Bloody hell," she said. "I knew the Ravnsfjalls were loaded, but to drive around with that much in the boot… There could be over a million there."

Hjalti Hentze had made the same calculation. He looked for a moment longer, then closed the lid of the attaché case and snapped the catches. He thought about Ári Niclasen's desire to play it safe.

"We'll need some evidence bags," he said. "And we'd better get the car taken in so it can be properly examined."

"You think there *was* a crime?"

"Do you?"

Annika Mortensen assessed the car for a moment. "I don't know. But it's bloody strange, whatever happened."

Hentze nodded. "I think so, too. So for the time being I think we'll do this by the book."

PART ONE

1

Tuesday/týsdagur

I DIDN'T SEE MUCH AS THE PLANE CAME IN TO VÁGAR airport. There was low cloud and I was seated over a wing. Once we'd landed I filed along the aisle with everyone else, down the metal steps and across to the terminal. There was no hurry.

Most of the other passengers seemed to be Faroese or Danish; dressed for business, or at least as if air travel was still a reason to turn out smartly. I hadn't gone that far, and I wondered if it set me apart to a passing glance, or whether the layers of foreignness I'd accrued over thirty-odd years were enough to cover the base metal beneath.

When I was a teenager it had been a conscious effort to adopt all those layers, taking on a new skin, covering any differentness. But it went back further than that, went deeper.

According to Ketty – my aunt – I'd refused to speak for the first three months I was with them. I was five years old – just – and when I finally broke my silence it was only in

English, refusing to acknowledge Faroese, or even Danish.

This was a product of trauma, the child psychologist had told Ketty and Peter, apparently. I don't remember, but I'd always thought it was probably more simple than that. Even aged five I'd have known I would never go back, so why cling to the language? Why single myself out with a name no one would pronounce in the right way? Only Ketty still sounded my first name with a Y, and who in England could be bothered to put an accent on Reyná?

Jan Reyna was easier. Jan Reyna was who I was.

When I'd arrived at their house, the day before I'd flown back to the Faroes, Ketty was on the phone. She was speaking Faroese and only looked up for a moment – enough to register I was there – before looking away to write something on a pad.

In the kitchen I found Peter. We shook hands, hugged and stepped back. Always the way.

Peter Sherland was sixty-eight, still a vigorous man with a grey-black goatee. *Daily Telegraph* crossword, Radio 4, three swims a week and the first signs of Parkinson's in the slight tremor of his left hand.

"I'm glad you came," he said. "Ketty's trying to find out more from the hospital – in Tórshavn," he added, although it was unnecessary.

I nodded – acknowledgement, but also a way of showing I didn't want to get into it yet. Peter took the hint.

"Coffee?" he asked.

"Yeah, thanks."

He moved to the coffee maker. This was the way Peter dealt with situations of whatever size – taking his time, never rushing into an opinion or judgement – unlike Ketty, who was always one for instinctive direct action. She made up her mind and spoke it, rarely backing down afterwards.

I knew I'd acquired a mixture of these traits, but it was Peter's way I'd always admired and aspired to, even when I heard myself speaking as Ketty would do. Maybe seeking to be like Peter was just a way of trying to show my appreciation for what he'd done: taking me in, the adoption, and then putting up with all the shit that came later. I still didn't know what it had cost him to suddenly have that troubled boy as part of his life. I'd never been able to ask, either. Instead I just tried to be measured.

"Did you have any trouble getting away?" Peter asked. He ferried two espressos to the kitchen table – one at a time because of his tremor.

"No, they can manage," I told him, momentarily regretting the lie.

He nodded, sat down. "Anything you can say?" Ever the solicitor.

I made a half shrug. "Not much. They made an arrest but there's not enough to charge yet."

He sipped his coffee.

"So listen—" he began, changing tone. But before he could finish, Ketty came into the kitchen.

I went over and kissed her on the cheek. She was still

a striking woman – high cheekbones, grey-blonde hair cut on an angle, blue eyes given to smiling, although they were serious now. She kissed me back, then stepped away.

"You have to go, Jan," she said without any preamble.

I wondered if I heard more of an accent now because she'd just been speaking her own language on the phone.

"What did they say?"

I moved back to my seat: a way to distance myself from the response.

"That he's seriously ill. It was a large stroke."

"Will he die?"

"They won't say that." She shook her head. "But when I said I was ringing for his son they said that they think his relatives should come."

I wondered if all hospitals adopted the same standard euphemisms.

"I can't do anything," I said.

"That's not the point." For a second her tone was annoyed, as if I was being wilfully stupid. "Not to go now…"

She was still standing and I knew she wouldn't sit down. That was what she was like. She'd stand firm until she got what she wanted or I left. There wouldn't be any compromise.

"I can't just pick up and leave," I said. Another lie.

"They won't let you go even if your father might die?" Her turn to be wilfully obtuse.

"Ketty—" Then I shook my head, negating it. "You can't bully me into going," I said. "Why the hell would I? I wouldn't even be thinking about it if he'd died."

That was true. Why go back, just to stand at a graveside?

But Signar Ravnsfjall wasn't dead. He was in limbo; at some halfway point on the scale, like the questions that had always been there, not yet asked or answered. The "yet" implied there was still time for it, but I doubted that. So why go back just to stand at a bedside?

"If Signar was dead it would be too late," Ketty said. "It would be different. Now you have a choice."

"I can live with that."

"Good. You'll have to." She said it with a decided nod: flat.

"Ketty…" Peter's tone was mildly reproachful.

But Ketty wouldn't shift. "You'll never know unless you see him."

"I don't need to know."

"Yes, you do. You don't see it – maybe you don't want to see it – but I do."

I drew a slow breath. In an interview room I usually know when the suspect across the table has reached the turning point. There will be a pause – the moment of balance – and if their next words are anything other than "no comment" you know that the truth will come out. It might still be slow or grudging, but the path has been chosen.

My own "no comment" would be to turn away now, pick up and go.

"I tried before," I said.

She shook her head. "You were seventeen," she said. "Try again."

* * *

Once the baggage carousel started to move my holdall appeared relatively quickly and I towed it past non-existent passport control and customs checks, then through the entrance hall to emerge from the low terminal building. Outside, people were already dispersing to cars and minibuses, but I paused under the overhanging shelter, wanting to give myself a moment of adjustment before moving on.

There was a sense of altitude here, and between breaks in the low, rolling grey cloud the sun glistened off the car park's wet tarmac. The air was cool, cold even, after the unseasonal September heat I'd been used to in England. The wind shepherded the clouds quickly across the bowl of sky between the undulating, rounded peaks of the surrounding mountains and fells. The landscape was treeless, brown-green. In places it was traced out by black strata of rock, as if the long-buried bones of the hills were gradually being exposed by erosion. I knew the feeling.

The second taxi I approached – a minivan – was free and I sat in the back behind the driver as a signal that I didn't want to talk. Instead I checked my phone as the van pulled out of the airport, then settled to watch the passing terrain: sculpted and weathered, often crossed by water in streams and cascades.

The smooth, sweeping road gave a sense of plunging through the landscape as if on a theme-park ride and I got the same feeling of make-believe when I looked at the villages and settlements as they passed, laid out in the valleys and inlets. The buildings were painted in primary colours, saturated by the patchy sunlight, as simple and angular as illustrations from a child's storybook. There was an underlying otherness to it all, it felt to me then – a vague foreignness that was hard to define, but a sense of uneasy familiarity, too.

Where from?

Was it a real recollection, or a memory of a childhood picture book? Either would have to have come from the time before Lýdia took me away from the islands, but now, as ever, I couldn't penetrate the void of childhood – not of living here, not of the first years in England. It was too far away and in the end I left it alone and simply watched the landscape going past, with no fixed point of reference and no sense of home. Because it wasn't.

2

BY THE TIME THE TAXI REACHED TÓRSHAVN THE BRIGHT patches of sunshine had given way to a grey drizzle. I persuaded the driver to wait while I dropped off my bags at the Hotel Streym, and then to take me on to the hospital. When we pulled up outside the block-like building I paid the driver off with crisp Danish notes from a bureau de change envelope and went in through sliding glass doors to look for the main desk.

The visiting hour had just started, I was told, and after getting directions, I took the lift to the third floor, navigating the Faroese signs as best I could until I reached a nurses' station and asked where I could find Signar Ravnsfjall.

The nurse was in her late twenties and took a moment to think herself into English. "I'm sorry, the visiting hour is for the family only," she said.

"I'm his son," I told her. "From England."

I knew that the last bit was clumsy: an attempt to distance myself from the claim of kinship and hold it at arm's length for a little while longer. "Ah. Okay," the nurse said. "At the moment the family are with him. Perhaps I can tell them you're here. You can come to the visiting room."

I followed her round a corner on to a corridor where she showed me into a glass-fronted room with firm-looking sofas and a view of the harbour. Leaving me there she went off, further along the corridor, but after a moment I returned to the doorway and waited. I didn't want to sit.

A couple of minutes later the nurse came out of a side room and returned along the corridor, passing me with a smile. Behind her I saw a man emerge from the room she'd just left. He cast a glance around, then headed towards me.

I knew without doubt who the man was. Magnus Ravnsfjall was in his late thirties and his resemblance to Signar was unmistakable. Father and son shared the same heavy-set, square build, the same slightly broad features and coarse hair, and watching him now I realised that Magnus was only a few years younger than Signar had been the last time I saw him. It gave me an odd sense that somehow time had sprung outwards, as if it had been compressed under pressure until now.

"Eg eiti Magnus Ravnsfjall. Hvat vilt tú her?"

Even though I didn't know what he was saying, the brisk, businesslike tone left no doubt that Magnus Ravnsfjall felt he was here to confront a disagreeable task.

I shook my head. "Sorry, I don't understand."

Coming to a halt Magnus looked at me more suspiciously. "I'm Magnus Ravnsfjall," he said.

"Jan Reyna." I held out my hand but Magnus ignored it.

"What is it you want here?"

For a moment I let the question hang, just long enough to show I wasn't impressed by the hostility. "I came to see your father," I said.

He frowned then, as if finally pinning down a deceit. "He is your father also," he said.

"Not really."

I shook my head, but if I'd hoped it might allay some of his suspicion, I was wrong. Instead it seemed to have the opposite effect as he set his shoulders, like an icebreaker that would plough its way through any opposition. And again I was struck by the similarity between him and his father. My lasting impression of Signar was as a bull of a man.

"There is nothing for you here," Magnus said then, as if he wanted to put the matter to rest once and for all.

Again, I shook my head, trying to get out of this groove and to relocate the exchange somewhere more neutral. "I don't want anything," I told him. "I got a message that he was seriously ill and—"

"Who was that from?"

"The message?"

"Yes."

"Does it matter?"

Along the corridor I became aware of another person – a woman, blonde, seemingly hesitant to intrude. That was all I saw in the short glance I made before turning back to Magnus.

"Listen, I don't want to interfere – that wasn't why I came."

"So I ask again," Magnus insisted. "What is it you want?"

"Just to visit, that's all."

"You don't see him for more than twenty years and now you arrive from nowhere? Why?" It was insistent and stubborn.

I started to draw a breath, but even as I did so I'd suddenly had enough of him. His intransigence made no sense, but more than that it was ridiculous, self-defeating. So instead I made a gesture, dismissive. "Okay, forget it," I said, turning away. "I'll come back later."

As I turned and started down the corridor Magnus said something in Faroese but I took no notice and kept going. At the end of the corridor I rounded the corner to the desk where the nurse was speaking on the phone.

While I waited for her to finish I made a conscious effort to settle my annoyance – as much at myself for not handling it better as at Magnus Ravnsfjall's obstinacy. But what had I expected – just to walk into a hospital room, take a look at Signar, lying there unconscious, and then simply walk away? Or had I had some child-like belief that there would have been a miraculous recovery, enabling him to... *what*?

The nurse hung up the phone.

"I'd like to speak to Sig— to my father's doctor about his condition," I said. "Is that possible?"

"I'm sorry, Dr Heinason isn't here now. Tomorrow, perhaps, you could call?"

"Could you give me the number?"

"Sure, of course."

She found a pad and wrote out a number, then handed

it to me. "We think he is better today," she added, as if in consolation. "A little."

I nodded. "Thank you. *Takk*."

I put the slip of paper in my wallet and headed away towards the lifts. When I got there I pressed the call button, then crossed to a window overlooking the car park below.

"Jan?" A woman's voice.

I turned, but not quickly.

"Yes?"

She was watching me with a faint crease of concern between her eyebrows, something that didn't lift entirely as I faced her. She was tall – maybe five ten – and dressed mostly in black and grey – trousers, boots, a large chunky-knit cardigan. Her blonde hair was pulled back in a ponytail and her features were strikingly Scandinavian with something of a determined set to her jaw. I guessed she was a little older than me, but knew it would take a while to be sure.

"I'm Fríða," she said, clearly expecting the name to be familiar to me.

"I'm sorry, I—"

"Fríða Sólsker," she said. Then by way of explanation: "My mother is Signar's sister, Estur."

I made the connection then. Estur Sólsker was the name Ketty most often quoted as her source of news or information from the Faroes, telling me despite my unwillingness to listen. And it had been Estur Sólsker who had called Ketty with the news of Signar's stroke.

"Yes, sorry. Of course," I said.

Fríða shook her head, dismissing the apology as unnecessary. She held out a slim hand, two silver rings, and her handshake was firm and warm.

"I remember you a little from when you lived here," she said. "Not much, just – er – *bits and pieces.*"

"I don't remember any of it," I said. "Not really."

She nodded, as if she thought that was possible. "You were a little younger than me," she said. "And it was a long time ago."

"Yeah."

She looked at me for a second, again as if she was assessing something, then she said, "I saw you speaking to Magnus."

"Right." Flat and dry.

"This is difficult for him. He's close to Signar and this has happened suddenly. They thought he might die."

"You don't need to explain," I said. It came out more pointed than I'd intended but Fríða just nodded.

"Do you know how he is?" I asked then. "Have you seen him?"

"Yes, for a short time. He's very sick, but maybe not so much as before. He has strength."

"Right." Again.

Beside us the lift arrived and as the doors opened Fríða seemed to decide something. "There's a café here," she said. "Would you like to have coffee?"

I hesitated, then nodded. "Sure."

The café was only moderately busy, a double-height space with a right-angle wall of glass which looked inland, over functional buildings on a hillside. We took our drinks to a circular aluminium table near the windows and sat on pale wood and steel chairs.

It seemed that, like me, Fríða Sólsker had decided to wait until we were seated before saying anything meaningful. It suited me. I wasn't used to thinking in terms of family connections and I needed time to adjust to thinking of Fríða Sólsker as my cousin.

She poured a single sachet of sugar into her black coffee and stirred it before looking up at me with a faintly apologetic smile. "I'm sorry," she said. "I think I have the advantage."

"How do you mean?"

"I think I might know more about you than the other way round. My mother told me you were coming but I didn't think you would arrive until later or I would have warned Magnus."

"Did he need to be warned?"

Fríða had an agile face and I saw the reaction to my abrasiveness. "Maybe that isn't the right word," she said. "I meant so he could get used to the idea. I don't think it's easy to meet a brother for the first time."

"Half-brother."

"Yes. Of course."

She conceded the point without issue and I knew I'd sounded unnecessarily pedantic. I made another effort to rein in my mood. Fríða had done nothing to deserve my poor mood, and she didn't have to be sitting across from me now.

"So, how long can you stay?" she asked. I knew she was giving me a way out.

"A few days – it depends. I'm not sure it was a good idea to come at all, though."

She shook her head. "Of course you should see him."

"You think I should fight my way in past Magnus?"

She seemed to consider that as a serious idea for a moment, then said, "Maybe I can help. I work here in the hospital some of the time, so if you would like to see Signar outside the visiting hours I think I can arrange it."

"What do you do?" The easy way to put off an acceptance or commitment.

"I'm a counsellor, mostly with children and young people," she said, but I hadn't distracted her from her original proposal. "So if you like I can ask Dr Heinason to meet you. He's Signar's consultant."

I knew I should accept the offer, not least because it would deal with everything at one time. The doctor could tell me the medical diagnosis, I could stand at the bedside and then I could leave. I'd have done what I came to do and there would be no need to cross paths with anyone else.

"Maybe that would be better," I said in the end. "If it's not a problem for you."

"No, not at all. Let me see what I can arrange with Hans – Dr Heinason – and then I can call you. Do you have a mobile phone number?"

"Sure." I searched out my wallet and took a card from it: work issue, but the only sort I had. "Thank you. I appreciate it."

35

Fríða looked at the card, but then seemed to decide to leave closer scrutiny until later. She put it away.

"So what else do you know?" I said then, leaving it open.

"About you?" She made a self-deprecating shrug. "Not really so much. My mother talks to Ketty and they tell each other their news. Some of it she tells me, but I don't always pay as much attention as she'd like."

She smiled as she said it and I nodded, letting myself relax a little. "I don't pay *any* attention," I said. "That's why Ketty stopped bothering years ago."

"We must disappoint them."

"I know I do."

I sipped my coffee and used it as a way to change the subject. "Do you know Magnus well?" I asked. "Are you friends?"

"No, I wouldn't say that," Fríða said, considering it seriously. "Of course, we are cousins, but I know Kristian a little better. His younger brother?" She looked at me to gauge my reaction, as if realising she'd made an assumption about how familiar I was with the family tree.

"Yeah, I know," I said, then I let a trace of amusement show through. "You can't help absorbing *some* information even if you're not interested."

"You're not interested in your family?"

She handled it deftly, with just the right lightness of tone. But I spent too much of my life planting my own leading questions to walk into that one. Unwilling to sound pedantic again I left my reflex answer unspoken. Instead I just shrugged and said, "How much did you hear of what Magnus said in the corridor?"

If she was disappointed that I'd dodged her question she didn't show it. "A little."

"So do you know what he meant when he said, 'There's nothing for you here'?"

"Perhaps." She hesitated, for the first time seemingly less at ease. "Do you know of Four Fjords?"

I shook my head. "No, what is it?"

"It's Signar's business. Fishing, salmon farms, fish processing, that sort of thing."

"I never thought about what he does or did for a living," I told her. "I knew it was something to do with fishing, but that's all. Is it a big company?"

"*Ja*, one of the biggest here. Signar is a wealthy man."

It was a new perspective on him – one that I hadn't even considered before. "So you think Magnus is worried that I came here to try and – what? Get money from Signar? Grab an inheritance if he dies?"

"No, I don't know that," Fríða said, quickly. "But as I said, this hasn't been an easy time for him. I'm sure he was surprised to see you, and after the way that Signar was found…"

"What way?"

Her hand paused on its way to her cup. "Oh. I thought you knew. He was found unconscious in his car at a place called Tjørnuvík. The police think he was there all night after his stroke, but no one knows why."

"Why he'd gone there?"

She nodded and because she didn't speak I knew that wasn't all of it.

"What else?" I asked.

She hesitated for a moment longer. "I was told there was a large amount of money in the car. Also a shotgun, and someone's blood."

It wasn't the answer I'd expected, although I didn't know what I *had* been expecting. Just not that.

Fríða watched me, as if she was concerned about what I might do with the information.

"Are the police investigating?" I asked, sitting back in my chair.

"*Ja*, I think so. Yesterday Magnus told me they had asked if anyone in the family knew why Signar was at Tjørnuvík, but I don't know more than that."

I nodded, still thinking it through, but before I could take it any further Fríða shifted and looked at her watch.

"I'm sorry, I have an appointment in a few minutes."

"No, of course," I said. "I appreciate you taking the time to talk to me."

"It's no problem." She said it as if it was to be expected and I believed her. "I will call you when I've talked to Hans about Signar. It will probably be the morning. Is that okay?"

"Sure," I said. "Thank you."

We stood up together. I picked up my coat but as I made to step aside Fríða hung back for a second. "Can I ask why you didn't tell Magnus how you knew Signar was ill?" she said.

I shrugged. "I didn't think it was any of his business."

"And you were annoyed with him."

"Yeah, that too."

She dipped her head, as if that much was cleared up. "I'll show you the way out," she said.

3

OUTSIDE THE HOSPITAL I GOT LUCKY AND PICKED UP A TAXI that had just dropped off a pair of elderly women with fixed chins and woollen coats. They linked arms and clung to each other as they went towards the building's entrance.

Back at the Hotel Streym I reclaimed my bags from the office and the manager – a neatly bearded guy in his thirties – waved away any need for form filling: my online booking was enough. He gave me a room key. "And there is a message for you," he said, handing me a slip of paper. "It was left by telephone about ten minutes ago."

I hadn't told anyone where I was staying, so getting a message was odd and I frowned at the paper: *Mr Reyna, please contact Kristian Ravnsfjall.* Beneath that there was a phone number and the time of the call.

News obviously travelled fast in the Ravnsfjall family – at least between my half-brothers – and I wondered if Kristian wanted to pick up where Magnus had left off with the warm welcome.

I thanked the manager, shoving the note in my pocket,

then I hauled my bag round the corner and up the tiled stairs.

My room was on the second floor along a windowless corridor. Inside it was clean and neat, two single beds and an Ikea-style desk. I hadn't wanted any more.

I hefted my holdall on to the bed nearest the window and dropped my coat next to it. The travelling had left me tired and the instinct to give in to the weariness – to simply stop the progress of the day – was strong. But I knew I wouldn't settle yet. Instead I sat down at the desk and used my mobile to dial the number on the message.

"*Ja? Kristian Ravnsfjall.*" His voice sounded brisk.

"This is Jan Reyna. You left a message for me at my hotel."

There was a moment's hesitation, then Kristian Ravnsfjall's voice shifted from neutral to more upbeat. "Jan, yes. Thank you for calling. When I knew you were here I thought I should make contact. I was hoping we could meet. Would that be all right?"

"Sure, if you like," I said.

If he registered the ambivalence in my voice he didn't let it show. Instead his tone seemed determinedly enthusiastic. After Magnus, it wasn't what I expected. "Great," he said. "Tonight? For a drink? Would that be okay?"

For a second I debated whether I wanted to meet two Ravnsfjall half-brothers in the same day, but in the end I said, "Fine. When and where?"

I jotted down the name of the place he told me and when he rang off I sat back, rubbed my eyes and looked out of the window. I ought to let Ketty know I'd arrived, but it would wait – an email, later; show I was a big boy, off on my own.

Beyond the road and the thin margin of land directly in front of the hotel there was a light blue sky over the choppy waters of a sound. In the distance a cluster of houses in the hollow back of a low island caught broken shreds of sunshine ahead of a more threatening sky. I had no idea what the island was called but I watched the light travel over the pretty-as-a-picture, make-believe little houses and wondered if the occupants knew that in reality they lived on a God-forsaken, rain-driven grey speck in the middle of the ocean that no one in the real world even knew existed, let alone gave a shit about...

And then, like a vignette round the edge of my thoughts, I recognised the faint loss of colour and nuance in what I was thinking and seeing. Usually I was ready to catch it at the first signs and portents, but this time it had come out of nowhere, or else I'd just been too distracted to notice the deepening greyness closing in. It had found a crack or a crevice to seep in through and now it was already spreading like a stain.

With a physical effort I made myself move then, standing and turning away from the window, knowing that if I didn't do it now I'd lose my chance. I needed an anchor to pull myself out; something I could fix on. I needed movement, and even as I recognised that, I was taking up my coat again, leaving the room and quickening my pace to try to step ahead of the black dog.

* * *

Hjalti Hentze was the only detective in CID who didn't have to share an office. His room was small – perhaps originally intended to be a store of some kind – but he'd been lucky enough to bag it when the station had transferred from the old building on Jónas Broncks gøta four years ago.

The plan for the reorganisation had been to put two CID officers in each of the new departmental offices, which all led off the same corridor. But this neat doubling up had not taken account of the fact that when the move occurred there was an odd number of detectives, which meant someone would be left alone in an office designed for two.

This mismatch had caused some upset to the plans of Inspector Remi Syderbø – who generally liked things as tidy as possible within his department – until Hentze had nobly volunteered to occupy the smaller space that no one else wanted. And wouldn't that also leave the larger office to serve a better purpose – a conference room, say? Weren't they a little short of those on the third floor?

So Hentze ended up with a small office to himself, and because the space was restricted he knew no one could be put in there with him at some later date. What did they call it – future-proofing? Hentze was the odd man out and that was how he preferred it. All this modern sharing was fine as far as it went, but he always suspected that it led to a certain uniformity of thinking and a naturally conservative consensus. A good way to keep your organisation running smoothly, perhaps, but a crap way of doing police work.

"Hjalti, are you busy?"

Ári Niclasen stood in the doorway of Hentze's office, a slightly harried expression on his face. The inspector was a tall man – a fishing rod – with a heavy lick of dark hair that always threatened to fall forward. Unlike Hentze, Ári Niclasen usually wore a suit – as he was doing today – or else something neatly casual but conservative. He was ten years younger than Hentze and occupied a spacious office with a view towards Nólsoy. He had also installed a new espresso machine, Hentze had noted somewhat enviously on his last visit there.

"No, just the usual," Hentze said, turning away from his keyboard. "Is there a problem?"

"I'm not sure. Hendrik has a British detective inspector called Reyna downstairs. He showed Hendrik his ID – he's on their homicide squad – and he's asking to see the officer in charge of the Ravnsfjall case."

"Is it official business?" Hentze asked, though he couldn't see how it would be.

Niclasen shook his head. "No. He says he's Signar Ravnsfjall's son."

Hentze sensed the discomfort this caused Ári, but couldn't tell whether it was because the man Reyna was a homicide detective or because he was related to Signar Ravnsfjall.

"I thought there were only two sons," Hentze said.

"So did I," Ári nodded. "And he doesn't speak Faroese apparently, but that's what he said."

He shifted uneasily, then made a vague gesture to Hentze's computer. "How are we doing on that – the Signar Ravnsfjall case? Did you turn up anything more?"

Hentze shook his head. "No one knows what he was doing out at Tjørnuvík and he's still in no condition to tell us what happened. But with no direct evidence of a crime taking place – and certainly none of robbery – I don't think there's much more we can do."

"Anything from Technical?"

"Not yet."

Still clearly uncomfortable, Niclasen pushed his hair lick back and made a decision. "Okay, will you do me a favour and talk to this guy Reyna? Give him the facts as you've just outlined them and see if there's anything we should – *consider*? Is that okay?"

Hentze nodded and stood up. "Sure," he said. "I don't mind that."

It might be an interesting insight on the Ravnsfjall family, too, he decided, but he didn't say so to Ári. The man looked unsettled enough as it was.

A uniformed officer with a square jaw and equally square shoulders showed me into a conference room on the second floor of the anonymous, flat-faced office block and asked me to wait. I'd walked past the building twice before spotting the small *Politi* logo on a sign by the uninviting front door. From the outside the place looked more like a tax office in Doncaster.

The conference room was furnished with two beech-effect tables pushed together in the centre, surrounded by half a dozen padded chairs. The partition walls were bare except for a poster-sized map of the islands and the place had the depersonalised feel of a space that didn't belong to anyone. There was no indication that it even belonged to a police station except for the two marked patrol cars in the car park outside.

I stood beside the window looking out at the cars for a while after the uniformed officer had left but there wasn't much to keep my attention. I didn't want to sit down, I didn't even want to be standing still, so when I'd taken all the distraction the car park had to offer I moved to study the map instead.

Set out brown-green against the sea's blue, the islands looked somehow Palaeolithic, like a shattered flint arrowhead laid out on a cloth, partially reconstructed. The names were all unfamiliar, leaving me to guess how to pronounce them in some cases, but even so I examined them all, traced roads and coastline. Anything to distract myself. I could feel the greying vignette withdrawing a little, but it wasn't gone yet.

Just as I was starting to get restless again, the door opened and this time a man in a dark-blue sweater and jeans came in. My first impression was that he was nearing fifty – if he hadn't already passed it – and although he came into the room with a casual familiarity, I also got the sense that it wasn't an entirely natural environment for him.

"Inspector Reyna? I'm Hjalti Hentze, CID."

I moved away from the map and shook the hand he offered: square and dry. "Thanks for seeing me," I said. "Is it Inspector or Sergeant...?"

Hentze waved the question away. "Here we don't worry so much about the ranks. In Denmark, yes, but in the Faroes no one is concerned. You are *ein politistur* – a police officer – and it's enough. Please."

He gestured me to sit, then moved to take the seat opposite, dropping heavily into the chair. His English wasn't bad – not quite as fluent as Fríða Sólsker's, but good enough that I knew he'd sidestepped the question about rank rather than just misunderstood it.

"I am told you wish to ask about Signar Ravnsfjall. He's your father?"

I nodded, wondering how many more times I'd have to reaffirm the connection. "Yes."

"But your last name is Reyna?"

"My mother's maiden name, except she used to spell it with an accent," I told him. "We left here when I was three."

"Ah. Okay," Hentze said, as if that put it out of the way. "So, what can I tell you?"

I made an effort to sound relaxed rather than inquisitorial. "I was told there was an investigation into the way Signar was found, so I wanted to ask about that – why you thought it was necessary. Is that possible?"

Hentze nodded. "Sure, I don't see why not."

He looked away for a moment, as if to order the information in his head, then started in on a chronological account of the incident as he'd dealt with it. He told it concisely, occasionally slowing when he searched for a phrase in English, but as far as I could tell he didn't seem to be withholding any salient details as he described the presence of the shotgun and cash – the equivalent of about a hundred thousand pounds sterling – and the possible bloodstains. "We have sent forensic samples to be examined in Copenhagen," he said. "But there are no results yet. Perhaps tomorrow."

"What about fingerprints? Were any found?"

"*Ja*, but so far they are only your father's."

Hentze sat back slightly, as if to signal that there was no more to say, and left me to absorb what I'd heard. He seemed in no hurry.

"The place he was found – Tjørnuvík? – what's it like?" I asked.

"*Chu-nu-wik*," he said, gently correcting my very poor pronunciation without making a big deal of doing so. "It's about thirty kilometres from here, at the north of this island." He cast round the room, then stood up and moved to the map. "Here."

I rose and followed him, looked at the place indicated by his finger.

"The village is small," Hentze told me. "But the car was in a— I don't know the English word: a place to stop by the road."

"A lay-by?"

"*Ja*. Here, on the headland. It isn't close to the village."

"And no one knows what he was doing there?"

As if the map had served its purpose Hentze stepped

away and leaned on a table. "No. I've asked his sons – the other sons – but no one in the family can think of a reason."

The implication was obvious, even though Hentze had been careful not to state it, and I thought back to my encounter with Magnus Ravnsfjall at the hospital. I wondered how he'd reacted to that line of questioning. Not well, I suspected.

"So do you think it was suspicious – that he was there doing something illegal?" I asked to clear up the ambiguity.

Hentze considered. "No, we can't say so for sure. There could be other explanations."

I nodded. Faced by a complete stranger, it was fair enough for Hentze to play it conservatively. I'd probably have done the same thing, but even so, I still wanted to get some indication of what he really thought and he was making me work hard to get it.

"You said the shotgun had been fired recently?"

"*Ja*, I think so. One shot only. The barrel was dirty and the used – *cartridge* – had not been removed."

Still neutral.

"And he had a graze on his head and knee from a fall of some kind. Or a push, or a fight," I added. It didn't prompt any greater response though, just a nod.

"So do you have a theory – a guess – about what happened?" I asked.

Hentze rubbed a hand over his chin, as if to indicate he thought it was a valid question, without necessarily endorsing it. Finally he said, "My police eye tells me the situation isn't usual, but without your father to explain I don't think I can say more."

He made an open-handed gesture and I knew it was as much of an answer as I was going to get. I couldn't tell whether he was maintaining a professional neutrality in order to conceal what he really thought, or because he didn't have a clue. He didn't come across as obtuse, but I recognised what was effectively a "no comment".

Time to go.

"Okay, well thanks for your time," I said. "If you get any more information will you let me know?"

I took a card from my wallet and handed it to him.

"Of course." Hentze nodded, then pushed himself upright from the table. "I'm walking outside. Let me take you."

I followed him along the modern, featureless corridor and through a heavy grey door which led out on to a landing and wooden stairs. Three flights below, the stairwell gave access to the main entrance and I expected Hentze to let me find my own way out. Instead, he set off down the stairs without reference to me, then along the ground floor corridor to the exit. He pushed the door open and stepped outside on to a concrete ramp, holding the door and waiting for me to join him.

"Do you smoke?" he asked when I stepped out. There was a breeze, but bright sunlight was reflected off the damp road in front of us.

"Not often now. I used to."

"I also stopped," Hentze said, slightly rueful. "But

sometimes it is – *useful* – to have a reason to stand outside, you know?"

When he cast me a sideways glance I knew what was going on. "Yeah, I think so," I said.

He nodded, considered the view for a moment. "You said you left here when you were three years old?"

On the surface it was conversational, but I knew it was an invitation to provide a final confirmation that he hadn't stepped outside for nothing. I said, "My mother left Signar and took me to Denmark, then England. I haven't been back since." Not the entire truth, but enough for the moment.

"Ah. Okay." Hentze nodded. "I have been to the UK – to Scotland – for seminars. Just two times. The speeches weren't so interesting, but there was a word I can't remember, for a guess – a feeling about an investigation. Do you know it?"

"A hunch?"

"Yes, that was it."

I took the cue. "You have a hunch about Signar?"

Hentze glanced up at the building behind us, as if to confirm he had left it. "Unofficially? For myself? Yes, of course." He turned to look at me. "The same as you, I think."

"If it was my case I'd think it was blackmail," I said baldly. "I can't think of another reason why anyone would go to an isolated spot with a briefcase full of cash and a gun. And if the gun's been fired and there's evidence of a struggle I'd think it was blackmail gone wrong."

"*Ja*, I think so." Hentze made an affirming gesture. "But I have nothing to prove it and the hospitals have seen no one with a shotgun injury, so I have a dead end."

He'd anticipated my next question so I reconsidered for a moment.

"Have you asked the family about blackmail? I mean, directly."

He looked off across the road, as if debating his reply. "It's a difficult thing," he said in the end. "If you say, 'I think there was blackmail,' you are also saying you think there is something a person wants to keep secret. It could be anything: personal or business – you understand what I mean? So it's difficult. Especially with *harra* Ravnsfjall."

"Why especially?"

Before Hentze could answer a man in a waterproof jacket approached. He climbed the steps and passed into the building with a nod towards Hentze and a mildly curious look at me. Hentze waited until he'd gone inside before speaking again.

"Signar Ravnsfjall has a large business. He knows many people in many places." He turned back to see if I understood. I did.

"So for now – until he can tell me what happened, or unless I discover something else – I have to wait."

Of course he did. If you've been told not to ask the obvious question, and if the family don't want to cooperate, it's bound to be a dead end.

"I understand," I said.

Hentze shrugged, as if he'd said nothing at all. "Where are you staying?" he asked.

"Just there. The Hotel Streym." I gestured to the

long, modern building, half clad in timber, half in silver grey steel, ten yards away. It still struck me as an unlikely, even ironic coincidence that the hotel had turned out to be next door to the police station.

"For how long?"

"I don't know yet. I only got here this afternoon. A few days, probably."

"Okay," Hentze said. "So it will be easy to contact you if there is news. And if there is anything you think of to help…"

I realised I'd decided to like him. He seemed like someone you could do business with, so I nodded to show him I got it. "I'll let you know," I said. "Thanks for talking to me."

I held out my hand, and although he seemed to find it an unexpected gesture he shook it.

"It's no problem," he said. "I'm sorry you had to come back because of these circumstances."

He sounded genuine about that, as if somewhere there had been a breach of etiquette. Then, with a brief nod, he turned away to open the door and go inside.

As the door closed behind him I looked out across the road for a moment. I still didn't know the name of the island on the far side of the grey sound water, but now that the light had shifted it didn't look so make-believe any more and I knew that the black dog had lifted. It might still be skulking nearby, but maybe I'd kicked it hard enough to stop it sniffing at my heels for a while.

4

I STILL HAD TIME TO KILL BEFORE I WENT TO MEET KRISTIAN Ravnsfjall so I went in search of something to eat. I'd picked up a free tourist map at the hotel but I didn't use it. I wanted to take the town as I found it, but despite the indecipherable signs and the underlying foreignness of the style and context of the buildings, what struck me most was the almost complete absence of people.

It was nearly seven o'clock now and the streets were deserted. It felt as if the entire population had withdrawn to safety; taking shelter from some imminent disaster or storm, leaving only strangers like me outside in my ignorance. It was a feeling I couldn't shake. What had I missed that everyone else knew?

The emptiness of the streets added a strange, otherworldly dimension to the unfamiliarity of the place. I'd been curious to see if anything would strike me as familiar from the last time I was here twenty-five years ago, but I'd retained no conscious memory of the place. Of course, all I'd really been interested in back then was a fight, which I'd got: knocked on my arse. What I'd wanted then had been easy, but wandering the abandoned streets made it even less clear what I hoped to achieve by coming here now.

I didn't like the lack of purpose, the absence of knowing what I was doing. If you're a copper the question of purpose is beautifully simple and defined: you want to know who did what. The *why* isn't important – unless, perhaps, it sheds light on the *who*. But more often than not, *why* doesn't matter. Why does someone kill a ten-year-old girl and leave her body in a stream? Who cares? What matters is who had the opportunity; who had the weapon; who left the DNA.

Sure, in the course of trying to find the *who* you might come across a few *whys* along the way – that your suspect had a thing for little girls; had been abused himself as a child; hated his wife or his life. But do you really care about any of that? Not particularly. All you care about is who's the right suspect.

Put into police terms like that, I knew who and I knew what. Forty-odd years ago Signar Ravnsfjall and Lýdia Reyná had married and conceived a child, but not in that order. Three years later they separated. Lýdia had left the islands and taken me with her: old enough to walk and to talk by then, little else.

All this I knew, and in police terms there was nothing left to answer: no mystery, no doubt. Those were the facts.

So why *was* I here?

Because it wasn't enough. I wanted a reason, but it was

a hard shift to make; to put aside the copper side of not caring about *why* and realise that it was the only question I was really interested in. It felt like I'd left solid ground and started to drift out to sea, where everything is fluid and changeable; pulled and distorted by the currents and tides of other people's interpretation. There were no facts to tie up to any more, and that's hard for a copper: it's not how we want things to be.

It wasn't how I wanted things to be either, but I was here now, and here I wasn't a copper any more. I'd have to get used to that, even if the idea was as foreign as the streets and their signs.

I ate in a restaurant called Marco Polo: dimly lit, silent and empty. From start to finish I was the sole customer, but the food was good and I left it deliberately late before paying the bill.

When I stepped outside again the streets still seemed preternaturally quiet – more so, if that was possible, and I heard a church clock chime the hour in an ornate, tinkly sort of way, somewhere distant across the town. At a stroll it took me only three or four minutes to walk back through the streets as far as the Café Natúr, an old building which parted the road around it a short distance from the harbour. Outside it was clad in black wood with a turf roof; inside there was a bare wooden floor and a bar which extended half the length of the room.

Fewer than half a dozen customers were scattered

amongst the tables and booths and a lone barmaid in a low-cut T-shirt was hanging newly washed glasses from the rack above the counter. She smiled as I went up to the bar, as if she was glad of the distraction, and seemed to take my pronunciation of "*Bjór*," as normal, which I was pretty sure it wasn't.

"Jan?"

I'd been aware of the man leaving a table by the window and crossing the room. Now I turned as Kristian Ravnsfjall held out his hand.

"I'm Kristian. It's good to meet you at last. Really good."

"You too," I said; an automatic response, not yet qualified.

We shook hands and Kristian clasped mine in both of his own for a moment, as if to emphasise his feelings.

He stood as tall as me, dressed in designer jeans and a smart-casual sweater under a sports jacket. He was good-looking the way many Scandinavians are, with healthy, athletic features and fair hair. It was receding a little at the temples but he wore it long enough to still give him a somewhat youthful appearance. I looked for any resemblance to Magnus but found little.

The barmaid brought my beer then, but as I reached for my wallet Kristian immediately stopped me. "Please. Don't think about it," he said. "This is from me."

"Okay, thanks."

He paid for the beer and we moved across to his table by the window. As I sat down I saw him looking at me openly before smiling again.

"I'm sorry," he said. "We're half-brothers, but I don't see it. I thought… I don't know." He shrugged, waved it away. "People see no similarity between Magnus and me either. You've met Magnus, yes?"

I nodded. "This afternoon at the hospital."

"It didn't go so well?" He framed it as a question, but only just.

"Did he say that?"

"He didn't have to. I saw him, and with Magnus you see what he's thinking on his face."

He paused for a moment, as if considering the implications of what he'd said, then he shifted. "Don't you think it's strange that we've never met before?"

"Not really. I've only been back once. You'd have been – I don't know, ten maybe?"

Kristian nodded. "I remember."

I frowned, not sure how he could. We hadn't met then. "You do?"

"Sure. You gave our father a black eye: we saw it. Someone gave Signar Ravnsfjall a black eye – that was a big thing. Even though we didn't know the details then, we knew he had been in a fight."

"It wasn't much of one," I said. "I hit him – two or three times – and then he hit *me* and that was it."

"And you've never spoken to him since then?"

"There was nothing to say."

Kristian seemed to consider this, then glanced around, perhaps assessing how public we were.

"Do you smoke?" he asked.

I shook my head. "Not any more."

"Lucky man. But I could use one. There's a smoking area at the back. Do you mind?"

I told him I didn't and we took our beers and crossed to the end of the room where Kristian held the door. Beyond it was a glassed-in terrace overlooking the street. It was furnished with aluminium furniture and a patio heater and there was no one else there.

Kristian chose a table close to the heater, waiting until we'd both sat down before striking a light on a brass Zippo and drawing on his cigarette.

"So tell me, are you married? Do you have kids?" he asked, exhaling smoke.

I shook my head. "Divorced. No kids."

"Ah. So we're in the same boat. I'm not divorced yet, but Anni and I split up three months ago. No kids either, thank God. Just Anni's daughter from before."

"How long were you married?"

"Seven years. You?"

"Eight."

Kristian nodded, as if acknowledging our shared experience. "Was it because of your work?" he asked. "Every time I see a police show on TV the detective has always split up with his wife because of his job. I think that must be an exaggeration for real life, but…"

"It doesn't help," I acknowledged. And because that was as far as I wanted to go I said, "What about Magnus – has he got a family?"

"*Oh ja*, he's the family man," Kristian said, as if it

couldn't be any other way. "He's married fifteen years with three kids. They are all brats, but that's okay because they're Signar's grandchildren. That's the important thing for Magnus: to keep the family line. You know what I mean? For the business." He tapped his cigarette on the ashtray as punctuation.

With someone else I'd have expected to hear an undertone of bitterness or resentment in that, but Kristian Ravnsfjall gave no sign of it. He had an easy, light manner of speaking; quick to add a self-deprecating gesture if he thought he'd said something too serious. He was a man who would be easy to like, I decided: easy to do business with probably, and perhaps easy to trust. I wasn't sure about doing any of that yet, but I did find myself speculating on how he and Magnus had turned out so different.

"So do you work for the business as well?" I said, conscious of the lull.

Kristian shook his head. "I used to, but I'm the second son. Magnus runs Four Fjords with Signar looking over his shoulder. They're a good team because they're so much the same." He paused, took a drag on his cigarette. "But Magnus and me, we don't do so well that way, so when I had the opportunity to make my own business a few years ago, that's what I did. I have one place at Vestmanna, another on Suðuroy."

"Doing what?"

"Aquaculture. We farm salmon: top quality, almost wild. We sell to the high-end markets all over the world – hotels, restaurants… They all say it's the best they can get." He made a wave-away motion, as if to distance the opinion. "We are not as large as Four Fjords, but it's going okay."

"I was told that Signar's business had made him a rich man. Is that true?"

"*Ja*, he's a rich man – at least on paper."

"So would it be usual for him to go around with a lot of cash in the boot of his car?"

Kristian gave me a slightly wry look. "You're being a police officer now?"

"Force of habit," I said, keeping it light. "The way he was found – the circumstances – seemed a bit odd that's all."

"You mean why he was out there at Tjørnuvík?"

I nodded. "Do you know?"

"No one does," he said with a shrug. "No one can figure it out."

"Who was the last person to see him on Sunday, do you know?"

"Magnus told me it was two guys on a boat in Runavík. Signar was there about five o'clock – the afternoon – but after that, no one has seen him."

"He didn't go home?"

"No," Kristian shook his head, but then seemed to recognise a need to elaborate. "My father often goes around to visit people: to talk, drink coffee, make the world right, you know what I mean? Sometimes he stays out into the evening, and on Sunday my mother went to bed early. She has a problem with her knee and her hip. They're painful, so she took pills and went to sleep. She didn't know till the morning that he wasn't there."

"Okay," I said, nodding. "That makes sense."

"You think there is something suspicious?"

He looked at me astutely and for a moment I debated whether to tell him about my meeting with Hentze before instinctively choosing not to. Instead I shrugged, as if I was considering it for the first time.

"I don't know," I said. "But in the circumstances… Could anyone have had a reason to blackmail Signar, do you think?"

I watched Kristian's face for any reaction, but all I got was a dry laugh. "Signar? No. He'd give them a punch in the mouth, maybe, but nothing else."

"So do you know why there'd be money and a shotgun in his car?"

He shrugged. "Knowing Signar, the money could have been for many things. He likes to do deals, you know? Off the accounts. And most people here have shotguns. I have two. I don't use them, but it's a tradition. In the old days people shot birds and hares, some still do."

"Right," I said, as if I accepted the logic of that.

Kristian stubbed out his cigarette. "Shall we go in? It's too cold out here to be comfortable."

We went back inside, but as we crossed the room towards the table we'd used earlier I noticed that Kristian's attention had been drawn by a slender girl at the bar. She was leaning on the counter talking to the barmaid, her long blonde hair hanging forward under a knitted black hat and obscuring most of her face.

For a moment Kristian seemed taken off-guard, but when he realised that I'd noticed the girl too he said, "Can you excuse me? I need to speak with her."

"Sure, of course," I nodded.

I continued on to the table and sat down as Kristian approached the girl and said something, causing her to turn sharply. For a second I saw guilty surprise in her movement, but when she saw it was Kristian she relaxed.

Even at a distance I could see she was striking; an animated face with fine features, about nineteen or twenty, I guessed. She spoke earnestly to Kristian and seemed to be explaining something, to which Kristian listened before responding. That prompted another explanation to which Kristian nodded again before seeming to remember the reason he was in the bar. He made a gesture towards me, said something to the girl and then headed to our table, obviously expecting the girl to follow, which she did.

"Jan, this is Elin Langgaard," he said as he approached. "Anni's daughter I told you about."

The girl came alongside Kristian and I stood up.

"Hi. Nice to meet you."

As I said it I revised her age down a little: somewhere around sixteen or seventeen, I guessed, though it was hard to be sure. She wasn't so much beautiful, I saw now – a slightly elfin quality ruled that out – but she had a face you wanted to watch, especially her eyes. They were an almost impossibly pale grey with slightly darker rings round the pupils; so unusual that it was hard not to fix on them.

"*Hey*," she said and shook my hand, confident and

composed. "This family is full of secrets, isn't it?"

"Is it?" I asked.

"Sure." She looked to Kristian, then back. "Like I never knew Kris had another brother in England until today."

"Well, we're only half-brothers," I told her.

"The good half or bad half?"

I didn't bother to stop a dry chuckle. "You'd have to ask Kristian. There's a lot about the family I don't know either."

She canted her head, still direct. "So you're here to find out?"

"Maybe," I nodded but left it open.

"You might have to work hard if you really want to find out everything," she said. "Faroese people never like to show what's really in their heads, you know?" Then before I could respond to that she shifted on her feet. "So is England a good place to live? I want to go there, to London, for some time to practise my English."

"It sounds pretty good already."

"*Takk*." She dipped her head in appreciation but I could tell that Kristian was restless and he cut in before the conversation could move on.

"I need to discuss something with Elin," he said. "Can you excuse us?"

"Sure, of course."

"Thanks. I won't be long." He looked to Elin, then started away.

She let him go a couple of steps before moving after him. "Welcome to the family," she said over her shoulder and gave me another brief smile before turning away.

I sat down again, sipped my beer and turned to look out of the window so it didn't seem as if I was watching them. It was growing dark outside, though, and in the reflection it wasn't hard to see them talking, off by the far wall. They had their backs turned but I could tell from his movements when Kristian took out his wallet.

Two minutes later they separated. I watched Elin leave by the side door – giving the briefest of waves in my direction – as Kristian returned to the table alone.

"I'm sorry about that," he said as he sat down. "Elin has had an argument with her mother and walked out of the house. I had to persuade her that if Anni found out she has been going to bars it wasn't going to make things any better."

He took a pull on what was left of his beer.

"How old is she – Elin?" I asked.

"Almost seventeen. I don't know, maybe it's a difficult age. She's not so happy about Anni and me separating, I think. She doesn't like their new house and Anni's not made things easy. Anyway, I gave her some money for a taxi and told her to go home. God knows if it will work. Maybe."

"What about her father, is he around?"

"No. He lives in Denmark. He's not interested." He said it definitively, then drained his glass to further emphasise the point. "Another?"

I shook my head. "No. Thanks. It's been a long day. I think I'll head back to the hotel."

For a moment I thought he was going to try to dissuade me, but then he nodded. "Sure, I understand. I'll walk with you a little way."

* * *

We left the bar and I walked ahead for a few paces on the narrow pavement until we crossed the road. It was fully dark now and the sky had cleared. There was only a light breeze and when we approached the innermost part of the harbour the shapes of the small boats moored there were caught by the shadowed reflections of lights in the motionless water.

Kristian paused to light a cigarette and I remembered something I'd thought about earlier. I said, "When you left the message for me at the hotel, how did you know where I was staying?"

He laughed. "When I knew you were here I did detective work, too," he said. "There are only four hotels in Tórshavn. It wasn't difficult."

"Right."

For a moment his attention seemed to shift. He drew on his cigarette but didn't move off again. Instead he gestured away, into the future.

"Will you call me if you want to have dinner while you're here? Or maybe you could come to see what we do at Vestmanna. Boats, fish farms; it's nothing new to people here, but I like to show off, you know? Come whenever you like."

"Okay. Thanks," I said. "But I don't know how long I'll stay. I'm going to see Signar tomorrow, but after that…"

"No, I understand. Of course."

For a moment I thought he looked disappointed, as

if I'd taken the easy way out. "To tell the truth, I was surprised you came now," he said.

"Oh? Why?"

He shrugged, as if it was obvious. "You use your mother's name and not Signar's, you've stayed away this long... I thought you had finished with the family."

Kristian Ravnsfjall might have made a good, instinctive copper, I decided then: the easy-going approach, the open questions and tacit invitation to respond. And although I still didn't feel entirely ready to try and explain my own uncertainties, I knew it was probably as close to an opportunity as I was going to get. What was there to lose? What did it matter?

"I suppose I had," I told him. "But in the circumstances..." I let the sentence trail off, then finally made it direct. "I wanted to find out about Signar and my mother. Do you know anything about that? Has Signar ever talked about why she left?"

"No, not really." Kristian shook his head, but looked away as if marshalling what information he had. "Of course, we knew – Magnus and me – that he was married before. We knew he had another son, but it wasn't talked about – not in detail, you know? I think maybe I asked questions when I was young, but because no one would say anything I realised it was a no-go area. So, all I know is what other people have said – you know, what you hear."

"Gossip?"

He nodded. "Behind the hand, people love to guess what they don't know. More so here, maybe – it's a small place."

"So what do they say?"

He hesitated as if he was reluctant to be associated with something he disliked. "Really, it's just… No one knows for sure: any of it. Okay? Always, it's what someone told someone who heard from someone else. It's not worth repeating."

"I'd like you to."

He flicked his cigarette and looked thoughtful for a moment. "Well, some people say that your mother had problems – mental problems – and that was why she went away. Others think that she had an affair, so maybe you were not Signar's son, and when he found out…" He looked at me to gauge my response.

I couldn't suppress a flat laugh. "That would be ironic."

Kristian frowned. "I don't know that word – *ironic*."

"I don't know how you'd translate it. It means it would be a like a bad joke."

"Ah, yes. I understand. But I don't think it's true."

"Why not?"

"Because if it was, Signar would have told you. He would have said it when you came before."

"You think?"

"I know. Listen, you challenged him: you gave him a black eye. Signar Ravnsfjall isn't a man to have that from anyone, and if you were not his son – or even if he thought it could be true – he would have told you then. I'm sure. I know him."

He paused, thinking about that, then looked at me. "Are you disappointed? Would it be easier if he wasn't your father also?"

"Probably."

He took it as seriously as I'd said it, then he tossed his cigarette away and said, "I'm glad to meet you at last."

"Me too."

I wasn't sure if he believed that, but he was too well mannered to let anything show. "Don't forget what I said about meeting again. Any time. You have my number. Okay?"

I nodded. "I'll remember."

"Good." He smiled and clapped me on the arm. "*Farvæl* then."

He moved away with long, easy strides and I watched him go for a few seconds before turning and heading out along the empty road past the ferry terminal. I shoved my hands in my jacket pockets and closed the coat around me. I had the urge to turn the conversation inside out and pick it over, but I knew it was too soon. I was still too close to things. They needed time to settle and I needed to gain some distance. I needed sleep.

5

Wednesday/mikudagur

PETUR BECH RODE THE QUAD BIKE DOWN THE SMOOTHLY tarmacked path, following the curve of the valley away from the river. It was still getting light and the sky held a trace of blue ahead of darker clouds to the west. In the trailer behind the quad a roll of wire netting, wooden posts and various tools clattered when the tarmac ran out and the track became rougher, stony gravel.

Out of a farmer's habit Bech cast his eye over the dark-green grass of the hillside to his left, looking for sheep and assessing the neatly mown but irregular patches of yellow where he had already cut hay, mostly on the higher slopes. There were still some areas to cut lower down – a job he should have been thinking about today if the bloody baler hadn't broken down. He'd have to cut the remaining hay soon if he was going to do it at all, but the drive belt he needed was on back order. If it wasn't in by tomorrow he'd ask Regin Larsen for the loan of his baler for a couple of days. That would be enough. In the meantime, at least the pen on the beach would finally get fixed.

The track ended and he was riding on the rich grey-black sand of Pollurin bay, only recently exposed by the receding tide. The sheep pen was further out, near the inlet on a flat area of grass, but as Petur Bech headed towards it his gaze followed the line of the water's edge and saw an incongruous object breaking the line of the sand.

The light was still poor for the distance and at first he thought it might be a large piece of driftwood, part of a telegraph pole perhaps. That would have been enough to send his grandfather – even his father – into a rush of anticipation. What you could do with a good piece of driftwood! It might make a gatepost, a roof truss, even firewood – all worth having for free in a place where every stick of timber had to be imported.

Old habits die hard, and because it was no trouble to go and look, Bech turned the bike towards the flotsam, giving it a bit of extra throttle and enjoying the smooth, even ride.

But it wasn't driftwood, he realised as he got closer. A seal? The thought lasted only a second and then he throttled back quickly. He let the quad bike run to a halt five metres away from the body, then he killed the engine and dismounted.

Farmers are used to the sight of death, from stillborn lambs to the old ewe that didn't have the strength to get out of a cleft in the rocks. So even though this was a person, Petur Bech had no qualms about approaching or any doubt that he was dead: a young man, in his twenties, he saw as he approached. His skin was pallid, blue-tinged, except where it was bruised and punctured in three different places on the side of his face.

Petur Bech recognised the wounds and didn't go closer. Instead, after a few seconds of silent contemplation and an inward, almost unconscious prayer – because old habits die hard – Petur Bech stepped away from the body, then turned and followed his footprints back to the bike. He didn't bother to take out his phone; there was never any reception down here. Instead, he started the engine and took the quad in a wide circle before heading back towards the path up to the farm.

I woke with sunlight coming round the edges of the blinds. I'd slept well enough, although I vaguely remembered surfacing at some point out of a confused dream which involved hospitals in airports and a hazy feeling of looking for someone without knowing who. No vast amount of analysis needed there.

I showered and dressed and remembered to pick up my phone as I went down to find breakfast. I ate alone in the dining room except for a scruffy-looking guy watching the TV at the far end of the room. By then the weather had turned and it was raining heavily outside. It didn't matter to me, though; I had no plan, except to wait for Fríða Sólsker to get in touch about visiting Signar. So I drank coffee and ate a pastry while I studied the Kort & Matrikelstyrelsen map book I'd bought yesterday in Tórshavn.

I've always had an affinity for maps. To me they have the quality of an absolute truth, only ever telling an objective story, whether you follow them on the ground or simply pore over them at a table. Words can always be subject to interpretation, but contours and places are unequivocal: *you are here*, nowhere else.

Even so, when I found the place called Tjørnuvík on the map there was nothing in the contours and symbols to tell me why Signar would have been found in a lay-by there, near the end of a road that terminated in a small village. And nor could I really guess at a reason, except for the obvious interpretation. But I knew that might well be too obvious – too pat – simply because it *was* an interpretation.

I was still thinking about it when my phone rang. It was a Faroes number.

"It's Hjalti Hentze," the voice said. "Are you busy? I think there could be something you would want to see – can you be outside the hotel in five minutes?"

If he didn't want to be more specific on the phone I decided not to press him so I said I could and went back to my room for my jacket.

Exactly five minutes later Hentze pulled up outside in a matt silver Volvo. I left the shelter of the hotel entrance and hurried across to the car through the rain.

"*Morgun*," Hentze said. "I'm sorry if this is sudden. Were you awake?"

"Having breakfast."

"Good. Okay." He nodded, then said, "There is a body on the beach at a place called Saksun. I'm sure that's of no interest to you, but it's not so far from Tjørnuvík and I remember you said you would like to see where your father was found."

His expression was completely deadpan, but I knew I'd said no such thing. I played along, though, and nodded. "Yes, sure."

"So if we have time maybe I could show you that, too... Maybe we won't, though. I can't promise. Is that okay?"

So, Hentze was crafty: enough to have a viable cover story to hand if he needed it, anyway.

"Sure, of course," I said. "I wasn't doing anything else."

"Okay," Hentze said, the understanding confirmed. "That's fine then. We can go."

We left Tórshavn on the coast road, driving through a place called Hoyvík before habitation fell away behind us. Hentze had the radio on in the background; a male voice was speaking calmly and without apparent emphasis for several minutes between records. I found it impossible to intuit any sort of meaning from the words.

Hentze said very little, seemingly content with his own thoughts and the driving, which to me was better than trying to make conversation for the length of the journey. I don't find silences awkward, only forced small talk.

The road was impeccably smooth and stayed with the shore; steep hillside slopes to the left and a long inlet of grey water on the right. The inlet – was it a fjord? I didn't know – was about quarter of a mile wide and on the far side the land was nearly vertical, rising up to the undulating, upper edge of a mountain draped in low, rolling mist.

Dozens of streams and some larger waterfalls cut through the dun, green and sodden yellow of the slope, carving their way down in incessant tumbling. I tried to estimate the height of their fall – eight hundred feet? A thousand maybe, if the size of the scattered buildings by the far shore was anything to go by. But I found the scale hard to grasp – as if I was being asked to accept two contradictory things at the same time: the size of the escarpment and its nearness. Somehow they didn't correspond.

A tunnel took the road through a mountainside in a wash of sodium light; the low rumble of approaching vehicles reflected off the rough-hewn rock walls. When we emerged on to the slope of a new valley two or three minutes later there was brighter sunlight and no rain. It felt oddly as if we'd made a passage between two worlds.

The transition seemed to mark a change in Hentze, too. He came out of his thoughts as if it had taken him this long to decide what to say, but now that he had, he didn't need any preamble.

"Did you bring your police identification with you? I should have asked before."

"Yeah, I've got it," I said. "Will I need it?"

"No, probably not. But just in case."

"Right."

I glanced at him, trying to weigh up what was really going on. Now we were moving there seemed no reason not to see how far Hentze could be drawn away from his cover story that this was really a trip to look at a lay-by.

"So what do you know about this body on the beach?" I asked.

"Not so much yet," he said, keeping his eyes on the road. "Usually these things are an accident, sometimes a suicide. How would you say it – a safe bet?" He looked at me for confirmation of the phrase. "Since 1988 we have had only two murders. You'd have no work."

"That might not be so bad."

"You think so?" He gave me a short, openly appraising look before turning his attention back to the road. "How many murders do you have to investigate in a year?"

"Personally? It depends how long the case lasts. Three or four maybe, including domestics."

"What is that?"

"Husbands and wives, cases within families."

"Okay, I see. And there are other murders that you don't work on?"

"Yeah. On my patch maybe twenty a year."

Hentze shook his head, as if considering the shortcomings of that other world I was describing. "Where do you live in England?" he asked.

"The Midlands – right in the middle."

"Not near the sea?"

"No, it's about as far away from it as you can get."

"Really?" He said it as if I'd confirmed a final deficiency. "That's a pity."

* * *

It had started to rain again by the time Hentze turned off the coast road twenty minutes later. We passed a cluster of houses and then the road narrowed to a single lane with a drop of a foot or more to soggy wet turf and boggy ground on either side. A meandering river cut deep into the dark-brown soil of the valley bottom, following the same route as the road.

Occasionally I spotted isolated concrete or stone sheds, most with rusting tin roofs, seemingly abandoned. There were no fields, no fences or walls – almost no sense that anyone had any use for this open, treeless landscape.

But it was the high, sculpted mountains on either side of the broad valley that took my attention the most as I tried to comprehend their scale. I wondered what living in this place did to your sense of personal meaning and importance. Did the overwhelming vastness press down on you – on your soul even – or did it make you expand against it?

Perhaps if you'd been brought up here you'd never give it a thought, but I couldn't see how that could be true: it would be like never noticing the sky or the sea.

Finally, after five or six miles, the road divided beside a lake and Hentze took the left-hand fork, going uphill. We passed two or three houses, the last one with tractors and farm implements scattered around it, and then I saw an empty police car parked where the road ended.

Hentze pulled in beside it, switched off the engine and gestured to a tarmacked footpath leading down a narrow valley beside a tumbling river.

"We'll walk from here," he said, then assessed my jeans. "Maybe you should have better trousers, though. It's cold *and* wet on the beach."

Outside the rain was heavier, more determined. Hentze pulled on waterproofs and handed me a spare pair of Gore-Tex trousers. He also took a camera from a padded case in the boot and stowed it inside his jacket.

We were about to set off down the path when I heard a quad bike start up somewhere out of sight. A short time later it appeared from the back of the nearest house and came our way. The man riding it was clad in waterproofs and wellingtons and when he saw us he waved and brought the quad round to a halt.

Hentze moved and spoke to the man, getting nods and gestures with the replies: an explanation of where, when and what, it seemed. Then Hentze indicated me and both men approached.

"This is Petur Bech," Hentze said by way of introduction as his phone rang. "He has the farm here. He found the body."

"Hi," I said. "Jan Reyna."

"You're from England?" Bech asked. "So you must be used to the rain."

"Not quite as much as here."

He laughed. "Two things would make the Faroes into paradise: no rain and no Danes. *Ja, Hjalti?*"

With a grin he looked to Hentze for agreement, but Hentze was still on his mobile. After a short exchange he rang off. "It was the doctor," he told me. "He is delayed but he says he'll be here in twenty minutes."

Turning to Bech, Hentze spoke Faroese again – a proposal and an agreement it seemed to me – and when it was done Bech handed Hentze a rucksack from the quad's trailer.

"Okay, we'll go now," Hentze said as Bech went back to the bike. "Petur will wait and give the doctor a ride to the beach."

"What's in the bag?"

"Coffee and sandwiches. Petur's wife made them for the boys on the beach while they waited."

"Nice of her."

"*Ja*, they are good people," Hentze said, as if it was perfectly natural. He started towards the path and I moved with him.

6

I STOOD WITH MY BACK TO THE WIND AS IT BUFFETED ITS WAY in through the inlet behind me. The narrow passage between the rock faces was the only break in the encircling mountain-sides, towering so far above that it felt more like being at the bottom of a chasm, instead of standing at sea level.

This well of a cove was perhaps a quarter of a mile across: a vast natural amphitheatre holding a lagoon of brown-tinged water, rippled and stirred by the gusting wind. The water lapped at the margin of the grey-black sand bar where I stood but it was impossible to guess how deep it might be further out: maybe shallow enough to wade through, or perhaps abyssally deep. And somehow this uncertainty only served to reinforce the sense of foreboding the place seemed to have, at least to me. It felt like a trap, for air and water and space. And for dead bodies. It was halfway to the underworld already.

Twenty yards away from me Hjalti Hentze was taking photographs of the body while the two uniformed officers looked on, sipping the coffee and eating the sandwiches sent down for them. They were a stoical pair, but given that they'd already been here for over an hour there wasn't much left to be excited about, and it wasn't going to be their case anyway.

I'd purposely kept my distance, partly because I didn't want to add my own footprints to those already around the body, but also so Hentze wouldn't feel as if he was under scrutiny. Not that it would have fazed the man very much, I suspected. Hentze didn't seem like the sort of man who let many things disconcert him.

His camera flashed a final time, then he stepped back and looked round before raising a hand and gesturing me in.

"His name is Tummas Gramm," he said as I approached. "I arrested him once, two years ago for possession of drugs. Would you like to look? There isn't any more we can do until the doctor gets here and says he is dead for the record."

He handed me a single latex glove and let me move towards the body alone.

Tummas Gramm was lying on his back, head slightly tilted to one side, eyes closed. He looked to be in his mid-to late twenties and it was clear from the way that the sand was sculpted around the margins of his body and clothes – hands, legs and hair – that he hadn't been moved since he'd come to rest here.

I circled the body, then squatted down beside his shoulder. As well as five smallish puncture wounds – bruised but washed clean by the sea water – Tummas Gramm's face also showed the wine-mark purple staining of hypostasis, the pooling of blood at the lower parts of the body after death. When I pressed the skin of the cheek with a gloved finger the colour remained fixed, which meant the blood had coagulated. That took about twelve hours.

After a few more seconds of looking I straightened and moved to look at the rest of the body. He was dressed in black jeans and a thick grey pullover which had ridden up, exposing part of the belly and a large wad of sodden cotton wool, stained pinkish brown. A sticking plaster still adhered to the cotton wool but not to the flesh. I lifted part of the wadding but without moving more of the clothing I couldn't see the wound it had been applied to. I put it back in position and stood up.

"So, what do you think about the body?" Hentze asked as I returned to where he stood waiting.

I waited a moment then said, "The lividity's set – the hypostasis?" I looked to see that he understood the word. "So he's been dead for more than twelve hours. Also, he wasn't in that position immediately after he died. I'd say he was lying face down for some time."

Hentze nodded. "The tide was high at four forty this morning. It could have moved the body here from somewhere else."

I looked towards the water at the edge of the sand bar, then towards the narrow, rocky inlet from the sea. "Do you think he could have been washed in from out there?"

"It's possible, but I don't think so," Hentze said. "It would take a long time to find the way in with the—" he searched for the word. "The movement of the water here – you know what I mean?"

82

"The currents?"

"Yes, currents. And he hasn't been long in the sea or there would be more damage from the fish and rocks. We see that sometimes – one time a year maybe. A person drowns and they sink to the bottom and stay there until the gasses of decomposition bring them back to the surface. But it's after days, maybe weeks. I don't think this is like that."

"No," I agreed. Then: "And you knew about the shotgun injury before we left Tórshavn – the pellets in his face?"

Hentze nodded. "Petur Bech knew what they were when he saw them. Of course, it doesn't mean that the injury here" – he indicated his torso – "is also from a shotgun. We will see."

The look on Hentze's face made it obvious that he was expecting me to say the most obvious thing now, so I did. There'd been no other reason for him bringing me here.

"So you'll have to look for a link to Signar's gun."

Hentze looked solemn. "It could be a coincidence, but yes, I think we will have to do that."

I thought so too. The circumstances around Signar being found with a discharged shotgun to hand, and now a guy with shotgun pellets in his face turning up dead on a beach *could* be coincidental. Could. But if it had been my case, confirming or refuting any link between the two would have been high on my list of objectives just then.

But before I could say anything else, the sound of an approaching engine made Hentze look away. Petur Bech's quad bike was coming down the path to the beach with two men astride it.

* * *

The doctor was a practical man in his forties called Olsen. It took him about ten seconds to pronounce that Tummas Gramm was dead and once it was official things started to happen more quickly.

At Hentze's request, the doctor secured plastic bags over Tummas Gramm's hands, feet and head before the body was moved. Then he and the two uniformed officers lifted the body from the sand and placed it on a polythene sheet, which the doctor and I had to hold in place against the wind. Finally, fully shrouded in plastic, Tummas Gramm was transferred to a body bag and the two uniforms lifted him into the trailer of the quad bike for the journey back to the top of the hill.

I took no part in this last part of the procedure. I was extraneous, so I wandered a little way off to look at an area of grass at the base of the cliff, only heading back when I heard the quad bike start up again. Hentze was waiting for me. The doctor was riding pillion with Petur Bech again and the uniformed officers had already started walking towards the path back to the farm.

"It's all done," Hentze told me. "There's an ambulance at the farm. It will take him to the mortuary in Tórshavn and the pathologist will do an examination this afternoon."

"A forensic pathologist?"

"No, we don't have one here, but if it's necessary someone can come from Denmark."

Considering this was a place that didn't reckon to have

more than one murder every twenty-odd years he seemed pretty untroubled about the fact that he might be looking at one now. Not that he seemed drawn to speculate or jump to any conclusion about the cause of Tummas Gramm's death. It was too soon for that, and the fact that Hentze knew it added to my growing feeling that the man was a decent copper.

We started back the way we had come, the wind pushing at our backs, and I let my gaze wander across the restless water to the landward side of the lagoon. On the far shore, close to the water, there was a steep-roofed building that looked as if it was in the process of being renovated. Above it and further round the curve of the shore a neater, tidier house with tarred clapboards and a turf roof was perched on a rare ledge of flat ground. There were no visible paths or tracks to either place.

"Does anyone live there?" I asked, gesturing towards the buildings.

Hentze followed my motion, then shook his head. "The old boathouse is being modernised. The other is only for holidays, I think. In summer many people come here to walk, to sit on the beach and enjoy themselves. It's a beautiful place isn't it?"

I cast a look upwards at the looming mountains and the over-spills of broken water running down their faces. *Beautiful* was not the word I would have chosen. To me the place still seemed forbidding, but maybe in summer it was different.

"Not an easy place to dump a body, though," I said.

"It'd be a long way to carry a dead weight."

I waited to see how Hentze would react to that, ready to back off if he seemed to view it as interference. He nodded thoughtfully, though.

"There are many easier places where you could just drop a body in the sea," he said. "But if he was here already... Is that what you're thinking?"

"It's just a thought."

"Yes. A good one," Hentze said. "We'll see."

By the time we got back to the car the rain had eased to a fine drizzle and the scene at the top of the hill had changed. Several cars and another quad bike were now parked on the road verges and half a dozen people were standing around, talking in knots and exchanging views with Petur Bech: his neighbours, I guessed – come to see what was happening.

Hentze confirmed it when he said, "The neighbours have come. I'll see what they say."

He seemed barely troubled by the walk we'd just done, whereas I was warm from the exertion and happy to lean on the car as he went off to circulate.

Ten minutes later, having spoken to everyone, he came back to me.

"No one has seen anything strange," he said. "The only thing, maybe, is that two days ago – on Monday morning – Noomi Simonsen from the other side of the valley saw someone at the boathouse. She thought he was a workman because he was moving things around outside."

"Could it have been Tummas Gramm?"

Hentze shook his head. "It was too far for her to give a description, but I've called the builder who does the work there. His men haven't been here for three weeks, so I think I would like to have a look."

We drove back to the fork in the road, then out along the other side of the valley, passing through a cluster of buildings – some modern, some built of stone and turf – before stopping where a temporary gate in the roadside fence marked the start of a track. From the muddy ruts in the wet grass it looked like the path had been made by the comings and goings of a quad bike, but not recently.

I followed Hentze's lead through the gate. He didn't hang about, walking with a purposeful stride as if he was used to travelling over rough terrain. Five minutes later we reached the narrow delta of grass where the boathouse stood about twenty yards from the shore. It was in the style of most of the Faroese houses I'd seen, with an undercroft of rendered stone and a first-floor living area above it, clad in neat wooden boards. From the outside at least it looked more or less complete, although the evidence of building work – barrels, cans and lengths of plastic piping and wood – were scattered in the grass all around and the wooden steps which led up to the first floor were still secured by scaffolding poles and roughly nailed cross-members.

Hentze still seemed keen to get on, climbing the steps and leaving me to look out across the bay for a minute. From here, without the cliffs bearing down, it felt less oppressive: more open and sweeping in scale. The inlet showed itself to be wider than I'd thought and across the intervening water I could see the spot where Tummas Gramm's body had been found, although from this distance and angle it was impossible to see any traces we'd left.

"Jan?"

I turned and looked upwards.

"Someone has been here," Hentze said from the top of the steps.

I crossed to them and went up to the platform at the top where Hentze was examining the door. It was unpainted plywood, scuffed and marked in places, clearly a temporary arrangement just to keep the elements out.

"Edvin, the builder, told me the door had a lock – on the outside, you know the sort?"

"A padlock?"

"Yeh, that's it."

He indicated a rectangular pattern of screw holes in the plywood at chest height, matched by four more on the door jamb. They all showed signs that the fixings had been levered out, rather than unscrewed.

"Maybe someone went in to see if there was anything worth stealing," I said.

"Maybe," Hentze concurred. "But here that would be unusual."

He contemplated the possibility for a moment longer, then reached out and opened the door, using his thumb at the very tip of the lever, I noted.

The door swung inwards and as we stepped inside I smelled wood and dust from the bare floorboards. All the windows except two at the far end of the room were obscured by black plastic bin bags, nailed in position, and as my eyes accustomed themselves to the gloom I saw that the place was pretty tidy for a building site. The floor had been swept and lengths of wood and blocks of foam insulation were neatly stacked against the walls.

Because my gaze was naturally drawn to the light from the far windows I saw the rumpled sleeping bag beneath them at the same time as Hentze, who started along the room to have a closer look.

I still didn't want to crowd him so I followed more slowly, casting my eye along the margins of the room until I reached a small, cast-iron stove where offcuts of wood were stacked up – not dropped or heaped up, but squared neatly by length. I put a hand to the stove. It was cold, but in the spilled ash below its door I saw two stray strands of cotton wool.

"There is a bag of food in tins here, and a jacket," Hentze said. He was standing over the sleeping bag now, pulling on a latex glove.

"The stove's been used, too," I told him.

I fished out the latex glove Hentze had given me earlier and squatted down to open the door of the stove. Inside, amongst the ash and partially burned wood, there were several wads of charred cotton wool and fabric; as if the stove had had insufficient heat to burn up the cloth before it had gone out.

"I think you should look at this," Hentze said.

I left the stove and crossed to what I saw now was a makeshift bed: a sleeping bag on top of layers of insulation foam. Hentze had lifted a khaki army-surplus coat off the sleeping bag and now he pointed to the spot where it had been. The navy-blue fabric of the sleeping bag was darkly stained over an area about the size of a football.

"Does this look like blood to you?" Hentze asked. His tone was serious and pensive, as if – despite our reason for being here – he hadn't expected to be looking at such a thing.

I nodded but kept my answer qualified. "It could be."

"Here, too, the same."

Hentze had the look of a man who knew an already poor day was probably going to get worse. He indicated the left side of the coat. The stain there approximately matched the one on the sleeping bag, although that didn't prove much. Transference could have gone either way.

He laid the coat carefully aside, stain uppermost, then looked at me. "So, there is a body out there and blood in here. I think there must be a connection."

"Yeah, there could be."

Hentze frowned. "You don't think so? Come, say what you think."

For the first time since I'd met him his tone was less than phlegmatic – a brief moment of irritation – and I realised I'd taken the neutrality too far.

"Someone I used to work with had a saying," I told him. "'If you don't know enough for a theory, don't make up a story instead.'"

I looked at him to see if he got it. His face remained set for a second, but finally he made a single, acknowledging nod. "You mean this doesn't prove Tummas Gramm was here."

"Not on its own, no. But if you can match the blood or fibres and DNA…"

"Okay," Hentze said, accepting it. "So if you were seeing this in your job in England, what would you do?"

I cast a look at the sleeping bag and then around the whole room. "I'd leave everything as it is," I said. "I'd seal the place off and get crime-scene examiners in to assess it."

Hentze considered that for a moment, then nodded. "Okay," he said. "I think you are right." Then he gestured at the coat. "But I think I am right too."

And from his expression I could see that it didn't make him happy to say it.

7

AFTER ARRANGING FOR SOMEONE TO COME OUT AND SECURE the boathouse with a new lock, and giving specific instructions that no one should enter the building, Hentze had driven back to Tórshavn in a sombre mood. He was grateful for the fact that the Englishman – which was how he still thought of Reyná – appeared content just to watch the passing landscape in silence.

The only interruption to that had been when Reyná received a phone call and paused part way through it to ask how long it would be before they were back. He had a meeting with Signar Ravnsfjall's doctor, he said, and Hentze told him he would drop him off at the hospital – half an hour, maybe less.

"How is your father?" he asked when Reyná came off the phone.

"The same, I think," Reyná said, matter-of-factly. "I haven't heard anything different."

Again Hentze registered the man's reluctance to be drawn into conversation about Signar Ravnsfjall, and despite the other things on his mind he remained curious about that. Why would someone who clearly had little or no relationship with his father come all this way to see him now he was unconscious in a hospital bed?

Reyná was a hard man to assess, though. He wasn't given to chatter and seemed to prefer keeping his thoughts to himself, which made it impossible for Hentze to judge whether the stiff and slightly distant impression he made was normal for him, or came from his reason for being here. Whichever it was, Hentze didn't object: the Englishman's reserve wasn't dissimilar to his own, and he would always rather have too little talk than too much.

Half an hour later, having dropped Reyná at the hospital and thanked him for his advice, Hentze climbed the station stairs, stopping off at the staff room to make coffee. It was past midday and he didn't think Ári Niclasen would be in the mood to offer him an espresso from the new machine in his office.

There were three people sitting round the staff-room table, chatting over their lunch. When Hentze entered they exchanged greetings and he moved to the worktop where Annika Mortensen was making tea – something herbal. When she offered him a teabag he wrinkled his nose. "How can you drink that stuff?"

"It's good for you."

"Huh."

Hentze made coffee instead – two heaped spoons of Nescafé, one of sugar.

"Do you still want to work with CID?" he asked Annika, his back to the others.

"Sure, of course, but I can't for another year."

"Pah," Hentze said, dismissing the regulation. "I need some information. Can you get on to Edvin Mohr, the builder in Kollafjørður? Ask him for a list of everyone he's employed to work on the boathouse at Saksun. He'll know what you're talking about. Also, find out from him who owns the boathouse."

"Is this to do with the body out there – the guy called Gramm?"

"Yeah, but don't spread it around, okay?" He indicated over his shoulder at the others.

Annika nodded. "Is it a murder?"

"I don't know yet. Just suspicious."

"Okay," Annika said. "Where will you be?"

"Upstairs with Ári."

On the third floor Hentze went along the main corridor to Ári Niclasen's office, which was about twice the size of Hentze's own, with several pot plants and a neat side table for the espresso machine. Niclasen didn't have to share his office either.

The door was open and when Hentze tapped on it Niclasen waved him in as if he'd been waiting. He looked agitated and didn't waste any time getting to the point.

"Why did you take the English detective out to Saksun?" he asked. "Did you clear it with anyone?"

"I didn't think there was any need," Hentze said equably. Although he hadn't been specifically invited to do so, he sat down in a leather armchair, which was less comfortable than it looked.

"So why was he there?" Ári asked again.

Hentze sipped his coffee. "I'd said I'd show him where Signar Ravnsfjall was found, but then the incident at Saksun came up. I didn't think there'd be a problem if he went along. He's a detective after all."

"Sure, yes, but not one of us."

"No, that's true." Hentze nodded, then sipped his coffee.

Ári Niclasen looked at him warily for a moment, as if weighing up whether to expend the effort to pursue the issue. In the end he evidently decided against it. "Okay, look, forget that for a minute," he said. "Tell me what you found. What does it look like?"

It took Hentze a couple of minutes to outline the basic facts: the identification of Tummas Gramm, the possible shotgun injury and the discovery of what might be bloodstains in the boathouse.

"So how does this link to Signar Ravnsfjall – or doesn't it?" Ári asked when he'd finished. "What are you thinking? Coincidence? Are they separate incidents or could Signar Ravnsfjall have shot this Tummas Gramm? Is that likely?"

For a second Hentze wondered whether to ask which of those questions Ári would like him to address first. He made a so-so gesture. "I think we should assume there *could* be a connection, but until we know how Gramm died, and whether it's his blood on Ravnsfjall's car we won't know for sure if it's all linked. I think we need a forensic pathologist to look at the body and a technical team to examine the boathouse."

"Our guys couldn't handle the boathouse?"

"Maybe," Hentze said, but without conviction. "But if it *is* a murder scene…"

He got the reaction he expected, seeing Ári Niclasen imagine the consequences of a major crime scene being less than fully investigated. Lifting fingerprints and taking samples was one thing, but the local officers weren't trained or qualified for in-depth scene analysis.

"The body's gone to the mortuary?" Ári asked in the end.

Hentze nodded. "I asked Dánjal to contact Gramm's family for a formal ID and I called Elisabet Hovgaard and said we'd need a PM as soon as possible."

Niclasen drew a pensive breath, then let it out. "Okay, first see what Elisabet says, then we'll decide about the technical team. I'm not asking for them to be flown out if Gramm died of natural causes. We're still supposed to be watching the budget."

"Okay."

"And what about this Reyná character? Where is he now?"

"He's gone to the hospital to see his father."

"Has Ravnsfjall come round? Is he up to talking?"

"Not as far as I know."

"Right. Okay. So the Englishman doesn't need to have any further involvement."

"As a matter of fact, he's Faroese," Hentze said. "And he does have experience with this kind of investigation."

"Well, whatever he is," Niclasen said with a note of irritation which then drifted easily into sarcasm. "You think we should put him on the payroll?"

Hentze knew that slightly acid tone was usually an indication that Ári was feeling pressured about something. Hentze wasn't sure what that might be, but he knew enough to tread carefully.

"I just think he might be able to give us more of an insight into what Signar Ravnsfjall might have been up to," he said equably. "More than we'll get from outside anyway. He wants to know what happened to his father, too, and if there *is* a link between that and Tummas Gramm…"

"*If.*"

"Yes, sure. I'm not jumping to any conclusions."

Ári Niclasen took a few seconds to consider that, then he straightened his shoulders. "Okay, but after this morning our priority has to be the death of Tummas Gramm. So, first and foremost, let's find out what Hovgaard says about the cause of death, then we'll decide on the next step."

"Okay, I'll get on it," Hentze said. "Is it okay if I also try and find out when and where Gramm was last seen alive?"

"Of course. And you'd better take someone to work with you."

"Dánjal?"

"If you like."

"Okay."

Hentze levered himself out of the armchair and carried his coffee to the door. He half expected Niclasen to throw in a last-minute caveat before he got there, but nothing came and Hentze went out, leaving the office door as it had been when he arrived.

It might be open to interpretation, of course, but he was fairly sure he could argue that Ári Niclasen hadn't specifically ruled out any further contact with Jan Reyná. Whether or not he would *need* further contact remained to be seen, but Hentze liked to keep his options open.

8

I WAS A COUPLE OF MINUTES EARLY WHEN I WALKED INTO THE hospital lobby, but Fríða Sólsker was already there. She greeted me warmly and then led the way to the ward. Walking beside her, I made a conscious effort to refocus my thoughts. Despite my resolution to be better prepared after yesterday, the distraction Hentze had provided that morning had made it too easy to avoid thinking about Signar.

At the nurses' station Fríða talked to the senior nurse in Faroese and when the nurse glanced at me I guessed I had been cited as the reason for this break with normal visiting protocol. I didn't understand the exchange beyond that, though, so I watched Fríða Sólsker instead. She was at ease here, but there was also a certain calmness about her – as if she was well practised at absorbing the reactions of others without letting her own reactions show. I wondered what sort of counsellor she was, exactly.

When she finished talking to the nurse, Fríða turned back to me with an expression which seemed to acknowledge that this wasn't going to be an easy situation.

"Hans – Dr Heinason – has been delayed for a few minutes but it's not a problem," she said. "We can see Signar now – unless you would rather wait?"

I shook his head. "No, that's fine."

We followed the corridor to the pale-wood door of a private room. Through the narrow window in the door I saw part of a hospital bed, the lower half of someone under the covers.

"Would you like me to come in with you?" Fríða asked. "I'm not sure if he will be able to understand English."

I hadn't considered the possibility that there might be a language problem; only that I still had no idea what I was going to say. "If you don't mind," I said.

"Of course not."

And then, as if to relieve me of the need to do so, she pushed the door open and held it as she went in.

Signar Ravnsfjall lay on the bed, supported by several pillows. My first reaction was that he looked like an old man; thinner and no longer bull-like, vulnerable and somehow marooned in the clinical surroundings.

I knew I shouldn't have been thrown by this, but it wasn't something I could control. And, again, I had the sensation of time springing outwards, decompressed. Yesterday I'd seen Magnus Ravnsfjall as the image of the Signar I remembered, but now I saw Signar as a premonition of what Magnus would be in thirty years: white-haired, thinner round the face, pale eyes milky. Perhaps Magnus wouldn't be brought down by a catastrophe in his brain, but he would only have to look at his father to see what else the future would hold.

"*Signar, tað er Fríða. Hvussu hevur tú tað í dag?*"

Fríða had moved to sit on the edge of the bed. She'd taken Signar's hand but it lay limp in her own, as if dead. Signar's eyes found her but there was no recognition, nothing to show any kind of understanding.

"*Her er ein komin at vitja teg. Tað er Jan. Hann er komin úr Onglandi.*"

Hearing my name, guessing what Fríða was saying, I walked around to the other side of the bed.

"Hello, Signar," I said.

Slowly the man's eyes traversed the space between Fríða and I. His open mouth moved weakly, closed to swallow, then fell open again. The reaction seemed to have no connection with his gaze.

"Do you remember me?" I said. "I'm Jan." I pronounced it with an unfamiliar *Y*.

For several seconds there was nothing, and then a faint frown, as if a message had taken this length of time to go down into the depths and send back a signal to the surface.

Fríða spoke again, patience in her voice. The old man continued to look at me and finally his mouth moved. The sound he made was breathy, laboured and barely audible, without strength. It might have been the ghosts of words.

"Can you tell what he's saying?" I asked, looking across at Fríða.

She shook her head. "It isn't really words."

On the bed cover Signar's right hand rocked a little, then fell still. His gaze wandered off into the middle distance.

So what did I say or do now? What *was* there to say or

do when there wasn't any way to know if I was even being understood, let alone recognised?

"Was he like this yesterday?" I asked Fríða. "The nurse said there'd been an improvement but..."

"No, he was more alert then," she said. "He's not so good today."

"I don't think he knows who I am."

"No, that's possible. I'm sorry."

Before I could frame a reply the door of the room opened and a man in a check shirt and chinos came in. He was in his late thirties with an easy-going manner to match the clothes. Fríða looked up and smiled at him. "Hey, Hans," she said. "This is Jan Reyná, Signar's son from England. Jan, Hans Heinason."

"Pleased to meet you," Heinason said, crossing the room to shake my hand.

"You too," I said. "Can you tell me how he is?"

"Sure," Heinason nodded. "Let me check the chart."

I understood the protocol and stepped back as the doctor glanced through Signar's chart, then moved to the bedside and talked to the old man for a few moments.

As before, Signar made no discernible response, but Heinason seemed used to it and the pattern of his speech was light and reassuring. When he finished he patted Signar's shoulder, stood back and turned to me. "Shall we go out for a moment?"

Fríða spoke to Signar, then placed his hand back on the bed cover and followed us out into the corridor. When the door closed I looked to Heinason. "How bad is it?" I asked.

"Pretty bad," Heinason admitted, as if this was a concession he wouldn't normally make. "He has lost the use of speech and most movement down his left side. Also some on the right, although that seems to be improving a little."

"What caused it, do you know?"

"It was what is called an ischemic stroke, which happens when blood supply to part of the brain is cut off by something like a clot blocking the blood vessels."

"Can you treat it? I mean, will he improve?"

Heinason's expression wasn't optimistic. "When the brain does not have oxygen for several minutes the tissue starts to die," he said. "Unfortunately, your father was not found for some time after he collapsed. We're not sure how long, but it was enough for the damage to be serious: we have seen this from the scans. However, he is a strong man and the brain is very smart at finding new pathways, so we don't give up hope."

"But recovery will be a long process," I said.

"Sure. It will be weeks or months, and also we don't know how far back he can come."

"Do you think he'll be able to communicate again?"

"It's possible, sure, but I can't promise. We just have to wait and see."

I nodded. "Thank you. I appreciate your honesty."

Heinason made a helpless expression. "I'm sorry it can't be better news, but we will do everything we can. Is there anything else I can tell you?"

"No, I don't think so," I said. "Thanks for taking the time to see me."

"It was no problem."

After a few words to Fríða, Heinason headed away down the corridor. I looked back at the door to Signar's room and knew I wouldn't go back, not today.

Seeming to interpret my look, Fríða said, "It must be hard to see him after so long."

"I don't know what I expected," I said, acknowledging it.

"Do you want to go back inside?"

I knew she was offering to go with me but I shook my head. "No, thanks, you've done enough."

"Okay, if you're sure."

I cast a look at the door to Signar's room, then turned away. We started back along the corridor.

"So, do you have plans for what you will do now – today?" Fríða asked after a moment.

"No, I hadn't got that far."

"Do you have time for lunch? There is something I'd like to talk to you about if you have time."

"Of course. I'd like to," I said, realising I meant it, not least because her offer removed any need to decide what to do next.

"Okay, good," Fríða said. "If you can wait five minutes while I go to my office, then we can go. Is that okay?"

"Sure. Take as long as you need."

It was nearly one o'clock by the time we entered Kaffi Húsið: a short drive from the hospital, followed by a brief walk along the harbour where the rain-specked water was flat, calm and clear around the boats, many of them wooden-hulled, small and traditional with graceful lines and bright paintwork.

The café was on the ground floor of a tall quayside building and there were only four other diners, two with laptops open in front of them as they ate. Fríða and I took a table by the window with a view of the harbour and once she'd interpreted the menu for me we made inconsequential conversation until the food came.

Fríða ate a pasta salad delicately and with precision. She waited until she'd almost finished before seeming to decide the moment was right to raise the subject I was sure she'd had in mind from the start.

"I brought you something," she said and reached into her shoulder bag.

She handed me a five-by-three photograph, which was obviously a reprinted copy. The paper was sharp and new, but the image was much older, faded, the colours washed out. It showed a boy aged about three with light-blond hair, wearing a dark sweater and trousers. He was sitting on an upturned bucket, looking at the camera. Beside him stood a girl in a plain skirt and cardigan with long hair tied back. She was looking down at the boy, as if saying something. There was nothing in the background to show where the photo had been taken – just an anonymous patch of grass.

"That's you and me," Fríða said as I studied the picture. "My father took it. I was seven, maybe eight. I think it was probably taken when you came to visit us."

I searched the picture, trying to see any resemblance

between the boy and myself. It was hard to tell, but I could see that the boy looked a lot like the photos I had of my mother.

"I've never seen myself at that age," I told her. "I didn't think there were any photos from before we left. My mother didn't have any."

"There may be some more," Fríða said. "I'm copying all the family photographs on to the computer, but it's a slow job and I don't spend enough time on it. I tried to get Matteus to help, but family history isn't so interesting when you're seventeen."

That was neatly dropped in. "He's your son?"

"Yes." She nodded but chose to leave it at that.

"Like I said yesterday, I don't really know anything about anyone – the family."

I made to hand the picture back but Fríða waved it away. "No, I brought it for you."

"Oh. Okay. *Takk*."

I put it into an inside pocket, using the time to form the question which obviously came next.

"How much do you know about my mother and Signar and why she left the islands?"

"Not very much," Fríða said, thinking about it. "In the family it has always been one of those things that people don't talk about, you know?"

I nodded. "I had a drink with Kristian last night. He said more or less the same thing."

She didn't seem surprised. "I'm glad you met him."

I wondered why "glad" but didn't pursue it. Instead I said, "So why do you think no one talks about Lýdia and Signar? Is it because something had happened between them?"

"Maybe, I don't know. But at the time that sort of thing – a husband and wife splitting up – would only have been talked about between adults. Things were different then – people had different attitudes here. We can still be very conservative even now – especially the older generations. So I think it would have been seen as a humiliation for Signar that Lýdia ran away. There would have been a lot of gossip, I'm sure."

"But that's what people think – that she ran away?"

"I think so, yes."

"Is that what Signar has said?"

"No, not to me. I've never talked to him about it, but my idea – my impression – is that when he married Sofia Winther later on, people saw it as a new start."

"You mean he wiped the slate clean."

"Yes, perhaps."

From the way she said it I could tell that she didn't entirely agree with that interpretation – or perhaps with the fact that I'd made it – but I followed through on the line of questioning.

"Do you know *when* they were married?"

"The year? No, I'm not sure. You want to know how long it was after your mother's death?"

It *was* what I'd wanted to know, but I realised now that I'd underestimated Fríða's astuteness, and also my own habit of adopting interview-room technique.

"I suppose so, yes. I'm sorry, I didn't mean to interrogate you."

Fríða shook her head and gave me an understanding

smile. "Don't worry, it's natural, I think."

"Because I'm a copper?"

"Because you want to know about your past. Wasn't that why you came here?"

"To be honest, I'm not sure. But yes, I suppose it must have been at least part of it."

She took a moment, then she said, "Yesterday you told me you don't remember anything about living in the islands: nothing at all?"

I shrugged. "Nothing that means very much. A few images – wallpaper on a bedroom wall – I think it was a bedroom; a house on a hillside with chickens in the garden, but I don't know where. Just stuff like that."

She nodded, as if that made sense. "How old were you when your mother died?"

"Five."

A slight pursing of her lips. "She committed suicide?"

It was almost a statement, not quite. "Yeah," I said.

"And you found her."

The same almost-statement. I didn't know how much she knew as fact but she seemed as familiar with the ways of leading people to talk as I was. I supposed she would be, given her job.

"So I'm told," I said with a nod. "I don't remember – or I've stopped myself."

Not true, not exactly. Better if it was, but some images won't shift. As vivid as blood on porcelain.

"I'm sorry," Fríða said then. "I didn't mean to interrogate you either."

I negated it with a shake of my head. "Maybe it's force of habit for both of us."

"Maybe." She smiled, acknowledging the point.

A waitress approached to ask if we'd finished and to clear the table. When she'd gone Fríða looked at her watch.

"Do you need to get back to work?" I asked.

"No, I've finished for today. I only work part-time at the hospital but I have shopping to do and I like to be home when Matteus finishes school. As a single parent I think it's a good thing to do, though not always possible."

She looked at me, assessing openly for a couple of seconds, then said, "Can I ask you a favour?"

"Of course. I think I owe you one."

"Would you visit my mother – Estur – while you're here? She was pleased that you'd come to see Signar and I know it would mean something if you visited her."

"You think?" The idea surprised me, though maybe it shouldn't have.

"Of course." She said it without doubt. "She asked me to tell you."

"Okay, sure," I said, finally letting myself fall into it. "Is it far? I could go this afternoon."

Fríða shook her head. "No, I'm sorry, I thought you knew. My parents live on Suðuroy, the southernmost island. You have to take the ferry and today it's too late. Tomorrow is better, though: you can get there and back in a day."

Too late to back out of it, and not sure I wanted to anyway, I put an easy-going expression on my face. "Tomorrow then."

* * *

I left Fríða outside the café, declining her offer of a lift back to the hotel by saying I wanted to walk and see some more of the town – the easy excuse and easier to explain than the fact that I wanted time to give the disturbed silt a chance to settle. I promised to call her tomorrow when I got back from Suðuroy and in the meantime she said she'd let her parents know that I'd be coming. As she headed towards her car I watched her loose, easy stride and wondered several things without any conclusion, then turned towards the town.

Even in the early afternoon the streets were almost as quiet as the previous evening and I walked without hurrying, feeling more confident that I could navigate my way to the hotel now that I'd orientated myself. The movement was enough to allow me to think about Signar without it taking my entire focus. That was what I needed: that was the silt.

Just by going into that hospital room I knew I'd been drawn into the complicity of sympathy and solicitude that always accompanies visits to the sick, no matter what animosities may have been present beforehand. *How're you feeling? You look a lot better. How's the food…?*

Sickness reduces us all to inanity, but I tried to work out if seeing Signar brought low and made helpless had changed my mind about anything else. Did the new vision of him as a sick, unresponsive old man wipe out the image I'd carried for the last twenty-five years, of the intractable, indomitable bull of a man? Had a few minutes erased and replaced the picture I'd always held as an incontrovertible truth?

But I couldn't decide. It was as if the two Signars – the one from my memory, the other from the present – bore no relationship to each other. I'd come looking for one and got the other. I should have known, but I hadn't. The old image was too strong.

The one thing I did know for certain now was that there would be no confrontation, and no possibility of demanding the facts from Signar himself. There'd be no rapprochement between us either. Even if Signar still had sufficient self-awareness buried inside his stroke-locked brain to want a reconciliation, he couldn't say or do anything to show it. So if there was to be any change of view it could only come from me. And even if I chose to make that shift I'd have no way of knowing whether it was reciprocated or not.

Was I ready for that one-sided commitment; that leap of faith?

Not right at this moment, no. I knew that. It was too soon and I hadn't come far enough – didn't know enough – to simply dismiss the last forty years. I needed more. I wanted evidence – something – to take me beyond a reasonable doubt.

I pushed myself to maintain my pace as I strode up a steep side street and when I reached the brow I recognised the road at the top from the previous night. Coming back to myself I felt the first lash of rain, blown in from the harbour.

I hadn't seen it coming and now, as the downpour grew suddenly stronger, I was caught out. I walked on quickly, hoping to find shelter, but within a couple of minutes my jeans were sodden and there was no point. I stopped hurrying. Some things are easier to accept than others.

9

ON THE FIVE-MINUTE DRIVE FROM THE POLICE STATION TO dr. Jakobsens gøta it started to rain heavily and Hentze listened carefully over the sound of the windscreen wipers and the downpour as Dánjal Michelsen told him about the identification of Tummas Gramm's body. Michelsen was in his early thirties with a shaved head and the gaunt, angular features of a brawler. It was a misleading, albeit sometimes useful, impression. In reality Dánjal Michelsen liked nothing better than to watch birds and wildlife.

"His father made the identification," Michelsen told Hentze. "He was pretty shaken up by it."

"Did you manage to get any more information about Tummas?" Sometimes after an identification like that people wanted – even needed – to talk.

"Yeah, he was pretty helpful," Michelsen said, flipping through his notebook. "The last time he saw Tummas was just over a week ago but that wasn't unusual. Him and his wife live in Sandavágur."

"Any other children?"

"One, a girl. She's at university in Denmark, apparently – training to be a nurse."

"Did he know Tummas was arrested for drug possession a couple of years ago?"

"Yeah, but *harra* Gramm said that was all in the past. He said Tummas had sorted himself out and wasn't into that sort of thing any more."

"Okay. Did you ask about Tummas's occupation?"

"Yes, he was a barman at the Café Natúr, worked there for the last two months. Before that he was a labourer; before that on the boats… You get the picture: always worked but never seemed to settle at anything, was what his father said."

"Whose boats did he work on, did he say?"

"No, I didn't ask."

"Okay, let's find out next time you talk to the family. Known friends and acquaintances?"

"I got a few names but his father said the people at the bar would probably know more."

"Good. Okay. We'll look into that after we've talked to the flatmate."

There was an empty parking bay directly opposite Tummas Gramm's address: above a shop selling women's clothing and knitwear. Hentze parked the Volvo neatly and pulled down the sun visor to display the word *Politi*. The town's parking wardens were a ferocious bunch.

He and Michelsen crossed the road through a stream of water on the tarmac and climbed the steel steps on the side of the building to the door of the flat. Hentze rang the bell and they waited, backs turned to the downpour. After a decent interval Michelsen pressed the bell again but there was still no response from inside. Hentze tried the door but it was locked.

"This guy Vang said he'd be here?"

"Yeah. He was at work but he said he'd come back. Didn't sound very happy about it, though."

"Okay, let's give him a few minutes," Hentze said. "We'll talk to the landlady while we wait."

The shop door buzzed when the two police officers entered, dripping on the carpet. Lit by halogen ceiling lamps it was warm inside and Hentze was careful not to stand too close to the racks of clothes and the stiffly posed mannequins in case he got them wet. He was no expert on fashion, but it seemed to him that the shop would cater for the more mature woman: the sort who had probably bought here for years.

From the rear of the shop a neatly turned-out woman in her fifties with permed hair emerged from a curtained area. Michelsen had already spoken to her on the phone and now Hentze introduced himself and asked if he could check a few facts about Tummas Gramm with her while they waited for her other tenant – Vang – to arrive.

It turned out that the woman – *frú* Marjun Jensen – was more than happy to talk. What with the rain and the end of the tourist season, she had had only one customer so far that day and she seemed to have built up a surfeit of unexpended chatter.

Naturally, she was upset at the news about Tummas,

she told Hentze. It was a terrible thing, especially for a young man. Of course, he'd only been renting the room for a few months; not as long as the other occupant, Janus Vang – such a good tenant – but Tummas had been no trouble either; paid his rent on time; didn't have parties. Would the officers like a cup of coffee while they waited? Did they have any idea how such an unexpected death could have occurred?

Hentze demurred on both counts and when he saw a man in his late twenties heading through the rain towards the side stairs he excused himself and went out with Michelsen to find Janus Vang letting himself into the flat.

"Do you think this will take long?" Vang wanted to know as he opened the door to the hallway. He was a thin man in a suit and tie with highly polished shoes. "I had to leave work and I can't be away for long."

"I appreciate that, thank you," Hentze said, catching Dánjal Michelsen's look. "It is important that we speak to you, though."

"Well I can't tell you much. His room's down there, on the right." Vang gestured down one branch of the hall. "Do you have a key? He kept it locked."

They didn't have a key so Michelsen went back down to the shop to ask *frú* Jensen while Hentze followed Vang into the sitting room. It was tidy, with a wooden floor and two relatively new sofas.

"So maybe you could tell me the last time you saw Tummas Gramm," Hentze said as Vang went to the kitchen area and poured a glass of juice from the fridge.

"I don't know," Vang said. "The weekend? Yes. Sunday. The afternoon. He went out. I suppose it was about three o'clock."

"And today's Wednesday. You haven't seen or heard him between Sunday and now?"

Vang shook his head. "No, but that doesn't mean he wasn't here. Look, we weren't friends or anything. I don't really know anything about him: he just rented the room. And he worked late – at the bar. You know about that?"

Hentze nodded. "Yes."

"So he came in late and slept late, and I go out early. Most weeks we didn't cross paths, except sometimes at the weekend."

"Did he say where he was going when you saw him on Sunday?"

"No, I don't think so. He just said something like 'see you later' and then he was gone."

"Okay." Hentze made a note. "Did he have a girlfriend, do you know – any visitors?"

"Not while I was here. I told you, I didn't know him. We didn't talk about stuff like that."

Vang came back to the sitting area carrying his glass. "Listen, is this serious? I mean, I know your colleague said his body had been found, but is that suspicious? I mean was it an accident or suicide or what?"

"At the moment we don't know," Hentze told him. "First we need to get the pathologist's report and that may take some time." He heard Dánjal coming back and stepped away to the hall. "Excuse me a moment."

CHRIS OULD

Dánjal Michelsen had a single key on a plastic fob and when Hentze joined him they went along to Tummas Gramm's room and unlocked the door.

The bedroom was a decent size but made smaller by the fact that Tummas Gramm had not been one for keeping things tidy. Clothes were piled on the floor, DVD cases scattered on a small desk around a laptop, magazines beside the bed. The room smelled of stale smoke, and by a window there was an ashtray with the stubs of several joints mixed with the other dog ends.

Hentze moved into the room, stepping carefully over the detritus.

"What are we looking for – a suicide note?" Michelsen asked.

Hentze shook his head. "I don't think so. I don't know yet. Drugs maybe." He picked up the end of a spliff from the ashtray. "He wasn't as reformed as his father said, at any rate. Just see if anything looks odd or out of place. Did they find any personal possessions on the body when they stripped him at the mortuary, do you know?"

"Only a lighter in his jeans pocket."

"So maybe we can find his wallet or mobile."

But he doubted it. And at the end of five minutes picking over the room they had found nothing more informative – or incriminating – than a small amount of hash in a tin, openly on view on a shelf, and three hardcore porn DVDs in the wardrobe.

Hentze hadn't really expected to find anything to leap out and furnish them with a reason why Tummas Gramm

118

had been found at Saksun. Such things were too good to be true.

He did consider trying to examine the laptop, but in the end he decided to bag it up and take it back to the station instead. Hentze was less than adept with electronics and knew it would be better to let someone else look at the machine, if it became necessary. Like making a thorough search of the room, that would depend on what the pathologist said.

There was a movement by the bedroom door and Janus Vang cleared his throat. "Will it be much longer? I need to get back."

Hentze sealed the evidence bag containing the laptop and turned round.

"No, I think we've finished here. Thank you."

"Are you taking that?" Vang asked, indicating the laptop.

"For the moment. Would you like a receipt?"

Vang shook his head. "It's nothing to do with me." He looked round the room with evident distaste. "Some people live like students even when they're not." And then, dismissing it: "So I can go?"

"Of course," Hentze said. "We may have to come back, but in the meantime would you stop anyone else coming in here?"

"No one else has a key, but yes, if that's what you want."

"Fine. Thank you."

Hentze signalled to Dánjal that they were done.

* * *

"I've put his clothes to dry in sterile conditions," Dr Elisabet Hovgaard told Hentze half an hour later as he closed the fire door behind them. "When they're ready I'll bag them for forensic examination."

They had come outside because Hovgaard wanted to smoke. Each of them had a coffee in a cardboard cup and when Hovgaard moved into the sunshine Hentze went with her. There was a glassy clarity in the air now that the rainstorm had passed and the concrete strip outside the mortuary's side door had a pleasant view down the hillside to the sea and the West Harbour.

"There's nothing else I can do," Hovgaard went on. "In view of his wounds and the way he was found it's certainly suspicious so he should have a full forensic PM. You'll need to get Peter or Anders in from Copenhagen."

She drew on her cigarette, then turned her head downwind to exhale. She was in her mid-fifties, short and rounded with dark hair cut in an angular, youthful bob. Hentze always felt comfortable in her presence because she was pragmatic and unemotional without being uncaring: the sort of person you knew wouldn't sugar-coat the pill. If you had to be ill, Hovgaard was the doctor you'd want – except for the fact that she was a pathologist and by the time you required her services it would be too late.

"Is there *anything* you can tell me?" Hentze asked.

Hovgaard nodded. "Well, he's dead. That's a start. You can have my preliminary findings if you like, but you'd see for yourself if you looked at the body. That's all I've done, more or less. White male, 1.8 metres tall, approximately 80 kilos, seems previously fit and healthy, good muscle tone. Bit of a looker, was he?"

"I don't know," Hentze said, momentarily thrown by the question. "Maybe. I hadn't thought about it. Why, does it matter?"

"Oh, no," Hovgaard said with an indifferent shrug. "It's just one of those things I think about while I'm looking them over: this one was a beauty; that one had a hard time of it; another should have smiled more... Now they're dead it's all the same, but it helps you keep things in perspective – to my way of thinking, at least."

Hentze nodded thoughtfully. "Yeh, I can see what you mean. Although you do have more opportunity to do that than most."

She fixed him with a beady eye. "Are you telling me I should get out more?"

"I wouldn't dream of it," Hentze said without a trace of flippancy. "Each to their own, I always say."

Elisabet Hovgaard nodded and sipped her coffee. "That's why I like you, Hjalti: you understand the basic human need for idiosyncrasies."

"I also need to understand what happened to him," Hentze said, attempting to get her back to the subject in hand. "Can you tell me anything about how he died?"

Hovgaard shook her head. "Without dissection, no, not definitively. Evidently he'd been in or near water post-mortem, so it's possible he drowned, but not likely I think. It's also possible he died of blood loss, but I doubt that, too."

"Why?"

"Because – and I don't know this from dissection, remember – it doesn't look to me as if the shotgun wound – if that's what it is, and let's say so for now because we all know that it is – the shotgun wound doesn't look severe enough to have caused major damage to any vital organs or vessels. Yes, it would have bled, but not so badly as to cause death. And from the cotton-wool wadding taped to the wound, either the victim or someone else was obviously tending the injury. If he'd come into hospital I'm pretty sure he'd have survived. He might have survived even *without* hospital, although leaving the pellets inside wouldn't be so good. Infection might have been an issue."

"So he was shot, but not fatally," Hentze said.

"So I believe."

"Did you find any other injuries that could have killed him?"

Hovgaard shook her head amidst a plume of smoke. "No, there's nothing obvious."

Hentze thought about that, then drank some coffee. "Can we go back to the shotgun wound? Is there anything you can say about it?"

Elisabet Hovgaard considered the question through another deep drag on her cigarette. "From the purely superficial examination I'd say it was caused at fairly close quarters, but not point-blank. I don't think he was hit by the full load of pellets either. It looks to me more like a glancing blow, you might say: perhaps aimed upwards from a low angle, which would also account for the injuries to his face."

"Could it have been self-inflicted?"

"No." On that she was definite.

"Could it have been an accident, then? While he was cleaning a gun or something like that?"

Hovgaard shrugged. "Sure, perhaps it slipped off a table or chair, struck the ground and went off. You *could* construct a scenario where something like that would be possible, but it would be a chance in a million: a really freak accident." She shook her head and looked at him. "Are you trying to avoid the most obvious explanation here, Hjalti?"

"No, not at all, but I think Ári will ask."

"*Psha.*"

"Yes, yes, okay," Hentze said, getting the message. "So would the injury have been enough to disable him or would he have been able to walk or drive afterwards?"

"Probably, yes. I don't doubt he was in pain, but maybe not so much as to incapacitate him."

"Okay," Hentze nodded, thinking it over. "You know what I'm going to ask now, right?"

"Time of death?"

"Can you say?"

Hovgaard made a so-so gesture. "It's difficult. Immersion in water throws things off – although his body *was* in the same physical position for about twelve hours immediately after death."

"The hypostasis?" Hentze asked.

"Precisely." She gave him a look of mock disapproval. "Have you been reading Wikipedia?"

"Not exactly. So, the time?"

She dropped her cigarette end and trod on it. "As accurately as I can assess – which isn't very – I'd say no less than forty-eight hours before you found him and no more than seventy-two."

"Anywhere between Sunday and Monday, then."

A nod. "Yes."

"Okay, thanks," Hentze said. "I'll tell Ári that we need a full forensic PM. He'll like that. He's already talking about the budget."

"There is one other thing," Hovgaard said, moving back towards the mortuary door and opening it. "His right shoulder is dislocated. I can't tell for certain, but from the lack of bruising or injury it probably happened after death, possibly from someone dragging the body by the arm." She looked back at him. "I only say it in case you need something else to convince Ári."

"Because it would mean that there was definitely another person involved at or around the time of his death?"

"I wouldn't want anyone to believe he simply went for a stroll on the beach and collapsed and died there. I think that's extremely unlikely."

Hentze nodded. "Thanks. But now that it's definitely suspicious, I'm sure Ári will want to make sure everything's done by the book: you can always rely on that."

10

IN THE NORMAL WAY OF THINGS I AVOID SHOPPING MALLS: they're depressing and claustrophobic for as many reasons as there are people inside them. But I'd wanted an excuse to use the car I'd hired from the hotel, to re-familiarise myself with driving on the wrong side of the road and to do something with even a vague sense of purpose, rather than just kill time. The idea of finding a gift to take when I went to see Estur Sólsker tomorrow – flowers or chocolates – provided enough of a pretext for that. It was probably an outdated and unnecessary gesture, but if it helped break the ice I didn't think it could hurt.

According to my town map the anonymous black warehouse of a building was the SMS shopping centre, but until I walked inside I was still uncertain: two floors under a high ceiling, a sleek clean-lined Scandinavian design of black steel and glass and a background swell of voices rolling off the hard surfaces.

The shop names were all unfamiliar, so I let myself fall into the unhurried strolling pace of those around me, assessing the windows I passed with no way to tell, more often than not, what the signs and advertising were enticing me to do.

This disconnection gave me some objectivity, but I still found it hard to gauge my real reaction to it all. The people were slim, healthy, good-looking. There was a sense of contentment and purpose in the adults – as if they knew they had a good life here – and a liveliness about the teenagers, compared to the often sullen or aggressive youths of home. Who wouldn't want to be a part of this smart, clean, ordered world if it was really as good as it looked?

But I also knew I was still a tourist, still skating over the surface. The more subtle and revealing signals that might tell a different story about the place were invisible to me, as inaccessible and unreadable as the language. It left me as much on the outside as I'd ever been, neither one thing nor the other.

I spent an hour wandering and observing, finally pausing to buy a box of gold-wrapped chocolates from a shop on the first floor. I could only go by their price and appearance, but they seemed classy enough and when the sales-girl volunteered to wrap the box in tissue paper I accepted with thanks and got a small red-ribbon bow added without asking.

I'd had enough of tourism by then, though, and I was making my way towards the exit when my phone rang. A woman's voice asked for me by name and told me she was calling from the office of Magnus Ravnsfjall at Four Fjords. Would I be able to meet with Magnus in half an hour?

For a moment I wondered if Magnus had been told about my visit to Signar that morning and wanted to tell me again to stay out of Ravnsfjall family affairs. But I pushed down the impulse to be offhand, and instead told the woman affably that half an hour would be fine if she gave me the address.

The offices of Four Fjords were not – as I'd expected – anywhere close to the harbour or the sea. Instead they were in a small, modern business park development on a hillside close to the ring road. The building itself looked more like a house than an office, with moulded steel cladding, a gabled roof and a porch over the entrance. A discreet pair of signs next to the door announced the occupants: Fagraberg Advokatar on the ground floor – a law firm, I guessed from the scales of justice logo – and Four Fjords on the first floor.

Inside I took the hollowly echoing stairs and emerged on a landing with a single door. Beyond that, in a large, open-plan space of exposed beams and pale wood flooring, a woman in her thirties looked up from her desk. When I introduced myself she nodded and smiled, telling me Magnus wouldn't be long; if I would care to take a seat, she would let him know I was there. Her English was very precise.

She showed me to a sofa and asked if I'd like coffee or water. I said, "*Nei, takk*," and as she left me I made a conscious effort not to check the time or let myself be irked by having to wait.

The place had the air of a show home. There were a couple of sea-orientated paintings on the walls and beside the sofa there was a glass coffee table where business magazines and a vase containing a single flower were immaculately laid out. If I disturbed the magazines I wondered how long it would be before the woman at the desk would straighten them again. Not very, I guessed. For all the prosperous minimalism, this didn't look like an office where there was very much else to occupy her.

A couple of minutes later an oak-framed door opened and Magnus Ravnsfjall came out. Unlike yesterday he was wearing a business suit, and just for a second I saw him adjust his expression before he came towards me. I stood up.

"Jan, thank you for coming."

The offer of a hand to shake came from Magnus this time – businesslike, automatic – but I accepted it. "It wasn't a problem," I said evenly.

"Good. I appreciate it," he said, a tad stiff. He seemed caught between acknowledging what had passed between us yesterday and the desire to move on. "Please, come in."

His office was almost as minimalist as the outer area, with a conference table – four seats either side – and an L-shaped desk in front of a leather executive chair. Magnus ignored the desk, though, and gestured me to a seat at the table before pulling one out for himself.

"So what can I do for you?" I asked as I settled myself. "I saw Signar this morning. You might know."

I knew I could have softened this, but I didn't want to give Magnus an easy way out or waste time getting to the point, so I waited for the reaction and for a moment thought I might get it. Magnus's jaw tightened, but then he said, "Is there a change?"

"I don't think so."

A nod. "I will see him this evening."

He drew a breath, then looked at me directly. "I thought we should talk again," he said. "Yesterday was not very productive."

"No? I learned quite a bit." Okay, I was allowed one gibe.

Magnus appeared to consider that, then chose to ignore it. "There is something else I want to ask you. Can you tell me why you were at Saksun this morning with the police?"

It wasn't what I'd expected as an opening gambit but I didn't let anything show. "Nothing official," I said.

"*Ja*, I understand. But there was a corpse, yes? A man called Tummas Gramm."

"Yes."

"And he had been shot."

It was a statement of fact, not a question, which was interesting. I wondered where Magnus had got his information but decided not to corroborate it. Instead I said, "I don't know the cause of death."

He thought about that briefly. "Okay, let me ask you then: do you think this dead man is there because of my father?"

It was the obvious question, but without knowing what Magnus wanted I still wasn't going to speculate. "If you mean, do I think Signar shot him, I've no idea," I said.

That wasn't enough for Magnus. "But last night you told Kristian that you thought my father was at Tjørnuvík because he would pay blackmail. You said that, didn't you?"

The previous night my impression had been that Kristian and Magnus weren't very close, but maybe I'd misjudged that if Kristian had told his brother this much.

"I said it might be a possibility, yes," I nodded. "Kristian didn't think so. If you know anything different, though…"

Magnus shook his head but remained silent for a few seconds, thinking. I let it run. I wanted to see how far he'd take it on his own, without prompting. It would be a good indicator of how much and what he was concerned about.

In the end he leaned forward and rested a hand on the table. "I think the police will try to connect my father to the corpse," he said. "You know what was in his car: a shotgun with one cartridge fired? It is too much of – two things happening at the same time."

"Coincidence?"

"*Ja*. It is too easy for the police to say they think there is a connection."

"Do you *know* that's what they're thinking, or are you just guessing?"

I saw a shadow of reluctance pass briefly over his face. "I know some things," he said. "And some people would like it – to make a connection between the two things."

"Why?"

This time Magnus's response was unequivocal. "Because Signar Ravnsfjall is a strong – no, a powerful man. So is his company. He is a good businessman, and some people they don't like that so much. You understand what I mean?"

"You mean they'd see this as a chance to stick the knife in?"

Magnus nodded. "Even if it is just talk, it does no good for his reputation. What's the word – rumours? They can still do harm even if there is no proof, even if nothing has happened."

"I suppose so," I said. "But what's that got to do with me? I told you yesterday, I only came here to see Signar. I've done that, so…"

"So you're not interested any more?" It was clear he didn't believe it. "Kristian told me you asked him questions about your mother and my father, when they were married."

"I didn't say anything to Kristian that I wouldn't have said to you if you'd bothered to listen yesterday."

I heard the acidic tone in my voice, too late to neutralise it. I saw Magnus stiffen in his seat and now I'd become the one who wouldn't back off, which was what I'd specifically intended to avoid.

"Look," I said, trying to draw it back a little. "I know you didn't get me here to organise a family reunion, okay? So why not just tell me what's on your mind."

Like the faint lag of an international call, Magnus seemed to take a moment to catch up with the end of the sentence. When he did he rubbed his chin, then said, "If it is what you want, I think the police here will keep you informed. You are also *ein politistur*, like them."

I frowned. "Are you saying they'll keep me informed because you've asked them to?"

"I don't have any control over the police, of course,"

Magnus said, distancing himself from that notion.

"But?"

"But I believe they will ask your ideas."

I sat back, taking my time. I didn't know enough to assess how far Magnus Ravnsfjall might be able to influence the local police, but clearly he thought he had or he could. Perhaps the relatively small scale of the islands would make it easier, when no one was further apart than two degrees of separation.

In the end I said, "And if they did talk to me, you'd want to be kept informed about what they're doing, is that the idea?"

Magnus shook his head. "I can hear the information," he said flatly. "It is *how* they look at things. Do you understand? My father cannot speak for himself, so it is very easy for others to say this or that happened because they want to think it. You must know this."

I nodded. "So you want someone to protect Signar's reputation," I said. "Okay, I get that. But so far there's nothing except coincidence to connect him to Tummas Gramm. So either the forensic evidence will prove a link between them, or it'll show there isn't one. Either way, there's nothing I can do about it."

"So you don't care?"

"I just said: there's nothing I can do."

"And that is why you went to Saksun this morning." Even with his accent the sarcasm came through. He didn't believe me.

I kept my face straight and said nothing for several

seconds. I'd tried to remain objective but I didn't like Magnus's superior attitude any more than I had before. The only difference now was that I had something he wanted and it gave me some leverage.

"*Do* you know why Signar went to Tjørnuvík with a million krónur in a briefcase?" I asked flatly.

"No, I don't know." The answer was definite and clear: either the truth or a well-practised lie.

"So when was the last time you saw him before he was found there?"

"At the church in Runavík on Sunday morning, for the service."

"Did Signar know Tummas Gramm?"

"No, I don't think so, but Gramm's father – Lias – is an employee for Four Fjords."

"Doing what?"

"He makes mechanical repairs on the boats."

"Here, in Tórshavn?"

"In Runavík. That is the head office."

As he said it my mobile rang, letting me leave the questioning in mid-air. I recognised the number.

"Reyna," I said.

"This is Hentze. May I speak to you for a minute?"

"I'm just leaving a meeting. Can I call you back?"

"Sure, of course."

"*Takk*. Bye." I rang off, gave it a second, then said, "I have to go."

I stood up, knowing it would force Magnus to the crux of the matter.

He rose. "So, we have an – *understanding*?"

"I understand what you *want*, but I think you're overestimating what I can do. You're also assuming I care about Signar's reputation."

"It is the family reputation as well."

I held back the broken-record response to that, left a pause where it would have been, then said, "If the police tell me something I don't mind passing it on to you, as long as I haven't been told in confidence. I'm not promising anything, though."

"Okay, I understand," he said with a nod, and to give him his due he at least had the grace to make it an acknowledgement that I'd offered a favour. In my head, though, I knew it was a qualified one. I didn't think Magnus Ravnsfjall was the sort of man who would see favours as currency; if I was right, he would only deal in the concrete, and then only according to his needs.

11

HENTZE STOOD IN FRONT OF THE TWO WHITEBOARDS IN THE small conference room, moodily assessing the layout of the information he'd written up in black marker pen. The blinds on the windows to the corridor were closed and he was alone. The dissatisfaction he felt didn't come from what he'd written on the boards, but from the murmur of voices through the thin wall separating him from the adjacent office. Ári Niclasen seemed to be speaking more than Jan Reyná, which didn't surprise Hentze, but he disliked this behind-the-hand way of doing things. He smelled politics and didn't like the aroma.

He turned away from the boards, paced for a moment. Something had happened while he'd been out. Something had shifted Ári's position from one of discouraging any contact with Reyná to one of getting Hentze to invite the man in.

Whatever the influencing factor had been, Hentze knew it wouldn't have been Ári's idea. He also doubted it came from Reyná, so it must have come from higher up –

the Chief, most likely. That was why he smelled politics, like a bad drain. And it was a distraction from what they should be thinking about.

Hentze turned back to the whiteboards in a conscious effort to refocus and assess the information again. On the left-hand board was a summary of the information they had on Tummas Gramm – age, occupation, address and so on – and beneath that was the scant information Elisabet Hovgaard had been willing to confirm, most of which Hentze felt obliged to follow with a question mark: time of death: 48/72 hrs; cause of death: gunshot wound (?); loss of blood (?); drowning (??).

On the right-hand board he had drawn a timeline of Gramm's known movements: Sunday (left home 15:00) to Wednesday (body found 07:45). Monday and Tuesday were conspicuously blank. This was what they needed to look at. Where had Tummas Gramm been – alive or dead – after he left home on Sunday?

He was wondering this when Annika Mortensen knocked on the door and came into the office. She had several sheets of paper in her hand and the air of someone who had spent time doing something they enjoyed.

"*Hey*," she said. "I've got the list of people who worked on the boathouse conversion at Saksun. I hope Edvin Mohr is faster at building than he is at searching his records."

"Great, thanks," Hentze said. "Is Tummas Gramm on there?"

"Yes. He worked for Mohr from April to August this year as a general labourer. He left because he got the job at Café

Natúr. Apparently he said he wanted to work in Tórshavn."

Hentze nodded. "It's harder to sell dope out in the sticks."

"You think that's what he was doing?"

"He has in the past. Who owns the boathouse, did you find out?"

"Yeah, it belongs to a woman from Denmark named Sonja Brygmann. She bought it two years ago. Mohr says she intends to use it as a summer home once it's finished."

"Okay," Hentze nodded. "Will you contact her and ask if she gave anyone permission to stay there over the last two weeks? I don't think it's likely, but just in case."

"Sure."

As she moved to the phone Dánjal Michelsen came in. "I've contacted most of the people on the list of Gramm's friends and acquaintances I got from his parents," he told Hentze. "The staff at the bar gave me a few other names, too."

"Did you get any more on his last known movements?"

"Yeah, I talked to the owner of the bar and the people who worked there over the weekend. Tummas worked from 6 p.m. on Saturday until 4 a.m. on Sunday when the bar closed. He stayed on for a drink and left about 5 a.m. So far no one I've spoken to saw him after that."

"That's a long shift, especially on a Saturday night."

Dánjal nodded. "According to the manager the staff are supposed to do twelve-hour shifts on Friday and Saturday, but Tummas was late. He rang in to say he'd had trouble with his car on the way back from Eysturoy."

"Eysturoy? What was he doing there?"

"I don't know. He didn't say."

"Okay."

Hentze moved to the boards and put in the new information on the timeline, although it didn't help move things forward. The last sighting of Gramm was still by Janus Vang on Sunday afternoon.

"Has anyone mentioned a girlfriend? Or a boyfriend? Was he straight or gay? Do we know?"

"Straight, I think," Michelsen said. "One of the bar staff said she thought he was seeing someone, but she'd never seen them together. Maybe the girlfriend lives on Eysturoy, if that's where he'd been."

"Maybe." Hentze stepped back from the board, looked it over again.

"Is there going to be a press statement – an appeal for information?" Dánjal Michelsen asked. "It might help."

"Ári's dealing with it," Hentze said, and he noticed that the conversation in the adjacent office seemed to have ended.

"So that is agreed then," Ári Niclasen said, as if he'd finally convinced himself. He stood up. "And of course, even unofficially, you understand that the details of the investigation will be – er – *confidential*."

"Of course," I said, standing. He'd almost tied himself in knots trying to make it clear that even though he was inviting my input, my access was entirely unofficial. It was also the third time he'd emphasised the need for confidentiality.

Of course, the language barrier didn't help and I could see that it was harder for Niclasen to be as subtle as he'd have liked with a limited vocabulary. I also got the impression that he was doing something he wouldn't necessarily have done of his own volition. That was another source of discomfort for him and I was tempted to mention Magnus Ravnsfjall's name just to see what sort of reaction it got. In the end I decided it might be better to wait.

I followed Niclasen out of the office and along to the one next door where Hjalti Hentze and two other officers – one a woman in uniform, the other a tough-looking guy in a leather jacket – were standing talking. They fell silent when Niclasen and I entered.

"This is Detective Inspector Jan Reyná from England," Niclasen said. "Annika Mortensen and Dánjal Michelsen. Inspector Reyná has agreed to give us advice if he can." He looked to Hentze. "Shall we go through it?"

I took a seat off to one side of the others and for the next five minutes Hentze outlined the information they'd collected. I said nothing but I paid attention, especially to what the pathologist had – or rather, hadn't – said.

I thought I detected a slight air of knowingness when Hentze told Niclasen that in the pathologist's opinion, the way the body was found was suspicious enough to require a full forensic examination, which she didn't feel qualified to do.

Niclasen took that in his stride. "Anders Toft will be here tomorrow," he said. "Also there will be a technical team to look at the boathouse and anything else we need.

What can you do while we wait?"

"There are still some people we need to speak with," Hentze said. "Gramm's friends. And we are looking for his car. He owned a blue Volkswagen Golf but there's no sign of it."

"Okay. Maybe the press statement will bring information," Niclasen said. "I will get it done so it can be on the news." He hesitated then, before finally nodding. "So I can leave you to it, okay?"

"Okay," Hentze said.

I waited until Niclasen had left the room, then stood up. "I need a cigarette," I told Hentze. "Can I smoke outside?"

"Sure," he said. "I'll show you the way."

Outside the front entrance to the station we stood, smokeless, where we'd talked yesterday. I said, "You know I didn't ask for this?"

"Yes, I thought that." Hentze nodded.

"And just so you know, I was with Magnus Ravnsfjall when you called earlier."

"Oh?" Hentze managed to keep a neutral expression.

"He said he thought someone from the police would get in touch with me. He seemed pretty sure."

I waited to see if Hentze understood the implication and saw from his clouded and troubled expression that he did. He mulled it over for a moment longer, then said, "Does Magnus Ravnsfjall think there is a connection between his father and Tummas Gramm?"

"He told me they didn't know each other, but apparently Tummas's father works for Four Fjords as a mechanic."

"I didn't know that."

"It might not mean anything."

"No. A lot of people work for Four Fjords in some way."

I wondered if there was a coded meaning in this, but without asking directly I couldn't be sure and I didn't want to put him on the spot. Instead I said, "Listen, I came in to see Niclasen because he asked me to, not because I think you need me or because I've got any right to interfere. I'm leaving in a few days anyway, and tomorrow I'm visiting my aunt on Suðuroy, so I'm not going to tread on your toes. If I can help, fine, but otherwise... I *don't* work for Magnus or Signar."

Hentze nodded. "Yes. I understand. *Takk*." He glanced away, then back. "Do you have any ideas, from what we have now?"

I shook my head. "You need the forensics and the post-mortem, otherwise it's just stories."

He got that. "Maybe by the time you come back tomorrow we'll have a theory," he said. "Then we'll see. Are you coming back inside?"

"No. I need to eat."

"Okay then." Unexpectedly he held out his hand to shake mine, as if we had just reached an unspoken agreement. "Have a good journey tomorrow: it won't be too rough. You might like Suðuroy, but the people are not like us here. They are a wild lot."

"Wild?"

"Sure. See how many have dark hair. They are the descendants of pirates from the Mediterranean and they all swear a lot."

As he turned away I was only partially sure he was joking.

Back inside the station Hjalti Hentze called Sóleyg to say he would be late – already was – then cast a rueful look at the clearing evening sky through the window. He had planned to dig up some potatoes and pull a few weeds when he got home, but that would have to wait now. There would have to be someone around in case the news report brought in information about Tummas Gramm's last movements. Hentze suspected that it would not, though. He was already sure that whoever had last seen Tummas Gramm alive would not want to speak with the police.

12

Thursday/hósdagur

THERE WAS RAIN IN THE AIR AS I MOVED OUT ON TO THE open stern deck of the ferry, *Smyril*. It was already throbbing its way out of Tórshavn harbour, leaving a blue-green and white arc of a wake.

From the deck I got a broad view of the receding town, spread out across the lower slopes of the encircling hills under a flat, overcast sky. The buildings seemed much more scattered from this distance, as if the town's toehold on the land was more tenuous than it was prepared to admit.

Turning my back to the breeze, I recognised the turquoise and charcoal-grey Lego buildings of the hospital passing to my left. I watched it and couldn't help picturing Signar somewhere inside. It was a strange thing to know exactly where he was all the time now: an alien concept when for so long he'd been simply an unknown, distant absence.

As the ship headed further out into deeper water the wind grew colder, but I ignored it for a while longer, watching the diminishing coastline as the low cloud cover blurred the distinction between rock and sky. But finally, as we passed beyond the southern tip of Streymoy, a light rain blew in and I shouldered my rucksack and went to seek shelter. I was tired of thinking – or not – anyway.

There was no announcement, but as the ferry passed into the elongated waters of Trongisvágsfjørður two hours later, the people around me in the lounge started to gather their possessions and migrate towards the stairwells. I took my cue from them and put away my iPad and the Bradt guidebook I'd bought yesterday, glad to have the enforced confinement lifted.

Ten minutes later the ramp in the stern of the ship went down with a clanking of steel plates and when it came to my turn I followed the lead of the others and drove down the ramp and on to the dock. At the exit to the terminal most of the other vehicles turned right, towards Tvøroyri, but I headed the other way, swearing when I messed up the gear change to third, but then settling down to the alien left-hand driving.

The sun was brighter than I'd seen it since I arrived – high, broken cloud with no threat of rain. The road was effortlessly smooth, like all the Faroese roads, and I was almost disappointed to slow down when I saw the sign for Porkeri after only ten miles or so. I made the hard, hairpin turn, then let the car drift down the hillside towards the village that sat in a fold of an inlet valley below.

"You can't miss it," Fríða Sólsker had told me. "It's the only yellow house on Skiparavegur."

Both these things turned out to be true, although in design the yellow house was exactly the same as its four neighbours: three storeys with pressed steel cladding, gable-roof bedrooms at the top and resolutely square windows.

There was something about the neat road and houses that I couldn't place for a moment, until I realised that they all looked virtually new. Nowhere was there any sign of age or decay: no litter, no potholes, no graffiti, no overgrown lawns. There might have been some somewhere, but I hadn't seen them yet and even when I stopped the car I still saw nothing to dispel the overarching impression of order and care.

I took my time retrieving the gift-wrapped chocolates from the passenger seat and walking up the neat laid-brick path to the house. I thought I'd seen movement in one of the first-floor windows and by the time I got to the door it was being opened by a man dressed in a white sweater and jeans. He was somewhere in his late sixties, perhaps seventy, I calculated: tall, bony, with that loose-limbed gangliness that such people have. His round glasses gave him a faintly scholarly air.

"*Hey*, welcome," he said with an easy smile. "You must be Jan. It's a pleasure to meet you. I'm Jens."

"It's good to meet you," I told him, shaking his hand.

"Come in, please. Estur's inside. She's been making lunch since breakfast, so I hope you brought your appetite."

He led the way up varnished wooden steps to the first

floor and into a sitting room furnished with a mixture of old, dark wooden furniture and modern leather recliners. One wall was given over to bookshelves and on the others there were several paintings – slightly primitive landscapes – and a collection of family photographs on a sideboard. The whole place looked as if it had been dusted and hoovered about ten minutes before.

"Estur, our visitor is here," Jens called towards another room and a moment later Estur Sólsker appeared, a woman of medium height, slightly plump in blue slacks and a white blouse. She had greying hair round a face inclined towards sternness, although she seemed to have made a decision to soften it now and smiled warmly at me.

"Jan, I'm so glad you came," she said, stepping forward to take hold of my hands. "Forty years since I saw you. That shouldn't be the way for a family."

There was just a slight tone of reproach and as she stood back to look at me again I had the feeling she was assessing whether I should be held responsible for the absence.

"I wanted to see you while I was here," I said, hoping to shift the subject. "And Ketty wouldn't have let me back in the house if I hadn't come. I thought you might like these." I handed her the box of chocolates. "I hope they're okay."

She took them, opened the ribbon to see inside, then looked up with a smile. "Thank you. Wonderful. Please, take off your coat. You'll have lunch with us, of course."

* * *

The dining-room table was set with half a dozen plates of cold meats, fish, cheese, a bowl of salad and a basket of home-made bread. I recognised Ketty's philosophy of entertaining – that it was better to offer too much than too little – and wondered if it was a generational thing, or peculiar to the Faroese.

When we were seated, Jens Sólsker said grace; it was as natural to him as it was alien to me. It took me a moment to catch on and I was glad the other two had bowed their heads first. I didn't go as far as uttering the "amen", but when they looked up it seemed sufficient to have appeared serious.

It was easy enough to make conversation over the meal just by letting myself be the subject of Estur's questions: when had I arrived and how had I met Fríða and Magnus? Had I also met Kristian? Yes? That was good. As you got older you realised how important family ties were. It was good that I was meeting my family after so long. These days, of course, it was easy to stay in contact and not so hard to get to the islands, either; not like the old times.

Again, I wondered if there was just a hint of reproach in that – or perhaps an explanation of past divisions – but I couldn't be sure. She seemed happy – perhaps even eager – to talk about Signar and to cast back in time, telling me about their childhood on Suðuroy and what their parents had been like. She recounted two or three anecdotes from childhood which seemed chosen to portray Signar as considerate, resourceful and if not perfect, then at least as good a brother as she could have wished for.

I listened and smiled and asked questions when it seemed

polite to do so, but I recognised the slightly rehearsed quality of the stories and wondered how many times Jens Sólsker had heard them. Although he didn't say too much, he didn't seem particularly retiring. Rather, he had a certain unhurried quality about him; not dissimilar to Fríða, I decided, as Estur brought the subject back to Signar's condition now. How had he seemed when I saw him?

I told her that it had been impossible to tell if Signar had known who I was, but when she looked worried I reported what Dr Heinason had said, making a point of a possible if partial recovery.

"Good. Good then," Estur nodded, seemingly reassured. "Signar is a strong man. He always was. This will not stop him. He will be back on his feet, I know it."

But as she said that I caught Jens Sólsker's eye for a moment and I had the feeling that he wasn't so sure that even Signar Ravnsfjall was strong enough for that.

When the meal was finished Estur refused all offers of help so Jens and I moved back to the sitting room while she made coffee. Out of politeness and some general curiosity I looked at the family photographs on the sideboard as Jens told me their names and relationships. They were hard to fully assimilate without any real context but it reminded me of the photo Fríða had given me. I took it out and showed it to Jens.

"Fríða gave me this yesterday. Do you remember where it was taken?"

Jens looked at the picture, then shook his head. "No, I'm sorry. Estur, do you know?"

Estur put down a tray of coffee and came to look. "Maybe Lýdia's parents' house at Lopra," she told me. "Your grandparents'. We all went there once for a party – perhaps a birthday. I don't remember now."

She moved to hand round the cups, then sat down. Before the conversation could turn in another direction I asked the question I'd been waiting to raise for a while. "I wanted to ask you what happened at that time – when my mother left the islands."

I addressed it to them both before looking back to Estur. I was pretty sure the answer would come from her and I saw that she had anticipated it.

"It's a long time ago," she said. "I don't think it matters so much. After all, we cannot change things."

"No, that's true." I nodded. "But I would like to know what you remember. I don't know very much about it and I'd like to understand – what happened when Signar found out she'd gone?"

I wasn't sure the tactic would work, but I was hoping that by framing the question around her brother she would want to champion him again.

"It was very sudden," she admitted in the end. "Signar didn't know what had happened."

"Lýdia didn't tell him she was leaving?"

"No." A shake of her head and a glance at Jens. "He was working on a boat, away for a few days, and when he came home you and Lýdia had gone."

She clearly hoped that would be the end of it, sipping her coffee as punctuation.

"She did leave a letter," Jens said; a gentle prompt, as if that detail was easy to forget.

"Oh. Yes," Estur said. "But it said only that she didn't want to stay here."

"She didn't say where she was going?" I asked.

"No. We didn't know where. Signar wrote to Ketty because he thought that was where Lýdia might go, but there was no answer... Perhaps the wrong address." The slight pause before that last was enough to say she didn't believe it.

"So was Signar worried about her?"

"Yes, of course," Estur said, as if there was no doubt. "About both of you. He didn't know what was wrong. But there was no news – not for a year – until he had a letter from Lýdia to say you were in England. As soon as it arrived he went on the next ferry to Aberdeen, then the train. He wanted to see you and be sure you were all right."

She pressed the last sentence, as if to counter the preconceptions she believed I would have.

"Did he find her?"

"Yes."

"And?"

"She wouldn't come home. That's all I know. When Signar came back he was—" She broke off to consider her choice of words, but didn't look to Jens for translation. "He was different."

"How?"

"Quiet. As if he had seen something he had not expected. He told me it was the end. Lýdia would not come back. That was all he said. We knew nothing more until we were told that Lýdia had died in Denmark and you were in England with Ketty and Peter."

She folded her hands and I knew she'd told me as much as she was going to volunteer, but I still had one more thing I wanted to clarify.

"What did he do then?"

A shrug. "It was agreed that you should live with Ketty and Peter."

"You mean that was what Signar wanted?"

She took a moment, then stood up, moved to take the tray of coffee things away. "It was what Ketty wanted," she said.

In the silence that followed while she left the room, Jens Sólsker slowly unfolded his long frame from the chair. "Perhaps you would like to look around the village," he said. "Have you seen it?"

I accepted the cue. "No, only from the road."

"Okay then, I'll show you. Let me tell Estur."

We left the house and walked down the gently sloping road towards the bay at a companionable pace past the neat, modern houses. But at the bottom of the hill I saw the first evidence that even here there was decay. A single-storey grey building with peeling paint and a rusting red roof stood beside the road. It had once been a village store; windows dark and blank, a lone box of Omo washing powder all that remained of its stock.

"Everyone can drive to the shops in Vágur or Tvøroyri," Jens told me by way of explanation. "The tunnel makes it easy. You came through it?"

I told him I had. If you used those tunnels every day I guessed their rock walls would eventually lose their worrying sense of constriction and slim margin for error. After a year, maybe.

"If you have time on the way back take the old coast road from Hov to Øravík instead," Jens told me. "There are some beautiful views across Trongisvágsfjørður. On a day like this it's better to be above ground, I think."

"On any day," I said, and he chuckled.

We passed a number of old boat sheds, their corrugated roofs rust red and eaten away at the edges, then took a ramp down to the side of the harbour where three commercial fishing vessels were tied up at the quay, other smaller ones resting on lines. Jens paused there, as if to give me the opportunity to look.

The curve of the inlet, the dark stone shoreline and almost motionless water were lit by bright sunshine, saturating the green of the surrounding headlands against the sky. Even though my mind was on other things, I recognised it as picture-postcard material, and in this light perhaps the prettiest place I had seen here. I took it in for a moment, then shifted.

"I didn't mean to upset Estur by asking about Signar and my mother," I said. It was an opening gambit to see how he'd react.

"No, it's natural you should ask. I understand," he said equably. "But for Estur, Signar has always been a hero: her big brother, yes? She doesn't wish to think badly of him."

"No, that's understandable," I acknowledged. "So how do you get on with him?"

Jens' expression was noncommittal. "Not so bad, I guess. You have to – what's the phrase? I can't remember. Get along together? For the family. But to me he is a man who likes to make himself bigger and all the time must be the winner." He glanced at me and gave a wry shrug. "Perhaps that is what makes him a successful businessman, while I was a teacher for thirty-five years."

"There's nothing wrong with that."

"No, of course not. It was what I wanted to do. And of course, Signar doesn't always get what he wants even with all his success."

"How do you mean?"

Jens considered for a moment, then said, "A few years ago he stood for election to the Kommuna – the municipal council – in Runavík. He was sure he would be elected because of his business there, but on voting day not so many people liked him as he thought. That is the good thing about a secret vote. Afterwards you may say, 'But of course I voted for you; it was all the others who did not.' Even so, it was a blow to his pride, I think."

"I can imagine," I said, thinking back to my conversation with Magnus yesterday. "So is he still political? Does he have influence with people?"

"He has stayed out of politics, but I think money is

always an influence," Jens said. We started walking again, along the harbour edge, still at a stroll.

"Until I got here I didn't know he was so well off," I said. "Did it all come from fishing?"

I'd had no specific reason to ask – just casual curiosity – but when Jens Sólsker didn't answer for a moment I cast a glance at him.

"Some people would say he made a good marriage," he said thoughtfully in the end. "I mean to Sofia."

"She had money?"

"*Ja*, some, I think. Before they married, Signar had just a share in a boat; afterwards he bought out the other partners. That was when he started to do well, although it caused some bad feeling later."

"Bad feeling with who?"

"The other partners. There was an idea that somehow Signar had not made a fair deal with them."

"You mean cheated them?"

"I don't know. One of the partners had died: an accident at sea. There was talk…" He shook his head, negating it. "It was a long time ago."

I thought it over for a moment. "Are any of the other partners still around? Maybe I could talk to them about Signar."

Jens chewed that over, then he said, "Pól Lydersen is the only one left now. He lives in Tvøroyri, with his eldest daughter I think. I can look for his address if you like, but today might not be so good. The family has had a death. Pól's grandson was found yesterday on a beach on Streymoy."

"Tummas Gramm?"

"You know of it?" He sounded surprised.

"Someone was telling me about it," I said, keeping it casual. "I think it was on the news. I don't suppose it happens very often."

"No." He looked away briefly, and when he turned back it seemed to me that he'd made a decision.

"I want to tell you two things Estur has not said," he told me. "The first is that when Lýdia left the islands with you it wasn't for the first time. Once before she went away, to Denmark. It was perhaps a year after you were born. She was away for a few weeks but I don't know really what it was about. All Signar would say was that she had gone for medical treatment."

"What sort of treatment? Was she ill?"

"I don't know. I had the idea it was private, you know?"

I nodded, not sure what, if anything, it meant. "What was the other thing?" I asked.

"It is something Estur doesn't know," Jens told me. "I would like it to remain between us. Can you agree to that?"

"Sure. Of course."

He nodded. "It happened shortly after we heard that Lýdia had died in Denmark and that you were now with her sister in England," he said. "Signar came to see me at the school. It was at the end of the day, before I went home. He was very serious. He said to me that he was going to England and wished to bring you back to live here, in the Faroes."

I frowned. "He said that?"

"Yes. I thought it was strange that he had come to tell

me this, but then he said that he had a proposal for me. If I agreed then you would come to live with my family. Of course, Signar said he would pay all the costs – food, clothes and so on – and he would also give me money so that we would be able to move to a bigger house. At the time where we lived was not so large."

"Did he say *why* he wanted you to take me in?"

"I asked him that. It was my first question. He said it would be better for everyone. I remember that phrase."

"What did he mean?"

Jens shook his head. "He wouldn't say more, just that he thought it would be the best way. He spoke like it was a matter of business, you know?"

"What did you *think* his reason was?"

With a shrug Jens said, "At first I thought it was because he would have to look after you on his own, but soon it was announced he would marry Sofia. So now I don't know. Perhaps she didn't want to be the stepmother."

I thought about that.

"So what did you tell Signar?" I asked in the end, although the answer was obvious.

"I said no." He looked at me. "I'm sorry if that was hard, but I had our own children, Fríða and Anna, to think of. Finn – our son – wasn't born then, but still…" He shifted. "Also it was— I had the feeling it was too much of a strange thing to do. Do you know what I mean? As if Signar wanted it to be a secret. I didn't think it was how things should be."

"And you didn't talk it over with Estur?"

"No. I knew she would want to say yes because it was Signar. She wouldn't think of anything else."

I thought he was right.

"How did Signar react when you said no?" I asked. "Did he try and change your mind?"

"No, he accepted it. He said he understood and thanked me for considering it. It was never mentioned between us again."

"And he went to England anyway?"

"*Ja*. It was just for a short time, I think. I don't know what happened, but I did write to tell Ketty. I thought she should know what he had said to me because she was looking after you. I got no reply for several months and then she wrote to say that she and Peter had adopted you, so I knew it was settled then. Are you okay?"

I realised I'd stopped walking and was staring out across the bay, not seeing it but rather absorbing what Jens Sólsker had said. I shook myself out of it and moved off again, thinking back to what Estur had implied earlier.

"So Estur thinks it was Ketty who stopped Signar bringing me back here," I said. "That's why she said it was what Ketty wanted."

Jens Sólsker nodded. "I think it has always been at the back of her mind and I'm sorry for that. But at the time..."

"No, I understand," I told him. "Thank you for telling me."

He looked at me, still with some concern. "Does it change how you think of him now, your father?"

I shook my head. "I don't know. It's too soon. I need to think about that."

13

AS HENTZE HAD SUSPECTED, THE NEWS COVERAGE OF tummas Gramm's body being found had not brought in any new information. There had been a few calls last night, but nothing useful, so this morning it was still a matter of waiting for forensics to arrive. To occupy the time Hentze had been to court to obtain a warrant for the phone company, obliging them to hand over details of all the calls Tummas had made or received on his missing mobile. It would probably take a day or two for the information to come through, but it was all he could do.

When the 12.15 flight from Copenhagen arrived at Vágar there was a car to take Anders Toft, the forensic pathologist, directly to the mortuary, and a van for the forensic team and their gear. By the time this arrived at Saksun, Hentze had already been waiting for twenty minutes, sitting in his car while the wind tossed spits of rain against the windscreen.

There were three forensic examiners in the team and as Hentze got out of his car he was glad to see Sophie Krogh was in charge. She was in her mid-thirties, with short hair and a lively face: just what you wanted to see at a crime scene because she was always resolutely upbeat – and she would talk to you, rather than writing everything out in a report first.

"Hey, Hjalti, this time you've got a proper job for us, eh?" Sophie said. She had a small amount of Faroese, but they spoke Danish to make life easier.

"I think so," Hentze told her. "I hope it's not another waste of time anyway."

The last time Sophie had been called in she'd only been on the ground for half an hour when the supposed victim of a break-in and assault decided to admit that she'd actually invited the alleged attacker home with her while drunk.

"Nah, don't worry," Sophie said. "I don't mind the trip, but I wish you'd chosen a weekend. I love Tórshavn on Friday and Saturday night: so many shy men like you to tease."

Hentze chuckled. It was a game she liked to play – trying to find out how far she'd have to go to shock him – based on the common Danish belief that all Faroese were prim and reserved. Hentze had no objection to it. He liked inventive people and the fact that Sophie Krogh was also openly gay meant he could safely disregard her most outrageous sexual references.

"I'm not shy," he told her. "I'm just thoughtful."

"Same thing," she shrugged. "What worries me, though, is what all you 'thoughtful' Faroese men are thinking *about*." And with that and a grin she went off to organise the equipment being unloaded from the van.

Once again Hentze enlisted Petur Bech's help to ferry the equipment down to the boathouse, using the track the builders had made during the summer. Bech clearly enjoyed the novelty of being part of the police team and his quad bike and trailer made the whole operation much quicker.

Rather than ride, Hentze walked the track with Sophie, who was smoking a final cigarette before they reached the scene.

"So, have you heard the latest trick by some female suspects in Copenhagen?" she asked.

"Of course not," Hentze said. "Tell me."

"Well, if the woman is arrested by a male officer she'll rub her right hand in her crotch while she's in the back of the patrol car – in secret, you know?"

She made a demonstration – thankfully on the outside of her jeans – and grinned at him.

"Then at the station she'll shake hands with the officer to show there are no hard feelings. Naturally, as soon as she's in custody she tells the sergeant that the arresting officer has groped her in the car. So then it's a complaint and they have to swab the man for DNA, and of course what do you find – lovely fresh quim juice, just like she said."

She looked to see what sort of reaction she'd get, but Hentze just nodded, deadpan. "It's a good tip," he said. "From now on I'll make sure always to wear gloves when I shake hands with Danish women."

"Ha!" Sophie said and pinched out her cigarette,

pushing the butt back into the pack. "So tell me what you've got here."

Being careful not to draw any conclusions or offer a theory, Hentze outlined as much as they knew about Tummas Gramm's body and the possible bloodstains in the boathouse. As he saw it, it came down to three things, he told Krogh: could the boathouse be connected to Tummas Gramm, was it the scene of a crime, and was there any evidence that anyone else had been there?

"You want the full works then?" Sophie said.

"Unless you can tell right away that I'm on the wrong track," Hentze said. "At the moment I don't know for sure what's linked to what, so we don't know what we should be investigating – if anything."

On the flat patch of ground at the end of the track he led her round to the bottom of the wooden steps that went up to the living space above the undercroft. "That's the only way in or out," he said.

"And you think there's a possibility that the body could have been moved from inside and dumped in the water?"

"If there was someone else involved, yes. Although it's also possible he walked there and collapsed."

"Okay, well, we'd better take a look at the steps first, then. How many people have been up there, that you know?"

"Three. Me and an English police officer, and Petur who put a new padlock on the door to secure the place. Is that a problem?"

Krogh shook her head. "No. We probably won't get any prints from the treads anyway, but it's useful to know. What about inside? Who's been in there?"

"Just me and Reyná – the Englishman. I told Petur to stay out."

"Okay, we'll need to take elimination prints later: fingers and footwear." She looked at him with a frown. "How are the Brits involved?"

"It's a long story. I'll explain later. Is there anything else I can do?"

"Nope, just leave us to it," Sophie Krogh told him. "Coffee and sandwiches laid on?"

"I'll make sure."

"That's also why I like coming here," she said with a grin. "I know you'll look after me."

Once Krogh and her team were at the boathouse there was nothing else Hentze could usefully do, so he took two uniformed officers and headed back along the valley to the villages of Hvalvík and Stremnes, where the road to Saksun met with route 10. He knew it was a long shot, but anyone going to Saksun had to pass through one of the villages, so it was just possible that a local resident might have seen Gramm or his car, which still hadn't been located.

For two hours Hentze and the two uniforms went door to door in the villages. Many of the houses were empty at that time of day, which made the enquiries less than conclusive, and by the time they'd visited them all they hadn't learned very much: a possible sighting of a blue car – or was it grey? – on Sunday evening; another of an unfamiliar man walking on the road – but was that Sunday or Monday? The informant couldn't recall. Certainly, however, no one had seen anything overtly suspicious and as he headed back to Saksun, Hentze hoped that Sophie Krogh had had time to make a first judgement about what she was looking at.

For a reason he couldn't place Hentze had a feeling – an instinct – that the enforced delay in getting things going was already working against them. He sensed that for all the time they plodded along the road of the investigation, something or someone else was sprinting. It worried him in a vague, shapeless way and made him feel uncharacteristically restless.

When Hentze got back to the boathouse he found that the forensics team had erected a tent on the grass to store samples out of the rain, and a small generator was throbbing nearby, cables trailing up the external steps to the door. The unnatural light from halogen lamps was visible inside and when Hentze sent word in to ask if it was okay to take a look he was told that it was, provided he suited up.

Five minutes later he climbed the steps in forensic overalls and paused at the door to put on plastic overshoes before going inside. The floodlights made the undivided space clinically bright and it seemed larger than the last time he'd been inside. The three crime-scene examiners were each concentrating on a different area: one on the stove, another on the rear of the room, and Sophie Krogh on the makeshift bed under the windows. She beckoned to Hentze and he walked over to her, being careful to tread only on the plastic stepping-stone plates put down to protect the floor.

"You're okay with this job," Sophie told him cheerfully. "Definitely not a waste of time."

"A crime scene?"

"I don't know if there was a crime, but someone was here who bled a lot. If your victim had a gunshot wound like you say, it could have been him."

"That's great," Hentze told her, meaning it. "What else can you say?"

"After only a couple of hours?" She gave him a mock reproachful look. "What are you, a yokel?"

All the same, she moved to indicate the khaki jacket that was bagged up beside the sleeping bag.

"The coat has a bloodstain, some of which came from lying on top of the blood here" – she gestured to the sleeping bag – "and some which came from an injury while the coat was being worn, I think."

"Can you tell if it's human blood, not from someone gutting fish or a hare?"

"I still need to test it in the lab, but that's my bet." She gestured away from the window. "We also have blood on partially burned cotton-wool wadding in the stove. You said your victim had a pad of cotton wool taped on his wound?"

"Yes."

"So we might be able to match the two."

She took a moment, then made a generalised motion with her hand. "It's interesting. This place has been lived in. There's a bucket at the back there for a toilet, some empty tins and rubbish in a plastic sack, and the stove had been used. The room's also been cleaned up at least twice – once before anything happened, then again afterwards. Both times were recent – less than a week ago, I'd say."

"But if someone was trying to remove the evidence, why did they leave the bloodstained coat and the sleeping bag?"

Sophie Krogh looked pensive for a moment. In the end she said, "You know, to me, I'm not sure they *were* trying to remove evidence. It feels more that this was a *home* – you know what I mean? – and that whoever was here wanted to keep it neat. They were house-proud."

"Are you serious?" Hentze asked. It seemed like a far-fetched idea.

But Sophie was serious, he could tell, and by way of explanation she said, "Okay, let me ask you: what do you do if your dog comes in and leaves mud all over the floor?"

"Wipe it up?"

"Exactly. So, there are several blood drops from the door to here, as if someone crossed the room bleeding. Most of the larger drops have been cleaned up, but not very thoroughly – with a rag maybe. By that time they'd started to dry, and there are smaller ones that were missed. To me that's tidying up – being domestic – not being forensically aware."

Hentze took the point. "So do you think there was one person here or more?"

"I can't say that for sure – it's possible that it was just one and that whoever left the blood cleaned the place up themselves, but I doubt it. We've got several sets of recent prints and from a first glance I'd say they belong to different people. We'll find out later. We might also have a couple of useable boot prints, though they'll probably turn out to be yours. Let's have a look."

Hentze held up a foot, awkwardly stork-like, so she could peel back the overshoe and look.

"Nope, not yours. Good. But let's get the others for elimination – your British detective? You were going to tell me about that."

Before Hentze could reply one of the other examiners called Krogh's name and beckoned her over.

"Okay, tell me later," Sophie said. "Over a beer. By then I should be able to give you the headlines."

"How long do you think it will all take?"

"Still hard to say. It's not a big space. Maybe by this evening we'll have most of it. Whether we've finished or not, I'll make sure the most significant samples are on the morning flight so we get a head start in the lab."

"Okay, thanks," Hentze said. "I'll leave you to get on, then."

"Are you going to see Anders now?"

"Yes."

"Okay," she tossed him a plastic vial. "See if he'll type this blood sample from the bedroll – it's okay, we've got plenty."

"Doesn't there have to be paperwork or something to go with it?"

"Sure, for the evidence. That's just unofficial, but if the type matches your victim at least you'll know a bit better where you stand, right?"

"Right. Thanks," Hentze said appreciatively. "That would help."

"Don't forget, beer later," she said.

14

WHEN WE GOT BACK TO THE HOUSE ESTUR HAD RECOVERED her cordial, welcoming manner, making no reference to our earlier conversation. Instead she offered to make more coffee, but I declined, telling her I didn't want to miss the ferry and I wanted to take Jens' advice and drive the old road back to look at the view. It was a useful excuse.

We parted, Estur extracting promises that I'd come and see them again, persuade Ketty and Peter to visit, keep in touch. It was hard to know how much she meant it and how much was simply what she felt was required from an aunt to a long-absent nephew, so I took it at face value.

Estur stayed in the sitting room but Jens Sólsker accompanied me down to the car. With his back to the house he gave me a slip of paper with Pól Lydersen's address on it. "From the telephone book," he said, before clapping me on the shoulder in farewell.

I turned the car and headed back down the hill. In the rear-view mirror I saw Jens returning towards the house and inevitably – predictably, I knew – I wondered who and what I would be now if Jens Sólsker had accepted Signar's offer of monthly payments and a bigger house in exchange for taking me in. As I reached the main road I knew it was pointless to speculate, though. It was too soon to evaluate how it changed my feelings towards Signar, if at all.

Later.

I turned the car north and headed for the tunnel rather than the slower coast road.

The street I was looking for – Traðarvegur on the outskirts of Tvøroyri – was easy enough to find, but by the time I'd located the house on the long road I was conscious that I was cutting it fine. If I missed the ferry I'd be stranded till tomorrow and getting someone to relax, to open up and speak freely wasn't something you could rush. Perhaps if they *wanted* to talk, yes; but there was no reason to think Pól Lydersen would want to do that, especially if he was mourning the death of his grandson.

For a moment, as I got out of the car, I balanced the possible insensitivity of the visit against the time it would take to come back here from Streymoy again. Perhaps rather than trying to ask questions – still only half formed in my head – it would be better to just get an idea of how helpful Pól Lydersen might be. If it seemed worthwhile I could always come back and talk to him in a couple of days. It seemed like the best compromise.

The house was built on a slope, with wooden steps up to a balcony that ran along the roadward side of the building.

There were several neatly tended pot plants near the door and a view over the fjord between the roofs of houses below.

The door was opened by a woman in her forties with a mug of tea in her hand. She had a faintly harried look, as if it had already been a difficult day.

"*Ja?*"

I spoke carefully, the memorised guidebook phrase. "*Góðan dag. Eg eiti Jan Reyná.* Do you speak English?"

"A little, *ja*. What can I do?"

"I'm looking for Pól Lydersen. Does he live here?"

"Yes. My father. But he is gone to the—" she sought the word. "To the ship, with my daughter."

"The ferry? *Smyril?*"

"*Ja.*" She looked at me suspiciously. "What do you want?"

"I wanted to ask him about my father. I was told they were friends."

"Who is your father?"

"Signar Ravnsfjall."

Now her suspicion seemed to be confirmed. She shook her head. "*Nei.*"

"He doesn't know him?"

"Not for a long time. *Orsaka meg.* I must go." She stepped back and made to close the door.

"*Takk fyri.*"

The woman said nothing. The door latched and I headed back to the steps.

* * *

At the ferry terminal there weren't as many vehicles waiting to board as there had been that morning and I was only about a dozen cars from the front of the queue. I felt more confident about the boarding process this time, and accepted the small ticket from the loading marshal before heading up the steel stairwell to the lounges.

The ship's turnaround was just as rapid as before. By the time I'd paid the fare at the shop and got coffee from the cafeteria we were already moving. I found a place in the forward lounge near a window and settled for a while.

I wanted to think. No, didn't exactly *want* to, but felt I should process what I'd learned: strip it back to the bones, free of the flesh of qualification and bias, and see what it came to.

So what *did* it amount to? I found a pen and calculated dates and sketched a meagre timeline on a blank page in the Bradt guidebook.

Signar had made two journeys to England, the first about a year after Lýdia and I had left. If Estur was right, he'd tried to persuade Lýdia to return to the Faroes with him and she had refused.

The second trip had been a little over three years later – weeks or months after my mother died; I couldn't be sure. Jens Sólsker had already turned down Signar's request to take me in, but Signar had gone to England anyway.

Why? Who had he seen there? What had he wanted?

I wondered if he'd made the same offer to Ketty and Peter that he had to Jens Sólsker. Or had he simply intended to take me away from them, only for them to refuse?

Whichever way it had been, Signar, the bull, had returned to the Faroes twice without his son. How would that have made him feel? Humiliated, angry, relieved? It was the one question I hadn't asked Jens Sólsker: *do you think Signar cared?*

I stared out of the window, unseeing. Could it be as simple, as clichéd, as that? Was that the real reason I was here now: to find out if Signar Ravnsfjall had ever actually cared what happened to me? And if that really was all I wanted to know, did it mean I was essentially no different to my seventeen-year-old self, still full of confused and unformed questions and anger?

But there *was* one difference: this time there would be no shouted confrontation on the quay, no accusations and no punches thrown. This time Signar would not – could not – knock me flat on my arse.

I'm not sure how long I sat there thinking. Long enough for the remains of my coffee to go cold, anyway. I swallowed a tepid mouthful and put the mug aside.

For a moment I thought about calling Ketty, but I knew any questions would sound accusatory. Too soon and not the right way. Let it all settle. Instead I got up from the table and shouldered my bag.

There were few enough people in the lounges that I reckoned there wouldn't be many men in their seventies travelling with their granddaughters. From a rough calculation based on the age of the woman at the house, the girl would be somewhere between her teens and early twenties and Pól Lydersen would be over seventy.

As it turned out she was nineteen or twenty, with crow-black hair down past her shoulders, reminding me of what Hentze had said about the people on Suðuroy having Mediterranean ancestors. The much older man with her had a weather-worn face, carved deep with lines and wind-tanned. His hair was completely white, topped by a peaked corduroy cap, which was slightly at odds with the more formal jacket and tie he was wearing.

They were the only people in a seating section near the ferry's shop. The girl was listening to an iPod, and the old man seemed content with his own thoughts until he saw me approaching.

"*Goðan dag,*" I said, pausing beside their table. "*Harra Pól Lydersen?*"

"*Ja?*" He looked curious, interested.

"My name's Jan Reyná," I said. "Do you speak English?"

"*Nei.*"

The man shook his head and looked to the girl beside him as she tugged her earphones free.

"I speak English," she said. "I'm his granddaughter, Halla Guttesen. Can I tell him what you want?"

"Sure. Thank you," I said. I explained that I'd been to Lydersen's house and been told that they were on the ferry, and since I was travelling back too...

The coincidence of it sounded more unlikely when I put it into words, but the girl didn't seem suspicious. "Ah, okay, I see," she said and turned to Lydersen to translate.

The old man looked at me quizzically, then finally nodded and said something in reply.

"He asks why you wanted to find him," Halla Guttesen said.

It was more awkward to explain than I would have liked, but I said, "I was told that your grandfather was a friend of my father's in the 1970s. I just wanted to ask him about that."

"Who is your father?"

"His name's Signar Ravnsfjall. He's in hospital at the moment so—"

I broke off as Pól Lydersen interrupted in Faroese, clearly impatient to know what was being said.

While the girl spoke to him I used the opportunity to sit down, as if there was enough of a connection to do so now. The conversation between the other two went back and forth for a minute or so before Pól Lydersen seemed to have finally said what he needed.

"He wants to know if you're the boy who was taken off the islands," Halla said. "Was your mother called Lýdia?"

I nodded, looking to Lydersen. "*Ja*, Lýdia Reyná was my mother."

Lydersen seemed to get that without translation because he spoke to his granddaughter again.

Finally the girl looked back to me. "He says he knew your mother when she was young. He liked her – he thought she was a nice person, you know?"

I nodded. "*Takk*."

"He also has heard that Signar Ravnsfjall is sick in the hospital," Halla said. "But he says he doesn't know him any more. Not for a long time. He doesn't know what he can say."

That was the nub of it, I knew. I wasn't even fully sure what I wanted to ask, and because of the language barrier there couldn't be any subtlety.

Slowly and choosing my words carefully, I explained that I hadn't seen Signar since I was young, and because Signar was now too ill to speak, I was trying to find out about his past. It was no more than interest – curiosity – I told the girl, but someone had said that her grandfather used to be partners with Signar on a fishing boat. Was that true? Could he tell me about that?

While the girl translated all this – not verbatim, but paraphrasing, I could tell – I watched Pól Lydersen's reaction. The old man listened carefully, slightly puzzled, it seemed, until close to the end when he started to speak again, this time with harder gestures and a more truculent tone. Even without understanding, I knew he was rehearsing an old argument or point of view.

The girl interrupted him a couple of times – seemingly for clarification – before finally turning to me. "I'm sorry," she told me. "He says he doesn't want to talk about it."

"Was that all he said?" I asked, knowing it wasn't.

She glanced at Lydersen and he said something, gesturing her to go on.

The girl seemed self-conscious now. "He says he wishes— He has no bad feeling towards you, but he says

CHRIS OULD

Signar Ravnsfjall was a cheat – *tjóvur*: a thief. Is that the right word?"

I nodded, careful not to show any significant reaction. "In what way? Did he cheat your grandfather?"

"That's what he says. And also the wife of a man called Eric Beder who had died. He says your father paid too little for their boat because he knew the wife was, er – *desperate* – for the money."

"Right," I said, still keeping it neutral. "So was that why they stopped being friends?"

Halla put the question to Lydersen, which brought a definite nod and some harder words from the old man.

"Yes. They haven't spoken since that time," Halla translated. "He says Signar Ravnsfjall made his money from the back of a dead man so he doesn't want to know him any more. It is finished."

I took a moment to think about that, debating whether to ask more. I hadn't decided before Pól Lydersen spoke again, still fervent. Halla Guttesen nodded, made a calming motion, spoke to me at the same time.

"I'm sorry. This is— It is an old story with him. He has had many years believing it. I don't know if it is true, but right now we also have problems in our family. It is not a good time. Can I ask you if that is enough?"

"Sure, of course," I said, seeing the awkwardness she felt and regretting making her feel it. "I'm sorry to have bothered you. I'll leave you alone." I stood up and dipped my head to Pól Lydersen. "*Stora takk fyri*. Thanks for talking to me."

I offered Lydersen my hand and the old man rose to shake it – a firm grip – as Halla translated. "He says it was good to meet Lýdia's son."

"You too," I said and bowed out.

I'd only gone a couple of steps when I heard Lydersen call after me. When I turned to look the man was still on his feet and he repeated what he'd just said.

"Sorry," I said, looking to Halla Guttesen. "Can you—"

She shook her head. "Don't worry, it wasn't important."

From the reluctance on her face I knew that wasn't true. "No, please tell me," I said.

She hesitated for a moment longer. "He said you can ask the police."

"About what?"

"About Eric Beder."

15

HJALTI HENTZE SAID NOTHING AS ÁRI NICLASEN SCANNED the sheets of paper. He wanted to give the other man time to absorb the details properly, so he sipped his coffee and stared passively out of the window.

Hentze had returned from the mortuary ten minutes ago after waiting while Anders Toft dictated his preliminary findings to a secretary borrowed from the hospital's admin department. Hentze knew he'd probably sounded a little terse when he'd told Toft that all he really required were the main facts and not every last observation – not yet, anyway. But Toft was a fairly forgiving soul and obliging enough, if he could be prevented from wandering off into anecdotes about similar cases he'd worked on. Unfortunately, the woman taking the dictation was rather pretty and Toft – a brush-headed, bespectacled little man – was also a bit of a goat, so the dictation wasn't entirely without distraction even then.

At his desk Ári Niclasen finally looked up.

"So until we get the full report we can't be certain," he said. "There are still tests to do."

"Yes," Hentze conceded. "But Anders doesn't expect them to contradict his preliminary conclusion."

"But they *could*?"

"He thinks it's very unlikely. You know Anders: if he had a reason to be cagey he'd say so."

"Hm," Niclasen said, looking back at the report for a moment. "Even so, maybe we should wait till we know for sure."

Hentze wasn't entirely sure why Ári Niclasen still seemed to be clinging to the hope that somehow or other this would all go away. Perhaps because it would simply make life easier if it did, or perhaps because Ári wasn't keen to revisit the disruption and inevitable scrutiny that a murder investigation would bring with it.

Five years ago there had been some implicit criticism of Ári's handling of the investigation into the disappearance of a Ukrainian woman, Vira Sirko – most notably because they had never got her fiancé to reveal what he'd done with her body. Even without that admission, the fiancé had been found guilty of murder – a verdict no one had ever really doubted – but the questions raised afterwards about the late start and length of the investigation, in addition to the failure to find the body, had all been a little barbed. They might have been more so if the convicted man hadn't been Ukrainian as well.

So, Hentze thought, perhaps Ári Niclasen was shying away from entering another murder case; like a sheep shies away from the electric fence when it remembers its first jolt. And no one could blame Ári for that; after all, homicide cases were not expected to be a major career feature for officers in the Faroes.

All the same, Hentze didn't see that they had any choice but to accept the situation for what it was. The B-negative blood in Signar Ravnsfjall's car – recently typed by the crime lab in Copenhagen – was rare. More than that, it was the same group as the blood on the bedroll in the boathouse, which was also the same as Tummas Gramm's. Furthermore, in Hentze's opinion, the preliminary PM report was unambiguous and holding off for the full test results would simply be postponing the inevitable.

"Listen," he told Niclasen. "Even if we don't *call* it murder just yet, there's still evidence that a third party was involved: the fingerprints from the boathouse; the disposal of the body; the dislocation of the arm, as well as the disappearance of Gramm's car. I think all that indicates that Gramm knew the other person – maybe he was even in partnership with them – so shouldn't our priority be to identify them?"

Niclasen put the report down on his desk. "Are you still connecting all this with Signar Ravnsfjall – blackmail or something like that?"

Hentze nodded. "Yes, for definite. The blood match means we *have* to link it to Ravnsfjall – not as Gramm's killer, obviously, but certainly as part of whatever led up to his death."

Ári Niclasen thought about that for a few seconds, then said, "Okay. For now – until we have the final forensic report – we treat it as probable murder: just between ourselves, but not for public consumption. If the press or anyone outside wants to know, we're still treating it as an unexplained death, understood?"

"Okay," Hentze said, not really worried about questions from reporters. That was Ári's area.

"And you'd better include the Englishman, Reyná, in that as well," Niclasen went on. "If his father's linked to a murder case – even indirectly – I don't think it's a good idea to tell him more than is strictly necessary."

Hentze frowned. "I thought there was—" He'd been about to say *I thought there was pressure to keep him involved*, but then reconsidered. "You don't think he might still be useful? Maybe more so now."

Niclasen shook his head. "I think he might be a complication we don't need – especially if this *is* a more complex case," he said. He considered for a moment, then said, "I thought I should be certain of his credentials, so I spoke to his superior officer, a Superintendent Kirkland, a couple of hours ago. It wasn't a very satisfactory conversation in most ways. He did confirm Reyná is *bona fide*, but he also told me that Reyná is currently suspended from duty, pending an inquiry."

"What sort of inquiry?"

"His superintendent wouldn't say: only that it related to an investigation from some months ago. So, as I said, perhaps we had better play safe and keep him at a distance. Just in case."

Hentze didn't reply for a moment, then he nodded. "Sure. Okay. Whatever you think."

16

IT WAS A LITTLE AFTER SEVEN O'CLOCK AND I'D BEEN BACK
at the hotel long enough to shower and start thinking about
walking into Tórshavn for a beer when Hentze called and
asked if we could talk. I'd assumed he wanted to meet in
the station, but as I approached it I saw him waiting on the
pavement by the steps.

"Hey," Hentze said. "How was your trip to Suðuroy?"

"Okay," I told him. "Interesting."

He seemed to get the idea that I wasn't ready to go
into detail yet and straightened up. "Do you feel like some
ordinary police work? There is someone I want to speak
with at the Café Natúr. Do you know it?"

"Yeah, I've been in there."

"Okay, good then," Hentze nodded. "And if we walk
we don't have to worry if we have a drink afterwards. Is
that okay with you?"

"Fine," I said, falling into step. And then, because I was
curious: "You wouldn't drive even after just one beer?"

"*Nei*, it would be risky," Hentze said. "And... *anti-social*

– is that the word? It's less expensive to take a taxi than to lose a job, but I can call my wife for a lift. She won't mind."

I was interested that for the first time Hentze seemed prepared to give an insight into his life. And because he seemed to only want small talk for the moment I said, "So how far away do you live?"

"Oh, only five kilometres, at Hvítanes. Sometimes I've even walked home, but not for a few years, I'll admit."

We paused at the kerb of a junction to let a car pull out of a steep side street and when we moved off again Hentze seemed to have passed one of the numerous invisible markers he seemed to use to separate his conversations and thought processes.

"So," he said, "we have the preliminary autopsy result from Dr Toft, the forensic pathologist. Do you want to guess?"

"Not natural causes," I said.

"No, and not from loss of blood. The wound was from a shotgun, as we thought, perhaps made twenty-four hours before death, but Toft agrees with Dr Hovgaard that it would not cause the death."

"Does he know what did then?" I asked.

"*Ja*, he says it was asphyxia."

That wasn't what I'd expected. "Drowning?"

Hentze shook his head. "*Nei*. He has to do all the laboratory tests for that, but there is no sign of it in the lungs. In Toft's opinion it was suffocation from something placed over the face – a pillow or cloth perhaps. There was force, too. There is bruising here" – he touched his bicep – "as if someone has held his arms down, perhaps with their *knæ* – er, knees – while sitting on top of him."

He glanced at me to see if I got the picture, then went on, "Toft also says that the body was certainly moved after death because the left shoulder is dislocated, as if he has been pulled along with the arm. So, we are looking for another person now, for sure."

"You'd have to be," I agreed. "What about forensics at the boathouse?"

"They have found blood and there are fingerprints and other marks from boots," Hentze said. "They will email the fingerprints to Denmark later and maybe we'll have a match by the morning."

"*If* they're in the database."

"Sure, but we can hope so."

He fell silent as we crossed the road beside a roundabout, as if giving me chance to absorb what he'd said. We cut round the corner to the harbourside road, past a slightly incongruous Italian restaurant and a fast-food takeaway beside it. Across the road at the ferry terminal the *Smyril* had long gone on the return to Suðuroy and its place had been taken by a much larger passenger ship called the *Norröna*. Hentze gestured towards it.

"That will be a problem for us maybe," he said. "The *Norröna* sails to Iceland and Denmark, so if someone wishes to leave here it's not so hard, even if they don't want to fly. And the person we are looking for has had three days to go."

I thought about that, then said, "I don't think they've run. Or if they have, it wasn't what they intended to do."

"Oh, why not?"

"Because whoever killed Gramm dragged the body to the beach to get rid of it. If they'd *intended* to run away they could have left it where it was, in the boathouse. It probably wouldn't have been found for weeks or months and by then they'd be long gone." I shook my head. "To me, trying to dispose of the body is something people do when they want to cover things up and pretend they didn't happen. They want the body to disappear so it can't be linked back to them and they can go on with their life."

"So if you're right, the killer moves the body because they are worried if it is found there we might be able to identify them. There could be a connection – like the owner, or the builder or someone who worked there."

"Yeah, possibly – or else just because the killer had been there and was worried that they'd left fingerprints or DNA."

"Have they planned this then, do you think – to kill Gramm and then get rid of his body?"

"I don't know." I shook my head. "It might explain why they suffocated him instead of using a gun or hitting him over the head with something heavy, though."

"Because they thought suffocation wouldn't show so much?"

I nodded. "You could ask the pathologist, but I bet it would be hard to tell he'd been suffocated after he'd been in the sea for a week. Even the shotgun wound might be hard to see after the fish had been at him."

"So if he had been found after a week or two in the sea

there would be nothing suspicious to look at," Hentze said.

"That's my guess."

Hentze drew an audible breath and looked disconsolately out across the harbour for a moment. "What sort of person thinks in that way?" he asked. "Someone who loses his temper and kills another – it's a bad thing to do, sure, but I understand how it could happen. But to decide that one way is better to kill someone than another, because it leaves not so many traces…"

He shook his head, as if the concept was as unfamiliar to him as the idea of walking on water or driving after a pint of beer. I wondered how he'd fare if he was a copper in some areas of Sheffield, Glasgow or London. By the same token I tried and failed to imagine myself doing the job here.

"So, is there a theory yet?" I asked.

Hentze took a breath then seemed to shake off his moment of disillusionment with the world.

"Now? Yes, because we also have results from the blood on your father's car. It is not his, but it is the same type as Tummas Gramm and the blood in the boathouse: B negative. Of course there would still need to be a DNA test to prove without doubt it belongs to Tummas, but…"

"But it would be one coincidence too far if it wasn't?"

"I think so, yes."

I nodded and thought it through. "So how are you hanging it together?" I asked.

"I think we have been correct since the start," Hentze said after a moment's consideration. "I think Tummas

Gramm met with Signar Ravnsfjall at Tjørnuvík on Sunday evening. Whatever the business they were doing, it didn't go well. Your father was knocked to the ground, so he injured his head and his knee, and Gramm was shot. An accident maybe, from the fall."

He looked to see how I reacted to that. I shook my head. "I doubt it," I said. "But go on."

"After he was shot Gramm went to the boathouse in Saksun. Perhaps he was taken there by someone who was with him at Tjørnuvík, perhaps he drove there himself and someone else came later. Either way, he didn't go to the hospital, so to me that says he was afraid of the questions he could be asked about the injury."

"Which means that whatever he was doing with Signar it was probably illegal," I said. "So we're back to blackmail."

"*Ja*, that is my feeling too," Hentze agreed. "Dr Toft cannot say exactly when Gramm was killed, but it was some time on Monday, he thinks. So, perhaps it was Monday night when the killer dragged his body to the water."

"What about motive for killing Gramm?" I asked. I already had my own idea but wanted to see if Hentze followed the same logic.

Hentze pursed his lips. "Perhaps because he now has the shotgun wound to his body, Gramm is a problem to the other person with him," he suggested. "Perhaps Gramm *wanted* to go to the hospital for help but his *makkarin* – his accomplice – thinks this is too dangerous. Your father may die because of what was done by them, and there is the blackmail as well. I don't think Gramm's accomplice would want the possibility of being found out, so to protect himself he kills Tummas and then gets rid of the body." He looked to see my response. "Do you agree?"

"It makes sense to me," I told him. "So now you need to know who might have been in on the blackmail with Tummas – friends, relatives... And was Tummas the one in charge – the one with the knowledge – or was it his partner?"

"I wonder if Tummas was the muscle, you know what I mean?" Hentze said thoughtfully. "He was a big guy, so maybe someone asks him to go with them to make sure there was no trouble from Signar."

"If that *was* why he was there it didn't work," I said. "Otherwise he wouldn't have been shot. Have you got anything else to go on?"

Hentze shook his head. "We must hope that the finger-prints will help. The other samples cannot go to Denmark until tomorrow's plane."

We'd crossed the road and were close to the inner harbour now, no one else in sight, the stillness of the small boats on the water absolute. Stray, lost raindrops made scattered ripples, which disappeared quickly. We weren't far from the Café Natúr but before we passed the last of the harbour I stopped walking, making the most of our relative privacy.

"There's another connection between Tummas Gramm and Signar," I said then. "I talked to my uncle on Suðuroy this afternoon and he told me that Signar fell out with his partner in a fishing boat – a man called Pól Lydersen. This was back in the seventies, but I talked to Lydersen as well and he still holds a grudge. He says Signar cheated him and the widow of their other partner, a man called Beder. He didn't say it in so many words but it was fairly obvious he thinks Signar was responsible for Beder's death."

Hentze made to speak, but I forestalled him for a moment. "I know, it was a long time ago, but there's something else. Pól Lydersen is – was – Tummas Gramm's grandfather. He was coming here on the ferry because of Tummas's death."

"I see," Hentze said with a serious nod. "So you think this could be the reason for blackmail? Tummas Gramm knows something from his grandfather and tries to blackmail Signar?"

"I don't know," I shrugged. "I just thought you should know there's a connection between Tummas and Signar. It might be worth asking Pól Lydersen about it, or looking into the death of Eric Beder. I don't know how easy that would be, though."

"I would have to look back in the records," Hentze said. "But it is something to think about. Thank you for telling me."

I shrugged the thanks away as unnecessary. "Is there anywhere around here that old guys – men Signar's age – hang out? A bar or a club, somewhere like that?"

"You want to ask questions about your father and Beder?" he asked, and I thought I heard a trace of caution in his voice.

"Not specifically," I said. "I don't know very much about Signar when he was younger. I just thought I'd see if I could find anyone who knew him then."

"And your mother also?"

I nodded. "Yeah – if anyone remembers."

"Because she took you away?"

He was astute, although I suspected he didn't like people to think so.

"There are some holes – some gaps in the story – I'd like to fill in," I admitted. "It's a long time ago, though. I don't suppose there are many people to ask any more."

Hentze seemed to consider that for a while, then he said, "Maybe you could try a place on the quay in the West Harbour. They call it the Underhouse. You can find it by the sign for fishing bait. The older men sit around talking, playing cards and drinking coffee. Some of them might know your father or remember your mother."

"Okay, thanks. I'll have a look."

Hentze glanced away, thoughtful for a second, then appeared to shift mental gears. "Come, let's have a drink," he said, starting off towards the bar again. I fell in beside him.

"Who is it that you need to talk to?" I asked.

"A man called Clementsen; one of the staff who worked in the bar with Tummas. We haven't been able to ask him questions about the weekend yet. It shouldn't take long."

The bar had almost as few patrons as the last time I had been in there with Kristian. Three Americans – two men and a woman – were occupying a table at the higher end of the room, their English conversation immediately catching my ear. They were making plans for tomorrow and didn't seem to care who knew it.

Hentze went to the opposite end of the bar where it curved round to terminate in the less furnished part of the room. The barman, unshaven, in his thirties and wearing a Föroyar Bjór branded polo shirt, appeared from a cubbyhole midway along the bar. I stood off a little way while Hentze did his business – or tried to. After a few seconds I could tell he was being given a dusty answer and it was confirmed when Hentze handed the barman a business card.

"No joy?" I asked as Hentze turned back to me.

"No. Clementsen isn't here. Tomorrow maybe. I've asked that he calls me."

The barman brought two beers to the end of the bar and I got my wallet out ahead of Hentze, who then seemed slightly embarrassed that he'd been too slow, but accepted with a nod of thanks.

We moved to a table and when we were seated Hentze raised his glass. "*Skál*."

"Cheers," I said.

We drank and as Hentze lowered his glass he said, "So now I must tell you something not so good."

There was a regretful note in his voice and my first thought was that Signar's condition must have worsened, until I realised that Hentze probably wouldn't have waited until now to tell me.

"Go on," I said.

Hentze straightened his face. "I spoke with Ári Niclasen

before I came to meet you. Because of the developments he thinks it is better if I don't tell you any more about the investigation. It is because of Tummas's blood on your father's car."

I understood the reasoning and should probably have seen it coming. If Signar had shot Tummas Gramm – even accidentally, even if he hadn't killed him – Niclasen would no longer view me as a disinterested party. From Niclasen's point of view, I couldn't possibly be objective, and in his place I'd probably have taken the same view.

"Okay," I said. "That's understandable."

But when I saw Hentze's expression, I knew that wasn't the end of it.

"Is that all?" I asked.

Hentze shifted in his chair, as if it was the source of his discomfort. He shook his head. "This afternoon Ári spoke to a man called Kirkland, a superintendent in your Homicide and Major Incident team."

Because it had come out of the blue it took me a second to realise what that meant. When I did I immediately resented Niclasen's intrusion.

"And?" I asked flatly, although I already knew the answer.

Hentze frowned, as if he'd misunderstood. "You don't know?"

"I don't know what Kirkland *told* him," I said levelly.

I saw more awkwardness flick across Hentze's face, as if he'd hoped to avoid this. "He told Ári that you had been suspended from your duties."

"Right," I said, nothing more. I wondered briefly

what had gone through Kirkland's mind when he'd got the call from Niclasen, but I could easily imagine the tone Kirkland would have adopted.

"Is it correct?" Hentze asked at length when I still hadn't reacted.

"More or less."

"What does that mean?"

"He didn't tell you?"

Hentze shook his head. "Ári said Kirkland would not tell him the details. He said it was an internal matter."

"Yeah, I bet he did," I said. Kirkland would happily have hidden behind protocol but he'd have let his silence speak volumes. He was a master at damning by insinuation.

"This Superintendent Kirkland doesn't like you?" he asked. "You don't get on?"

"Not so you'd notice."

"So if it would make you look bad to say a little but not more, that's what he'd do?"

"Probably," I said. Then I gestured it away. "Listen, forget it. It doesn't matter. Now I know, I'll keep out of your way."

Hentze made a dissatisfied face. "That isn't— Why don't you speak for yourself? At least here. If something isn't as it should be…"

I shook his head. "It's my business," I told him. "And anyway, whatever I said, you'd still only have my side of it. So…"

I picked up my beer, took a mouthful, then set it aside. "You can tell Niclasen you frightened me off," I said, then I pushed my chair back and stood up.

Hentze made an open-handed gesture. "Maybe you should let me decide what I believe."

I could see that he meant it to be sincere, but at that moment the good intentions were way off the mark. I felt too exposed, though perhaps not for the reason Hentze might have thought.

"Okay, if you want something I'll tell you a joke," I said.

"A joke?" he frowned, as if he thought he might have misinterpreted the word.

"There are two friends walking down the road one night after work," I said. "Up ahead they see a guy called Smith, who they both know. When they reach Smith one of the men hits him – as hard as he can. Smith falls down and the first guy hits him again. The second guy looks at the first guy and says, 'Why did you do that?' But the first guy just shrugs and says, 'Because he deserved it.'"

Hentze looked at me seriously for a moment. "For a joke, that's not so funny," he said.

"No," I agreed.

"So which man are you?"

"Why do you think I'm either?"

"But if you weren't..."

"And how do you know that Smith *didn't* deserve it," I said. Then I shook my head again, because I knew that saying anything had been a mistake.

"It's just a joke – a story," I said. "Not even a very good one; not even accurate."

I stood up and made to turn away, until it occurred to

me that it was getting to be a habit, this walking away: first Magnus at the hospital, now Hentze. And Hentze deserved it less.

"Listen," I said. "It's not personal, okay? This."

"If you say so."

I nodded. "Maybe I'll see you later," I said, and with that I headed for the door. Outside I walked briskly, hard-heeled. Fuck Kirkland, and fuck Niclasen, too, for good measure.

I walked hard and fumed until I was back on the road to the hotel, Yviri við Strond. It ought not to have bothered me that much, but it did. It's hard to shake off the instinct for privacy when you've lived it so long, but even so I was shaken by the strength of my reaction.

It wasn't that I cared if Niclasen knew about the suspension. It made no difference. What had bitten me was that the separation between the compartments of my life had been breached, and I knew Kirkland would think he'd gained some kind of insight. I could imagine he had feigned concern: *The Faroe Islands? His father? An investigation?* A little information would be enough. A little went a long way with Kirkland: he was that kind of man.

By the time I reached the hotel I'd slowed and had started to wind down, let it go. There was no other choice. But I wasn't ready to go in yet: to spend the rest of the evening watching sub-titled imports on the TV with duty-free gin, so instead I kept walking — a stroll now, slightly more measured.

It was still light enough, although the sun was low and invisible behind the clouds, and after a while I came to a gravelled car park which butted up to the rocky shore. For want of any better destination I turned in and headed for the edge of the water.

The only vehicle on the rough patch of ground was a large, old-fashioned lorry, painted a uniform cream. It looked as if it might once have been a military vehicle. The long cabin on the back had been converted into living quarters. Through its yellow-lit windows I glimpsed bottles in a rack, red upholstery and wooden cladding. At the back a stable door was half open, allowing the sound of a jazz quartet out into the air.

I passed behind the truck and on to the tussocky grass, which formed the margin between land and high-water mark. I stepped down on to the rocks, taking several broad strides between boulders until I came to a natural halt. I let my gaze wander along the hump-backed outline of the island opposite. It was called Nólsoy, I knew now: once home to a local hero, Nólsoy Páll, who had challenged the Danish trade monopoly in the 1700s. I'd been reading the guidebook. I was becoming a mine of information.

I went further out on to the rocks, down on to a flat ledge where the sea rolled and chopped irritatedly. There was a small tangle of driftwood caught in a gully and a length of nylon rope trailing into the water, writhing slowly, disappearing into the deep. I resisted the impulse to haul it in. I didn't want to know what was on the other end.

Instead I leaned on a rock and wished I still smoked.

This was one of those moments for it. Instead I just shoved my hands in my pockets and looked at the view until my phone rang. It was Fríða. I'd forgotten to call her as I'd said I would.

"How was your visit?" she asked after we'd each said hello.

"Okay," I said, but realised it sounded too noncommittal. "Good, I think. It was nice to meet them."

"My mother told me you took her chocolates. She liked that."

"I wasn't sure," I said. "But I'm glad if she did."

Neither of us spoke for a moment, then she said, "Where are you?"

"Out for a walk. By the sea."

"Ah. I thought I could hear something." There was another, briefer pause, as if she was considering whether where I was made a difference to what she said next. "I wondered if you would like to have dinner with us – me and Matteus – tomorrow evening. If you still have the car. I have found some more photos you might like to see."

"I'd like that," I said, which was unexpectedly true.

"You can come to the house? It's at Leynar on the road 612, but it can be difficult to find so I could send you a text with directions."

I told her that would be a help and she said to arrive any time after five. I asked if I could bring anything but she said that wasn't necessary; she'd see me tomorrow.

I rang off and heard a raised voice behind me. When I turned my head to look I saw a man in his thirties leaving the cabin of the parked truck, shouting at someone still inside. An argument: a domestic, recognisable in any language.

The man didn't stop or look my way. He didn't know I was there. He strode away towards the road with anger in every step. Maybe it was an evening for it.

But my own mood had settled and after a moment or two I started back over the rocks. There was no point staying there any longer, between the water and land. It was getting darker and the symbolism was too easy.

As I walked across the car park I caught a glimpse of a woman in the living quarters on the back of the truck. She was holding a cigarette at a distance from her body and swaying with the music, which still issued from the open door. Her eyes were closed and for the brief moment I saw her she looked almost serene.

I trod lightly on the gravel as I went past. I didn't want to break her spell.

PART TWO

1

Friday/fríggjadagur

AT SEVEN THIRTY HENTZE TOOK THE STEPS TO THE BACK door of the station and touched his security fob to the sensor. When the lock clicked he tugged the door open and its steel frame grated on a stray pebble. It made him wince.

He held the door open until Dánjal Michelsen caught up and they went in together. Dánjal hadn't seemed to mind the request for a lift – he passed Hvítanes on his way to work anyway – but Hentze still felt guilty for having to ask. It wasn't the way he liked to operate.

The truth was, he'd known he should go home at least an hour before he'd actually left the Hvonn bar last night. He hadn't even wanted to drink more than a glass, maybe two, but because he hadn't really been in the mood for socialising he'd gone past that, just to try and lift his mood. The result was that he'd slept badly and had to get up twice in the night. Now he felt dehydrated and mildly below par. God knew what time Sophie Krogh had gone to bed, or what state she'd be in this morning.

Hentze and Dánjal separated on the first floor and Hentze went to the staff room to make a coffee – his third of the day – before heading up to the incident room.

When he got there he could hear Ári Niclasen talking to someone in the adjacent office but he didn't go to see who. Instead he went into the incident room quietly and moved a chair round so he could sit in front of the whiteboards and assess them as a whole. He sipped his coffee and wished he'd taken a couple of paracetamols as Sóleyg had advised.

He sat there for five minutes, reabsorbing and re-evaluating what they knew about Tummas Gramm's murder, before the door of the office opened and Ári came in, followed by Sophie Krogh. Today Ári was wearing a suit.

"Oh, you're here," Ári said, as if he'd been expecting something different.

"Uh-huh," Hentze nodded.

"Morning, Hjalti," Sophie said, lively and bright when she intuited his slightly impaired state. He simply lifted a hand in response and she grinned.

"I want to look at what we've got before we have a full briefing," Ári said, addressing Hentze. "But before I forget, did you speak to Reyná last night?"

"Yeh." Hentze nodded and then sipped the last of his coffee.

"And?"

"He said to tell you that I'd frightened him off."

Ári frowned. "What does that mean?"

202

"That he doesn't expect us to involve him any more, I suppose."

"Okay, good then. I think we can manage without his input, don't you?"

"I guess so," Hentze said without conviction and Ári reacted exactly as Hentze had known he would.

"Why not?" he asked, a frown of concern returning to his face. "Did he tell you something else?"

"Not exactly," Hentze said. "But I've had chance to think about it and I still believe Gramm was trying to blackmail Signar Ravnsfjall. Therefore, to identify Gramm's killer, I think we need to find out what the blackmail was about and our best chance of that is – or was – from someone inside the Ravnsfjall family: someone like Reyná, with no vested interest in hushing things up."

"Well it's too late for that now," Niclasen said, clearly wanting to move on. "And anyway, I wouldn't trust a corrupt officer."

Hentze stiffened. "Who said he was corrupt?"

"He's under suspension, isn't he? What else would it be for?"

"It could be any number of things."

But Niclasen wasn't having it. "Well, whatever it was doesn't matter," he said. "We have to think of the bigger picture. Say we get someone to trial and the defence brings up the involvement of a suspended officer, a foreigner with no jurisdiction. It's a minefield… No, it's better this way."

There was a knock on the door and one of the civilian staff came in, bringing a sheet of paper to Niclasen.

CHRIS OULD

During the distraction Hentze glanced at Sophie Krogh
but she was studying her fingernails in the way people do
when they pretend not to notice a couple having a private
row in public.

"Okay, this changes things," Ári announced then.
"Some of the prints from the boathouse have been matched
to a Nóa Petur Lisberg."

He handed the paper to Hentze. It was an email from
someone at the technical lab in Copenhagen. The reference
numbers didn't mean anything to him, but Sophie Krogh
had already moved to a table and opened her laptop. "Can
you tell us where the prints came from?" Hentze asked,
moving to stand beside her.

"Give me a second."

Her fingers flitted across the keyboard and trackpad,
opened documents and sub-files while she glanced at the email.

"Okay, yes," she said in the end. "The identified prints
are from one of the windows, a sheet of insulation and an
empty tin of ham."

"Anything from Tummas Gramm?" Hentze asked.

Sophie Krogh shook her head. "No, there are no
matching prints."

"But Gramm *was* there," Niclasen said, suddenly
looking worried and seeking confirmation.

"I'm pretty sure, yes," Sophie told him. "All the
evidence points to it, but until we get the DNA and fibre
analysis I can't tell you with *absolute* certainty. I'd be really
surprised if the analysis doesn't agree with that, though."

"Right, okay. So we have a suspect," Niclasen said with

satisfaction, turning to Hentze. "We need to bring Nóa Lisberg in for questioning, and let's pull his record to see who we're dealing with."

Hentze nodded, but before he could do anything more Sophie looked up from her laptop. "There are also several prints they couldn't identify. Most are old – probably left by the builders – but there's a partial palm print from the end window that was more recent. It isn't from Nóa Lisberg or Tummas Gramm."

"What? A third person?" Niclasen asked. "How can that be?"

Hentze saw his satisfaction evaporate, which had been Sophie Krogh's intention, he was sure.

"I'm just telling you what's there," Sophie said with a shrug. "The palm print is fairly recent, but whether it was left at the same time as the rest of the evidence I can't say."

"Is there any other evidence for another person being there?"

"Not yet. Hair and fibres might show something, but we'll have to wait for the lab analysis on that."

Ári Niclasen considered that unhappily for a moment, but then seemed to solve the problem. "Well, if there was someone else there we can find out when we bring Lisberg in. Let's have a full briefing in" – he checked his watch – "ten minutes. Is that enough time to get Lisberg's details?"

"Sure," Hentze said.

"Good. Ten minutes, then." He turned and headed out.

Once he was gone Hentze looked back to Sophie. "Are you serious about a third person being involved, or were you just giving Ári a hard time?"

"He's a pompous arse," Sophie declared. "But yes, there could have been someone else there. If the boathouse was locked up before your suspects broke in then it would follow that any recent prints belonged to them."

Hentze thought it over. "Can you stay? We might need forensics, depending what we find at Lisberg's address."

"Sure, no problem," Sophie said happily. "But if we miss the afternoon flight it's another overnight. And from the look of you I'm not sure you could survive that."

"Leave me alone," Hentze said, moving off towards a computer terminal. "It's still early."

By eight twenty they were on the move: Niclasen, Hentze and Dánjal Michelsen in one vehicle, two uniformed officers following in a patrol car.

Hentze had noted that Ári was wearing his pistol, which didn't improve the cut of his suit. Hentze himself was not armed, despite the edict that CID officers were required to carry a weapon while on duty. He had rarely carried his service pistol since he came out of uniform nearly twenty years ago and looking at Nóa Lisberg's criminal record had not persuaded him that it was necessary today.

That record, such as it was, consisted of a single charge of public drunkenness and minor assault against Nóa Lisberg. It had happened six months ago when Lisberg was eighteen years old and a student. The incident appeared to be a Friday-night brawl on Niels Finsens gøta, but both Lisberg's statement and that of the victim had been contradictory. The victim – a man in his twenties who had suffered a black eye and a few other bruises – claimed the attack was unprovoked; Lisberg said he had been goaded. In the end, though, Nóa Lisberg had pleaded guilty in court and a moderate fine had been levied. He was not exactly a career criminal, nor even a real delinquent.

Nóa Lisberg's address was in Argir, on the southern side of Tórshavn, linked to it by a single road and a bridge over the Sandá river. It was a relatively small house, one of a cluster on the hillside which faced east across the channel towards Nólsoy. The Lisberg house did not have the view, though. It faced the houses opposite and occupied a plot that was barely larger than the footprint of the building itself.

When Dánjal stopped the car Ári Niclasen was first out. He waited for the others to follow, then headed determinedly for the front door. A good thirty seconds after he knocked, the door was opened by a woman in her early forties. She wore jeans and a sweatshirt and had, Hentze thought, the look of someone who didn't sleep well; dark under the eyes, hair and make-up only cursorily brushed and applied.

The woman was clearly unsettled by their unexpected arrival, but she confirmed that this was the home of Nóa Lisberg; she was his mother but he wasn't there. What was this all about?

"It's a serious matter, I'm afraid," Ári told her. "May we come in?"

Reluctantly *frú* Lisberg stood back and allowed them

to file inside, leading them from the hall to a sitting room. Hentze could see immediately from the furniture and aged carpet that this was not a wealthy family. The place was clean and tidy, but gave the distinct impression that things were being encouraged to last.

When invited to do so, *frú* Lisberg sat down in an armchair with worn arms and looked up at Ári Niclasen as if the submissive position was something she assumed automatically in the presence of men in suits. She didn't challenge him, only nodded as he explained that they needed to satisfy themselves that her son wasn't on the premises and that he needed to ask her some questions.

Hentze and Dánjal made the search, although Hentze already knew they wouldn't find Nóa Lisberg hiding in a wardrobe or under a bed: his mother wouldn't have been able to carry off the lie. Even so, he went upstairs – wooden steps, carpet on the landing, doors half open to a bedroom and bathroom. A second flight of stairs led up to an attic bedroom and Hentze took them, leaving Dánjal to check the other floor.

The attic room was unmistakably Nóa Lisberg's – from the CDs and DVDs on the shelves to the posters on the walls. There was a low bed, a TV on a swivel stand and a wardrobe, doors standing open. The bed was unmade and Hentze pulled back the rumpled quilt to check for residual warmth. There was none. That didn't necessarily mean anything, but the closed room also lacked the slightly stale air of one which had recently been slept in and Hentze was satisfied that Nóa Lisberg had not been here last night.

Turning away from the bed he moved to look at a desk beside the dormer window. There was an open laptop, surrounded by papers and notebooks, and scattered around were sketches and various artwork projects. After taking a cursory glance at a couple of the notebooks, Hentze allowed his eye to be drawn to the wall behind the desk.

Here most of the white-painted plaster had been filled with complex and scrupulously neat illustrations; outlined with pencil then carefully and colourfully painted in: flowers, a petrol pump, Celtic designs, geometric shapes, single words and a few slogans. All the parts of this mural were interconnected, as if they'd grown organically one from another; it must have taken hours of concentration. All the same, it didn't tell Hentze a lot: just that Nóa Lisberg clearly had an artistic bent and an eye for detail.

By the time Hentze returned to the sitting room Ári was seated on the sofa, questioning Anna Lisberg. When he saw Hentze he stood up and accompanied him out into the hall.

"Anything suspicious in the room?" Ári asked.

"Not that I can see, but it would need a detailed search. There's a laptop, though, so it might be a good idea to get it looked at."

"Okay, I'll arrange that. His mother says she hasn't seen or heard from the boy since last Saturday. Apparently he left without taking anything except his wallet and phone and he hasn't been answering that."

"Does he have a car?"

"No. He can drive but he uses his old man's when he lets him. The father's name is Eli; he's a warehouseman at the Miklagarður supermarket. I think you should get him back here so you can talk to him as well. We need statements from both parents – as detailed as possible, okay? I'll go back and coordinate from the station. We'll need an all-units alert and checks on the ferries and airport."

"Okay," Hentze said, not entirely surprised that Ári was leaving him to take statements now there was no arrest to be made. Hentze was happy to stay and ask questions, though, not least because he'd started to wonder why Nóa Lisberg had gone missing from home on Saturday, three days *before* Tummas Gramm had been killed.

He didn't mention that to Ári, though. Instead he gestured through the open front door to the patrol car in the street. "Can we send the other car away? There's no need to have all the neighbours looking to see what's going on."

"Don't worry, they can give me a lift back to the station," Niclasen told him. "Just make sure you let me know straight away if you find out anything useful."

"Sure, of course," Hentze said.

As Niclasen headed outside Hentze took a moment. His headache still hadn't fully abated but he tried to ignore it and went back into the sitting room. He smiled at the woman sitting uncertainly in the armchair. "*Frú* Lisberg, I'm Hjalti Hentze," he said. "I don't suppose you could offer me and my colleague a cup of coffee, could you?"

2

I'D EXPECTED TO FIND SOME FAULT WITH THE DAY — SOME lingering aftermath; a rebound of my mood from last night – but in the bright sunshine there was nothing, and I knew enough to take the day as it came.

There had been an email from Kirkland when I'd checked the iPad over breakfast but I'd deleted it without reading, along with the rest of the spam. Whatever he'd said, I knew he'd have made the mistake of thinking I cared. Instead, once I'd eaten I drove into town and walked round to the West Harbour, enjoying the brightness.

On the quay a man in white overalls was selling vacuum-packed fish fillets to a gaggle of pensioners, who examined the packets charily, as if assessing their true value. Wandering past them I let my gaze run ahead, along a line of tall, steep-gabled buildings until I found the hand-painted sign whose picture more than the words indicated the place was selling fishing bait.

The sign was the only thing Hentze had specified as a way to identify the place he'd called the Underhouse, but I didn't think there could be many alternatives so I crossed towards it. A heavy metal door was propped open and inside there was an alcove-like space with a few shelves of fishing accessories, a couple of framed black-and-white photos of old Tórshavn and some notices fastened to the whitewashed walls. There was no one in attendance so I went in and scuffed my feet on the concrete floor to see if I could attract any attention.

In the rear corner there was a doorway leading back into some inner sanctum, it seemed, and after a few seconds a short-set, grey-haired guy with a moustache emerged, as if he was on door duty.

"*Hey. Kann eg hjálpa tær?*" he asked.

"*Orsaka meg. Duga tygum enskt?*"

"English? *Nei*. Little."

"*Eg eiti Jan Reyná,*" I said. "I'm looking for someone who might have known a man called Eric Beder."

Before I got close to the end of it I knew I'd lost him and there was nothing in my phrasebook Faroese vocabulary to come close to putting it across. All I could do was repeat the name as a question: "Eric Beder?"

He shook his head, but before I could write it off he said something incomprehensible and gestured me to follow him through the rear doorway. I followed, wondering what sort of Aladdin's cave I was passing into.

The back room was larger than I'd expected, lit by a couple of harsh strip lights, which gave it the feel of a cellar or vault. It was furnished with a junk-shop assortment of tables and chairs, populated by a dozen or so men: some neatly turned out, others more relaxed in dungarees and sweaters, none of them under fifty. Their voices rose and fell against the echo off the brick walls: card-playing and card banter – amused or hectoring – at a couple of tables; dominoes and coffee at another.

It was a den, not often broached by outsiders; I could tell that just from the sideways, curious looks that came my way as I followed the duty guardian to a small, coffee-making counter where a guy in his sixties was drying mugs with a tea towel. It wasn't a thing he was naturally designed to use. His large, square hands were too big for the mugs he was drying and his belly pulled a blue-and-white-striped apron tight against its ties.

He listened as the man from the shop spoke and gestured to me, then he turned his heavy-jowled head to make a nod of greeting.

"Hey," he said. "Can I help you? My name is Óli. Jens thinks you look for some person here. Is that correct?"

The guy from the shop departed – back to guard the entrance, no doubt – and I nodded. "*Ja*. A friend told me I might find someone here who knew a man called Eric Beder from Suðuroy. He died a long time ago: the 1970s."

I watched his face to see if he understood, and whether the name tripped any recognition. There was a faint flicker but nothing more.

"You say this man is dead?" the man called Óli asked.

"*Ja*. But I'm trying to find out *how* he died. I think it was some kind of accident at sea."

"Ah, okay, I understand."

He nodded but didn't move and I knew I hadn't given enough, so I shifted and took out my warrant card, flipping it open so he could see it. "My name's Reyna," I said. "I'm a British police officer. I'd appreciate any help you can give me."

That got me a short-lived frown as he looked at the ID.

"You think—" Then he broke off, realising he'd started down the wrong translation path. He tried again. "Is this an investigation?"

"No, not officially," I said, trying to make it sound unthreatening. "It's personal – for me. It's to do with my family."

He seemed to consider that for a moment, then made up his mind and looked round the room. "I think the only person here from Suðuroy is Páll Thomsen. He was born there. Let me ask him if he has heard of this man. Eric Beder, yes?"

"That's right. Thanks."

He started to come round the counter and gestured at his mugs. "If you like coffee, help yourself. It is free but there is the tin for giving money – the, er, charity – yes?"

"Okay. *Takk fyri.*"

To cover the wait while the man called Óli crossed the room and interrupted the card players I went round the counter and poured coffee into a mug from the glass jug on the hot plate. I pushed a fifty-króna note into the slot of the Reyði Krossur tin beside it and looked for sugar.

I kept an eye on the exchange at the card table, but even by the time I'd located a carton of creamer and stirred that in, too, the conference at the card table was still going on. From a distance it had the look of a debate, shifting back and forth between the players; a sense that something new had come along to add a bit of variety to the day — something to be chewed over and savoured, not rushed.

Because time didn't seem to be of the essence, I cast round, then moved to a small side table with two chairs and sat down to wait. A white-haired guy at the domino table gave me an accepting nod before looking back to his game. I was an object of curiosity, but seemingly harmless enough.

About five minutes later Óli left the card table at the same time as the man he'd first spoken to there. Óli came my way, while the other man ducked out into the shop. He was thumbing a mobile as he went.

"Your coffee's okay?" Óli asked as he parked himself sideways on the chair opposite me, his back against the wall.

"Fine. Thanks."

"Good." He looked me over for a second, then said, "I asked Páll for this man, Beder. He doesn't know him until I say there was an accident, then he thinks he remembers."

"That was Páll?" I asked, indicating the doorway.

"*Ja.* He has gone to make a telephone call – 'call' is correct? Yes?"

I nodded. "Who to?"

"To his *systkinabarn* – I don't know in English. The son of his father's sister."

"Cousin," I said.

"*Ja?* Okay. The cousin is on Suðuroy so we see if he knows."

"Okay, thanks. I appreciate it."

He shrugged. "Sure. Why not?" Then he made a faintly regretful expression. "Of course, there must be a cost, too."

"Cost?"

"Sure. A British policeman is not here every day. So now, of course, everyone thinks: how did you find us?"

He let a small trace of amusement wallow round the corners of his fleshy mouth until he saw that I understood he was trying to trade: one story for another.

"Are you a secret society?" I asked, playing it back, but deflecting it a little at the same time.

He laughed then. "*Nei, nei.* Except for some who are here to hide from their wives, but that is only two or three. The rest of us, our wives are happy we are gone out of the way. They don't care."

"They don't know what they're missing," I said, going with the flow of it, looking round at the den.

"Oh, no, they do," he said, grinning. "We are a lot of us old guys – pensioners, *ja*? – with nothing to do. Why do our women want us in the house all day? So, to help them, we come here and tell each other how we would all make the world better if we were the ones in charge, you know?"

I chuckled and nodded. "You put the world to rights."

"Of course. That is why we call this place the *Undirhúsið* – Underhouse." He gestured at the brick ceiling. "Upstairs, the bosses; down here the ordinary guys who know how things *should* be. Here we solve all problems."

We chatted like that for ten minutes or so, about

how long had I been in the islands and how did I like it here, what had I seen? It was companionable enough – interrupted only when Óli went to get us more coffee. I was a new friend – something novel to make conversation about when I was gone – and that was okay. *Sure. Why not?*

I expected him to work his way round to asking the real question – about my interest in Eric Beder – but it didn't come. Instead I sensed the same polite respect for privacy that seemed to run just under the surface of most Faroese. They might *like* to know more, but would never be impolite enough to ask if you didn't volunteer.

And then, just as Óli was in the middle of describing the trials and tribulations of the small car-repair business he used to run, the man he'd called Páll Thomsen came back into the room and approached our table. He was a trim, wiry man and it was easy to see that he was pleased with himself. He didn't speak English, though, so after we'd smiled and exchanged "*Hey*s" he turned to Óli and gave a report in Faroese.

It went on for a while, with questions from Óli and several different names being mentioned. They ran like a list, and I got the impression that Páll Thomsen had talked to a succession of people before he'd finally tracked down the one he wanted.

At the end of this run-down, Óli nodded and looked satisfied. Páll Thomsen returned to his card game with a smile and a nod and Óli said, "So, the man you need to see is called Rói Eysturberg. It should be easy for you to talk to him, I think: he was a police officer, also."

"He knew Eric Beder?"

"No, that I don't know. But he was the police officer in Suðuroy when Eric Beder died and he tells Páll he will talk to you. He is in Vestmanna now and if you want to be there before midday he can talk."

"That's great, thank you," I said. "Do you have an address?"

"No, that isn't needed. Look for the tourist information office. You can't miss it. Eysturberg is at the harbour beside it: he works on his boat." He gave me a knowing grin. "I think maybe a boat is *his* Underhouse, you know?"

"Every man needs one," I said. "*Takk fyri, Óli.*"

Eli Lisberg had not taken off his windcheater, only unzipped it halfway, as if he didn't intend to stay long before returning to work. He sat in the armchair by the window like a man braced for a stormy passage, Hentze thought: not an overly large man, but one whose general demeanour spoke of being used to commanding a space, especially his own sitting room.

By contrast, Hentze was perched easily on the edge of the sofa, the third point in the triangle between Eli Lisberg and his wife. Dánjal Michelsen was keeping out of the way at the dining table in the adjoining room. Hentze didn't need to look to know he was making quiet notes.

"Can you tell me if it's usual for Nóa to disappear – to go off like this – for several days without being in contact with you?" Hentze asked, addressing the question initially to Eli Lisberg but glancing at Anna to gauge her reaction as well. She clasped her hands more tightly in her lap, thin-lipped, worried.

"No," Eli Lisberg said, before his wife could answer the question. "But it doesn't surprise me. Not these days."

"Oh? Why not?" Hentze asked, keeping it open.

"Because it's typical of him," Lisberg said flatly, as if that was an end to it as far as he was concerned.

It wasn't an unusual reaction, Hentze knew. Called home from work to find policemen in your sitting room, you're going to be cautious – suspicious, even. You'll watch what you say and guard your privacy jealously until you find out what they want and then maybe you'll talk to them, maybe you won't: it will depend on how far they want to dig into the things you hold private.

Because of this, Hentze had deliberately kept their reason for wanting to talk to Nóa Lisberg as generalised as possible, while at the same time emphasising that it wasn't a trivial matter: in connection with a break-in and possible assault, he had said. Both were broadly accurate interpretations of the situation, but ones which avoided using the inflammatory words "crime scene" or "murder".

But even without such words being used, Eli Lisberg's reaction to the policemen in his sitting room seemed to go beyond the ordinary aversion to having strangers delving into his life. To Hentze, his stony reaction appeared to run deeper than that, which made Hentze more interested to find out what was at the bottom of it.

"Typical?" he asked, feigning innocence. "But if he hasn't done it before..."

For a moment Eli Lisberg didn't react to the bait. But then, as if he could no longer tolerate being still, his hands seized the arms of his chair and he pushed himself up, abruptly, then paced to the window.

"He has no respect any more," he told Hentze over his shoulder. "No— No manners; no organisation or plan for his life. First he does so little work for his exams that he doesn't get his university place and then, when we want to know what he is going to do with himself – get a job, go back to study again – he won't give any answer. Nothing! Instead all he does is lock himself in his room, or spend his time hanging around town, coming and going at all hours, day and night."

Even from behind, Hentze could tell Lisberg was glaring at the small patch of lawn and the street beyond it: an angry and frustrated man who could no longer work out what he was supposed to do with a son who didn't conform.

"Do you know who he might have been hanging around *with*?" Hentze asked. "Has he mentioned their names at all?"

"Mention?" The word seemed to dredge up more resentment in Eli Lisberg. He turned away from the window to look down on Hentze. "He doesn't *mention* anything to *us* any more. Oh no! Not even a 'hello' or 'goodbye' most of the time. Too busy for that: too busy with God knows what, but still, too busy."

"I know what you mean. They can be a pain at that age," Hentze said, as if he shared the other man's experience. "They want independence but at the same time they think everything should just fall into their laps."

"Sure, everything for free and easy," Lisberg nodded tersely. "Always."

"So does he have an allowance? Do you give him money each month or does he have some kind of part-time job?"

"He had a holiday job, but that was a couple of years ago. Nothing since then. He was *supposed* to be studying." Lisberg glanced at his wife, then back at Hentze. "Anna gives him money – too much, if you ask me."

Hentze shifted his gaze briefly to Anna Lisberg. Since her husband had returned from work she had said almost nothing. Not such an uncommon thing, the wife who defers to the husband in all important matters, especially in front of strangers. Still, Eli Lisberg's presence seemed to have flattened her even more than theirs had, and now Hentze felt it might be useful to separate them, just while he tried to ascertain whether he had got as much as he could from them both.

He looked back to Eli Lisberg. "Perhaps I could ask you to go through what you remember about the last time you saw Nóa," he said, standing up and signalling to Dánjal. "If you can do that in here with Officer Michelsen, *frú* Lisberg can do the same thing with me in the kitchen. Is that all right with you?"

Lisberg hesitated for a moment, then nodded. "If that's what's necessary," he said.

"Thank you. I'm sure it won't take us long. *frú* Lisberg?" And Hentze extended a hand.

* * *

In the kitchen Anna Lisberg fiddled with the dishes on the drainer as she spoke. She kept her voice down, Hentze noted. Through the thin wooden door it was quite easy to hear the sound of her husband's voice in the other room.

"It's only since a year ago that he became... difficult; different," Anna Lisberg said earnestly, as if she wanted Hentze to realise that so far he had heard only one aspect of the story.

"He had trouble sleeping," she went on. "I thought it might be his nerves – perhaps worrying about his exams. I tried to get him to see the doctor about it, but he wouldn't go. He said he didn't want sleeping pills or chemicals interfering with his mind. He needed a *clear* head, he said: nothing to pollute his ideas. He wouldn't take so much as an aspirin."

"What sort of ideas?" Hentze asked. "School work and that kind of thing?"

"I don't know. He always had projects. He drew things, wrote things, kept dozens of notebooks. That was why I couldn't understand how he failed his exams. All that work, but... It didn't seem to count for anything."

"I see," Hentze nodded, sympathetically. "I saw notebooks in his room. Do you think it would be possible for me to borrow one or two? I'll make sure they're returned, but they might give us some idea about where he might have gone, or who he's with."

"Well, I don't know," Anna Lisberg hesitated with a glance towards the kitchen door and the unseen presence of her husband beyond it. "I suppose it would be all right, if it would help."

"Thank you," Hentze said. "I know it must be a great worry for you, wondering where he is, but we will do our best to locate him."

Anna Lisberg's lips tightened, as if it was hard to hold back the words that had built up behind them. Finally, she seized up a cloth from the worktop and used it to scrub at an invisible mark on the counter.

"I wanted to report him missing after the weekend," she said. "But Eli said it wasn't necessary: not to get everyone worked up and asking questions. He said Nóa would come home soon enough when he ran out of cash or clean clothes. But that was a week ago now."

"Is there anything you can remember that might have triggered him to go – or to stay away? Any kind of argument perhaps?"

"No. Nothing more than— Nothing I can think of."

Nothing more than the usual. It told Hentze a lot.

"Do you— Will he be in trouble; when you find him?" Anna Lisberg asked. She was twisting the cloth nervously between her hands. "I know he's had problems with the police before – the fight and…" She shook her head. "But he really isn't like that, not really. He's just confused. That's what I believe. That's the way he seems to me – not bad, just confused."

"I'm sure we can sort it out," Hentze told her, placing a comforting hand on her arm. "Try not to worry unduly, okay? Let's see what we can do."

* * *

Five minutes later, Hentze and Dánjal Michelsen left the house, following Eli Lisberg as he headed back to his car, back to work. From the sitting-room window Anna Lisberg watched them go for a moment, before turning away.

Dánjal took the driver's seat without being asked. As he settled beside him, Hentze put the evidence bag containing Nóa Lisberg's laptop on the footwell, then opened a notebook he'd taken from the bedroom at the same time. It was black and hard-backed, plain paper: thick and easy to flick through it.

"You really think there'll be anything useful in there?" Michelsen asked. "Looks a bit weird to me."

Under Hentze's thumb a page from the centre of the notebook was filled with blocks of neat but quickly executed words linked by arrows to other passages and to competent but rather incomprehensible sketches and diagrams.

"I'm not thinking so much of *what* he's written – more what it shows about him," Hentze said. He closed the notebook and took out his phone. "Come on, let's get the laptop to Sophie before she leaves for the plane."

3

MY NEW FRIEND ÓLI HAD BEEN RIGHT: YOU COULDN'T MISS the tourist information centre. As the road to Vestmanna curved around the hillside on its descent to the bay I could pick out the tall white letters on the corrugated roof of the building from half a mile away. They stood out in the sunlight, but further out to the west over the neighbouring coastline there was a band of grey cloud rolling closer.

I turned off the main road before it entered the town, slowing down and following a side road towards a semi-industrial-looking collection of steel commercial buildings with little or nothing to show their purpose. I was getting used to the fact that half the places I saw remained anonymous and impossible to interpret, though, and it bothered me less. Inside these unidentifiable, precisely designed buildings there might be production lines or offices, or maybe nothing at all. Whatever the case, it was none of my business – or anyone else's – to know. Private; discreet; without show. The Faroese way.

The tourist information building was almost as

anonymous as the others – at least from ground level where you couldn't see the lettering on the roof. Beyond it was an outcrop of land, man-made possibly, from the look of the black boulders reinforcing its edges, and to the right was a small marina of boats. I parked the car parallel to the water's edge on a patch of gravel and pulled on my jacket as I strolled out to take a look. The wind off the water was chilly, despite the sunshine.

The marina was embraced by a sea wall and held thirty or forty boats of differing sizes and design, moored to two wooden jetties. Some of the boats were no more than twelve feet long, wooden and open to the elements, but others went to twice that, with partly or fully enclosed cabins.

I had no real experience of boats so it was hard to tell whether these were just pleasure craft or if they had any commercial purpose. Most of them looked too neat and clean to be fishing vessels, but I saw no sign of life – commercial or otherwise – as I walked out as far as the second jetty. When I paused there I realised I'd been stupid for not getting the name of Rói Eysturberg's boat. For all I knew now he might have sailed off or changed his mind about seeing me and gone home.

Vaguely irritated with myself I turned back, wondering if the tourist information office might be any help, but as I got level with the first jetty there was a shout from somewhere off to my left.

"Are you Reyná?"

I didn't see him until he stepped up from the boat and on to the jetty: a sinewy man in blue jeans and thick sweater with knee-high waders turned down at the top. I waved an acknowledgement and headed towards him down the gangplank, treading carefully on the damp wood.

By the time I reached his boat, halfway along the jetty, he'd gone back on board and was sitting on an upturned plastic crate, cleaning something on his lap with a dirty rag.

"*Harra* Eysturberg?" I asked.

"I'm Eysturberg," he said, looking up briefly. "Come aboard."

The boat was about eighteen feet long, wooden, with an open cabin at the front. I negotiated the step across to the narrow strip of deck beside the cabin, then stepped down to the open well of the boat where he was sitting. Not a pleasure boat, I could tell from the worn deck boards and the lingering smell of fish. The cover of a box-like hatch in the centre of the boat was folded back, revealing the engine, and a small toolbox was open beside it.

"*Hey*," I said holding out a hand. "Jan Reyna."

He looked, then gestured to the oil on his hand. "I'm not so clean," he said.

At a guess, he was in his mid-sixties, hair greying under a wool hat. His face had a tendency to the round, but his blue-grey eyes were sharp and watchful.

"I appreciate you taking the time to talk to me," I said, moving back a step to rest against the side of the boat. "It looks like you're busy."

"Not so much. I have some time." He looked back to the thing he was cleaning. It appeared to be some kind of pump.

"I know your father," he said then. "Signar Ravnsfjall. Correct?"

He glanced up and I nodded. "How did you know?"

Eysturberg shrugged. "One plus two plus three. The man Thomsen said you wanted to know about, Eric Beder. Beder died in November 1977, and his wife – Maiken – was dead ten years later from cancer. There were no children so who would be interested in him now? And the name – Reyná – is not so common. Only one family I know of, and one of them was married to Signar Ravnsfjall before she left here." He looked up at me. "So, that is what I think – how I put it in order: that and other things."

"Well it saved me explaining," I said, keeping it light.

"You think?" he asked drily.

Before I could answer he stood up and went off to the cabin – perhaps for effect, perhaps because he really did need the new piece of rag he came back with. Either way, I took it as time I was being given to decide what to say next. I opted for the direct approach because I got the impression that Rói Eysturberg would respond best to that.

"I'm trying to find out about my father's early life," I told him. "And yesterday I talked to someone who said that Signar had been in business with Eric Beder back in the seventies. According to the man I spoke to, there was some bad feeling between Beder and Signar – something to do with shares in a boat?"

I let the last bit of that drift up into a question and left it hanging there to see what would happen.

"Who was this – your informer?"

I debated, but not for very long. By now I knew we were fencing: Eysturberg, with his knowledge, probing to see how much I wanted it and what I might give in exchange.

"His name's Pól Lydersen," I said. "I met him on the ferry to Tórshavn."

"*Ja*, I thought so," Eysturberg said. He cleared his throat, then went back to cleaning his pump.

I waited: the copper's oldest ploy. It doesn't always work, not if you're faced with someone who doesn't mind silence, but the one thing that went in my favour was knowing I wouldn't have been there if Eysturberg wasn't at least considering talking to me.

"Are you British now, then?" Eysturberg asked, finally, without looking up.

"They seem to think so."

"What sort of police officer?"

"Detective."

"Huh."

Without seeing his expression that was a hard one to interpret, so I didn't.

More silence. More cleaning, but not for quite as long this time.

"So," Eysturberg said in the end. "You will have stirred up some gossip at the Underhouse this morning. You know that, eh? Got them interested? Like a gang of old women."

"I'm not too worried. I didn't say much."

"You think so? Listen— Hear that?" He cupped a hand to his ear, then dropped his voice to a stage whisper. "Eric Beder... Eric Beder... Eric Beder... You can hear it from here."

I wasn't sure whether I was supposed to be amused or chastised, so it was difficult to navigate a response. In the end I opted for a simple, acknowledging nod. "Does it matter?" I asked.

"Not to me. Not to your father either, I suppose. It didn't worry him at the time."

"In 1977?"

"*Ja.*"

"So what can you tell me about that?"

Eysturberg considered, then stopped his cleaning and put the pump aside on the deck, wiping his hands with the rag.

"I was born on Suðuroy," he said. "I was there my first ten years as a police officer, but my wife is from Streymoy, so in the end we moved here." He made a shrug, then dismissed it. "So, these are the facts that I know – that I remember, okay?"

I nodded.

"Okay. In November 1977 we – the police – have a report that Eric Beder has fallen overboard from a boat, *Vesturlíð*. The man with him on the boat is Signar Ravnsfjall and he reports this accident over the radio so that other boats can help to look for Beder. But it is dark, in the evening, and after two hours – maybe three – they know Beder is dead. It is impossible that in the night and at that time of the year he can survive, so there is nothing more they can do.

"When Signar Ravnsfjall returns to Vágur after the search he makes a report of the accident. He says he and Beder are on their way back to the harbour when Beder goes to do some job on the deck. Signar Ravnsfjall is at the wheel and for maybe twenty minutes he thinks nothing is wrong until he calls to Beder and no one replies. When he goes to the stern Beder is gone and more than that he doesn't know." Eysturberg paused, looked at me to see if I understood. "At sea these things happen. It's a dangerous place."

I nodded to show I got it. "There was no explanation – no cause for an accident?" I asked.

"*Nei*. There is a *krani* – a crane – in the stern for lifting. Ravnsfjall says it was loose, to move, so maybe it swings round… We don't know. All we can do is make the report and that's it."

He broke off for a moment, drew a breath and looked off across the water. In the distance I saw that the grey cloud was as close as the mountains across the sound now.

"Perhaps six weeks later – I think after Christmas – a body is found at Víkarbyrgi," Eysturberg resumed. "It was washed up on the beach and cannot be recognised, but from the clothes it is identified as Eric Beder and an examination is done. You understand, there is a lot of decay so it is not possible to say for sure about the cause of death, but one thing the examination shows is a crack in the skull. Here."

He raised his hand to the back of his head and patted his hat.

"So, that is when we start to hear rumours – gossip, yes? Three men had shares in the *Vesturlíð* – Signar Ravnsfjall, Eric Beder and Pól Lydersen. Now that Beder is dead, Signar Ravnsfjall wishes to buy Beder's share from his widow, and also from Lydersen. But Lydersen doesn't like this. He says the price is unfair – that Ravnsfjall is using the opportunity to buy cheap."

"Was he?"

Eysturberg shrugged. "Perhaps. I don't know. It is not police business."

"So… Then what?" I asked, because I knew that wasn't the end of it.

"Then Lydersen says more," Eysturberg said. "To anyone who will listen he says that Eric Beder did not want to sell his share of the boat and he believes Beder did not die as an accident. Instead he says that Signar Ravnsfjall has hit him with something to kill him and then put his body over the side."

I shifted against the bulwark of the boat. "Was there any evidence to support that?"

"No, nothing," Rói Eysturberg was definite.

"But you – the police – couldn't know for sure what *did* happen."

"No, that is true. But neither could Lydersen. All anyone knows is what Signar Ravnsfjall has said in his statement."

"So what happened – about these allegations?"

Eysturberg considered his next statement before making it. "Pól Lydersen will not let it sleep. He says these things in public, he complains to the police to say things are wrong… So at last the inspector at the station looks at all the papers again – the statements, the doctor's report – and then he tells Lydersen that there is no evidence for what he is saying. He goes further, also. He warns

Lydersen that if he does not be quiet now he might find he is in trouble."

"'Trouble'? In what way?"

"With the lawyers, maybe, for saying accusations with no proof – or perhaps with Signar Ravnsfjall himself. He was not happy to hear what Lydersen was saying, you know?"

He gave me a significant look to see that I took his meaning and I did. I could imagine Signar confronting Pól Lydersen about his loose talk of murder. I could also imagine that it wasn't an encounter Lydersen would have enjoyed when Signar was in his prime.

"So what happened in the end – about Lydersen and the boat?" I asked, although I already had a pretty good idea.

Eysturberg cocked his head. "At the end? – Maiken Beder sold her share to your father, and then Lydersen sold also. Soon after that Signar Ravnsfjall took the boat to sail from Runavík instead of Tvøroyri and he has been there ever since. It is where his second wife is from, Sofia Winther."

I thought that over for a moment. "Do you remember if there was any other gossip?" I asked. "Anything about my mother, Lýdia, for example – maybe about why she'd gone away?"

Eysturberg shrugged. "There is always gossip. If you are a detective you know that."

"Sometimes it can be useful, though. Did you know her?"

"*Ja*, a little. To see in the shop or the street. She was a beautiful young woman."

He shifted, looked away, then picked up the pump

from the deck and rose from his crate to start tinkering with the engine. I could tell he was nearing the limit of his cooperation and I used the time to think it through and frame a last question.

"As far as you know, is there anything about Eric Beder's death that could have been, I don't know – hidden or kept secret – until now? Anything that would have made a difference to the case if it had been known at the time?"

Eysturberg glanced up briefly from the engine. "Is that why you came to see me?"

I nodded. "More or less."

I could see him putting that together – one plus two plus three – and then he shook his head.

"No," he said leaving no room for debate. "Unless Signar Ravnsfjall says something different now, nothing is changed. It was an accident at sea. No one can say – can prove – it was not. I'm sure of that."

4

"WELL?" ÁRI NICLASEN ASKED AS HENTZE ENTERED THE incident room. The other officers were busy either writing reports or talking on the phone.

"Fine," Hentze said, knowing full well that wasn't what Niclasen had been asking.

"I mean, is there any idea where Nóa Lisberg might be?" Niclasen said.

Hentze shook his head. "As you know, he hasn't been home since Saturday according to his parents, and having talked to them I think they're telling the truth. From what I could tell, Nóa Lisberg and his father haven't been getting on so well recently – which could account for the absence – but his mother is definitely worried. If she knew where he was I think she'd have told me."

"Is she worried because he's missing or because she thinks he could be a murderer?"

"I didn't mention the connection to Tummas Gramm or his death," Hentze said. "Just that we needed to talk to Nóa about a possible assault."

CHRIS OULD

He moved away from Niclasen in order to take off his coat. It was a useful diversion, too. In truth he was still a little irked that Ári hadn't stayed long enough to have heard all this for himself: it would have saved time. On the other hand, Hentze knew he'd probably got a far better idea of the Lisberg family than he would have if Ári had been leading the questioning. Not one for subtlety and nuance, was Ári: he'd rather hit a single question hard and persistently, even if the hammer was too big for the job.

"So what sort of impression did you get of him then?" Niclasen pressed. "Did you pick up on anything that would support the idea that Lisberg killed Gramm?"

"On the surface? No I don't think so," Hentze said, hanging his coat on the back of a chair. "I'm not saying he *didn't* do it, but apart from that one minor brawl there's nothing to indicate that he's given to violence: maybe the opposite, in fact."

"In what way?"

Hentze shrugged. "He seems to be the artistic type; a bit wrapped up in himself, too, maybe."

Whether that pleased or disheartened Niclasen it was hard to tell. He absorbed it and seemed to add it to a mental checklist as he shifted his tall, awkward frame.

"Okay, well, I have to go and brief Remi now, so push on here, okay? Names and addresses of Nóa Lisberg's friends and associates, anyone he might have spoken to or seen in the last few days. And his phone. Don't forget that."

So saying, Niclasen moved off towards the door.

"Did you get anything from the ferries or airport yet?" Hentze called after him.

"Only the airport. It was a negative. He hasn't left by plane."

Hentze let him go. He was pretty sure that Nóa Lisberg hadn't left by ferry either, but it was only a feeling – to go along with one or two others, slowly making themselves comfortable in his gut. He weighed the notebook from Nóa Lisberg's room in his hand for a moment, then put it aside and turned to address the others in the room.

"All right everyone, let's pull things together and see where we are," he announced. "Annika: we need to talk to Nóa's school – he left this year but let's track down his teachers and classmates; Oddur, let's see if he's on Facebook or any other social media sites; and Dánjal, let's get a warrant to get hold of his phone records. Okay?" He looked round at the desks. "Hasn't anyone brought a flask of coffee up here yet?"

As a gesture, and partly out of mild curiosity, I'd offered to buy lunch for Rói Eysturberg, but he'd declined. Relatively politely, he'd made it clear that he'd said as much as he felt like saying – to me and perhaps to anyone else for the day. So I'd left him tinkering with his boat and walked back to the tourist information building where a sign outside announced its business in a very un-Faroese manner.

I ate at the restaurant inside: a modern, characterless place whose only up side was an all-you-can-eat buffet for eighty-nine krónur and a view across the sound to the mountains beyond. The cloud had finally rolled in and brought a light drizzle to damp down the tarmac and flatten the colour of the water. Inside, a long table at the far end of the room was occupied by twenty or so suited businessmen and a couple of women in neat skirts, all anonymous enough that this could have been the monthly get-together of bank managers, dentists or the local chamber of commerce.

What I did know was that I'd come here chasing the wrong theory. It had been a simple enough idea – that Tummas Gramm had learned something from his grandfather, Pól Lydersen, with which he thought he could blackmail Signar. Simple but wrong, it seemed now.

Whatever the circumstances of Eric Beder's death in 1977, Rói Eysturberg had summed it up definitively: no one but Signar could know what happened on the boat, so there was no room for blackmail. There was no room, either, for a one-plus-two-plus-three chain of reasons that would explain the link between Signar and Tummas Gramm. I'd tried out the blackmail-from-the-past angle and it didn't fit, so there was nothing left to do.

Well, not quite true. Back in Tórshavn I was pretty sure Hjalti Hentze would still be trying to figure out why Tummas Gramm's blood was on the door of Signar's car, and how that connected with Gramm's body being found on a beach. But it wasn't something I could take a part in any more, even if I'd been that way inclined. NMP: Not My Problem. I was out. I'd done my bit. The only thing

I had to think about now was how to occupy myself until going to Fríða Sólsker's house.

The buffet was fair, but not special enough to encourage you to linger or debate how much you could eat, and once I'd finished I made up my mind to be a tourist, since I was here anyway. I picked up a leaflet about Vestmanna on my way out of the restaurant and scanned it as I set off to walk around the harbour and on into the town.

The list of attractions and facilities in the town was thin, but I was going to treat myself to them all, I decided. I started by admiring the hydroelectric power station whose yellow and red metal walls made it look like a Meccano creation, then – further into town – there was the Eik Bank; perhaps closed, perhaps not. Naturally, it was hard to tell.

And, of course, as I strolled along the up-and-down road, there was no one else in sight, not on the street or behind the grey-glassed windows of the houses I passed. Bright potted plants and mailboxes with names on them were all clearly designed to give an impression of neat, ordered occupation, but I wasn't fooled. No one was home.

Where did they go? What did they do with their lives?

I couldn't shake the notion that everything around me might just be some kind of bizarre theme park: a model town, like the Gulliver's Kingdom I'd been taken to as a kid – a perfect, idealised representation of English life, but fifty years out of date.

Was this the same, except that everything here was built on a 1:1 scale? You couldn't stride over the houses, or touch the top of the church steeple, but I still couldn't shake the impression that I was the only one who didn't know it was all a carefully tended illusion. Even the few people I'd met could be the staff, simply hired in to maintain the place, to switch the lights on at night, draw the curtains, keep the houses and buildings painted, clean and orderly.

Like I said, once this notion had taken root it was a hard thing to shift, although in terms of the illusion the Kommuna building let the side down a little. Overlooking the harbour there was a light on behind one of the windows and for a moment I thought I saw someone inside. The pastel blue-and-white utilitarian architecture was a tad shabby, too – perhaps missed from the list of essential maintenance projects. Nearby a pristine white church made up for it, though: perfect white boards and black window frames. The graves around it were freshly tended and trimmed, too, so even the dead could rest in idealised neatness and—

And I was being unfair.

I felt disconnected here, perhaps more than anywhere I'd been. Maybe it was because I hadn't got an easy answer from Rói Eysturberg, or because I felt the black dog scratching at the door, but whatever it was, my growing sourness was unjust. *I* was the outsider. *I* was the one who'd chosen to come here, so I had no right to feel either sour or resentful because it was different and unknown. No, I was the one in the wrong and I needed a distraction, however slight.

* * *

Midway through the afternoon Hjalti Hentze took a call on his mobile from Simon Clementsen, the barman from Café Natúr he'd tried to speak to the previous evening when he was with Reyná. Clementsen had just come in to work and been told that Hentze wanted to speak with him.

For a moment Hentze debated whether to simply ask his questions on the phone. They were straightforward enough that he could do that, but for the last hour Ári Niclasen had been breathing down people's necks – literally at times – and Hentze didn't like it. It was almost as if Ári was afraid he would miss something if he didn't peer over everyone's shoulder, which was rubbish, of course, but still annoying. So, when he saw that Ári was distracted by a spreadsheet on Oddur's computer, Hentze told Clementsen that he would be along to see him shortly, then ducked out of the incident room before Ári could notice.

The Café Natúr bar wasn't busy – just a couple of customers sitting together – and when Hentze arrived Clementsen was cleaning the coffee machine. He was in his late twenties with gelled hair and blond stubble and bold black tattoos on his upper arm; probably acquired in Denmark, Hentze guessed as he introduced himself.

"You want to know about Tummas?" Simon Clementsen asked. "Shit, that was a bad thing. I didn't believe it when I saw it on the TV. Do you know what happened yet?"

Although the discovery of Tummas Gramm's body had been reported on Kringvarp Føroya and in *Sosialurin*, the police department had managed to maintain the impression – without actually saying as much – that it was still being treated as accidental. Hentze didn't think the charade could last much longer – too many people were working on the investigation now – but he was happy to let Ári Niclasen and Remi Syderbø have the headache over that. He wasn't going to be the one who blew it, so in answer to Clementsen's question he said, "We're still looking into it. At the moment we're just trying to account for his last movements."

"Well, the last time I saw him was Saturday night, in here," Clementsen said. "He was working. I wasn't supposed to be, but I did a couple of hours to help him out."

"It was busy?"

"Well, not so much then." He hesitated as if debating the wisdom of saying any more. "I don't suppose it matters now," he said. "I wouldn't have mentioned it before in case Pauli found out – the owner? We're not supposed to swap shifts, but I was here and Tummas asked if I'd stand in for him, just for a couple of hours. He needed to sort something out – personal stuff, I dunno."

"What time was this?"

"About ten, maybe a bit before."

"And when did Tummas get back?"

"Just after midnight – in time for the rush, like he'd promised. I thought he might leave me to it, but he didn't."

"And you don't know where he went?"

"No. He just said it was personal."

"Could it have been to buy or sell drugs? We know he sometimes did that."

"No, man," Clementsen said, distancing himself. "I don't know about anything like that."

Hentze mulled it over. It was something and nothing. They already knew that Tummas had been at the bar at closing time, around four on Sunday morning, so if he'd nipped out for a while – whatever the reason – it didn't seem to affect anything.

"Okay, well, thanks for your help," Hentze said. "And just while I think about it I don't suppose you know this guy, do you?" He fished out a copy of Nóa Lisberg's arrest photograph. It was nearly a year old but still a good likeness, Anna Lisberg had said.

"Nóa?" Clementsen said. "Sure, I've seen him in here. I don't know him so well – just to say hi, you know? Why?"

"It's another case we're working on," Hentze told him. "He's missing and his parents are worried. Have you seen him recently?"

"No, I'm not sure. Sorry." Clementsen shrugged.

Hentze caught the lie, though. He remained still, waited. After a few seconds Clementsen shifted uneasily.

"Okay, Saturday. That was the last time," he admitted.

"Okay," Hentze nodded without a trace of censure. "Go on."

Reluctantly Clementsen said: "He came in here in a bit of a state. He was looking for Tummas."

"They knew each other?"

Clementsen nodded. "They hung out sometimes. Listen, I don't want to get him in any trouble, you know?"

"You won't. Why was he in a state?"

Clementsen sucked his teeth for a second. "He'd been in some sort of fight. I dunno the ins and outs, okay? He had some blood on the front of his shirt, seemed pretty upset. He was looking for Tummas and they went off over there." He gestured to the corner near the entrance to the toilets. "I don't know what was said but Tummas looked like he was – you know – calming Nóa down. Nóa was waving his hands around a lot: like I said, pretty worked up."

"Was that when Tummas asked you to take over behind the bar for him?"

Simon Clementsen nodded. "He said he needed to get Nóa sorted out."

At the wheel of the boat Kristian Ravnsfjall seemed completely at ease. He stood easily, feet apart, knees relaxed to accommodate the movement of the swell, while the engine throbbed away rhythmically beneath the deck. I'd been his excuse to abandon the office, with its smooth desk and climate-controlled air, and get out into the real world. You could sense the relief – the liberation – just from looking at him.

He'd sounded pleased to hear from me – a little surprised, too – when I called him and said I was in Vestmanna and could take him up on the invitation to look at his business if he wasn't too busy.

"Sure," he said. "Of course. Where are you? I'll come and pick you up."

"No, there's no need; I could do with the walk," I told

him. "Give me directions and I'll get there."

The logo for Kristian's company – Atlantic Aquaculture – was a leaping salmon over blue waves. It was etched into a brushed-steel plate beside the door of a new, single-storey building with a turf roof, which was almost but not quite at the end of the road around Vestmanna bay.

Inside it was a three-room operation: not as highly designed as Magnus's offices in Tórshavn, nor as big. But the young woman in the outer office was brighter and chirpier than Magnus's receptionist, and looked as if she had much more to do than just straighten magazines.

Kristian greeted me with a warm handshake, introduced me as his brother – not *half*-brother, I noticed – to his PA, a rather stern-looking woman in her fifties called Astrid, and then showed me into a smallish conference room with two leather sofas. We drank coffee while he asked what I'd been doing since he last saw me, and although I deliberately left some details vague and generalised it didn't seem to worry him. He talked about his company, too, but like me, he seemed glad of a distraction and to welcome the intrusion of something different.

It was an amiable, easy-going conversation, interrupted a couple of times by phone calls, which prompted a slightly irritable reaction from Kristian. I got the impression the calls were business which had to be dealt with, but after the third he'd had enough and announced to Astrid that he was going to show me the operational end of the company and it didn't matter who called; he was out and unreachable.

I thought I saw a slight doubt about the wisdom of

that cross Astrid's face, but she accepted it and Kristian led me outside.

We were heading back now, as Kristian subtly adjusted the course of the boat. He had shown me the sea pens in the sound – massive circles of net tens of yards across – paired up in a block of six; I'd stood on the pontoon raft beside them and seen the slow-circling iridescent shapes of the salmon rising and falling together like some sort of endless fairground ride, and I'd noted the genuine sense of achievement – pride – Kristian seemed to have in all this. It was almost boyish and hard not to appreciate, even if I couldn't quite raise the same passion for thousands of fish.

"How old were you when you first learned how to handle a boat?" I asked him, raising my voice over the throb of the engine.

"To steer? As soon as I was high enough to see where I was going," he grinned. "I stood on a box. Magnus the same. There is no choice in our family: it's the business, so you learn."

"Did Signar ever talk about how he started up in business?"

"I guess, sometimes," Kristian said with a nod. "Always it was hard, you know, in the old days. Not like today. We all have it easy." He gave a sardonic laugh.

"He started with one boat?"

"*Vesturlíð*, yeh. Magnus and I both learned how to sail and to fish from her when we were kids. Signar kept her for many years, even after she was too small to be useful to the company any more. That wasn't usual for him, to be – what's the word – sentimental. Why do you ask?"

"No real reason. Just interested."

He gave me a wry look to say he didn't entirely believe that. "Are you still doing detective work?"

"No – just trying to fill in the gaps – the history."

He seemed to accept that and looked away to adjust his course.

"I've heard no more from the police," he said then. "Do you think that means they have stopped being interested in what he was doing at Tjørnuvík?"

"I'm not sure."

"Not even after finding the body of the man on the beach – Tummas Gramm?"

I had to refocus a little and assume that whatever Kristian knew he'd got it from Magnus. It was logical that they would talk. Kristian might even share Magnus's desire to protect the family name from unwarranted gossip and scandal. I didn't want to talk out of turn about Hentze's ongoing investigation, but there again, I wasn't exactly privy to the latest developments. I was at least a day behind, out of the loop.

"The last thing I heard from the police, they had forensic evidence to connect Tummas Gramm with Signar's car," I told him. "But Gramm died after Signar was found and there may have been other people involved in that."

"So they still don't know why Gramm was with Signar?"

"Not as far as I know. Can you think of any reason?"

"*Nei*, I don't know the man, but it has Magnus in a bad mood. He doesn't like not to be in control of things. Just like Signar."

"Have you seen him recently – Signar?"

"No. I might go to visit him later." He looked away with a dissatisfied expression. "I don't know if there is any point, though. What is there to say when there's no reply? You sit there and feel uncomfortable and you wonder how long it is before you have done your duty so you can leave. At least before this you always knew he would have something to say whether you like it or not. Now, nothing."

I watched him as he spoke, but it was impossible to read what he was thinking.

"So, how was it you were in Vestmanna today?" he asked, as if he should have thought to ask sooner.

"You made me curious," I told him.

"Really?"

"Sure. And Fríða's invited me to dinner, so I was coming this way anyway."

He cast me a look. "You like her?"

"Sure," I said, not sure if there was anything behind the question. "She's been very friendly – helpful."

He nodded. "She's one of the people in the family I like the best. She does things the way she wants to do them and doesn't care what people think or say."

"Like?"

He considered. "Well, with her son, Matteus. There's no father – well, there must be, sure – but no one knows who. She worked in Denmark for a few years and when she came home Matteus was with her, two years old. He had her last name and as far as I know she has never said who his father is."

"Any reason she should?"

"No, of course not." He shook his head. "It's her business. But here you still have to be strong to push your way through what people will say, the way they give you a look, even today."

It was an echo of what Magnus had said: the importance of reputation and propriety, or at least the appearance of it. It was one of those things – the growing list of things – about these people that I still found hard to fully understand.

Five minutes later Kristian let the boat glide up to the dock where a shabby Portakabin was the business end of Atlantic Aquaculture. Inside, the place was scruffy and worn, with boots and sou'westers, boat tackle and equipment scattered around.

Kristian introduced me to a couple of men in bibbed waders who tended the fish pens and they discussed a few practical matters as he shrugged off his heavy wool jacket, revealing the smart-casual office clothes beneath.

It might just have been my imagination, but walking back to the office Kristian seemed to lose some of his previous ease, as if he'd left the thing he really enjoyed for something that was more of a burden.

"Say *hey* to Fríða for me," he said when I told him I'd

better head back to the car rather than come inside again.

I said I would, then remembered something. "Can you tell me where I can get a bottle of wine to take with me? I looked in a shop back there – *Skivan* – but they didn't have anything."

He laughed. "No, you can't buy alcohol except pissbeer. Real stuff is only at the state shop and they're closed now. But I think I can help. Come in."

Astrid immediately waved phone messages as we entered. She seemed concerned, maybe mildly disapproving when Kristian refused to listen until he'd searched for and found a bottle of wine, dusty from storage.

"Take it as a gift," he said, handing it to me. "It's left from a reception we had to bring in investors from Denmark. It's not so bad actually: better than they were. Will it do?"

I said it would, thanked him – for it, and the boat trip – and said goodbye. I thought I sensed some regret that he wasn't leaving to go to dinner as well, but I could see that Astrid wasn't going to let him out again for a while.

By the end of the afternoon Hjalti Hentze began to think he had something: not a lot yet, it was true, but at least a start. It no longer felt as if he was scrabbling to find any kind of purchase on the disparate facts, but that he'd managed to put a few into some sort of tentative order.

When he'd returned from talking to Clementsen at the Café Natúr his first action had been to check for any reports of fights or assaults between 6 p.m. and 11 p.m. the previous Saturday night. There were none. Undeterred, he sent round an email to everyone who had been on duty that night in case they had attended an incident but hadn't needed to make an arrest or bring charges. The results of that would take longer to come in, owing to shift patterns and days off, but that was okay. In the meantime he started to work up a timeline and sketch out his thoughts on a pad of paper.

All this he did from his own office, away from the distracting activity of the incident room and Ári Niclasen's mother-of-the-bride anxiety, popping in and out all the time. It was not the all-inclusive, file-sharing, open-plan approach favoured these days, but it was the way Hentze worked best.

Eventually, however, Annika found him.

"Ári's going spare looking for you," she told him.

"I'm not hard to find – clearly," Hentze said.

"He thinks you're still out. Your phone's off."

It wasn't off, but on silent. Hentze had been ignoring its periodic vibrations on the desk. Now he picked it up and switched the ringtone back on.

"Have you two fallen out?" Annika asked.

The question surprised Hentze, not least because he thought he'd been discreet about his growing irritation with Ári. "I don't think so," he said. "Why?"

Annika Mortensen shrugged. "I just wondered."

Hentze picked up his pad of paper and stood. "Let's get everyone together."

* * *

In the incident room the blinds on the inner corridor were down and the door was closed. Hentze had added several bulletpoints and connecting lines to the whiteboards on the wall. He waited until everyone was paying attention before starting his summation. Off to one side of the room Ári Niclasen was sitting on a chair looking judicial; prepared to be convinced by what was said, but not necessarily without question.

"Because Nóa Lisberg and Tummas Gramm were seen together on Saturday night we now have a definite link between them," Hentze was saying. "I think this is important."

"We had that connection before, though, didn't we?" Ári said, just a hint that he thought they were going over old ground. "From the fingerprints at the boathouse."

"No," Hentze shook his head. "We had Lisberg's prints and what seems likely to be Gramm's blood, but there was nothing to say they were contemporaneous. Lisberg could have been there before or after Gramm. But now we know they were together on Saturday night, so we've established beyond doubt that they knew each other."

Ári pursed his lips but chose to keep quiet, so Hentze moved to indicate his extension to the timeline and went on. "Clementsen says Nóa came into the bar at about ten. He was upset, having been in a fight, apparently. He was looking for Tummas. Again, I think this is significant. Then, after Nóa and Tummas had spoken in private, Tummas asked Clementsen to take over his shift so he could 'sort Nóa out'. That's a quote. How Tummas intended to sort him out, we don't know. But whatever happened, Tummas left with Nóa and was gone for a couple of hours, returning at about midnight." Hentze looked back at the team. "So the question is, what happened to Nóa? Where did Tummas take him?"

"In two hours he could have driven him to Saksun and got back to the bar," Dánjal Michelsen said. "Gramm knew the boathouse would be empty because he'd been working on it for Edvin Mohr."

"True. You could be right," Hentze said. "But if so, *why* did Tummas take Nóa there? That's the question. Why take Nóa to the boathouse and not to his parents' house, or even back to Tummas's own flat, say? That was a lot closer, a lot better furnished. If Nóa just needed a place to crash, why take him to somewhere as isolated as Saksun?"

"Maybe Nóa wanted to be out of the way," Annika said. "Maybe he was afraid of someone – the person he'd had a fight with, perhaps. Maybe he wanted to hide."

"Yes, that's possible." Hentze nodded and wrote up the word "*Afraid?*" on the board. "You went to his old school, didn't you? What sort of impression do we have of him from that?"

Annika checked her notes. "His teachers say he's intelligent, but they noticed a change in the last year he was there: lack of attention, absences, low grades, disrespect. Some of the pupils we talked to said more or less the same thing: he became a bit of a loner, sulky, preoccupied. He didn't want to mix."

"Any particular friends or enemies?"

"Not specifically, though a lot of his classmates have left for university so it's hard to be sure."

"What about the previous assault charge?" Dánjal suggested. "It could be worth checking on the guy Lisberg thumped twelve months ago – to see where he was last Saturday. Maybe there was an ongoing feud between them."

"Good, yes. Let's find out," Hentze said. Then he turned to Ári. "We know Lisberg didn't leave on the *Norröna* now, or by air, which means he's still here. So do we make a media appeal for information regarding his whereabouts?"

Niclasen unfolded his legs and sat forward. "No," he said flatly. "We're being badgered for more information about Gramm's death as it is. They know there was a post-mortem and a forensic investigation, so I'm going to make a statement – low-key – saying the results are still inconclusive. But if we follow that immediately with an appeal for information on Lisberg, everyone will jump to the obvious conclusion."

"Does that matter?" Hentze asked. "It is a murder investigation."

"Yes, I think it does. Going public will tell Lisberg we're on to him and could drive him deeper into hiding. I think our best course of action is to say nothing publicly and maintain that our interest in him is simply as a missing person. Then we wait for him to show himself, or to use his bank card or mobile."

"So we do nothing?" Hentze said. He didn't mind a hint of scepticism creeping in.

"No, of course not," Ári responded. "We follow up all the lines of enquiry we've already started and I think we should also cross-reference anyone known to both Tummas Gramm *and* Nóa Lisberg, no matter how distantly. Okay?"

Hentze nodded. "Okay, but in addition can we pull in some uniformed officers to start checking outbuildings and garages for Tummas Gramm's car? It's still not been found and it's hard to dump something that size unobtrusively, so I think it's been put under cover."

"Are you serious?" Ári asked. "You want to look in every barn and shed on the islands? There must be hundreds. You know we haven't got that sort of manpower."

"Well, maybe we could request that any officer called to a property with a shed or outbuilding should check it while they're there," Hentze suggested. "They're already on alert for the car, so…"

"Sure, okay," Niclasen said, as if keen to get off the topic. "Just as long as we don't make it look like we're so desperate that we're clutching at straws."

Hentze couldn't see that searching outbuildings was any more or less desperate than simply waiting and hoping that Nóa Lisberg would inadvertently give himself away, but he didn't say so. Instead, once they'd run through the rest of the investigation's housekeeping and allocated tasks, he followed Ári out of the incident room towards his office.

"I still think we should be trying to find out how Nóa Lisberg and Tummas Gramm connect to Signar Ravnsfjall," he told Niclasen. "It goes back to what I said before: if we find out what the blackmail was about we might get an indication of other areas we should be examining."

"If there *was* blackmail. That's far from certain."

"Sure, yes, but if there was…"

Niclasen frowned. "I suppose you'd also want to involve the Englishman Reyná again, too."

"No, I think that ship has sailed."

"Really?" Niclasen sounded irritable now. "Do you know he's been asking questions in Vestmanna about the investigation of a death – a case of drowning reported by Signar Ravnsfjall from the 1970s?"

"Really?" Hentze said. "No, I had no idea."

Ári Niclasen didn't bother to hide his doubt about that. "It's not something to do with this investigation, then?"

"Not as far as I know," Hentze said. By now he had sifted various caches of information in his head and recalled that Ári had an uncle – perhaps a great uncle or second cousin – who was a retired police officer in Vestmanna. Name of Eysturberg, if he remembered correctly.

"No, well, I hope not," Ári was saying. "Listen, let's just keep ourselves focused on Lisberg and Gramm, okay? Never mind distractions about blackmail and so on. When we find Lisberg we can ask him everything we want to know."

If they could find him without actually looking, Hentze thought drily as Ári went into his office. To him it seemed like a very big *if*, though.

5

LEYNAR WAS A COLLECTION OF HOUSES STRUNG OUT ALONG the road. They overlooked a beach of grey-black sand held in the crook of a V-shaped inlet where waves were running in ahead of the strengthening wind. It was still a while until sunset, but the light already felt exhausted.

I stood on the decking outside Fríða Sólsker's house and admired the view. It was probably the best in the village, given that the house was built on the rocks directly above the beach. Next to it was a smaller cottage – the guest house, Fríða had called it – mirroring the dark tarred weatherboards and turf roof of its big brother. Both were neat and well maintained.

I'd come out to have a look at the scenery at Fríða's suggestion – a tactful way of getting me out of the kitchen when, a few minutes after my arrival, she needed to juggle things between ovens.

"It's sheep stew," she told me.

"Lamb?"

"*Nei*. Er— mutton. The older sheep, from a friend. I

thought of making dried haddock and whale blubber with potatoes. It's traditional – very tasty – but I wasn't sure you were ready to be so Faroese again just yet."

"Are you teasing me?"

"A little."

"Okay, just so I know."

So I'd made myself scarce, taking my bottle of beer to watch the waves running in. There was salt in the air and I wondered how many summer days – or any days – there were when the Faroese weather was good enough that you could sit out here comfortably on the two wooden chairs. Few, I suspected.

In my pocket my phone rang. I took it out and glanced at the screen at the same time as the glass door slid open behind me. Fríða came out on to the deck, wrapping her knitted cardigan closer around her. Her hair was confined in a French braid.

The phone rang again.

"Do you need to answer that?" she asked, ready to step back if I wanted privacy.

I shook my head and rejected the call. I wasn't any more interested in anything Kirkland had to say over the phone than I had been in his email that morning.

"It's only work," I told her, dropping the phone back in my pocket. "Not important."

"Oh. Okay." She closed the door behind her and came to stand beside me. "I put your wine in the refrigerator," she said.

"I don't know how good it is. Does Kristian have good

taste?" When I'd told her how I'd come by it she'd been amused – or rather, I took it that my inexperience of island ways was the source of amusement.

"Sure, I think so," she nodded. "I'm sure it will be good enough to make a toast to your homecoming." Then, seeing my reaction, she added, "Is that the wrong thing to say?"

I waved it away. "No, it's fine. But after this I'd better stick to water. I gather the drink-driving laws here are different to England."

"Yeh, sure, but you don't have to worry about it. Unless you prefer to drive back tonight, you can stay in the guest house."

I'd been ready for a beer when I arrived, and willing to risk just the one, but the prospect of an otherwise abstemious evening didn't greatly appeal – or rather, the attraction of being able to relax was greater.

"Are you sure that's not putting you out?" I asked.

"No, of course not. That's what it's for," Fríða said matter-of-factly. "In summer I rent it out to holidaymakers. The rest of the time it's for friends. And Matteus goes there when we need a break from each other, or if he wants a little privacy for him and Marna – his girlfriend."

"That's pretty enlightened of you."

She gave me a curious look. "You think? To me it's better they have a warm, safe place rather than a cold bus shelter somewhere."

"I have a few good memories of bus shelters."

"Really?" she asked, raising an eyebrow. Sometimes it was hard to know when she was being ironic.

"Well, no, perhaps not so good, thinking back on it," I admitted. "I don't want to cramp his style, though."

"You won't. Tonight he can take Marna home. It's fine."

"Okay, well, if you're sure. Thanks," I said.

From inside the house there was the sound of a door banging closed.

"That will be them. Shall we go in? I'll introduce you."

Matteus Sólsker had the same deep-seated Scandinavian looks as his mother, although his hair was a shade darker. He was good-looking enough to be confident, but self-aware enough that it wasn't an issue. He also shared Fríða's tendency to frown when he was thinking about something. His girlfriend, Marna, seemed more playful and a little less serious, her auburn hair cut in an angular bob. They seemed well matched and comfortable with one another and I gathered they had been going out together for nearly a year, although they'd known each other for longer.

Over dinner at a nicely aged wooden table they chatted away to me, Fríða and between themselves, sticking to English except for short, personal asides. I was a source of interest and, inevitably, the conversation came round to the fact that I was one of them, but also – irrevocably – an outsider.

I didn't particularly mind being the object of curiosity. To a degree it carried the conversation along, with the inevitable comparisons and requests for clarifications on both sides, as well as diversions into linguistic anomalies like the silent ð in Faroese. I gave them some amusement with my pronunciation of place names, and once they'd worked out where I was talking about they were able to correct me – gently – so that Tvøroyri became "Twuh-ruh-ruh" and Suðuroy "Soo-uh-roy".

Both Matteus and Marna were that teenage mix of interest in the wider world, while also being slightly wary of the unknown. They seemed to have a deep-seated sense of connection to the islands, but at the same time it was tempered by the knowledge that the horizons and opportunities weren't as great as those on offer on the mainland. When I asked if they'd return after university or choose to stay in Denmark they both said it was too early to know and would depend what careers they chose.

"Fríða says you are a homicide officer," Marna said. "Don't you work on anything else?"

"No, usually just murder."

"That must be grim," Matteus said, clearly giving it some thought.

"It can be."

"Not always?"

"No, it's a mixture of things: the grim stuff, yes; but you get a buzz – get wrapped up in it – because you want to find out what happened."

"Matts talked to the cops at school today," Marna said, mostly directed to Fríða. "Has he told you?"

Fríða shook her head and frowned. "What happened?"

"Oh, it wasn't so much. Just a regular investigation," Matteus said. "They asked for anyone who knew Nóa Lisberg."

"Nóa from the swimming team?"

"*Ja*. He's missing. No one's seen him for a week."

"Could you tell them anything? Have you seen him?"

"Not really since he stopped being on the team, and then he left school, so…" He shrugged. "They talked to all the team, though, and the teachers."

"They also asked you about the guy who died on the beach, didn't they?" Marna said, prompting him, as if he'd left out the most interesting detail.

Matteus gave her a brief disapproving frown. "They asked us not to talk about it," he said. And then, to Fríða in mitigation: "They only wanted to know if I'd heard Nóa talk about him, but he didn't to me."

I was paying polite attention, but the reference to the beach made me curious. "Do you mean Tummas Gramm?" I asked.

"*Ja*."

"Was the officer at the school called Hjalti Hentze?"

"No, a woman. I don't remember her name. Sorry."

"It doesn't matter, I was just being nosey – curious," I added when I saw that he didn't know the word.

I *was* curious about the connection, though – if there was one. It didn't seem as if a run-of-the-mill missing-person enquiry would be linked to Tummas Gramm for no reason, and I wondered if Hentze and his team had made a step forward. Preliminary forensics would – should – be in by now, so it was possible that something had thrown up a connection to the missing Nóa Lisberg. The fact that he *was* missing might be significant, too:

more so if he was being seen as a potential suspect.

I realised I'd drifted out of the conversation. When I refocused Marna was speaking, more or less to Matteus.

"I think he is sitting on top of a mountain," she said. "Or by a lake, to talk with himself. It is the kind of thing he would do – did they talk to Elin? She would tell them."

"I don't know," Matteus said.

"Did you tell them her name?"

"*Nei*," Matteus shook his head, and I got the sense that it was something he'd prefer not to have got into. But Marna was enjoying the novelty.

"You should have," she said. "After the way he was with her. That was very weird. You said so yourself."

Matteus shrugged, as if he didn't remember, and he chose to eat rather than respond.

"Which Elin are you talking about?" Fríða asked, more out of politeness than real curiosity it seemed.

"Elin Langgaard. Nóa was—" Marna searched for the word. "Obsessed – crazy about her, you know? All the time watching and looking at her. Of course, I think she likes it, although she says she wishes he would stop. Even if he is not old enough for her, I think she thinks it's cool to have the attention."

"Well, she's pretty," Fríða said. And then a tad pointedly, "Her stepfather is Jan's brother."

Marna glanced at me quickly, then down at her plate and coloured a little, as if she realised she might have spoken out of turn. "Oh, okay," she said.

I felt a bit sorry for her; the family dinner with her

boyfriend's mother and an unknown foreigner was probably tough enough without wandering into the minefield of family relationships. I turned to Fríða and said, "I met her – Elin – when I was having a drink with Kristian the night I arrived. Her mother is Anni, is that right?"

"Yes. Anni Langgaard."

"Right. I think I'm starting to get some of the family tree sorted out now."

She chuckled and stood up to start clearing the dishes. "There is a lot to look at if you feel like it. In the last hundred years our population has trebled, so if you go back far enough we all meet somewhere."

Fríða refused my offer of help to clear away, getting Matteus to give her a hand. Marna and I moved through to the sitting room where a couple of logs were burning in a small stove, damped down so there wasn't much flame.

Conscious Marna might still be feeling reticent about her faux pas, I asked about the film she and Matteus were going to see that evening and she seemed to relax. The director was clever, she said, but not as cool as he thought he was. She expected the film to miss the point of the book it was based on and asked if I'd read it. I admitted I hadn't even heard of it but used the opportunity to shift the topic.

"Can I ask you about something?"

"Sure."

"How well do you know Elin Langgaard?"

I sensed her reluctance return a little.

"Oh, not so well," she said. "We have some of the same classes at school, that's all."

"So what did you mean when you said Nóa Lisberg wasn't old enough for her?"

"Oh, nothing."

Which never means what it says, and she seemed to realise that as soon as she said it. "I just mean she isn't interested in the boys at school, you know? She is— She thinks she is more grown up than that."

"She likes older men?"

"No, I don't know. She likes to flirt. If it's an older guy… They're easy, you know?"

I did know. Even from the short meeting with Elin Langgaard in Café Natúr I could see how that would go.

"Have you seen her flirt with anyone in particular?"

It was mostly idle curiosity; perhaps just a desire to get a more rounded picture, but I saw a flash of embarrassment as Marna shook her head. "There is— Just gossip that's all. Really."

I knew I was making her uncomfortable, which wasn't very nice of me, so I just nodded and changed the subject. I did wonder what would make a fairly confident, fairly forthright teenage girl embarrassed, though. Perhaps just being cross-questioned by a stranger, and a man at that. Perhaps.

Matteus and Marna left for the cinema a few minutes later, taking Fríða's car with promises to drive carefully. When they'd gone Fríða came to join me in the sitting room, bringing the wine from the table. She topped up my glass and then settled comfortably in a leather armchair, tucking her legs up beneath her. Outside the glass door the deck was invisible in the darkness but there was a faint band of moon-greyed clouds high up.

"How long were you with Kristian this afternoon?" she asked as a way of restarting the conversation.

"A couple of hours, I suppose. He took me out to look at his fish pens. I got the impression he'd rather be sailing a boat than running the business."

She nodded. "I think that might be true. He is never as happy in the office as Magnus, I think. Magnus likes to do deals and be interested in the politics – to have control of things – but Kris is more straightforward."

"More down to earth?"

"Yeh." She tilted her head slightly. "Have you thought what you might have been doing if you had stayed here? Do you think you would be like Kristian or Magnus?"

"You mean do I think I'd have been part of the business, or out sailing boats?" I shook my head. "I don't know; it's too hard to imagine."

"You can only imagine yourself as a police officer?"

"Maybe it's just *lack* of imagination," I said. "But while we're talking about jobs, can I ask you something?"

"Sure, go ahead."

"The other day when we met at the hospital, why did you say you were a counsellor rather than a psychotherapist?" I saw the question as it crossed her face. "Google," I said.

"Ah. Okay."

She gave it a moment, as if deciding how she felt about that, but in the end she returned to my original question without showing her decision. "I suppose it's because to say 'counsellor' is not so threatening to some people. Also, it's a better interpretation of what I do, I think."

"You mean to advise people rather than to treat them?"

"Yeh, maybe – although really it is both at the same time."

"And mostly with kids?"

She nodded. "Young people often find it the hardest time in their life. They have to find a way to live in a world they don't understand yet, and if they also have psychological problems or there have been upsetting things happening to them…"

It sounded familiar.

"Would you have put me in that category when I was a kid, then?" I asked.

"From what I know? Yes, sure," she said without hesitation. "I would have thought it was a good idea to make sure you were okay – in case you needed help, you know?"

I nodded. "They did," I told her. "I didn't like it much. I thought it was a waste of time, but maybe it worked."

"You're not sure?"

"Well, I haven't killed anyone yet – or myself – so I suppose it must have."

I'd meant it as a quip – a way to duck out of the subject – but I saw her assessing look linger for a moment.

"Yes, that's always a good start." She nodded, although

I knew she wasn't really sharing the joke, only going along with it because she'd read my intention.

"So tell me about your visit to Suðuroy yesterday," she said. "They were pleased to see you, by the way."

It was a more open way of dealing with the dead end and moving past it than I would probably have used, but why not? It was refreshing not to have the awkward transition, and I liked the honesty of it.

So I told her about my impressions of the island, and of her mother and father, and the conversation wandered around that for a while, as they do. Then it prompted her to uncurl from the armchair and fetch an album of photographs from her study upstairs. She laid it out on the coffee table and sat beside me on the sofa to turn to pages flagged with sticky tags.

She had found two more photographs of me, at about the same age as I was in the one she'd given me the other day, and further back in the album – earlier in time – there was another, of my mother standing with her arm round Signar on a stone quay. It was in black and white and was dated in white ink underneath: *Signar & Lýdia, august 1971*. They were both smiling, but Signar looked slightly uncomfortable.

"Do you know where it is?" I asked.

"No. Perhaps Suðuroy."

I did some mental arithmetic and worked out that Lýdia would have been eighteen, Signar about twenty-five. For some reason I'd never really realised the age difference between them before, or the fact that they had been a couple when Lýdia was still quite young. Given when I was born it had to be the case, but even so it surprised me. I studied the picture for a little longer, then sat back.

"Your father told me that Lýdia went to Denmark for medical treatment about a year after I was born, so in about 1973," I said. "Do you know anything about that?"

Fríða shook her head. "What sort of treatment?"

"He doesn't know. I'd like to find out, though. Do you think that's possible? Would there still be medical records from that long ago, or would it be possible to find out who her doctor was? He might still be alive."

Too many questions: bad interview technique. Fríða seemed to think through them one by one, then nodded and sipped her wine as punctuation.

"You think you will find out why she committed suicide?" she asked.

I shrugged. "I wondered if she had a history of depression or some other mental illness."

"Do you have a reason to think that she did?"

I didn't answer immediately. She wasn't pressing me to.

"Maybe," I said, and left it for her to infer what she wanted from that. "I'd just like to know more."

"To understand."

"Yeah."

And then I left a silence. Because it was tempting to say other things, and the silence was deciding whether I was ready to say them. And the longer I didn't the further away they went. Because I know interview technique.

"Would you be able to find out about her records?" I asked then. "I'm sorry to keep asking for favours."

"No, don't worry about it," she said. "I don't know if records are kept from so long ago, but I will ask."

"*Takk*."

Later, but not late, when the wine was finished and the stove needed another log or none, I said I wouldn't keep her up any longer.

She took me through to the side door of the house and put the external light on so I could see to cross the short distance to the door of the guest house.

"I hope you sleep well," she said.

"Thanks," I said. "For the meal and the company. I enjoyed it."

"Me too." Then she gave me a slightly wan smile. "Don't think too much, okay?"

"Why do you say that?"

She shrugged. "I think you do."

And in the moment when you hesitate about what is and isn't the way to say goodnight, she said it and touched my arm as she turned away.

The door of the guest house was unlocked.

Inside I found the light switch and went up the stairs. There was one bedroom and an adjacent bathroom. On the bed there was a clean towel with a toothbrush and tube of toothpaste on top, still in their boxes. There was no sign of any personal items in the bathroom and when I checked the drawers of the dressing table they were also empty. I wasn't sure why I'd looked.

6

Saturday/leygardagur

UPSTAIRS SÓLEYG WAS STILL ASLEEP AND HENTZE POTTERED quietly round the kitchen in his socks while he made and drank his first coffee of the day. In the grey, rainy morning light he tidied up and absently watered the potted basil on the windowsill, letting his mind wander as he did so. When he finally put on his boots and coat he checked to make sure there was enough coffee in the pot for when Sóleyg came down and then he left quietly through the back door.

He knew there had been no developments – no progress – since the previous evening because there had been no phone call. Even so, various elements of the case had risen above others and become clearer in his mind overnight. Foremost of those was the most obvious one: if the investigation into Tummas Gramm's death was going to move forward they needed to find and to speak with Nóa Lisberg as soon as possible.

Okay, so maybe he didn't need to be a detective

to work that one out, but he had also spent part of the previous evening reading through the notebook he had taken from Nóa Lisberg's bedroom, and it had been a strange experience. It was also one that had convinced him that they needed to do more than just sit back and wait until Nóa Lisberg showed himself. Rather, they ought to be making every effort to find him, even if that meant publicising the case.

To Hentze, Ári Niclasen's reluctance to do that felt misjudged. Of course people might put two and two together and realise they wanted to speak to Lisberg in connection with Gramm's death, but so what? People would be far more likely to notice and report the boy if they thought he was a murder suspect. So wasn't it better to have the whole population on the lookout, rather than just relying on the chance that a passing patrol car would spot him? Surely there was no need to make life even more difficult for themselves.

In the station the CID corridor had its usual Saturday-morning quiet and when Hentze looked in at Ári's office it was, unsurprisingly, still empty. The incident room wasn't, however, and although the team had been slimmed down since yesterday, Dánjal, Annika and Oddur were at the desks.

Once they'd all got coffee, Hentze called a brief conference to get the latest progress reports, the most significant of which was an email from the technical lab in Copenhagen. It confirmed that the DNA in the blood samples from Signar Ravnsfjall's car, and from the boathouse at Saksun had both come from Tummas Gramm.

It wasn't exactly a new development, but it at least allowed Hentze to use a black marker and reinforce the connecting lines between these elements on the whiteboards.

There was no news yet on the laptops belonging to Tummas Gramm and Nóa Lisberg, so when the conference ended Hentze rang the lab and asked for Sophie Krogh. She wasn't there, but after a couple of transfers he was finally able to speak with a lab manager in Technical Investigation who confirmed that the laptops had been logged in for analysis and would probably be looked at tomorrow or Monday. Did Hentze want to bump up their priority – along with the cost – or was he happy to wait? Hentze told the lab manager to put them through as a matter of urgency, ignoring the fact that Ári was supposed to approve the budget for such things.

By the time Ári Niclasen came in at nine thirty – dressed down in jeans and a sweater – Hentze was waiting for him, ready to state his case even before Ári had taken off his coat.

"There haven't been any significant developments overnight," he said, tapping his notepad. "The DNA tests confirmed what we suspected – that it *was* Tummas Gramm's blood on Signar Ravnsfjall's car and also in the boathouse. We've also been given Nóa Lisberg's phone records, but they're not much help. No calls made and no texts sent in the last seven days."

"Can they triangulate the phone's position?" Ári asked, finally taking the chair behind his desk.

"No, it's not active. Either he's taken the battery out

or it's simply gone flat. Dánjal's asked the phone company to let us know if it becomes active again, but I wouldn't want to rely on it as a way of locating him. Other than that, we're down to looking at the minutiae and chasing a few loose ends."

"Okay," Niclasen said, as if he was giving that serious consideration. "So is there anything we've missed? Anything we should be looking at and aren't?"

Hentze knew this was his opening, but he didn't rush at it. "To be honest," he said, "I think we should seriously consider the possibility that Lisberg's being hidden: I mean that someone is *helping* him to stay out of sight, giving him somewhere to stay, feeding him and so on. If that *is* the case, he might be able to remain out of sight for weeks, which clearly isn't what we want."

"No, clearly," Ári agreed. "But at least we know he can't leave the islands."

"True," Hentze nodded. "But even so I think we should reconsider going public. At least that way anyone sheltering him will be under no illusion that he's just left home to get away from Mum and Dad. In my opinion we need to make it clear that Lisberg is a suspect in a serious case and that anyone sheltering him is potentially aiding a criminal."

For a moment Ári Niclasen looked as if he was about to respond, but then he seemed to think better of it and got up to go to his espresso machine instead. He checked the water level, pushed a button, then turned back to Hentze.

"And what if that doesn't flush him out? Have you thought about that? What if he's holed up on his own in a shepherd's hut somewhere, living off the land? We don't know whether he's capable of that, but if he is he could stay out there for God knows how long – and he'll have an added incentive to do that if he thinks he's being hunted. Then we'll have a situation where everyone knows we're looking for him but we can't bring him in. How will that make us look?"

So that was it, Hentze realised. It was the Vira Sirko case again, except this time it wasn't the failure to locate a body that Ári feared; it was the spotlight of attention that any public announcement would inevitably bring. If days or a week passed and they *still* couldn't catch their man – a boy, actually… No, that was the last thing Ári would want: it would be an open invitation for criticism from all sides if a teenage fugitive continued to evade them. The whole population would look on and wonder how hard it could be.

"Does it really matter how it looks?" Hentze said in response to Ári's last question. "I mean, it won't be any better if we keep quiet but take a month to find him. As soon as he *is* found it'll be obvious how long we took."

"Maybe, but at least then we'll have him in custody," Niclasen said flatly. "It will be over."

"And if there was a third person involved, in the blackmail and the murder?" Hentze asked. "Someone we don't know about? They could be leaving the islands right now. They could be gone already."

He hoped that the spectre of an escaped suspect might touch a nerve, but Ári shook his head, no longer open to argument. "I'm not convinced. If there *was* blackmail it seems much more likely to me that Lisberg and Gramm cooked it up between them. It's plain and straightforward and it fits what we know. I don't see any need to complicate things on pure speculation."

"The forensics at the boathouse—"

"Aren't definitive," Ári cut him off, sounding tetchy now. "One partial print, wasn't that what Sophie Krogh said? Impossible to be sure when it was made."

Hentze said nothing and, as if he realised his tone might have been a tad too peremptory, Ári looked at his watch. "Listen," he said. "I'm going to see Remi in a minute. He asked for an update so I'll see if he'll get us some more uniform support for roadside checks and canvassing of outlying shops and petrol stations with Lisberg's photo. Even if Lisberg's gone to ground he'll still need to buy supplies. I'll also mention your idea about searching barns and outbuildings for Gramm's car, okay?"

Hentze nodded. "That would be something." There was a vague chance that as chief, Remi Syderbø might decide to press ahead more actively, but Hentze had little faith in Ári's advocacy for it.

"Okay then," Ári said, as if the tiff had been settled amicably after all. He glanced at the espresso machine with a look of mild regret that he'd missed his opportunity to use it, then switched it off. "I'll look in when I've finished," he said.

I'd woken early, partly because of the unfamiliar bed, partly because I'd set the alarm on my mobile. I washed and dressed and went downstairs. The guest-house kitchen was small – recently cleaned, well equipped: just right for a holiday let. There was a jar of Nescafé on the worktop so I made a cup – black because the fridge was empty – and drank it looking out of the bay windows of the sitting room. Then I went to see if anyone was moving in Fríða's house.

Matteus was in the kitchen, still wearing his pyjama trousers and a long-sleeved T-shirt as he browsed Facebook on a laptop. We exchanged good mornings and chatted a little about the film he'd seen last night: Marna hadn't been impressed but he'd thought it was okay.

A couple of minutes later Fríða came in to make coffee. She'd already been out for a run, come back and had a shower, which made me revise my definition of early rising and made her laugh when I told her so.

I drank another coffee to be sociable, but declined the offer of breakfast and said I ought to be going. Fríða went with me to the hall and waited while I put on my coat.

"I won't forget about Lýdia's medical records," she said.

"Thanks."

"When do you leave?"

"Tuesday afternoon."

"Ah. Okay."

I couldn't read that. Regardless, I said, "Listen, can I buy you dinner before I go? Monday?"

"Sure, that would be nice. Can I check my diary and let you know?"

"Of course."

"Will you see Magnus or Kristian again before you go, too?"

I knew she was leaving Signar off the options on purpose. "Maybe, I'm not sure," I said, but since we were on the subject I went on: "I meant to ask last night: do you know why Kristian split up with Anni?"

She shook her head. "Not really. I think it's just one of those things: some marriages run out of energy."

"Or put it all into fighting." I nodded. "But it wasn't an affair or anything like that?"

"No, I don't know." A slight frown. "Why?"

I shrugged. "I just wondered. Like I said, I like him, but I don't know him."

Then a phone began to ring and Matteus was calling Fríða from the kitchen.

"I'd better go," I said. "Thanks again for last night."

"You're welcome."

Outside I strode back up the hill to the car.

Hentze had kept some small hope that Remi Syderbø would either put in an appearance in the incident room, or at least express some concern about the pace and direction of the investigation, but apparently Ári Niclasen's meeting with him had been reassuring enough that he didn't feel it necessary. Twenty minutes later Ári was gone, although he'd emphasised that he would be on call if there were any significant developments.

"You think he'll have his phone on while he's at the

match?" Dánjal asked sardonically, once Ári had departed.

Hentze gave him a look, but then his own phone rang and gave him an excuse not to make comment.

"Hentze."

"It's Jan Reyna. Are you busy?"

"No, not so much."

There was a brief pause. "Okay, well, I've got some information you might be interested in. It's nothing concrete but it might be useful if you're free for five minutes. I'm at the hotel."

"Okay, sure," Hentze said. "I'll come now."

"Okay. I'm in the dining room."

Hentze rang off, looked round the room, then made a decision. "Okay, listen," he said to the others. "There's not enough to keep four of us occupied here. I have to go out, but we only need one person here in case something comes in. Any volunteers?"

"I don't mind," Annika said. "Dánjal and Oddur have got kids. I can carry on with these phone lists."

"Okay, thanks," Hentze nodded. "I'll be back in a while."

He collected his coat and headed out. He was on the last flight of stairs down to ground level when he passed Heri Kalsø coming the other way.

"Hey, Heri," Hentze nodded.

"Hey," Kalsø said, pausing. "I was coming to see you about your email. Are you still interested in fights and assaults from last Saturday?"

Hentze stopped, turned back. "Yes, why? Did you attend one?"

"Sort of. I was having a burger at Emilia's and a guy came in out of the rain. When he saw me he said there'd been a fight in the car park by the Nólsoy ferry quay: one guy had got a bloody nose and the other had run off."

"Did you go to look?"

"Sure, though I reckoned it would be a waste of time if it was all over. Anyway, I drove down there and looked around and there was a guy sitting in his car holding a tissue to his nose. He had the light on inside, you know? So I went over and tapped on the window and asked if everything was all right. He said everything was fine: he just had a nosebleed. I asked if he was sure it wasn't a fight; did he want to report anything? 'No,' he says, 'it's nothing. No fight, just a nose bleed.' I knew it wasn't true, but what could I do? So I left."

"You didn't know him? Did you ask his name?"

"No, there didn't seem any need. I did write down the car licence, though."

He patted his jacket pocket, then took out his notebook.

"Why? I mean, if nothing was wrong?"

Heri shrugged. "Just to be safe, I guess. Just in case – you know. Do you want it?"

Hentze nodded. "Will you do me a favour and find out who it belongs to, then give me a call?"

"Sure, no problem. By the way, is Annika still on your team?"

"Yes, she's in the incident room."

"Mind if I drop in for a word with her? She sent me a text saying she wanted to see me."

"Are things looking up again with you two now, then?"

"I dunno," Heri said with a shrug. "But at least she's not completely ignoring me any more."

"Well, good luck," Hentze said. "Don't forget to check that car licence."

"I won't."

"Thanks."

As Heri Kalsø headed upwards with a spring in his step, Hentze took the last couple of stairs and headed for the exit.

I saw Hentze come along the parking area in front of the hotel through the windows in the dining room. I was the only person there; showered, changed and breakfasted. I'd been starting my first coffee when I called him; I was getting another from the pump-flask on the breakfast bar when he came in.

"*Morgun*," I said. "Coffee?"

"*Takk*."

When we were sorted on that front we sat at a table by the window. I was trying to read his mood but couldn't, so in the end I went for a direct approach. "Are you interested in a teenager called Nóa Lisberg?" I asked. "In relation to Tummas Gramm's death?"

Hentze cocked his head as if that wasn't what he'd expected. "A little, yes. How do you know?"

I told him briefly about my dinner with Fríða, Matteus and Marna and said that Matteus had talked to a police officer at school the previous day.

"Did he tell you something he didn't tell us?" Hentze asked.

"No – not specifically anyway," I said. "But while we were talking something came up that you may or may not already know. When I thought about it, it seemed as if it might be relevant – *if* you've got a reason to link this Lisberg guy to Tummas Gramm."

Hentze considered that, but not for very long. "Nóa Lisberg's fingerprints were found in the boathouse," he said. "I think he was there with Tummas."

"Right," I said, weighing that up. "In that case I think there's a circle of association. Do you use the phrase?"

"No, but I understand. Go on."

I nodded. "Okay. Signar connects to Tummas Gramm at Tjørnuvík through the blood on Signar's car; Gramm connects to Lisberg at the boathouse; Lisberg connects to a girl called Elin Langgaard; Elin Langgaard connects to Kristian Ravnsfjall because she's his stepdaughter; and then Kristian connects back to Signar."

Hentze didn't say anything for a while. He blinked a couple of times, looked off in the distance, frowned a little.

In the end he said, "Why is there a link between Nóa Lisberg and this girl, Elin Langgaard?"

"Apparently he is, or was, obsessed with her. That's not my word. From what I can gather, it was serious – I mean, he took it seriously but she wasn't interested, or said she wasn't."

Hentze looked thoughtful. "So what do you think this gives us?"

"I don't know," I said, because I didn't. "But I don't know all the facts either. It *does* give you a way of associating all the people you know about, though."

While he was still considering that his mobile rang. "*Ja, Heri?*"

He didn't need to move away to talk privately: what he said was in Faroese and he didn't say much. When he finished he rang off, put the phone away, then looked at me.

"How do you feel?" he asked.

"About what?"

"Police work," he said, then immediately answered his own question. "I think it should be done properly or why do we bother? But we're not doing anything with this case. There's no energy, no commitment."

He shook his head, exasperated, then abruptly pushed back his chair. It made a God-awful scrape. "So, I have had enough," he told me. "Do you want to come?"

"Where?"

"To see Elin Langgaard."

"Why?"

"As you said, you don't know all the picture. Last Saturday night at ten o'clock Nóa Lisberg went to see Tummas Gramm because he'd been involved in a fight." He indicated his phone. "That was information that also last Saturday night Kristian Ravnsfjall was assaulted in the car park by the harbour. It happened a few minutes before ten o'clock."

7

WE DROVE BELOW MIST. ROILING CLOUD FILLED THE GAPS between mountaintops, not quite descending to the road in the valley but placing a murky, overcast lid on the world.

Unusually for him, Hentze talked most of the way. But this wasn't chat; it was – or might as well have been – a briefing. I got the sense that he'd had a lot of it bottled up and that running through it now was a way of reassessing and re-ordering some of the component pieces: the forensic results; the lead on Nóa Lisberg; and the fact that the search for him was being hampered. I could see why he'd seemed frustrated back at the hotel. He was a straightforward man, a straightforward copper, and he was being prevented from doing the straightforward, most logical thing for his investigation: going public. He didn't like it, and I didn't blame him.

"You still think Lisberg's the prime suspect for Gramm's murder, then?" I asked.

He chewed that over for a moment. "Ári thinks so," he said then. "So, perhaps he's right. But my feeling – my hunch – is that it's not so likely. We know a third person was at the boathouse, so for me it's important to find Lisberg and ask him who that was."

"Because they'd be a more likely killer than Lisberg."

"It's what we need to find out."

Eventually we turned off route 40 and headed downhill into a valley and the village of Kvívík. The smooth, unmarked tarmac twisted and turned between the houses – maybe a hundred all told, with a modern church and a barn-like school high up, overlooking the rest of the valley.

Anni and Elin Langgaard's house was on the far side of the energetic river that bisected the village, cascading over a rocky bed. The house looked new, set on a plot hardly bigger than its own dimensions at the foot of the valley's slope. It was neat but relatively small compared with many of the houses around it. A red Ford Focus was parked on the short drive. Hentze parked his own car on the road below the house and stopped the engine.

"Do you want me to wait here?" I asked him.

He looked surprised. "Why?"

"Aren't I *persona non grata* as far as Niclasen's concerned?"

"Ári's not here. Besides, you know the girl."

"I only met her once."

"Still."

I shrugged. "Okay then."

I let Hentze lead, up steps to a side door at first-floor level, above the undercroft. Alongside the steps there were a couple of wooden pallets, some offcuts of builder's timber and a stack of floor tiles, half-heartedly tidied away.

The door was opened by a woman in jeans and a well-fitting sweater, the sleeves pushed back on her arms. She was about forty, certainly not much beyond that, with dark auburn hair, cut straight below her shoulders. She had high cheekbones, verging on sharp, and a faintly closed-down expression as if she was getting used to bad news.

Hentze introduced himself in Faroese, and then me. I saw her catch my name with recognition and wondered if my being Kristian's half-brother might be a problem. From what I'd picked up, Anni Langgaard's split with Kristian hadn't been, or wasn't, without its lingering tension.

She nodded to me, though, polite if not warm. "I have heard Kristian speak about you," she said. "Please, come in."

It was warm in the house. We entered through a small lobby to the kitchen. Beyond that there was a single room with a dining table at one end, a sofa and armchair in front of a TV at the other. Although it was neat it gave the impression that the furniture had not been bought with the size of this space in mind. That's what break-ups do.

Still in Faroese, Hentze was telling Anni why we were there and I heard Elin's name and a confirmation from her mother. She gestured us through to the sitting room and went off down a short hallway. At the far end she tapped on a door and called Elin's name.

Hentze and I said nothing as we moved into the living room and waited. I unzipped my jacket. It was uncomfortably warm.

Maybe thirty seconds later Anni reappeared with Elin

following her. Another girl, about the same age but slightly rounder in the face and not as confident in her movements, tagged along behind. They were both wearing strappy, sleeveless tops and their fingernails were freshly varnished. That seemed to be what we had interrupted.

Hentze did a further round of introductions. The other girl was called Silja Midjord, I learned, but Elin Langgaard didn't need to be reminded who I was. I'd wondered if she'd want to acknowledge that we'd met before, given where and when it had happened, but she obviously didn't see it as a problem.

"*Hey*, Jan," she said, as if she'd been looking forward to the next time we met. "It's good to see you again."

"You too," I said, returning her smile.

"Jan is Kris's secret brother," she told Silja. There was a slight air of mischief in the way she said it, as if she enjoyed the phrase.

With the five of us there, the room seemed crowded and the sofa and single armchair weren't enough to accommodate everyone. Hentze gestured to the dining table and asked Anni if we could sit there. It wasn't a bad trick. No one was left standing and the table also lent a slightly more businesslike air to the proceedings. That seemed to suit Anni Langgaard, too. I got the impression she wanted to get this over with.

When we were finally seated, Hentze came to the point.

"Let me say again that there is nothing to be worried about," he told Anni. "We are here because we have information that Elin knows a boy called Nóa Lisberg. He is missing and we are trying to find where he could be."

He'd looked to Elin at the end of this and her response was an immediate and definite shake of her head. "*Nei*. I don't know. I don't care as long as he stays away."

"Oh?" Hentze did a good job of mild surprise. "Why is that?"

"He's crazy: weird, you know? Not in a good way. He has a— He is a stalker."

"To you?"

"Sure. Yes."

She looked to her mother and switched to Faroese but it was easy to tell that she was asking Anni to confirm what she was saying. Anni Langgaard did so and added more: an explanation and grievance, it seemed when Hentze asked further questions.

I caught the odd, easily distinguishable word – *telefon*, *hús*, *skúli* – but knew better than to interrupt the flow. Instead I glanced at Silja who was following this closely, a slight look of concern on her face. When she caught me looking at her she made a small, self-conscious dip of her head but the concern didn't go away.

After a couple of minutes Hentze nodded, as if he'd got the picture now. He turned to Silja and switched back to English.

"Silja, did you also know about these problems with Nóa?"

"*Ja*. It was— From Elin, *ja*. But also other people know it."

"Ah, okay, I see."

I caught the slight lull he left and took the cue. I turned to Elin. "Did Kristian know that Nóa had been bothering you?" I asked.

She made a conservative nod. "A little, yes. But I didn't want to make it sound very serious, you know? It was just a nuisance."

"Has he met Nóa? Does he know him?"

There was a fractional pause, then she shook her head. "No, I don't think so. When we were at the other house before— before we moved here, Nóa wouldn't have come. He would be afraid if Kris was at home."

"Has Nóa been here, to this house?" Hentze asked.

"No," Elin shook her head. "I haven't seen him from when he left school: not for months. I don't want to. Maybe he's left the islands. That would be good."

Hentze nodded as if it was a reasonable point. "Yes, it's something we're checking," he said. "And you can't think of anywhere else he might have gone – friends maybe?"

"*Nei*."

"Okay, well then, I think we can leave you to your day. We just have to check these things, you understand."

"Sure," Elin said. "It's no problem."

Hentze stood up, bringing the interview to an end. The rest of us followed suit, but as he went towards the kitchen with Anni Langgaard I held back, just a little, when Elin spoke to me.

"Are you going to be with the Faroes police now?" she asked. Again that slightly playful manner, as if that would be an interesting thing for me to do.

"I'm just keeping Hjalti company," I said. "He's been showing me round."

"Do policemen always hang out with other policemen, even on holiday?"

"Sure," I said, keeping it light. "Sometimes we even paint each other's fingernails."

I wiggled imaginary wet nails camply and that made her laugh.

Hentze and I walked the short distance back to the car. Apart from "*farvæl*" and "*takk fyri*" to Anni Langgaard and Elin, Hentze hadn't said anything as we left.

"Have you seen Kvívík before?" he asked as he opened the car door.

I told him I hadn't.

"Okay, I'll show you the harbour."

He drove for little more than a minute, following the slope of the road downhill, then parked on a pristine area of tarmac, neatly laid out with parking slots and not another car in sight. There was a fine mist in the air and the constant background sound of the river, tumbling the last few yards to its liberation. Behind us there was another church with a squat square spire. Beside it was a stunted, wind-bowed thicket of scrubby trees inside a neat stone wall. The trees could have been a hundred years old but they would never get any taller: the wind kept them permanently clipped and bowed.

We strolled away from the car and Hentze didn't bother to lock it, I noticed.

"How much did you understand about Nóa Lisberg?" he asked then.

"Just that he'd made a nuisance of himself."

"*Ja*. Maybe a little more than that. He has called Elin, sent her SMS messages and letters, gone to places where she would be. He says they are supposed to be together and sometimes he was upset – angry – when she told him to leave her alone."

"Do you think she encouraged him?"

"No, she says not." He looked at me. "You don't think so?"

I made a so-so gesture. "Last night a girl who knows Elin from school told me Elin might have enjoyed the attention – having someone obsessed with her. But she also said that Nóa wasn't Elin's type."

"Oh? What is her type?"

"Older men."

He knew I wasn't saying it without reason, but for the moment he seemed content to let me take my time before saying more, if I chose to.

We walked past some boathouses: sheds with slatted doors facing a ramp down to the harbour. The heavy concrete of the sea walls had the look of Second World War architecture: the same heavy lines, redoubtable and defensive. I waited until we'd got to the main harbour wall before deciding what to say.

"Do you still think blackmail is at the bottom of all this?" I asked. I wanted confirmation that Hentze was thinking the same way I was.

"*Ja*, for me I think it's certain," he said flatly. "I think it is the key. Anyone who was involved in that could have killed Tummas Gramm."

I nodded. "I was distracted by thinking the blackmail could have been about something in Signar's past," I said. "But what if it wasn't? What if the blackmail was about something else that Signar wouldn't want to be made public?"

"But still something to do with the family?"

"Yeah."

I had to make up my mind now. I either said it or shut up.

I said, "From what I can tell, Kristian's separation from Anni hasn't been good. I get the feeling that there's more under the surface than just irreconcilable differences."

"Another woman?"

"Or a girl."

He looked at me but didn't break our stroll. He wasn't going to say anything now; he'd just let me lay it out.

"What if Kristian had an affair with Elin?" I said. "There are hints that it might have happened: the way she acts with him, the fact that she's supposed to like older, more sophisticated men. And to sleep with your stepdaughter: that would definitely blow a marriage apart with a lot of bitterness."

"*If* his wife knew," Hentze said with a nod. "Then yes."

I made an open, casting-away gesture. "It's not solid. I'm not saying that. It's a guess. But – if it was true – I don't think it would be something the Ravnsfjall family would want to be public. So, that's a secret, a basis for blackmail... but what if it's not completely secret because

Nóa Lisberg finds out? Maybe he sees Elin and Kristian together somewhere while he's following her around; maybe she makes him suspicious by something she says... I don't know. But however it happens, Nóa knows or guesses the secret. Maybe he's upset, maybe he's angry, but he tells his mate Tummas and Tummas immediately sees a way to make a profit: 'Give us a million krónur or we tell everyone what's been going on.' And that gives you the chain of association, from Kristian through Elin to Tummas Gramm."

I paused, looked down, kicked a stray pebble off the quay into the water. Hentze still hadn't said anything.

I said, "The only thing I don't like is that it only works if you believe that Kristian or Signar would be willing to pay that much money to keep it quiet. An affair would be hard to prove unless there was some incriminating evidence like photos, but even then... Would they really pay a million just to stop gossip – to protect the family name?"

I looked up at him to see he was thinking. After a while he said, "How old is Elin, do you know?"

"I think Kristian said she was nearly seventeen. Old enough anyway."

He shook his head. "*Nei.* No – here and in Denmark the *straffeloven*, the penal law, is the same. The legal age for sex is fifteen – unless it is with a guardian or teacher, or a stepfather. Then the age must be eighteen. There is a prison sentence of up to four years."

I let out a breath. "Shit."

"Yeh. So, I think this *would* be enough for blackmail.

And it is not just the crime." He gestured broadly towards the village. "Here it's a very hard thing to live with that known about you. Impossible maybe."

There were no more pebbles to kick so I walked on a little way. Hentze fell in alongside me.

"Do you know the phrase 'devil's advocate'?" I asked him.

"To speak on the side of evil?"

"Yeah. So if I play devil's advocate, we don't know that there *was* or is an affair between Kristian and Elin: we're just guessing. We don't know what proof Tummas Gramm or Nóa Lisberg might have had, or why they'd try to blackmail Signar rather than Kristian."

Hentze nodded and thought about that as we approached the end of the quay. It was like a hooked arm, holding the calmer, flatter water in place. On the concrete there were the remains of several fish, filleted down to their spines, heads and tails still intact; baleful, open mouths and glassy eyes.

"Without knowing if any of this is true, there's a break in your chain," Hentze said in the end. "We could ask Elin Langgaard if there is an affair, but even if she says it's true, she probably can't tell us about the blackmail." He glanced my way. "Do you think Kristian Ravnsfjall would talk to me?"

I shook my head. "I wouldn't if I was him. I'd deny it, all the way."

"Even to you?"

I'd known it was coming, of course. I said, "I don't know.

But he'd have to have some reason to tell me: some incentive. It won't be enough that I've got no jurisdiction here."

"You want to offer him a deal?"

"No, but something – even if it's just advance warning of what he's going to face."

"Is that how you work in England?"

I was fairly sure what he was alluding to and it took me a moment to decide how to respond. In the end I kept the answer pragmatic.

"What's your most immediate case here?" I said. "The murder, or a guy who fucked his sixteen-year-old stepdaughter?"

He winced at the vulgarity, but I'd used it deliberately.

"The murder, of course." He glanced away and then back. "But I can't ignore the other if there has been an offence."

I shook my head. "I'm not saying you should hide or ignore it," I told him. "But if the murder's your main focus of interest right now, then anything else could be left until that's sorted out. You need Kristian's side of the story to find out if anyone besides Gramm and Lisberg was involved in the blackmail, but what the blackmail was *about* is a side issue."

"For now."

"Sure, for now."

For a moment Hentze thought it over, then he made up his mind. "Okay," he said. "If you talk to Kristian Ravnsfjall to find out what he knows, I will do what I can to hold things as they are. But I can't make a promise. If

Ári asks I may have to tell him. That's the best I can do."

I knew that it was.

"I'll call Kristian," I said. "But I can't make any promises either."

And I moved off, back along the quay.

8

IT WAS UNSATISFACTORY BUT THERE WAS NOTHING TO BE
done about it. Kristian Ravnsfjall hadn't answered his
phone, and even though Reyná had left a message there
had still been no response by the time Hentze dropped
him back at the Hotel Streym.

Agreeing that Reyná would let him know when he *had*
spoken to Kristian Ravnsfjall, Hentze drove along Yviri við
Strond past the police station. On a momentary impulse,
however, he ignored the turn that would take him round to
the back of the station, and carried on to the roundabout
where he headed up Jónas Broncks gøta instead.

Half an hour and a short diversion later he entered the
mortuary just as Elisabet Hovgaard was disposing of her
surgical gloves. Behind her at the dissection table a lab
technician – a gawky young man no older than his mid-
twenties – was sewing up a deep Y-shaped incision in the
torso of a man in his fifties. The face of the corpse seemed
vaguely familiar to Hentze, although it was hard to be sure
at this angle.

"Jákup Lützen," Elisabet Hovgaard said, seeming to intuit Hentze's question.

"From Kaldbak?"

"You knew him?"

"I arrested him for drunk driving – it must be nearly thirty years ago."

"You remember all your arrests, even from when you were in uniform?" She seemed curious rather than amused.

"Only because I was new on the job," Hentze said with a shrug. "And because I arrested him three times in as many weeks – each time for alcohol-related incidents. His mother kept calling and telling us he was drunk again and would we do something about it, so... The last time I took him in he'd just slaughtered a sheep. He'd done a terrible job and he still had the knife in his hand, covered in blood. I thought he was going to use it on me."

"Well, you had the last laugh," Elisabet told him. "The alcohol killed *him* instead: chronic cirrhosis of the liver, along with arteries as hard as drain pipes." She moved to the sink to wash her hands. "So, what are you doing here – apart from renewing old acquaintanceships?"

"I could ask you the same thing. I called at your house but Johan said you'd come in to work."

"Well, you know what they say: find a job you enjoy and you'll never work again. How's *your* job by the way?"

"I'm working on it," Hentze said. "That's why I'm here."

"Right."

She finished drying her hands, took a pack of Prince cigarettes from her pocket and nodded for him to accompany her to the side door. "Well, go on then," she said. "Now we've established we've both abandoned our spouses on a Saturday, work away."

She pushed the bar on the door and stepped outside, lighting up as Hentze followed her.

"Tummas Gramm, the guy from the beach. Would you say he was strong?"

"Relatively so, yes, I suppose," Elisabet nodded. "He was well muscled, anyway."

"And he weighed about eighty kilos, right?" Hentze went on.

"If you say so. I can't remember exactly."

"Okay. So, in your opinion, would he have been weakened enough by his injuries that it would have been easy for someone smaller and lighter to smother him?"

"That's impossible to say. It depends on the circumstances."

"Okay, let me put it another way then: if someone weaker and lighter *had* tried to smother him, wouldn't you expect to see more evidence that Gramm had put up a fight? More bruising, say, because he'd struggled or used his fists?"

"You *might* see more bruising or defensive injuries." Hovgaard nodded. "But not for certain. If he was asleep or unconscious then he might have been smothered before he knew it was happening." She narrowed her eyes at him suspiciously. "Are you trying to make the circumstances fit a particular suspect – or exclude one?"

"I just want to know if it's possible – likely – that

someone smaller, lighter and weaker than Gramm could have smothered him."

"Of course they could. Anything's possible, you know that. I wouldn't rule it out, but at the same time I wouldn't say there was any specific evidence that they had either. Have you asked Anders?"

"There's no point. He'll just say what you have – except he'd probably say it by telling me that the absence of ballet shoes on Gramm's feet doesn't prove he *wasn't* a ballet dancer, or some such nonsense. You know what he's like."

"Well if you know all that why are you bothering me?"

Hentze heaved a sigh, waving the question away. "I don't know," he said.

Elisabet Hovgaard considered him then, as she exhaled a plume of smoke. "Is the case going so badly?" she asked.

"Badly?" Hentze shook his head. "No. At the moment it isn't going at all."

A few minutes later, as he walked back to his car, he got a call from Annika in the office.

"We've just had a notification from the Eik Bank that Tummas Gramm's cash card was used at the Miðlon Bónus store last night at 19.47," she told him. "The amount was five hundred and thirty-six krónur."

"Have there been any other transactions?"

"No, just that. It has to be Nóa, right?"

"It certainly wasn't Gramm."

The Miðlon Bónus supermarket was on the outskirts of Tórshavn, easily accessible, which meant Nóa Lisberg could have travelled there from anywhere, especially if he was using Tummas Gramm's car. It made it a little more likely that he was still somewhere on Streymoy, then, but that was about it.

"Hjalti?" Annika said.

"Yeh, I'm here. Can you go to the store? Find out who the cashier was, what was bought and get a description of the person who used the card. Better yet, take Nóa Lisberg's photo and see if anyone recognises him, and check CCTV if they have it."

"Okay," Annika said. "Do you want me to get someone in to cover the office while I'm doing that?"

Hentze checked his watch and realised he was running late. "No, just make sure the answerphone's on. I'll be back in an hour."

He unlocked the Volvo and got in.

He arrived five minutes late – slowed by the Saturday traffic – and parked at Vaglið, walking briskly to the coffee and craft shop on the square. Fríða Sólsker was already there, a cappuccino on the table in front of her, but no other distraction like a book or a phone to fill the time.

"Sorry I'm late," Hentze said after they'd greeted each other. He glanced at the other tables, two of them occupied. "Do you mind if we sit outside?"

"No, of course not."

Fríða didn't show any visible sign that she thought it an odd request and while she collected her things Hentze ordered a cappuccino for himself. Outside they took the single metal table and two chairs under the shop's awning. It was chilly but dry and they both kept their coats on.

"How've you been? How's Sóleyg?" Fríða asked as Hentze finally settled.

"Fine. We're both good," Hentze said, slightly conscious that he was making the response a tad brighter than normal. "Things are okay."

"Good, I'm glad," Fríða said, an encouraging smile to go with it, but perhaps just a hint that she was taking him at his word.

Hentze didn't mind that. He had always found Fríða Sólsker to be scrupulously objective, perhaps just because of her job. We all have professional faces, he thought, and wondered – not for the first time – if Fríða Sólsker would be substantially different in an off-duty context. He'd never find out, of course, because there would always be a professional history between them.

"I'm sorry to bother you with this," Hentze said then, taking the opportunity to shift the subject. "But you're the only person I know who might give me some ideas – at least, without going through official channels."

"Is it to do with an investigation?" Fríða asked.

"Yeh, but as I said on the phone, it's something I'd like to get an opinion on before I take it any further."

From his pocket he removed Nóa Lisberg's notebook, wrapped in a clear plastic bag, and handed it to her. "Can I ask you to have a look at this? Obviously I don't expect you to read it all, but a first impression…"

"Sure, okay," Fríða said.

The shop owner brought Hentze's coffee and he sipped it patiently as Fríða thumbed through the book, stopping occasionally to examine a page in more detail.

Hentze, of course, had had much more time to examine it the previous night and he'd found the perplexing collection of designs, sketches and writings oddly unsettling. A few might have been copied from other sources, but most seemed to be Nóa Lisberg's own creations; some abandoned mid-sentence and some written on scraps of paper and pasted in.

None of it had told Hentze anything specifically relevant to the Gramm case, but if – as they seemed to be – the contents of the book were an extension of Nóa Lisberg's thoughts, then it seemed to Hentze that those thoughts were extremely troubled and confused.

Finally, after perhaps five minutes of reading, Fríða reached the end of the book and closed it with some deliberation.

"Okay, what would you like me to say?" she asked.

"In your opinion, would you say it was— Do you think the person who wrote that could have some kind of mental illness?"

Fríða laughed. "Just from this? No, I couldn't tell you, not without a lot of additional context."

Hentze nodded, as if he'd expected nothing different. "If I tell you that there were five or six other notebooks like that, and that the behaviour of the young man who wrote them has changed a lot over the last few months? According to his mother he's become isolated, uncommunicative and there's some evidence of obsessive behaviour towards a girl he knows."

Fríða didn't answer immediately but Hentze saw there was a vague hint of a frown.

"How old is he?" she asked.

"Eighteen, nearly nineteen. He's also been missing from home for a week."

"Are you talking about Nóa Lisberg?"

"How did you know? Is he one of your patients?"

Fríða shook her head. "A police officer visited the high school yesterday to ask about him. Matteus was talking about it at dinner last night. Your name came up, too."

"Mine? Why?"

"Jan asked if you were the officer at the school: Jan Reyná, my cousin."

"Ah," Hentze said as it became clear. "I didn't know."

"I gather he's been talking to you about his father."

Hentze nodded, opting for a generalised response. "Yes. He also gave us some advice over the death of the man who was found at Saksun." He shifted a little. "Look, if this is awkward…"

"No, not at all. Unless it is for you."

Hentze shook his head, glanced round. "No, but if we can keep it in confidence, I can tell you that Nóa Lisberg may be linked to a murder. I say 'maybe' because for myself I'm not sure. That's why I was hoping you could advise me about his mental state. It could make a difference to our approach if he's schizophrenic, bipolar…"

"It would take hours of sessions with him to establish if

he was suffering from a mental illness," Fríða said. "It isn't a diagnosis you can make quickly, although it's quite common for those illnesses to manifest themselves at his age."

"So it's possible."

"Possible, yes. Likely, I can't say." She saw Hentze's slightly disappointed look and relented a little. "But tentatively, from what you say, and from this" – she tapped the book – "there's a chance he may be psychotic. Only a chance, mind you. It's highly unprofessional to say even that."

Hentze frowned. "Isn't that worse – being psychotic?"

"No, not necessarily. Psychosis is a symptom, if you like. It means only that he might suffer some degree of detachment from reality. The degree is important. It can be mild – just a little oddness or eccentricity – through to delusions, hallucinations or violence."

Hentze thought about that. "In that state, would he be capable of making a complicated plan and carrying it out over several days or weeks?"

Fríða shook her head. "I'm sorry, Hjalti, that really is an impossible question to answer."

"I seem to be asking a lot of them this morning," Hentze said ruefully. He rubbed his chin. "Could he be dangerous?"

"To others? Perhaps, but again…"

Hentze nodded. "To himself then?"

Here Fríða was more definite. "Yes. A recent study found that adolescents who reported psychotic symptoms were seventy times more likely to attempt suicide. That would be my major concern, even on so little evidence."

"It's mine, also," Hentze said. And it was – more so now than it had been before. "Thank you for your help. I feel better knowing the possibilities, at least."

"They *are* only possibilities," Fríða said. "But if you need help when you find him – if you think you need someone to assess him – let me know. I might have to pass it to a more specialised colleague, but I can probably speed that up."

"Thanks, I appreciate it," Hentze nodded. He placed Nóa Lisberg's notebook back in its plastic bag and put it away.

"Is Jan also involved in this case?" Fríða asked then.

"A little, yeh," Hentze said. And since she'd brought up his name again he felt entitled to ask, "Did you know him at all, before he came back here?"

"Only as a child. His mother left with him while he was still small."

"Was there anything – I don't know – odd about all that, do you know?" Hentze asked. "He told me he was looking for information about what happened at that time, but…"

He shrugged and left it open, knowing he might be asking something she'd consider private.

"She died young: his mother," Fríða said after a moment. "I think it's understandable that he'd want to know more about her."

"Yeh, I suppose so," Hentze said, knowing it was only half an answer, but unwilling to press it further. Instead he finished his coffee, thanked Fríða again for her time and took his leave.

* * *

"I guessed tuna would be okay," Annika said, placing the roll on the desk in front of him, then moving round to sit opposite him with her own sandwich.

"Did you make it?"

"Sure."

"Thanks." He'd staved off hunger with coffee but now he was glad of something more substantial. "How did you get on at Bónus?"

"Pretty good. Having the time of the transaction helped. I was able to get the manager to go through the records and identify the cashier. She was working today, too, and she identified Nóa immediately."

"Why immediately? She must see hundreds of faces every day. Did he stand out in some way?"

"Yeh, she said he looked like a tramp."

"And here we have a lot of them for comparison," Hentze said drily. "Do we know what he bought?"

"Yep."

She handed him a sheet of paper. There were about forty items listed. Hentze ran his eye down them as he ate. The list was almost entirely tinned food, apart from a loaf of bread. Nothing chilled, nothing fresh. However, at the bottom of the list there were also two bars of soap, two toothbrushes, two tubes of toothpaste, a bottle of shampoo and a comb.

"Like Nóa's ark, eh?" Annika said. "Two of everything – toiletries, anyway."

"Huh," Hentze said. "But the cashier said he looked like a tramp."

"Maybe that's why he wanted all the stuff: to clean himself up – or if he's with someone else."

The same thought had occurred to Hentze. It could fit with his idea that someone was sheltering Nóa, but then, if he felt the need to hide, why had he gone out to the store to buy groceries? That didn't make sense: either you were hiding or you weren't.

Of course, given that there had been no publicity, thanks to Ári, it was possible that Nóa might not realise he was being actively sought. In which case he wouldn't necessarily see it as dangerous to go to the Bónus store or use Tummas Gramm's cash card. But in that case, why would he hide out in the first place? The puzzle went round in a circle, chasing its tail.

"Hjalti?"

"Hmm?" He realised Annika had asked him a question and that he hadn't heard it.

"I said, what do you want me to do next?"

She had finished her sandwich and his was only half eaten.

"Nothing," he said. "Why don't you knock off? I'll be here for a while; I'm waiting for a call." And he would think better if he had the place to himself.

"Are you sure?"

"Yeh."

"Okay, thanks." She got up and crossed the office to collect her coat.

"Did Heri find you earlier, by the way?"

"Yeh." She gave him a mischievous smile. "I'm letting him take me out for dinner tonight – at Hafnia."

"Ouch."

"It was his suggestion."

Because he could think of too many possible replies Hentze just shook his head sardonically, which made her laugh. "See you later," she said, heading for the door.

"Yeh, bye. Enjoy the meal," Hentze said. By then he had started to re-read Nóa Lisberg's shopping list.

9

THROUGH THE BLINDS ON THE WINDOW AT THE END OF THE booth I could see the ferry-terminal block. It stood out in the darkness, starkly lit and oddly clinical for all its glass walls. Closer, the single-file thread of car lights leaving the terminal divided as they reached the roundabout, turning right for the ring road, left for the town centre. The *Smyril* had docked about five minutes ago and I'd watched it approaching the harbour from the quayside before heading to the Toscana restaurant.

The place wasn't busy – less than half full – and when the waitress offered the choice of table or booth I took the booth, said I was waiting for someone and ordered a beer.

Meeting there had been Kristian's idea. When he'd finally returned the message I'd left that morning he told me he was on Suðuroy and wouldn't be back until nine that evening. How about a drink and something to eat? It wouldn't have been my choice, but I hadn't wanted to make a big play of wanting somewhere more private, so I told him I'd see him there.

I'd called Hentze and told him how things stood, and although I knew he'd have liked to move things further and faster than that, he accepted the delay as unavoidable. He wanted to open his case out, but that could only happen if Kristian confirmed that there had been blackmail over an affair with Elin, so until I could talk to him there was nothing to be done.

In some ways I was glad of the delay, though. I wanted some distance to work out where my loyalties lay – if I had any. I still wasn't sure if I did, or whom they would favour. I understood what Hentze was up against, but it wasn't my case. And, like I'd told Fríða, I liked Kristian well enough, but I didn't really know him. It left me a long way from being my half-brother's keeper.

So I was still somewhere in the middle – still unresolved – and halfway through my beer when Kristian arrived. He seemed a little weary, explaining a problem with salmon pens between ordering drinks and a pizza to share. I didn't want to eat, but for the sake of occupying the booth I agreed. When the waitress brought his gin and tonic he finally seemed to settle, toying with the ice, but I wanted to tackle the reason for being there before anyone got too comfortable.

"Listen," I said. "I need to ask you something."

"That sounds serious." It was light and untroubled.

"It could be. Have you spoken to Anni or Elin today?"

He frowned. "No, why?"

"I was with Hjalti Hentze from the police this morning. We went to see Elin because there could be a link between

CHRIS OULD

her and Tummas Gramm, the guy who was found on the beach at Saksun."

Kristian made to speak, but I held him off for a moment. "It involves you, too: your relationship with Elin."

"I don't understand."

I didn't say anything immediately, just to give him chance to start figuring it out, but after a few seconds I said, "Look, it's up to you. You don't have to tell me anything. Or you can tell me what you like and I'll promise you it won't go any further. But Hentze is working on a murder, so I don't think it will go away."

"I don't understand," he said again. "He thinks I had something to do with that – the murder?"

"Did you?"

"No. Shit. Of course not."

"Okay – but it still leaves you and Elin."

He was still for a moment, but then he moved sideways abruptly, slid out of the booth. For a second I thought he might head for the door, but instead he crossed to the bar. He had to wait to be served but that didn't matter. I knew he needed to work it out in his head.

Finally, when the youth behind the counter had poured the drink, Kristian returned to the table. He brought a new beer for me, another gin and tonic for himself. I'd seen the double shot going in.

He didn't look at me until he'd settled again and taken a drink.

"How did you know?"

"I didn't, but certain things fit together that way."

He took a long breath, let it out. "Is there anything I can do?" he said then. "I mean to stop it. What if I say it's not true?"

"That there wasn't anything between you two?" I asked, to make sure we were talking about the same thing.

He nodded.

"Will Elin back you up if you say that?"

"I don't know. Maybe if— I don't know." Then he shook his head. "Fuck."

He looked down at his drink, not seeing it really, even as he knocked half of it back. He had that owlish, disconnected look that people sometimes have when unexpected events suddenly collide with normality. They know it's happened, but the full extent of the impact hasn't hit them yet. Their old life – their plans and expectations – still seems to exist. They haven't fully given up that redundant reality for the new one, with its car crash, its death or its loss.

"How long did it go on for?" I asked. "Or is it still going on?"

"No," he shook his head immediately. "No, I stopped it. It was a few months." He made a sour noise. "Long enough, right?"

"Did Anni know?"

"Shit, no."

"It wasn't the reason you separated?"

Another shake of his head. "It was the sign – the *symptom* – not the reason. Anni and me, we had been— It wasn't good for a long time."

"How did Elin react when you stopped it?"

He shrugged, resigned. "She was upset. There were tears, some... I don't know. She'd thought because I'd left Anni it was more, you know? So, for a couple of weeks I made sure I stayed away. In the end she knew it was— that I was serious. Then it was okay."

"And then someone tried to blackmail you over it – is that right?"

A nod.

"Do you know who?"

"No. Of course not."

There didn't have to be any *of course not* about it, but I let it go.

"Okay, tell me about the blackmail then. How did they approach you?"

He ran a hand through his hair. "It was the beginning of this month, the first Saturday, in the morning. There was a text message. It said, 'I know what you have done.' Just that."

"In English?"

"What? No. No, in Danish."

"Okay. Then what?"

He took another drink, then put the glass down slightly further away than it had been, as if he wanted to ration himself.

"I thought it was a joke or a mistake. I didn't think it was for me. I thought someone had the wrong number. But the next day there was another. It said, 'I know about you and the girl. There is proof. It will cost you.'"

He glanced up to see how I was taking this. I said, "What did you do?"

"Nothing." His voice was empty. "I thought— I don't know. I thought maybe it still wasn't for me. Or maybe if I do nothing they'll think they've used the wrong number. That was what I hoped, right? I was telling myself that. But then on Monday morning as I went to work there was another message. It said, 'Elin Langgaard. Be ready to pay.'"

His hand went to his drink again. Being a few extra inches away made no difference. He took a single swallow and started speaking even before the glass was back on the table.

"I threw up," he said. "Outside the office. I couldn't stop shaking. When I was inside I couldn't get it out of my head, you know? The whole thing is going round and round. In the end I told Astrid I was sick and went home."

"Did you reply to the texts?"

He shook his head. "I kept thinking about it. I tried to think what I could say, but what *could* I say? They said there was proof so if I told them I didn't know what they were talking about…"

The hopelessness in his face reflected the impossibility of the situation he was reliving.

"And then there was nothing for two days," he said. "I didn't know what was happening. Not until the Thursday morning. I got a text saying they wanted a million krónur, to be left in a bag under the radio mast at Tjørnuvík. It was to be put there at 10 p.m. on Sunday night. They said no tricks, no police, or they would know. This is one chance only. I was to text 'OK' to show I agreed."

The pizza came and the waitress asked if we had

everything we needed. Kristian looked vaguely nauseous as he glanced at the food. He asked her for another gin and tonic – large – and she went away.

"You'd better eat something," I told him.

For a second he looked as if he was about to argue, but then he picked up a slice. He bit into it and chewed as if he was eating ashes.

"Were all the texts in Danish?" I asked. It was something to keep it neutral for a while.

"Yeh." He nodded, swallowed hard. "I thought it was perhaps a way to be confusing on purpose, but lots of people speak Danish here."

"Have you still got the messages on your phone?"

He shook his head. "No, I erased them. I didn't want— Afterwards I didn't want any evidence. I kept the number they came from, though. Do you want it?"

I nodded and he took out his phone. I put the number he read out into my own.

"Will it— What will you do with it?" he asked.

"It'll be a pay as you go, a disposable," I told him. "There'll be no way to trace it, but Hentze might want to try."

I was pretty sure the phone would be at the bottom of the sea or in landfill by now. And unless they were stupid they'd have been careful to only put the battery into the handset and activate it when they needed to send a text, making it impossible to triangulate a location. Blackmail demands in the digital age have no fingerprints, no forensics on envelopes, no postmarks; nothing except an untraceable, disposable phone number.

The waitress brought Kristian's new drink – his third – and he knocked back the old one so she could take the glass. I didn't know what his alcohol tolerance was, but at this rate I was going to find out.

"So tell me what happened about the money," I said. "How did Signar get involved?"

He put his pizza crust aside, wiped his hands, kept hold of the napkin. "I didn't have the money," he said. "After Anni and I separated… There were a lot of expenses. The business has everything else in it, but not cash – not that much, anyway. Don't get me wrong, we're doing okay, but not a huge success yet. It takes time."

"So you couldn't pay."

"No. I thought of calling them, to say that; maybe to offer less. But then I knew it was stupid. Why should they bargain? So I went to see Signar."

"How did he take it?"

Kristian shook his head at the memory. "He told me I was a fool, worse than that. I'd never seen him so angry. For a time I thought he would tell me to get out, go to hell. In the end, though, he starts to ask questions; he makes me tell him everything and I just have to do it, you know? Then, when it's over, I just asked him: can he give me the money? I told him: that's all I need. And he says no. He says, how do we know that there is proof? How do we know they will go away if we pay once? No. Instead, he says *he* will go to Tjørnuvík and he will be there when they come for the money. When he sees them he will get from them what they have – if there *is* proof – and if not, to hell with them. Fuck them."

I could imagine it; not from seeing Signar in his hospital bed, but from the time, years ago, when he'd still been a bull. I knew that was the way he would have been. It couldn't have been different.

"So what did you say?" I asked, just for the sake of it.

"I tried to argue, but his mind was set, so in the end I agreed," he said flatly. "What else? It's his way or nothing. I said I'd go with him but he wouldn't allow that either. He says I've done enough damage; he will take charge now. That's it: go home. Do nothing. He will tell me when it is done."

Telling the story seemed to have left a bad taste in his mouth and he raised his glass, sipped from it this time.

"What about Magnus?" I said. "Did he – does he – know about this?"

"No." Kristian shook his head. "I thought Signar might tell him, but I don't think so now. Magnus would have said something, I'm sure."

I thought so, too. "What about afterwards – since Sunday night? Have you had any contact from the blackmailers?"

"No." Then he frowned. "How could I? If it was the guy, Tummas Gramm, from the beach – if he was dead…"

"I'm pretty sure he wasn't doing it alone," I told him. "Hentze doesn't think so either."

"Not—? You think someone else?"

It took him by surprise and I could see it had wiped out the single, small cause for hope that he must have been nurturing. If Gramm was the blackmailer and Gramm was dead, then at least that put an end to things. Something might even be salvaged, but only if Gramm had been acting alone.

For a moment Kristian was still, then he slid part way out of the booth. "I need a cigarette. Can we get out of here?"

"Sure, go ahead," I told him. "I'll sort this out."

He nodded and slid the rest of the way out of the booth quickly, then reached back for his drink. I looked for the waitress and when I managed to catch her eye I signalled to her, then looked out of the window between the slats of the blinds. Outside on the wooden deck Kristian was hunched over his cupped hands, lighting up.

"Was everything okay for you?" the girl asked when she came to the table. She looked at the barely touched pizza. "Shall I put this in a box?"

"*Nei, takk*. Just the bill please."

When I got outside Kristian was standing on the decking that fronted the restaurant. He was looking out across the docks at the lights of the *Smyril* but he turned away when he heard the door close behind me.

"Well, that was fun," he said drily. "All nights out should be so good, eh? A nice meal, a few drinks, some conversation with family or friends."

I wondered if the fresh air had hit the gin, or whether this was just his way of coping. Whichever it was, I wanted to get to the end now, before he shut down and withdrew. He might not, but most people do after they've shown themselves raw. They need time to pull back into themselves, restore some kind of dignity, even if it's only in their heads.

"So what do you want me to do now?" he asked. "Is your friend Hentze waiting to speak to me?"

He made a play of looking round.

"I expect he'll talk to you if you want," I said. "But if I were you I'd leave it. He doesn't need to follow it up – at least, not yet. For now it'll be enough if he knows why Tummas Gramm was with Signar at Tjørnuvík. It gives him a context for the investigation."

"I'm pleased to be of help, then."

I ignored the sarcasm because I didn't think he was entitled to it. "Are you sure no one else knew about you and Elin?"

"You think I wanted to tell people about it? No. I told no one."

"What about a boy – a teenager – called Nóa Lisberg? How do you know him?"

Kristian shook his head and exhaled smoke. "I don't."

"So why did he attack you in the car park a week ago?"

He looked at me for a couple of seconds. "Jesus, you know everything, don't you?" he said bitterly.

"Listen," I said. "You can get mad with me if you want – I won't break. But the more you hold back the less you help yourself. Just don't pretend it's my fault, though."

His cigarettes and lighter were on the metal table beside him. For no good reason I reached out for the pack, shook one out, lit it. On the second pull I looked up again.

"I don't know Lisberg," Kristian said then. "I'd seen him. He was at Elin's school. She talked about him sometimes, saying he was – what do you call it – a pest?

He kept calling her, wanting to see her."

"And she wasn't interested?"

"*Nei*. She thought he was too weird, too strange. He was a joke to her."

"So what happened last Saturday?"

"Nothing – I mean, I don't know. It was the same as tonight. I'd come back from Suðuroy on the *Smyril* and I thought I'd walk into town for a drink. I left the car over there in the car park and I was walking away when this guy comes from nowhere. Straight away he's hitting me. We struggled for a few seconds. I tried to push him away but then he hit my nose and I saw lights and tasted blood and then he stopped."

"Did he say anything?"

"No, nothing. That was why it was so strange, so sudden. And then he was running away, so I don't know what happened."

He took a final drag on his cigarette and tossed it into the darkness. "You can believe me or not, but that's how it was."

I didn't believe him, not entirely. He'd told me about the attack because I already knew, but I had the feeling that there had been something else to it, too. I couldn't tell what, though, so I left it. In the end he might tell me, but for now keeping something to himself was his way of staying in control.

Then he reached out, picked up his cigarettes and pocketed them. "So, are you coming?" he said, gesturing away.

"Where to?"

"To get another drink," he said, heading for the steps. "That's what Saturday nights are for, isn't it?"

He had every intention of getting drunk, that much was obvious. He switched to straight Scotch when we got to the Hvonn bar, close to the West Harbour waterfront, but I stuck to beer and didn't attempt to keep up with him. It didn't matter. He was drinking to prove a point of some kind, like it was a punishment or a penance. He didn't say much, but in the noise of the bar that didn't matter either: I was only there because I felt responsible for the situation.

Instead I watched the people. Even on their night out there seemed to be something innately conservative about the Faroese: the middle-aged rubbing shoulders with the twenty-somethings; the men in smart-casual jackets and ties above jeans and chinos and polished shoes; the younger women in short jackets, tight jeans and woollen scarves. No micro skirts, no plunging necklines, no six-inch heels; no macho display of tattooed biceps under short-sleeved shirts. It was as if, sure, they came out for a good time, but still there were elements of propriety and practical considerations that went without saying. I got the feeling that these people would no more fight or pass out in the gutter than they would put their feet up in church tomorrow morning.

Kristian had left the bar for a smoke. I looked at my watch, then at my beer. I didn't want any more. I'd had enough in more ways than one and now Kristian was outside it might be easier to get him to go home. I went out to join him.

"*Hey*," he greeted me amiably, as if we hadn't seen each other in a while. "You want a cigarette? Go ahead."

He held out the pack and I took one, easier than refusing. He lit it for me with a slight sway.

"*Takk*."

He grinned. "Your Faroese is pretty good now. Like a local."

I nodded towards the road. "You feel like moving on?"

"Why? Don't you like this place? Here," – he glanced round but there was no one nearby – "I want to tell you. About Elin. You *want* to know, right?"

"Listen—" I started, but got no further.

"*Ja!* Yeh, you do." He waved a hand. "You think I was the first, eh? You think she didn't know – what she was doing? No, no. No way. She knows *exactly* the right thing to do. You know what I mean?"

I did, but right then I'd heard enough. He was either too drunk to reason with, or pretending he was as an excuse to let himself off the hook.

"Listen, you need to go home before you say something you regret," I told him. "I'll get you a taxi if you come now."

"*Nei, nei*," he said, gesturing widely. "It's too *early*."

"It's too late," I told him. "Are you coming?"

He ignored the question. "How was your meal with Fríða? What do you think about her? She— She looks good, eh? You think you can get something there?"

"I think you'd better be quiet," I said. It was too sharp, though, and I shouldn't have been drawn.

"Oh-oh! I hit a nail on the head," Kristian laughed.

I gave him a flat look. "Go home," I told him, then started away.

Behind me he called out in Faroese. It didn't matter what. I kept going, up the hill past the Kommuna and the taxis parked at the junction.

In a way he'd helped. Until that evening he'd been too easy to like and it had been too easy to make the connection because of that. In the morning he'd want to be a nice guy again. He'd be sorry for getting drunk and being an arsehole; sorrier still for ever letting temptation get the better of him, however that had happened with Elin.

If I believed him, it had been a recent, short-lived affair.

If I believed him, she hadn't exactly discouraged him, either.

If I believed him.

I wasn't blind. I wasn't stupid. But whatever the circumstances, they made no difference. There are rules. They're there for a reason. They're there to protect. There's no excuse when you break them, which Kristian had.

So that was it: black and white – the colours coppers like best. I wasn't going to go looking for grey. In a couple of days I was leaving and none of this would go with me. I didn't need any more baggage.

10

Sunday/sunnudagur

SEVERAL TIMES AS HE NEGOTIATED THE PATROL CAR through the streets of Kvívík, Heri Kalsø raised a hand to acknowledge the nods from the villagers making their way to church. It was damp but not raining and most people were carrying their Bibles in their hands.

Heri had started the morning feeling good, even if he was a little tired and certainly stiff in a few places. Last night had been just like old times: the meal, a few drinks, the easy-going conversation. Even though Annika had been very clear that it was just a dinner date – a try-out, to see how it went – it had felt natural and relaxed: just like old times when they'd first been getting together.

Heri knew Annika was a woman of her word, so he hadn't expected any more than that; perhaps an affectionate kiss as they separated on leaving the restaurant – so he was surprised, albeit very pleasantly surprised, to have spent half the night wrapped up in some of the fiercest love-making he had ever experienced. Not just once, but three times. That was how inventive Annika had been, all the while hardly saying a word except to instruct him this way or that.

There was no doubt it had been fantastic, but then, with time to think once he'd set out on the quiet Sunday patrol, he couldn't help wondering where it left him. Or them. *Was* there even a "them" again now?

Heri couldn't work out what he should think. What did it mean that Annika had left silently, and without disturbing his exhausted sleep, at some point after one in the morning? She'd left no note, sent no text message, had even washed up and put away her wine glass. So what was he supposed to read into all that? What was he supposed to do? Should he call her or not? Should he assume they were back together again or… what?

Heri Kalsø didn't ask a lot from relationships, but God, he hated all this intuitive stuff. Why couldn't people – but women most especially – simply say what they expected from him?

As he stopped the patrol car across the drive of the house, Heri took a moment to check his phone again to see if he'd missed a text from Annika. He hadn't, so he made an effort to shift his thoughts to his reason for being here and got out of the car.

She must have been watching for his arrival because Anni Langgaard was already standing in the open doorway as Heri climbed the steps.

"*Frú* Langgaard? I'm Heri Kalsø. You called us about a missing person?"

"Yes, she's my daughter, Elin. Come in."

From her accent Heri realised the woman was Danish, and her manner was rather peremptory as she went back inside, gesturing him to follow. He did so, closing the door behind him, then moving into the kitchen. He looked round to see if anyone else was there, but it seemed not.

"She's been gone since last night," Anni Langgaard said, clearly keen to focus his attention. "I think something has happened to her."

"Okay, let me get some details from you, okay?" Heri said, taking out his pocketbook. "How old is Elin?"

"Sixteen."

"And her full name?"

"Elin Signe Langgaard."

"Okay. And when did you see her last?"

"Yesterday – last night, I just told you." She moved distractedly, taking a pace to the side, then turning back. "At about eight thirty she left here to go to her friend's house – Silja Midjord. She lives on Junkaravegur. I didn't think— I thought she was still there until I called her to see when she was going to come home. There was no answer on her phone, so then I called Silja's house and her mother told me they hadn't seen Elin at all."

"I see." Heri nodded. "Well, perhaps she changed her mind and went to see someone else instead. Is there anyone else nearby she might have gone to, do you know?"

"Here? No. And anyway, why would she? If she said she was going to Silja's why would she go somewhere else? She goes there all the time."

"Well, there might be several reasons," Heri said. He was trying to be reassuring, but Anni Langgaard seemed determined to make it difficult.

"Does she have a boyfriend, do you know?" Heri asked.

"No. Not— No one she's mentioned."

Anni Langgaard looked away for a moment, then she seemed to make up her mind about something. "I think you'd better speak to an officer called Hjalti Hentze," she said decidedly. "He's in CID."

"Yes, I know Hjalti," Heri said, "but I'm not sure—"

"He was here yesterday," Anni Langgaard said, cutting him off. "It was about a boy they want to find: Nóa Lisberg. I think Detective Hentze ought to know what's happened now. I think *he* should deal with it."

Heri considered for a moment. Anni Langgaard was clearly a rather high-handed woman, and a tad too used to getting her own way. But while he would normally have resisted – politely – any attempt to tell him how to do his job, the fact that Hjalti Hentze might be involved slightly mitigated his impulse to stick rigidly to protocol.

"Very well, let me see if I can speak to him," he said. "Although, being Sunday there's a good chance he won't be on duty."

I was getting used to the stairwell of the police station by now; enough to find my way to the third floor where Hentze was waiting beside one of the blank, battleship-grey metal doors. The place seemed deserted.

"*Morgun*," he said.

"*Morgun*," I nodded. "You're on your own?"

"*Ja*. Ári may come in later, but if there's no progress…" He shrugged and held the door wider so I could pass through.

We went along the corridor to the incident room. Nothing appeared to have changed much since the last time I'd been there except for the whiteboards. Alongside the photograph of Tummas Gramm there was one of Nóa Lisberg.

"Coffee?" Hentze asked.

"Sure, thanks."

While he poured it from a flask I moved to look at the information and the timeline on the boards. Some parts of it were easier to understand than others because the facts would be the same in any language: time, place, name. Where my word recognition fell down was on the short, probably abbreviated phrases, mostly ending in question marks.

Hentze came across and gave me a mug of coffee. The mug was yellow with a green logo and the word *Landsverk* on it.

"You want me to translate anything?" Hentze asked. He meant the whiteboards, not the mug.

I shook my head, turned away from the boards and leaned on a desk.

"Kristian confirmed the affair," I told him, because I knew that was what he wanted to get to. "He said it lasted a few weeks and then he ended it. He didn't say when exactly it ended but I think it was about three months ago, when he split up from his wife."

"What was his mood when you asked him about it?"

"Not happy. What would you expect? He knows what it means."

"But there was blackmail?"

"Yeah."

I outlined what Kristian had told me, boiling it down to the bulletpoints; most of them concerning the blackmail demands via text message and how Signar had reacted when Kristian went to him for help. Hentze listened attentively and, except for the phone number Kristian had received the texts from, he made no attempt to write any of it down.

"I think Signar went out to Tjørnuvík looking for trouble," I said. "He was going to face them down – I mean, he wanted to confront whoever it was, rather than just leave the cash there."

"Which is why the money was in the trunk of the car." Hentze nodded. "He would only give it to them if he had no choice. He was hoping he could scare them away."

"That's my guess," I agreed. "So when Tummas Gramm arrives to pick up the money it's not there and Signar is waiting. Signar tackles him and he has the shotgun to make his point. There's an argument, Signar is knocked down, the gun goes off and Tummas is wounded. Or the other way round. It doesn't matter. Tummas manages to get back to his car and drive away – or maybe Nóa Lisberg drives for him. Signar gets back into his car but before he can leave he has a stroke."

"Yes, I think you're right," Hentze said. He walked

over to the whiteboard. "Except for Nóa Lisberg being there. I don't think he was a part of the blackmail."

I frowned. "Why not?"

"For one thing because I don't think he is— I don't know the word. I mean, I think he has mental problems. Yesterday I talked to Fríða Sólsker about him."

For some reason it surprised me that he hadn't mentioned this before, but it was easy to forget that Hentze was a man who played his cards close to his chest.

I nodded to acknowledge I knew Fríða. "What did she say?" I asked.

"I showed her a book of Nóa's writing and told her some things people have said about the way he's behaved. She didn't like to say anything for sure without all the facts, but she did say it's possible that Nóa is psychotic – that he might be seeing everything in a way that's only real in his head."

"You mean he could be delusional?"

"If that's the word. I don't know." He thought for a second, then moved on. "A second reason I don't think Nóa is part of the blackmail is because he attacked Kristian Ravnsfjall on Saturday night. To me that doesn't make sense if he thought he was going to get money from Kristian the next day."

"But he *was* with Tummas at the boathouse after Tummas was shot."

"Sure, yes," Hentze said. "But I have a theory about that. We know Nóa was obsessed with Elin Langgaard – he thinks he is in love with her, yes? Okay, so if he found out what she's doing with Kristian, maybe he's angry and jealous when he sees him in the car park. His feelings boil up, and he attacks him. But then, because he is afraid of what he has done – perhaps because he's scared someone has called the police – he goes to his friend Tummas who is working at the bar. He says, 'Help me, I've hit Kristian Ravnsfjall because he's having sex with Elin.' When Tummas hears this he knows it's not good: if Nóa shouts about it to everyone it will spoil the whole blackmail plan. Do you agree?"

"Yeah, go ahead," I said. It made sense to me and I could sense his satisfaction at finally piecing it together.

"Okay. So, if Tummas knows that Nóa could spoil the blackmail plan, what would he do? He would want to get Nóa out of the way: to keep him quiet until after the blackmail price is paid the next day. So, Tummas takes Nóa to the boathouse at Saksun. He knows it is a safe place, and without a car Nóa would have a hard time to leave. I don't know – maybe he tells Nóa he must hide, that the cops will look for him, or that Kristian will come after him. Whatever he says he tries to scare Nóa so he will stay there."

"Yeah, that could work," I said. "Especially if you don't think Nóa is particularly rational. And when the blackmail goes wrong and Tummas is shot, he goes to the boathouse because it's nearby. He doesn't want to risk going to the hospital and he thinks he'll have Nóa to help and look after him."

"That's what I think," Hentze said with a satisfied nod. "That's my theory."

I looked at the board. "It makes Nóa a strong circumstantial suspect for killing Tummas."

"Circumstantial, yes, but I don't believe that was what happened. I think there was a third person – someone who was in the blackmail with Tummas. The forensics at the boathouse indicate that someone else was there, and my feeling is the same. When things went wrong I think this third person came to the boathouse and suffocated Tummas because he was a risk of exposing what they had done."

I thought about that. If Nóa hadn't been part of the blackmail plot, Hentze was right: it removed at least one motive for him to kill Tummas Gramm. "So what happened to Nóa?" I asked.

"Yeh, that's a good question." Hentze nodded solemnly.

"You know he could be dead, right?" I said. "If your third person killed Tummas to protect himself he wouldn't want Nóa running round as a witness either."

"That is my worry," Hentze said. "If Nóa is also dead it would explain why he has disappeared. And without him we have no way to find the third man. But now we know Nóa was alive until two nights ago at least because he was seen at the supermarket buying food."

As he said it his mobile rang. He looked at the screen and didn't seem to recognise the number.

"Excuse me," he said, answering the call. "*Ja? Hentze. Hey, Heri. Hvat kann eg hjálpa tær við?*"

He spoke for a minute or so, asked a couple of questions, then agreed something and rang off.

"That was Heri Kalsø, a uniformed officer," Hentze

told me. "He's at Anni Langgaard's house. Elin Langgaard is missing, since eight thirty last night. What time did you leave Kristian Ravnsfjall last night?"

I knew what he was thinking. "About half past eleven. He'd had a fair bit to drink."

He nodded. "Okay. Heri says Anni has called Kristian and Elin isn't there. I think we had better go out to Kvívík, but first I need to get some people here."

He made a couple of calls before we left the building: not flustered or alarmed, but matter-of-fact. His tone was briefly apologetic for interrupting their Sunday, then slipped into what sounded like tasking. If he had an opinion on what might have happened it seemed as if he was keeping it to himself, which was no bad thing and he went up another notch in my estimation.

"This is getting to be a habit," he said as we got into his car at the back of the station. "Is that the right phrase?"

"Yeah," I said, to both comments. "You sure you want me to come?"

"Now I do," he said, starting the engine. "Now I think you and I are the only two who think the same way on this case."

"One dead and two missing?"

"*Ja*. I don't think even Ári can say we should wait and see what happens now."

"You didn't call him in?"

"No, for now just Dánjal and Annika, until we know what we have."

* * *

A rain squall hit us as we drove along Kaldbaksfjørður, lashing hard at the car until we entered the protection of the tunnel. On the radio a sombre bell tolled and a flat, melancholic voice started to read out a series of names. After a minute or so I figured out what it was.

Hentze nodded when I asked. "It's the names of those who have died recently; their age, where they lived."

"That's cheerful. Do they do that every Sunday morning?"

"Yeh. In a minute there will be a church service." He reached down and muted the radio. "Do you go to church?"

I shook my head. "No. Do you?"

"No, not for a long time. God and I fell out."

It struck me as an odd thing to say, and for a moment I wondered if it was intended as an invitation to ask more. But then he shifted, reached down and retuned the radio.

"I want to think about the blackmail again," he said. "In my opinion it's the strongest lead, but I also wonder what proof they had of the affair. The text messages to Kristian Ravnsfjall didn't say what it was?"

"No – at least, that's what he said."

"You think he's keeping something back?"

"I didn't think so. It's possible, though."

"What proof would *you* want?"

"To blackmail someone?" I shrugged. "Photos or video. It would have to show beyond a doubt that Kristian was having sex with Elin, though, otherwise it's deniable."

"So how could they get that?"

"Covert surveillance, maybe. Or if Kristian or Elin had taken photos… Someone hacks a computer and there they are."

Hentze nodded. "There's another possibility, too," he said.

"Elin?"

"*Ja.*"

I thought about that. It wasn't beyond the bounds of credibility, but it dragged a lot of other things along in its wake.

"Maybe," I said. "But it's a big leap."

He nodded, conceding the point. "Yeh, maybe too big until we know what's happened to her."

11

ANNI LANGGAARD'S BODY LANGUAGE WAS CLOSED. HER hair was pulled back tightly into a ponytail and she held her arms across her body, leaning slightly forward, but at an angle on the sofa, as if to deflect a cold draught. Sometimes there really was one when Officer Kalsø stepped outside to use his radio.

"What was the argument about?" Hentze asked. He'd taken the armchair and seemed at pains to pitch his level of concern just right. I was on a dining chair, listening but separate.

"The usual things," Anni said. "She asked for money to go out and I said no. Then it became about all the other things that she doesn't like here: it is too small, there is no life... Everything."

Hentze nodded. "And then what happened?"

"She says she will go to Silja's house. 'There they have room to breathe,' she says. She would rather be with Silja."

"Are they best friends?"

Anni shifted, drew herself closer. "Only because Silja is

337

stupid. She doesn't know when she is being used."

"What do you mean?"

"That she is useful to Elin. That's all. That's how Elin is. She only thinks of what *she* needs and if people can give her that."

She broke off and stood up then, took a couple of determined steps before turning back to Hentze as if the movement wasn't a solution. She spoke again, more rapidly and in Faroese this time, as if she'd lost patience with the limitations of English. Her tone was annoyed and clearly resentful. I wasn't in any doubt that it was Elin she was blaming.

Hentze asked a couple more questions and then the back door opened again and this time Heri Kalsø had another officer with him. Hentze glanced their way, then used it as an opportunity to break off from his questions. He stood up and came across to me.

"I think it would be useful to speak to Silja," he said. "If Heri goes with you, can you see what she knows? You know what we're interested in."

I knew what he meant. "Sure," I said, standing up.

Outside I followed Heri Kalsø to his patrol car and got in for the short drive across to the other side of the village. I didn't know what Hentze had told him, but he didn't seem put out that he'd been asked to take me along rather than being entrusted with the task on his own. His English was okay but rusty, and like a lot of coppers I suspected he had a sixth sense for something that might turn out to be more interesting than his usual calls.

Silja Midjord's house was large and well placed on a spur of road that had a fine view down over the harbour. It had a white roof and weatherboards, with a first-floor balcony. A silver Mitsubishi Shogun was parked in front of it.

We'd passed a couple of family groups walking uphill on the road and by the time Kalsø had parked and we'd got out of the car the foremost of these was only a few yards away: two adults, a girl of about twelve, and Silja.

"They are coming from the church," Kalsø told me.

The wind had picked up and there were dashes of rain in the harder gusts. Kalsø and I stood with our backs towards it and waited for Silja and her family. I saw Silja recognise me as they approached, but I let Kalsø make the initial introductions and explanation in Faroese, only getting involved when Silja's father – Martin Midjord – gave me a curious look. He was about my age, clean-cut and lean. His wife was a perfect match.

"An English policeman?" he asked, looking me over with interest. "That's unusual here."

"It's only temporary," I told him, happy to leave it vague.

"Like an exchange student?"

"Yes, pretty much."

"Ah, okay then," he said, apparently satisfied. "So it's about Elin, *ja*? Come inside."

We went in and upstairs to a sitting room with large picture windows and several oil paintings on the walls. Compared with Anni Langgaard's house it was spacious and airy and in the course of the conversation while we got settled I learned that Martin Midjord was an architect, his wife a schoolteacher. Martin came to sit with Silja on the sofa, while Marie Midjord kept their other daughter out of the way.

Anni Langgaard's call to the house earlier that morning had already made them aware that all might not be well, so I explained briefly that Elin had left her own house last night, saying she was coming here. I watched Silja's reaction to that as I said it and caught just a hint of apprehension: a look that suggested she was hoping none of this would go too far.

As far as Martin Midjord was concerned it was a worry that Elin had gone missing, but perhaps not surprising, he intimated. It must have been hard on her, the split between Anni and Kristian – unfortunate and to be regretted – although he didn't know either of them well.

Through this Silja said as little as necessary. She told me that she hadn't seen or spoken to Elin since yesterday at Anni's house, but that Elin had seemed to be in a good mood when she left. She hadn't said anything about meeting anyone last night, or that she might come over to see Silja. She had no idea where Elin might have gone, none at all.

I nodded and took it all seriously, and when it seemed that we had pretty much got to the end of it I accepted her father's offer of a coffee. "I'll ask Maria to make some fresh," he said.

He got up from the sofa beside Silja and headed towards the kitchen. As he did so I caught Kalsø's eye and flicked a glance after Martin Midjord, hoping Kalsø would take my meaning. It took him a second, but then he seemed to get it because he said something in Faroese and went after the other man.

I waited until they'd both left the room, then I looked back to Silja.

"Now can you tell me what you didn't want your dad to hear?" I asked.

She tried to look puzzled but we both knew it hadn't come off. "I don't understand."

"Is it something about Elin? Something she's been doing?"

She hesitated.

"It's important for us to know," I told her. "But I don't have to tell anyone else."

"She— Sometimes she tells Anni she's coming to stay here, but she doesn't."

"How often? A lot?"

"In the summer it was more. Not so much after."

"When was the last time?"

"Maybe two weeks."

"Did she tell you where she was really going when she was supposed to be with you?"

Silja's reluctance came back and she lowered her head and picked at the cuff of her sleeve.

"I think she met a boyfriend."

"Do you know his name?"

"*Nei, eg veit ikki*. I don't know. She wouldn't tell me."

"That doesn't sound like the teenage girls I've come

across," I said. "Usually they want to tell their best friends everything about the boys they're dating."

She shook her head, then looked up again. "I'm not her best friend. No one is. Elin is— At school she is the cool girl, but she can be nasty too, you know? She can be mad at you if you don't do what she likes. You understand what I mean?"

"Yeah, I think so."

She left her sleeve alone and gave me an uncertain look. "Will she be in trouble now?"

"No, I don't think so. We just need to find her to be sure she's all right. But don't worry about it, okay?"

She nodded, not entirely convinced, then glanced away when her father and Kalsø returned.

"And there's nothing else you can tell me?" I asked for her father's benefit.

"No. I'm sorry."

"Okay. *Takk*."

I let Kalsø take a list of Elin's closest friends from Silja, not trusting that I'd get spellings and accents correct, and sipped a coffee in the kitchen with Martin and Maria Midjord.

"Is there anything we can do for Anni?" Maria asked me.

"I don't think so at the moment," I told them. "Do you know her well?"

Maria shook her head. "Not so much. She has only lived here for a few months, but as neighbours if we can help…"

"I don't think I would want to be in her place, you know?" Martin said.

I feigned mild surprise and asked why not. He said

because Elin was "lively", then glanced at his wife for confirmation. Yes, that was the word, they both agreed. Of course, they wouldn't want to say anything negative about the girl; she was always polite and well spoken when she was here – but lively. There was just enough allusion that I could read the subtext, if I was so inclined.

When Kalsø had finished, Martin Midjord accompanied us down to the patrol car and stood looking after us as Kalsø drove away.

"Did she tell you anything in secret?" Kalsø asked, casting me a glance.

I shrugged to keep it low key and vague. "Not much. She thinks Elin might have a boyfriend."

He nodded. "I would think so," he said.

Up ahead I saw a man in his sixties walking along the road in the same direction as us. He stood in to the side for a moment, but when he saw the police markings he stepped out again and held up a hand to flag us down. In his other hand he was carrying an incongruous red leather bag.

Kalsø stopped the car and wound down the window. Rain and wind buffeted in as the man came around to his side.

"*Hey hey, hvat er hent?*" Kalsø asked as the man leaned down.

The older guy said something, indicating the bag and gesturing back along the road. He talked for a minute or so and I heard Elin Langgaard's name in amongst it before he passed the bag in through the window to Kalsø.

"*Alt í lagi, bíða eitt sindur,*" Kalsø said. He turned to me. "He says he found this bag near his house when he went to church. There is a purse inside. It belongs to Elin Langgaard, so he was taking it to her house."

The bag was a medium-sized duffel type with a drawstring and two shoulder straps. The leather was damp and it was wetter and stained darker on one side, perhaps from lying on the ground. I asked Kalsø if he had a surgical glove and when he produced one from his jacket I pulled it on and opened the bag. Inside there was a nylon wallet and a mobile as well as a hairbrush, make-up bag and a pack of Prince cigarettes. I took out the wallet and looked inside long enough to confirm it was Elin's.

"Can he show us where he found it?" I asked Kalsø.

"Sure, his house is just back there."

The man, whose name was Johannesen, lived in a modest house on a slope near a turn in the road. There was no garden outside, but he indicated a patch of overgrown grass beside three steps down from the road where the bag had been lying. Apparently he would have taken it back to Elin sooner, but he'd been on his way to church when he found it and thought it could wait until afterwards. No one apart from him had touched it and he hadn't heard or seen anything unusual outside the house the previous night.

Johannesen's house didn't have a direct line of sight to Anni Langgaard's, but it was less than three hundred yards between the two along the road: probably a couple of minutes' walk if you were a teenager who'd banged out of the house in a strop. I knew because I walked it, looking for anything else that might have been dropped, lost or thrown along the road. But there was nothing, and by the time I arrived at the Langgaard house Hentze was outside with Kalsø. Two more marked cars had arrived and Elin's bag was in a clear plastic evidence bag on the bonnet of Kalsø's car.

Hentze moved to meet me. His expression was serious and troubled.

"Did Silja tell you anything?"

"Only that Elin used her as an alibi so she could spend nights away from home sometimes. More in the summer, not so much recently."

"I guess we know who she was seeing then," Hentze said. "What about the bag? What do you think?"

I shook my head. "A girl doesn't just lose her bag with her wallet and phone still inside it."

"No," he agreed flatly. "You think she was made to go with someone by force?"

"If it was my guess, yes. I can't see any other scenario where she wouldn't have kept the bag with her or come back to look for it as soon as she realised it was gone."

Hentze drew a breath then let it out. "Then we have to think of Nóa Lisberg," he said. "It could be someone else, of course, but he has to be very probable." He cast a look back at the house while he thought for a moment. "So, if he *has* taken Elin, what worries me now is that we can't know what he will do. If he's had some kind of a dream in his head about her and then suddenly that dream is broken because she doesn't say or do the right thing, how will he react? Will he be angry, or violent or depressed?"

I could see the possible scenarios playing out in Hentze's head because they were in mine, too.

"Have you ever had your own case like this?" he asked.

I nodded. "A couple of abductions; but not exactly like this."

"That's a pity." He forced a thin smile. "I hoped you'd have the solution."

I shrugged. "You need publicity and men on the ground, there's no other way."

"Even if we don't know where to look?" He gestured up at the sodden, open hillsides around us. "There's a lot of space here."

"Yeah," I conceded. "But he's not going to be out in the open, is he? If he did take Elin he had somewhere to go: a house or a building like the boathouse at Saksun. I'd lay money on it."

He nodded. "So all we have to do is find the place," he said drily. "Okay, then. Now at least no one can say that we have time to wait and see."

12

ÁRI NICLASEN HAD LISTENED WITH A MIXTURE OF distraction and growing unrest as Hentze told him about Elin Langgaard's disappearance. He stood up and paced between his desk and the window, periodically casting glances outside.

Hentze deliberately kept his report brief and to the point: the time Elin Langgaard had left her house; how her bag had been found, apparently discarded; and the fact that neither calls to her friends nor the door-to-door questioning of neighbours had brought any new information regarding her whereabouts. The bottom line was that Elin Langgaard hadn't been seen or heard from for nearly eighteen hours, and when the circumstances were coupled with Nóa Lisberg's known obsession with the girl it could only lead to one realistic conclusion.

"We've also had another notification from the bank that Tummas Gramm's cash card was used at the petrol station near Leynar at six thirty last night. Oddur's gone to check it out but we have to assume it was Nóa, which puts him only a few kilometres from Kvívík a couple of hours before Elin Langgaard disappeared."

He looked to see Ári's reaction, but the man didn't say anything. He had come to a halt, looking out of the window, his long, awkward frame barely at rest.

"In my opinion that only supports the theory that he's taken her somewhere," Hentze continued, spelling it out. "We can only guess why, but yesterday I spoke to a psychotherapist I know and she thinks it's possible that Lisberg is showing symptoms of mental illness: perhaps psychosis. If that *is* the case we don't know what he might do."

"Who is that, the expert?" Ári asked, as if the answer would determine his reaction.

"Her name's Fríða Sólsker," Hentze said. "She works at the hospital."

For a moment Hentze saw the temptation to question the circumstances of his contact with Fríða cross the other man's mind, but instead Ári let it go.

"And she says Lisberg is dangerous?" he asked.

"She said it's *possible*. Of course, it's not certain, but I think we have to assume the worst."

Ári Niclasen didn't respond. Instead he turned away to look at the grey-black view through the glass, and Hentze found himself wondering if this final piece of information had caused the other man to shut down altogether.

Until then he'd understood that Ári wanted to avoid putting himself and the investigation under the spotlight for as long as possible. After the Vira Sirko case that was understandable. But now was the time – exactly the time,

Hentze was convinced – when they needed to disregard the past and make firm, focused decisions. Elin Langgaard's disappearance had changed things completely, but Ári's continued resistance to acknowledging that left Hentze wondering if his superior had reached the limits of what he was able to deal with.

He gave it a couple of seconds, and when Niclasen still didn't move Hentze tried to put some reconciliation in his tone. "Listen Ári, I'm not trying to tell you how to respond to this but I think we have to see this situation for what it is now."

Finally Niclasen turned away from the window.

"For what *you* think it is," he said. He sounded tetchy and tightly wound.

"Yeh, okay, for what *I* think it is," Hentze conceded. "But what's the alternative? The girl's missing, possibly in danger. To do nothing isn't an option."

He didn't add "any more" to the end of the sentence, but he knew from the way Ári Niclasen jerked his head – as if stung – that he'd heard it just the same.

"So what's your solution?" Niclasen said. "What's your plan of action?"

I'd expected the wind and the rain to pass over because that seemed to be the usual way of it here. But instead it had got worse, and we'd made the return drive from Kvívík under unrelenting black cloud, with bullets of rain splattering the windscreen. By the time we got back to the police station there was no sky, only heavy black cloud, and some of the street lights had come on.

In the incident room Hentze's team were back and at work. A new board had been started for the details of Elin Langgaard's disappearance and as soon as we got in Hentze called everyone together for a briefing. He didn't bother with English – no more than I would have in his place. He wanted to get the team moving as a matter of urgency and when he left the room about five minutes later I could guess where he was going.

He was gone for about quarter of an hour and I kept myself out of the way, conscious that I didn't belong and couldn't contribute anything. I'd already made up my mind to leave them to it as soon as Hentze got back, but I didn't get the chance. Instead, when he returned it was only to lean in at the door to locate me.

"Can you come?" he asked, and then he was gone.

I followed him along the corridor. When I saw that he was heading for Ári Niclasen's office I wondered if Hentze knew what he was doing. Niclasen had been pretty quick to put me at a distance as soon as he'd spoken to Kirkland, so I couldn't see him exactly welcoming anything I might have to say now. But maybe I'd got it wrong. Maybe he'd reconsidered.

Inside the office Niclasen was standing beside his desk. He wore an open-necked shirt under a sweater and was looking at a couple of print-outs – more for show than for information, it seemed to me, because he put them aside as soon as I entered. "You agree with Hjalti about this?" he asked without preamble.

I closed the door and glanced towards Hentze, but he didn't look my way.

"If you mean, do I agree that Elin Langgaard's been abducted, yes," I told him.

Niclasen's tone made it clear that he wasn't prepared to accept that just because I'd said it. He waved a hand at his papers. "You don't think she could have gone with someone because she wanted to?"

I shrugged because I wasn't going to fight. "And just left her bag? It's possible, but it doesn't seem likely to me."

"So your opinion is also that she is in danger?"

"I think she could be, yes."

He didn't like it, but I could tell the assessment was no surprise to him either. For the sake of show he went back round his desk and sat down before speaking again.

"Hjalti says you have dealt with situations similar to this in the past. Is that true?"

"Similar, yes – not exactly the same, though."

"So, what would you do now?"

I took a moment, then said, "If you really don't know where Lisberg might have taken her – if he has taken her – I'd go public. I'd get something out on TV and radio as soon as I could."

"To say what?"

"Nothing specific at first. Just that Elin is missing and you have reason to think she might be with Nóa Lisberg. I'd make it an appeal for her to come home, or at least get in touch with her mother: say she isn't in trouble, but that everyone wants to know she's okay."

Niclasen considered that for a moment.

"And what if Lisberg sees it? You don't think he'll react badly?"

"I don't think you can predict *how* he'll react," I said. "But if you keep the statement neutral – just make it an appeal for Elin to get in touch and say she's all right – you won't have said anything to directly alarm him and it will let the public know that they're missing."

Niclasen took a moment, then nodded. "Okay. *Takk fyri*," he said.

I took it as a dismissal but before I could make more than a half-turn to the door Hentze said, "Will you tell the others I'll be there in a few minutes?"

I saw Niclasen cast him a look, but he said nothing.

"Sure," I said, and made for the door.

When Hentze came back into the incident room I was standing in front of a large-scale map of the islands, looking at the area around Kvívík and following the lines of the roads to and from it.

"Ári's gone up to see Remi Syderbø – the boss," Hentze said before I even asked the question. "He's agreed that we should make a public statement now, but he has to make sure Remi is okay with that."

I nodded. "Anything else? What about searches?"

Hentze shook his head and gestured to the windows. Outside the wind-driven rain was as hard as before and the sky was several shades darker.

"The weather forecast is bad and it would be dark before we could organise anything. Besides, without knowing where to start looking... By tomorrow there may be some information from the publicity and while we wait we can look at the CCTV from the land tunnels last night, and also the electronic toll registers from the sea tunnels to Vágar or Kunoy."

"You still think he's using Tummas Gramm's car?"

"There are no reports of other cars stolen – it would be unusual if there were – so yes, I think so. Ári can give out the car registration in his statement and maybe someone will have seen it."

"Sounds like you've got it covered then," I said. "I'll get out of your way, but if you want me I'll be at the hotel. Just let me know."

I made to leave, but instead Hentze held up a hand.

"It would help me if you stayed – if you have nothing else to do." He smiled thinly. "We can use another brain, and also you know the whole case."

When he said that I knew what he was getting at but I was slightly surprised.

"You didn't tell Niclasen about Elin and Kristian?" I asked.

Hentze shook his head, as if he'd already considered the idea and dismissed it.

"*Nei*," he said and shifted a little as if he was assessing the best form of words to use next. "At the moment I think it would only be a – distraction. I think we need to concentrate only on finding Elin now, you know?"

I wasn't sure I did know and it struck me as a slightly off-kilter thing to say, but from his look I knew he was inviting me to read something into it that he wasn't prepared to acknowledge or specify, at least not out loud.

"Okay, it's your party," I told him. "You *have* sent someone to check she isn't with Kristian, though, right?"

"*Ja*, of course." He nodded. "I sent a uniform. Because he's her stepfather it's natural to check, but she isn't there. Kristian says he hasn't seen her and he was worried when he heard she was missing."

Then Annika Mortensen approached and took Hentze's attention for a moment. While he was distracted I wondered whether Elin's disappearance would worry Kristian more than knowing what she might say when she was found. It wasn't anything I could guess at, though, so when Hentze had finished talking to Annika I left it alone.

"So what can I do, then?" I asked him. "Make coffee?"

"I think maybe you're a little too qualified for that. How is your writing?"

"In Faroese? About as good as my reading and speaking."

He shook his head. "No, in English will do. We need to write the statement for Ári to give to the media. If Remi says okay we can have it on the TV news at six o'clock. Come on, I'll find you a desk."

The single bulb had flickered and dimmed. She looked up as it glowed red for a couple of seconds and then finally went out. In the quick fall of darkness she felt the room contract around her. Sitting on the mattress she drew up her knees, waiting to see what would happen.

Nothing did.

It was hard to know how long she waited. She thought he'd come, if only to explain or reassure her, but there was nothing. The darkness continued. There was only the sound of the wind and the rain on the corrugated iron roof above her head.

She knew she'd handled it badly before. She'd thought she could make him do what she wanted by standing up to him; demanding, claiming her rights, raising her voice, loud and strident.

The force of the slap had stunned her into silence. She'd staggered back, felt a hot numbness slowly followed by a hard burning in her cheek. No one had ever struck her like that before and she was still too surprised to resist when she felt him tug at her, dragging her, the movement gathering pace so she couldn't hold back as he bundled her up the stairs, along the corridor to the bedroom.

What was he saying? She couldn't tell. The muttering, mumbling of his words didn't even seem to be directed at her.

It wasn't until she saw the door that she finally started to resist. She tried to throw off his grip, but she'd left it too late and he had too much purpose. At the doorway they struggled. She swung her free hand in an effort to strike him but he caught that wrist too, then pushed her, forcing her through, finally letting go as she stumbled backwards.

And then she heard the door slam closed and the quick scrape of a key turning.

At first she'd tried to find a way out. The lock on the door was an old-fashioned box lock, but there was nothing she could use to loosen the screws that held it in place. The window was nailed shut. One of the three nails had split the wooden frame but it still wouldn't budge. She thought about breaking the glass, but although she couldn't see down to the ground directly below she could estimate the distance: too far. And she knew he'd hear the sound and come.

The view through the glass was one of a sloping hillside and sky: nothing else; no landmarks to give a clue where she was, no one to see her. Even so, she kept looking. At least here she could see out, not like the ground floor with the boards over the windows and the perpetual gloom.

The last time she'd seen him was in the late afternoon. The light was already dimming outside: rain and growing wind. When he came into the room he seemed uncertain, distracted, as if he'd spent the intervening time trying to solve a problem and had come up with the answer: a covered plate of food.

He'd switched on the light and held out the plate for her to take, but she'd refused; as if refusing was a way of denying him something he wanted. But the petulance hadn't worked any better than her earlier strident demands. Instead, after her second rejection, he'd simply taken the plate away again without speaking, and locked the door.

Hungry but still nurturing her resentment she had curled up on the mattress, pulling the duvet round her for warmth. In the end she had slept, waking again only when it was dark outside and the storm seemed to be at its height.

In the light of the single bulb, suspended from the ceiling, the room seemed even more bare and depressing. How long would he keep her here? How could she bear it?

She made her decision then. When he came back she would play along, whatever it was he wanted her to do. Just enough: enough to convince him she could be trusted and allowed out of the room. There were ways. He wanted her, didn't he? He must do, why else was she here? She'd let him fuck her if that's what it took; if that was all he was after. She knew she could convince him she wanted it too. What would it matter if it meant she got out of here?

But he didn't come and after the light dimmed and went out the darkness remained, constricting the space around her, growing heavier and closer.

Unable to sit still any longer she felt her way to the edge of the mattress and stood up, groping blindly for the wall then navigating by touch, along to her right until she reached the door. She felt the smoothness of the paint over the planks, the ledge and brace, found the door knob and tried it again, just as before. It rattled against the keeper but was still locked.

Tentatively she turned her head and put her ear to the wood, straining to listen. She could hear nothing beyond the noise of the wind and the rain on the roof.

Finally she stood back a little, swallowed to clear her throat and called out.

"Nóa?"

Too hesitant, not loud enough. She tried again, a shout this time to carry over the gale: "Nóa? Are you there?"

Still nothing.

She started to feel a surge of panic now. What if he'd just left her here? What if she was trapped in the dark and no one would come? No one knew she was there.

She hammered on the door with the flats of her hands this time, shouting as loud as she could: just his name.

There was no reply, no sound she could hear that wasn't the wind and rain. Nothing. Nothing. Nothing.

She felt the panic well up again and she turned round. There was just a little difference in the darkness – the shape of the window – and she crossed to it quickly, as a diver might rise to the surface, desperate to reach air. She pressed her hands to the glass, straining to see anything beyond it.

Nothing.

The thin pane was cold, a fragile barrier. She remembered the view downwards and recoiled from it until she thought about the alternative, of remaining here, trapped.

Finally, mind made up, she bent down and fumbled with the laces on one of her boots; tugged at it until it came off. She didn't care if he came now. She didn't care if the noise brought him. Even that would be something.

Grasping the boot by the toe she positioned herself so she could swing it at the glass. It hit with a thud, but nothing else. Not hard enough. She moved back a little, swung it again with more force.

The glass smashed and she felt a sudden, cold draught of air before she swung the boot again and again.

Through the momentary blur of the rain on the windscreen Linda Eliasen thought the movement in the headlights must be a sheep and instinctively she took her foot off the accelerator. But almost immediately she saw that it wasn't a sheep but a person, a person on hands and knees in the centre of the narrow road; the paleness of a raised face and then the motion of a waving, exhausted arm.

Linda Eliasen hit the brakes, although she hadn't been travelling very fast. The tyres skidded, the car lurched, came to an abrupt halt.

"Dear Jesus!" she said, unable for a moment to understand how such a thing could really be true and in front of her. But the girl – it *was* a girl, she realised, soaked, bedraggled, long blonde hair hanging down in rats' tails round her face – raised her hand again and used it to shield her eyes from the headlights for a moment before the effort became too great and she slumped on the tarmac.

Hurriedly, Linda opened her door, pushed it against the weight of the wind and struggled around it before running the twenty metres or so along the road to the prone figure.

"Are you all right? What's happened?" she asked. The words had to be shouted over the noise of the storm.

There was no response. Perhaps the girl hadn't heard.

The woman put a hand on the girl's shoulder. "Are you hurt? What are you doing here?"

The girl's entire body was racked by shivering but finally she raised her head to look up. She said something but Linda Eliasen couldn't tell what it was. "What?"

She leaned in closer.

"Please," the girl said.

360

13

OUT HERE WE WERE IN THE MIDDLE OF NOWHERE. I'D LOST any sense of direction and distance almost as soon as we'd left the lit roads around Tórshavn, Dánjal Michelsen driving at speed. All I knew was that we were on the west side of the island and after some hairpin bends the last place we'd passed through was called Velbastaður.

Now we inhabited a small circle of light, cast by the cars and the ambulance on the narrow section of road, and the wind was made visible by the rain it dashed through the headlight beams.

In the back of the ambulance Elin Langgaard was wrapped in two foil survival blankets but her teeth were still chattering and her body was racked by uncontrollable shivering, whether from shock or exposure I couldn't tell. Probably both.

She seemed to have retreated into herself, paying no attention as the paramedic fastened a dressing over the long, jagged cut down the outside of her forearm. Beside her Hentze squatted down and spoke reassuringly as he asked his questions, but Elin barely focused on him and he had to lean in close to her in order to hear the few words she said. Finally he stood up and patted her shoulder before moving away. Elin didn't react.

"How is she?" I asked when he came over to me.

"She can't say very much: just 'Nóa was in the house'. The paramedic says it's shock. She has a bad cut on her arm and her ankle is hurt – maybe broken. She said she smashed a window to get out."

By the time he'd finished speaking Dánjal Michelsen was coming our way, leaving a woman in a hooded coat in the shelter of the tailgate of her car. All three of us turned our backs to the wind.

"Her name's Linda Eliasen," Michelsen said in English, for my benefit. "She says Elin was coming from that direction." He gestured along the road into the darkness beyond the car's headlights.

"She didn't see any sign of Nóa Lisberg?" Hentze asked.

"*Nei*, nothing. The girl was on her own."

Hentze assessed that for a moment, then dropped back into Faroese as he gave Michelsen a series of instructions: concise and without hesitation, voice only raised because of the wind and the rain. It took less than a minute and at the end of it Michelsen nodded an okay and headed off quickly towards the patrol cars.

"I'm sorry," Hentze said, turning back to me. "In Faroese is faster."

I waved it away. "What're you going to do?"

He gestured us back towards the car we'd arrived in and

we started moving as he spoke. "Dánjal will go with Elin to the hospital. One car will stay here to stop anyone coming or going. The other will come with me along the road."

"Where does it go?"

"A place called Syðradalur, maybe four kilometres from here, but it's only one farm. There the road stops."

"You think she came that far?"

Hentze shook his head. "Not from there, no, but along the way there are two or three buildings near the road. They used to be empty, but it's a long time since I saw them."

We got to the car and a uniformed cop trotted up and had a quick confab with Hentze, then handed over a bulky, yellow flashlight – the million-candlelight type – before jogging back to his partner in the patrol car. Hentze checked the flashlight, aiming it down at the ground, then switched it off.

"Do you want me to take that, or to drive?" I asked him.

He cast me a glance. "Are you happy to come? I can't ask it."

"I've come this far," I said.

There was a second's deliberation, then he nodded. "Okay, *takk*."

He handed me the flashlight and opened the driver's door to get in.

Hentze drove at a steady 20 kph and the patrol car matched it, about twenty yards behind us. The rain had started to ease off, but the wind still buffeted the car in bad-tempered gusts, although that wasn't the reason for the moderate speed. Instead we were both watching for any sign of another person on the road or its edges; any sign of movement that wasn't the wind.

I found myself straining forward, closer to the windscreen in an effort to see. There was nothing, though, only the black of the tarmac in the headlights and the wind-flattened grass on the verges. Even with the lights on full beam, anything or anyone down in the gullies beside the tarmac or just a few yards to the left or the right of the road would be invisible.

Neither of us said anything, until Hentze spotted a patch of light-coloured gravel broaching the verge up ahead on the left.

"The first place," he said and let the car drift to a halt.

He left the engine running and the lights on, and as we got out the patrol car pulled up behind. I moved round the car and flicked the switch on the flashlight, aiming it into the wind. It bored a hole in the darkness and I played it over a steep slope dropping away from the road.

Almost immediately the light picked out a single-storey, cast-concrete building about the size of a garage. There was a single, empty doorway and a corrugated iron roof, rusted to holes in several places, their edges flapping in the wind. I focused the beam on the doorway again. There was no sign of life.

"You'd have to be pretty desperate to use that for shelter," I called out to Hentze over the wind.

"Yeh, I think so too, and Elin said a house."

He looked for a moment longer then signalled the other cops that we were moving again as the wind pushed us back to the car.

We drove on as before and it was hard to estimate the distance we'd covered with no landmarks and no world beyond the cast of the headlights. After a couple of minutes I saw a chevron sign marking a sharp turn and in the darkness it felt like the road might simply take us off into emptiness.

"I thought we should have reached the next place by now," Hentze said after a few moments.

"Could we have passed it?"

"I don't think so. Maybe. No. There."

I looked and saw what appeared to be a lay-by, scooped out on the left-hand side of the road. At its centre were two wooden posts marking the start of an unmetalled track. Hentze pulled the car in beside them, tyres rolling over loose stones, and we got out again.

As before there was a steep slope and I let the flashlight beam follow the track downwards until it levelled out about fifty yards below and gave out on to a flat shelf of land. Off to the left there was the white of a building: a gable end and back wall and a new-looking roof.

"Want to look?" I asked Hentze.

He nodded. "I think so."

"You'd better have this then."

I handed him the flashlight and took his Maglite in exchange as the two uniformed officers joined us with their own torches. Briefly, Hentze introduced them as Einar Geil and Esmar Dimon. Dimon was the older of the two; more experienced, I could tell. Geil was in his mid-twenties, stocky and keen to be moving.

We started down the track and Hentze played the flashlight over the emerging side and back of the house. There was a chimney above the gable end but no windows or doors and no movement. The whitewash on the gable was flaked off in several places and damp-looking concrete showed through.

Even against the wind it didn't take much more than a minute to reach the flat ground and we rounded the building to the front, giving the corner a wide berth. Hentze shone the flashlight round in an arc over the open ground in front of the house, briefly pausing when the beam reflected off the rear lights of a car beside an outbuilding made of stone and turf, then moving on to the frontage of the house. It was neatly symmetrical with windows either side of a doorway and a dormer window, central in the roof. The ground-floor windows were boarded up with plywood on the inside, but the door was open and above the undulating roar of the wind I could hear an intermittent banging as it swung back against a wall.

We stopped as a group and I looked to Hentze. "Didn't you say Elin broke a window to get out?" I asked, aiming the Maglite over each one. They were all intact.

"That was what she said. Maybe there are more. Will you look around the outside? Einar will go with you."

I couldn't tell if he had any ulterior motive for that, but I nodded. "Okay, sure."

As Hentze headed for the front door of the house, Einar Geil and I moved towards the car. He didn't seem inclined to talk but played his torch over the ground ahead of us, then strode out a little ahead of me as he centred the beam on the rear window of the car. Definitely keen.

I recognised the car's number plate as Tummas Gramm's Golf and let Geil look it over, turning my attention instead to the outbuilding beyond it. It wasn't much bigger than a shed but solidly built out of stone, with a rough plank door which stood slightly ajar. I played the Maglite beam on the gap as I approached, and as I did so the light caught a patch of denim jeans and the tan leather of a boot. I gave it a moment. The boot didn't move.

"*Hey*," I called out. "Nóa?"

There was no reaction but by now Geil had come the last few yards at a brief jog.

"You see something?"

"Behind the door, on the ground."

"Okay."

He took hold of the edge of the door, glanced at me then hauled it open a couple of feet before it grated on the ground and wedged itself. By then I'd stepped forward to shine the torch inside, braced for the reaction until I saw that there wasn't going to be one.

"*Skrapa*," Geil said.

I'd looked at Nóa Lisberg's photograph on the incident room whiteboards for long enough to know I'd recognise him if I saw him. Unfortunately I wasn't looking at the side of his face anyone would recognise now.

He was lying on his back, legs at awkward angles in the cramped space, one arm flung wide, the other near the barrels of a side-by-side shotgun, which lay across his thigh. The last shot from the gun had taken the right side of his face away: cheek bone, eye socket and upper jaw. In their absence the bloody mess of the remaining tissue and bone glistened wetly in the wash of the torch. There was a pool of blood on the stone floor beneath his head. It hadn't been there long.

After a moment I moved the light away, then took a half-step to the side to get a look at what remained of his face. It was Nóa Lisberg.

Geil hadn't moved, and because I knew he wouldn't I stepped closer, ducking my head under the low roof, watching where I put my feet. I leaned down and reached in to check Nóa Lisberg's carotid pulse – the left side, not the right. There was no reason for checking, except that it's what you do in those circumstances, for the recently dead. It's procedure. In twenty-odd years I'd done it five times before and I could list them all.

I felt nothing. My fingers were cold, though, so I gave it a few seconds and glanced up at Geil. He still hadn't moved.

"You'd better fetch Hjalti," I told him.

It broke the spell. "He's Lisberg?" he asked.

"Yeah. Get Hjalti, okay?"

"Sure. Okay."

With a touch of relief, he stepped back from the doorway and started away towards the house. I looked down again, ready to step back myself. A bubble of blood swelled slowly, then deflated in Nóa Lisberg's nostril.

I took my hand away from his jaw and refocused the light. It could just have been the natural settling and deflating of the lungs, but when the bubble rose again a few seconds later I knew that it wasn't.

"Geil!" I shouted over the wind noise and shone the torch towards him as he heard me.

"He's breathing. Get an ambulance."

He called something back that I couldn't understand until he cupped a hand to his ear.

"For fuck's sake." I moved to the doorway and yelled again. "He's still alive. Get a bloody ambulance! Fast, man!"

14

DÁNJAL MICHELSEN DISLIKED HOSPITALS. THEY GAVE HIM A feeling of ill-defined anxiety and made him jumpy. His wife's twenty-four-hour labour with their last child had almost reduced him to a nervous wreck before Elias had finally bawled at the new world.

Being Sunday night the emergency department was quiet, so there had been no shortage of staff to move in and tend to Elin Langgaard when she'd arrived. She had mild hypothermia, a laceration to her forearm that would require stitches, and a suspected broken ankle, the registrar informed Dánjal about ten minutes later. None of it was life-threatening.

A while later Anni Langgaard had arrived, brought in from home by a uniformed officer, and had been taken into her daughter's cubicle by a nurse. While the curtain was back Michelsen had caught a momentary glimpse of the doctor stitching Elin Langgaard's arm and he'd looked away quickly. The thought, never mind the reality, of needles in flesh had always made him feel lightheaded.

Now, when the doctor emerged from the cubicle, Dánjal Michelsen felt safe to intercept him as the man made for the administration desk.

"Doctor? How is she?"

The doctor was a self-confident man in his early thirties. "She'll be okay. The cut in her arm was deepest higher up but there doesn't seem to be any nerve damage. She needs an X-ray of her ankle and after we've assessed that we'll probably admit her for observation. It's not strictly necessary, but after what she's been through… It was on the news that she was missing."

Dánjal nodded but didn't take up the invitation to provide more detail about exactly what Elin Langgaard had been through. Instead he said, "Is it okay if I ask her a few questions now?"

"Sure. She's on morphine, though, so she may be a little out of it."

In the cubicle Elin Langgaard was now dressed in a hospital gown with a thermal blanket covering her from chest to knees. Below it her left ankle was bruised and swollen.

She looked a lot younger than she had in the photograph her mother had provided when she was still missing, Dánjal thought, pale and without make-up; her hair had dried uncombed. There was a cannula in the back of her left hand, connected to a drip – Dánjal looked away quickly – and the cut on her right forearm had been dressed from elbow to wrist.

Dánjal introduced himself, noticing that there was no physical contact between mother and daughter; no hand-holding or hair-smoothing as there often was in these circumstances. Anni Langgaard might have been waiting for a bus, he thought.

"I'd just like to ask a few questions, if you're up to it," he said, addressing Elin.

"Does it have to be now? Can't it wait?" Anni said, although she seemed to lack the spirit to put any real feeling behind it.

"It's nothing too much," Dánjal told her. "Just so we have an idea of what happened." He looked to Elin again. "Is that okay? Elin?"

Elin had a slightly disconnected look but when she realised she was being spoken to she nodded. "I don't mind," she said absently.

"Good, thank you," Dánjal said. He drew up the nearest chair and sat down.

"So, can you tell me where you were since last night?"

"Last night?"

"When you left home."

"Oh. At the house."

"Which house?"

She seemed to have difficulty remembering. "I don't know. I don't know where it is. Nóa took me there."

"Nóa Lisberg?"

She nodded, then frowned, as if at the memory of something strange. "He was waiting. It was dark. He said I had to go with him. I didn't want to. I was going to see Silja…"

Her expression clouded and became less disconnected. "I tried to walk away but he wouldn't let me. He grabbed me and— He put his hand over my mouth. I struggled. I hit him, but he— He pushed me into the boot of the car – locked it. I shouted but when he started to drive…"

She shook her head, tears welling in her eyes, and looked round for her mother, reached out a hand. After a moment Anni Langgaard took her daughter's fingers in her own, but now it was the older woman's expression that seemed slightly distant – disconnected – to Dánjal Michelsen. She seemed oddly unmoved.

They tell you to put pressure on a wound to stop the bleeding, but with Nóa Lisberg there was nowhere you could apply pressure to. Without wanting to move him and risk making things worse, all we'd been able to do was wrap jackets around him for warmth and gently press some first-aid dressings into the hole in his head. We took turns monitoring the faintest of pulses and hoping it would keep going.

Twenty minutes later the ambulance arrived and we got out of the paramedics' way, glad to hand over the responsibility. Hentze and I crossed to Tummas Gramm's Golf and Hentze retrieved the shotgun from where it had been placed on the bonnet, out of harm's way. It was broken now but the shells were still in place and someone had had the common sense to place it in an evidence bag.

"It's a cheap gun," Hentze said, looking it over for a

moment before lowering it and turning at me. "Do you think it's as it looks?"

"A suicide attempt? Yeah, I'd say so."

"Where was the gun when you found him?"

"Here, across his legs," I indicated across myself then took out my phone. "You can see better on here."

I swiped the screen.

"You took photographs?"

"A couple – for reference."

He didn't ask whether that was before or after I'd discovered Lisberg was alive, but I knew he was wondering. I held out the phone and he looked.

"I think I got his best side," I said.

It took him a second, then he accepted the joke with a short, dry laugh. "Yeh, I think so."

I put the phone away. "Did you find anything in the house?"

"No, not so much. It looks like he lived there for a few days."

Then his own phone rang. He pulled it out, looked at the screen. "Ári," he told me, then gestured to the house. "I think Elin was in the bedroom if you want to look."

He dug in a pocket and passed me a pair of surgical gloves and I left him to speak to Niclasen.

Someone had closed the front door, probably to stop it banging in the wind, and I did the same once I was inside, casting the torch beam round the interior, scaring up shadows.

There wasn't a lot there to see; a single ground-floor

space was divided by a partly boarded stud-wall frame, with a sagging sofa and a few pieces of junk-shop furniture at one end and a half-finished kitchen area at the other. It was obviously a work in progress, but just about habitable if you didn't mind living a bit rough.

Upstairs there had been more building work: new chipboard floors and recently plastered walls. The stairs led to a short corridor with two bedrooms and a bathroom off it. The first bedroom I looked in was being used to store a variety of building materials and tools, but the one at the far end of the corridor had a mattress on the floor and a chair on its side. They interested me less than the window in the gable end wall, though, and I crossed the room carefully to look at it.

The window was broken – the glass smashed entirely out of the frame except for small, jagged pieces – and a duvet had been draped over the lower edge, presumably to cover the remains of the glass. Hanging down outside, the duvet was sodden, twisting and flapping in the wind.

If the door had been locked and the window wouldn't open then breaking the glass had been the only way to get out. To the ground below it was probably about eight or ten feet: enough to twist or break an ankle if you fell badly, the shards of glass enough to cut you as you climbed out. It explained Elin's injuries and made sense of the way she'd said she escaped.

Then, from the ground floor, I heard Hentze calling my name and made my way back downstairs.

Outside the ambulance was already moving away.

* * *

"So, it's finished then," Niclasen said. In the warmth of his office he was addressing Hentze more than me and wasn't quite able to keep a note of satisfaction out of his voice.

"Lisberg was psychotic, as you said," Niclasen went on. "First he killed Tummas Gramm and then he kidnapped Elin Langgaard. When he realised he had no way out he tried to kill himself. Yes?"

I could see Hentze didn't like the oversimplification, but in the end he dipped his head a little. "If you leave out the details, yes."

"Do any of the details make it different? Do they change it?"

"No, not at the moment. But we still need to speak with Elin Langgaard to get her full story. The doctor has said she can talk better in the morning, and of course, if Nóa Lisberg survives…"

"What do they think about that?"

"You know doctors. He's having surgery and the best they will say is that the chances are thin. No one knows why he didn't die already, but if he lives twenty-four hours he may be okay."

"'Okay'?"

"Alive, at least."

"Ah."

Niclasen mulled that over for a second, then looked at me. I could see him debate whether to ask my opinion and decide against it. Instead he said, "Thank you for your help with this case."

I nodded. "No problem," I said.

He couldn't read anything into that, so he left it alone and looked back to Hentze.

"I'll put out a statement to say Elin and Lisberg have been found. It will stop people calling us to say they think they have seen them. It's a pity we had to go public in the first place, but never mind." He waved it away magnanimously. "And tomorrow we can give more details, okay?"

"Okay," Hentze nodded.

"Good then."

It was our cue to leave.

We walked back to the incident room. Dánjal Michelsen was there, talking to a uniform officer from one of the patrol cars, and a couple of the CID people were still taking calls. Everyone else had sat back a little, though, now it was over. There would still be tidying up to do, but I recognised the sense of easing up now the pressure of the live case had gone.

"I don't think we can do much more tonight," Hentze said, referring to the room. "It can wait till tomorrow."

I nodded. "You want to get a drink?"

He hesitated, then shook his head. "*Nei. Takk.* Tomorrow maybe."

"Okay. It's my last day here anyway. My flight's on Tuesday."

"Yes, of course." For a moment he seemed in two minds about something, then he said, "There is something we should talk about before that: your brother."

"Okay."

"Let me buy you breakfast in the morning. Would that be all right?"

I said it would and we agreed the time and place, then I left him to his people and headed for the stairs. While I was taking them my phone rang and Kristian's name was on the screen. I thought about answering for a second, then didn't. By the time I reached the bottom of the stairs it had stopped ringing.

Outside the wind was finally abating: still a few ragged gusts and a little drizzle, but calmer. I looked at my watch. It was only ten o'clock. It felt later.

As I descended the steps to the pavement I thought about walking into Tórshavn for a beer but I didn't feel like doing it alone. If I was going to drink solo it would be gin in the hotel room. I was hungry, though, so I went as far as the fast-food hut opposite the ferry terminal and bought a burger. I ate it walking back towards the hotel.

He was standing on the tile step outside the front door, sheltered from the wind as he smoked.

"How long have you been here?"

Kristian shrugged. "Maybe an hour."

"Out here?"

"*Nei*, inside. I know the owner. I only came out to smoke. I was going to call you again when I'd finished." He dug in his pocket, held out the pack. "Do you want one?"

I did but I shook my head.

For a second he seemed faintly disappointed, but then he put the pack away and nodded to the police station. "Were you there?"

"Yeah."

"How is she – Elin? Do you know? Have you seen her?"

"No, but as far as I know she'll be all right. She cut her arm and broke her ankle in a fall."

"Shit." He glanced away and then back. "But that's all? Everything else— She isn't hurt more than that?"

I wasn't sure how much to read into his apparent concern. It seemed genuine enough, but I didn't completely dismiss the idea that it might have been put on a little for my benefit, too.

"They're keeping her in overnight for observation," I said. "I think she'll be able to go home sometime tomorrow."

"And Anni's with her?"

"Yeah."

He took a breath, let it out. "Thank you," he said. Then he tossed his cigarette away. "Listen, can we go for a beer? I'd like to talk."

"I don't feel like drinking," I said. "We can talk inside, though, if you want."

I could tell he'd have liked it better if I'd agreed to the beer, but he accepted it with a nod. "Sure, that's fine," he said, and he pulled the door open.

We sat in the dining room. Most of the lights were off but the kettle and coffee sachets had been left out on the side table so I made a cup before I joined Kristian, even though it wasn't really what I wanted.

He hadn't shaved for a couple of days and he was rubbing a hand over the stubble, distracted, when I shrugged off my coat and tossed it over the back of a nearby chair.

"How much do you know about what's happened?" I asked him.

He made an open gesture with his hand. "An officer came to my flat this morning to see if Elin was there, then nothing until I saw the news. Anni wouldn't answer my calls."

"How did you know Elin was in hospital?"

"An officer called me and said she'd been found and taken there. I didn't want to go if Anni would react badly, so…" He let it tail off, then shifted. "Can you say what happened? The guy on the news – Niclasen – said they thought she was with Nóa Lisberg."

"She was," I said. "He abducted her – forced her to go with him."

I told him the salient details then, including the fact that Nóa had tried to kill himself. It was almost as pat as Niclasen's precis and Kristian listened without interrupting, toying with a sachet of sugar on the tabletop.

"So what will happen now?" he asked when I finished.

"They'll check the details, see if it hangs together. If it does, and if Nóa Lisberg lives and recovers enough, I suppose he'll go to trial, but I reckon that's a long way off."

It wasn't what he'd meant. I knew that, but I didn't feel like giving anything away for free any more. Talking about Nóa Lisberg had put the picture of his ruined face back in my head.

"It was just Nóa and Tummas Gramm, then?" Kristian asked. "That's what they think?"

"You mean the blackmail?"

He nodded. "Will it come out? I mean, if Gramm is dead and Nóa's— If he can't talk?"

I took a few seconds, as if thinking about it. I sipped my coffee, though it still wasn't what I wanted. "Tell me what proof they had," I said then. "There must have been something. They must have had something to make you take it seriously."

He shook his head. "No, I told you. They only said they knew about Elin."

I didn't bother to hide what I thought.

"You don't believe me?" he said.

"No."

"*For helviti!* Why wouldn't I tell you?"

"Because everyone lies to policemen. Big lies, small lies. Sometimes it doesn't matter, sometimes it does."

"I *told* you how it was," he said, sounding more irritable now. "You think that was an easy thing to do? This is everything to me."

"To *you*, yeah."

"What? You think it's wrong if I see— If there could be a way out of this shit?"

But the note of anger and frustration had a slightly rehearsed quality, as if he knew it was what I'd expect to hear if he was telling the truth. Maybe he was, but I didn't care any more. I'd had enough of him. I pushed the coffee away.

"Listen, I spent a long time looking at a kid with a hole in the side of his head this evening. No eye, no ear, no jaw, just a bloody big hole. So now I want a shower and a large gin and tonic. And a cigarette. But I can't have a cigarette, so just fuck off and leave me alone, okay?"

I stood up, picked up my coat, headed towards the stairs. I didn't expect him to call or come after me and he didn't. He had that much sense.

15

Monday/mánadagur

IT WAS A LITTLE AFTER SEVEN AND THE GREY FIRST LIGHT was still weak and undecided as Hjalti Hentze negotiated the sharp bends down to the coast road towards Syðradalur. The tarmac was wet and the Volvo's wipers beat intermittently. He drove without hurry – leisurely almost – because that was the way he had decided to do things this morning: slowly and thoughtfully.

Once he'd made the hard turn onto route 536 at Velbastaður and left the scattered buildings behind, Hentze slowed even further, down to 20 kph, as he looked for the place where Elin Langgaard had been found last night, finally identifying it by the tyre marks on the soft road verges where vehicles had turned round. At that point he reset the trip counter on the dashboard and allowed the car to pick up speed again.

When he reached the gravelled entrance to the track above the house a couple of minutes later the trip counter read 2.6 km and he did some calculations in his head. At a reasonable pace it might take him about half an hour to walk that distance. In the dark of last night's storm, with a broken ankle, how long might it have taken Elin Langgaard? At least twice that, he decided; probably more like three times, so no less than ninety minutes. He drew no conclusion, just stored it away as he left the car and headed down to the house.

In the daylight it was easier to appreciate the position of the building in the landscape. It occupied a horseshoe depression carved out of the hillside, and from the road it was nearly hidden – only the ridge of the roof and the chimney showing. Beyond the building and its level ground the slope continued until it fell away in an invisible cliff and then there was nothing but slate-grey sea and whitecaps between this land and Koltur, three kilometres away. With the low cloud concealing the peak of Kolturshamar mountain, the outline of the island reminded Hentze of a whale.

And then he was in front of the house and he stopped thinking about whales and turned to consider the building instead.

It was commensurate with Hentze's slow, thoughtful mood that his examination of the house, inside and out, took nearly an hour. Sometimes he returned to look at something again, conscious that he was compiling an inventory in his head; not just of objects and details like the box of shotgun cartridges in a kitchen cupboard, but of his impressions and questions arising from them.

Why, for instance, would you board up perfectly good windows so that even in daylight it would be dark inside? To protect them? Perhaps. But in that case it would be more logical to put the boards on the outside. Here they were fastened to the inside of the frames, and secured with large galvanised nails. He counted ten in one board, nine in the other – some badly driven and bent over – and the boards had been poorly cut without any skill or accuracy.

After a while he went upstairs and examined the bedroom that stored building materials, and then the bathroom. It was easier to see here because the windows were not obscured and the grey morning light was sufficient without the aid of a torch. He was drawn again to the windows, though: each one showing the protruding heads of more nails, hammered through the frames to prevent opening. Why?

In the final bedroom, the one used to imprison Elin Langgaard, he raised the sodden duvet, which still hung out of the broken window, to look at the sill beneath it. Three nails, imprisoning her, forcing her to break the window in order to escape. But by now he did not believe that confinement had been the intention – at least not the *only* intention – for securing the windows like this.

When he'd finally finished his examination of the interior, Hentze went outside again and crossed the short distance to the *hjallur* shed where Reyná had found Nóa Lisberg.

The door of the shed had been secured on a rusty hasp and now Hentze opened it as far as it would go, shining his torch to the back where it picked out a small generator with a jerry can beside it. An electrical cable snaked from the generator and disappeared into a steel pipe buried in the floor, presumably going underground to the house.

Ducking under the low door frame Hentze went inside. There had been too many people and too much disturbance last night to worry much about forensics now, but when he reached the generator he was more cautious as he examined it, noting that the position of the kill switch was to *off*, then unscrewing the cap of the petrol tank and peering inside. Half full, as was the jerry can, he found, when he felt its weight.

He stood looking at the generator for a full minute before finally heading outside. He locked the door of the house, pocketed the key and walked back up the track to his car. There, sitting crosswise on the driver's seat, looking out over the house to Koltur in the distance, he made a series of phone calls before manoeuvring the car round and heading back towards Tórshavn. He was already missing the Monday morning briefing, but it was too late to worry about that.

Breakfast at the restaurant of the Hotel Tórshavn was only for residents I was told as I tried to walk in, but when I indicated Hentze at a table beside a window the problem dissolved. Of course, that was fine.

"Are you an honorary resident or did you stay here last night?" I asked as I sat down.

Hentze made a shrug. "They don't mind if I drop in sometimes. Nowhere else is open yet," he said. "What do you call it – an advantage of the job?"

"A 'perk', yeah."

The place wasn't very busy and we were well away from a group of lively American tourists at a long table in the opposite corner. There was a good view of the harbour and although Hentze had already eaten he pressed me to take more than just coffee, so I ordered scrambled eggs: easy and simple.

"Is there any news on Nóa Lisberg's condition?" I asked when the waitress departed.

He nodded. "Last night they operated for six hours. It isn't good, but he is still alive."

"Is he conscious?"

"*Nei*, they think there is brain damage. Would you believe not just from the gunshot? They think from hitting the back of his head on the wall or the floor." He looked rueful. "I don't think he will be able to tell us what happened for a long time – maybe never."

"Does that mean you think something *did* happen?" I said. "I mean, more than him just going out to the shed and putting a gun in his mouth when he realised how much trouble he was in?"

Hentze chewed the question over, as if he was deciding whether he liked the taste.

"I think there's more, yes," he said in the end.

"Why?"

"Because nothing that happened yesterday has

changed my mind about Nóa Lisberg," he said flatly. "It took our attention away, but I still do not think he killed Tummas Gramm."

"Your third man at the boathouse theory?"

"Yeh, the third man."

As he said it the waitress brought my eggs. I thanked her and when she went away I picked up my fork and looked back to Hentze. "Okay, so convince me."

For a moment he seemed to gather his thoughts, then he nodded and laid it out for me.

"Let us say that there *is* a third man and he kills Tummas at the boathouse to stop him exposing the blackmail plan. Yes?"

I nodded, chewing.

"Okay. Yesterday you asked what happened to Nóa after that. Well, now I think he saw the murder, or realised what had been done, and he was afraid. I think he took Tummas's car and drove away from the boathouse and from the third man because he thought he also could be killed."

He toyed with his cup for a second. "So, Nóa is scared and very mixed up in his head. He is too afraid to come to the police. He wants to hide – just like at the boathouse – but where? Then he thinks of the house at Syðradalur."

He saw my objection before I could start to make it.

"I have checked: the Syðradalur house belonged to a man named Bjarki Gramm who died two years ago. Bjarki was Tummas Gramm's grandfather. Oddur is still looking for the details, but if Tummas Gramm owned it or used it, it's easy to think that Nóa could know about the place. Maybe he has even been there before with his friend Tummas."

I nodded. "Okay, that's possible."

"So, it is a good place to hide, Nóa thinks," Hentze went on. "And that's where he goes. He buys food at the Miðlon Bónus shop on Friday – we know this because he used his bank card, and also to buy petrol on Saturday. Why not? He doesn't know we are looking for him: there has been no publicity. He isn't hiding from us – the police – he is hiding from someone else. You saw the boards over the windows of the house? I have looked again this morning. Every window is nailed closed. To me this says Nóa wanted protection – to stop someone getting in – and if that is true it would mean that he was still afraid."

"Of the third man."

"*Ja.*"

I thought about it. It wasn't strong but it wasn't impossible either. "Are you saying that's who shot him, then? You don't think he did it himself?"

"No, I don't know. Maybe it's as it looks, but I think we should ask the question, to see if it's possible another way round. I think we should be looking for evidence one way or the other."

"What does Ári Niclasen think about that?"

Hentze made a moue. "I haven't seen him today. I went to Syðradalur for another look and then I came here."

We both knew he was being coy.

"So you're dodging him," I said. "You're keeping out of his way so he can't tell you to leave it alone."

"*Ja*, maybe a little," Hentze acknowledged. "You were there last night. He has a neat case."

"So why rock the boat?" I asked. "Niclasen's the SIO – the senior investigating officer – so if he calls time on it too soon and then something comes back to bite him on the arse later it's not your problem. Unless you're trying to protect him from himself."

"Protect him? No."

"So what is it then?"

He frowned. "What's the way you say it? If a job is started…"

"'If a job's worth doing it's worth doing well'?"

"*Ja*. I think so. And if we don't do it well then someone who has committed a murder – maybe two murders if Nóa doesn't live – will have got away."

It wasn't a bullshit, politically correct answer. I could see he believed it and I had a feeling it summed up his whole philosophy of life.

"And Niclasen's not up to the job," I said. "At least, not a case like this."

Hentze took a moment, shifting in his chair.

"Why is it that you were suspended from your job?" he asked. "Because you told a few people what you thought?"

I laughed. "Yeah, something like that."

"I believe it." He nodded, poker-faced.

I finished my eggs, which had been good, and let him drink his coffee.

"You'll need to find something that proves someone else was involved besides Gramm and Lisberg," I said, stating the obvious. "Without it…"

He nodded. "I've asked Sophie Krogh to come to look at the house."

"Without telling Niclasen?"

"I hope she'll be here before he finds out. But in case she isn't, or in case she can't find anything, do you think Kristian Ravnsfjall will talk to me now about the blackmail?"

That was really what breakfast had been about. He still hoped that details about the blackmail could lead him to his third man.

"I doubt it," I said. "He came to my hotel last night and he could already see a way out if there was no one left to talk." I nodded towards the American tourists, who were leaving their table now. "They'd call it *plausible deniability*."

Hentze sighed, disappointed but not surprised. "Yes, I can see that."

"You could ask Elin, though," I said. "If you tackle it right she might confirm it – unless you still think she might have been in on it: part of the blackmail."

"Do you?"

I'd gone back and forth on that a couple of times before she was found, but I hadn't been able to reach a conclusion based on anything more than the balance of probability.

"No. It's possible, but I don't think so," I told him.

He accepted that. "Annika's with Elin now to take a statement, but I'd like to ask her about some things I saw at the house before she leaves hospital. Maybe that will tell us something." He sank the remains of his coffee and put the cup aside. "Can you come?"

"To see Elin? You want a scapegoat?"

He frowned. "I don't know that word."

"Someone to blame when Niclasen finds out you've gone off the reservation and fucked up his neat case."

Unexpectedly he laughed at that, lightening up for a moment. "Sure, that's exactly what I need."

"Okay, then – since you bought breakfast."

"And because you think I'm right?"

"About Niclasen's theory being too easy? Yeah, I'd say so."

16

WE MET ANNIKA MORTENSEN IN A VISITORS' ROOM IN THE
hospital, and if she thought it was odd that Hentze had
me along with him she didn't show it. She was brisk and
engaged, seeming pleased that Hentze had kept her involved
in the case. I hadn't had much to do with her over the past
couple of days – no more than I'd really had much to do
with anyone else on the investigation – but all the same, I'd
got the feeling that she and Hentze had an easy rapport.

There was a brief catching up in Faroese between them
and I heard Niclasen's name a couple of times amongst the
questions and answers. Then, out of courtesy, Hentze moved
into English as Annika went back through the notes she'd
made during the interview and gave us the bulletpoints.

"What do you think of Elin?" he asked. "How did she
seem to you?"

Annika considered it briefly. "I would say she's a smart
girl, maybe used to getting what she wants. I think that was
what made this more shocking for her."

"Because she wasn't in control?"

Annika nodded. "She said a lot that Nóa was acting weird or crazy and didn't make sense to her."

"Was she kept in the bedroom all the time?" I asked.

"*Nei*. She says for the first night, but in the morning he told her to come downstairs. He gave her books and magazines to read while he watched her."

"Watched her reading?"

"Yeh. She said it was weird. He would sit and look at her, for a long time. She said something—" Annika looked at her notes for a moment. "Yeh, she said it was like he was trying to make everything seem normal – like playing at being grown ups when you're a kid, you know?"

She looked to me to see if I understood what she was getting at.

"In English we'd say 'playing house'."

"*Ja*, like that. Then, in the afternoon yesterday, she demanded that he let her go. She'd had enough, she told him. She tried to walk out and he hit her across the face, then took her to the bedroom and locked the door again."

"She had spoiled his dream – the fantasy," Hentze said with a thoughtful nod. "Is there anything else?"

"Not so much, although she told me that Nóa talked a lot about being safe: she was safe there; everything was okay; he was going to look after her and they would be safe. Elin says it was a big thing to him."

"Safe from what?" Hentze asked.

"She doesn't know: he wouldn't say."

Hentze looked at me. "Kristian?"

I just shrugged because I didn't have an opinion:

anything was possible if Nóa Lisberg really had been delusional. He could have thought the kitchen forks or the pixies were out to get him.

Hentze considered for a couple of seconds, then moved on, looking back to Annika.

"Did you ask if Nóa tried to have sex with her?"

"*Ja*, I asked," Annika nodded. "She said no, not at all, nothing like that."

"Do you think she was saying that because she doesn't want us to know?"

Annika thought about that, but then her answer was definite. "No, I think it's the truth. You know how some teenagers will be embarrassed when you mention sex? Elin isn't like that. She told me she thought he would want sex – she was expecting it – and so she was surprised – relieved, of course – when he didn't. She thought it was strange."

"So do I," Hentze said, glancing at me. "We know he had an obsession with her. He'd said he was in love with her, and now – when he has her in a place where there is nothing to stop him – he doesn't do anything. Does that make sense?"

"Maybe," I said. "We don't know his motive for abducting her in the first place. But if he had some kind of delusion about saving her, being a hero and keeping her safe, then forcing himself on her – raping her – wouldn't be doing that, would it? He'd be the one hurting her and it would break the fantasy."

"Isn't it the fantasy of a rapist that his victim enjoys it?"

"For some, maybe. But you're not being consistent. If

you don't think Nóa's a murderer, why do you think he could be a rapist?"

"No, you're right," Hentze said. "And it's beside the point."

He checked his watch, shifted, looked to Annika. "We should go and see her, but just tell me: was there any time when you thought maybe she wasn't telling the truth or maybe hiding something?"

Annika thought about it, then shook her head. "*Nei*, I think she was telling the truth."

"Okay, good," Hentze said. "Let's hope she continues."

Annika led us down the corridor towards Elin's room, but as we approached I saw Anni Langgaard with Magnus in the hallway outside the closed door. Magnus was already making to move away, but it didn't look like a parting of relatives, or even ex-relatives – more like the end of a business transaction.

When he saw us Magnus was only momentarily wrong-footed, then came on with shoulders set. Behind him Anni went into the room.

"Maybe you two should go ahead," I told Hentze.

He knew what I meant and they went on without me, passing Magnus with a brief acknowledgement.

I slowed up and stopped by a window, glanced at the view, waiting for Magnus to reach me. He was dressed in a suit that might have cost less than my monthly salary. There was an immaculate cream raincoat over his arm and in his free hand he carried an oxblood leather attaché case.

"*Morgun*," I said when he was close enough. "Have you just been in to see Elin?"

He nodded and stopped, although I could tell it wasn't what he'd have chosen to do. "Yes, for a short time."

"How is she?"

"Okay, I think. She can go home soon – this morning."

"That's good."

"Yes, I think so."

I nodded but didn't say anything. I let the silence grow awkward, as if I hadn't noticed, and eventually Magnus couldn't resist it any longer.

"So, are you here with the police officers or...?" he asked. Along the corridor Hentze and Annika were going into Elin's room.

"In a way."

That didn't make him any happier, but when I didn't elaborate he said, "Maybe— Do you have a few minutes? There is something I would like to discuss with you. Perhaps outside?"

"Sure," I said, amiably. "If you like."

"Okay. *Takk*."

I let him lead and we retraced the route Hentze and I had come in by, but brisker. Magnus made no small talk to cover the distance. Instead, now that he'd set this in motion, I got the feeling he was only interested in getting to the nub of it with the least possible delay.

On the ground floor we crossed the reception area and

exited through the glass doors, then went a few more steps until we were clear of the building and the few people coming and going. Finally then, at the edge of a swathe of grass, Magnus seemed to decide we'd come far enough. He put his attaché case down and turned to face me.

"I think I should tell you the situation," he said. "So things are clear, yes?"

"Okay," I said. "Go ahead."

This didn't come easy to him, I could see that from the way he curled and uncurled his fingers, as if he was easing a cramp.

"Last night Kristian came to see me," he said then. "He told me he had talked to you, also – about Elin."

"You mean about the fact he'd been screwing her?"

He nodded but the word hurt him – or maybe it was just the way I'd come out and said it, without bothering to dress it up. For a moment a dark frown crossed his face and I wondered if his reaction to Kristian's confession had been the same as Signar's.

"And the blackmail?" I said, pressing it further. "He told you about that as well?"

"Yes."

Tight-lipped, he looked away for a moment and pushed a hand into his pocket, leaving it there, as if he could hold the subject out of sight. By the time he looked at me directly again he'd composed his expression into one of flat business.

He said, "I think I should tell you that I have made an agreement with Kristian that Four Fjords will buy out his company. The finances of his business have been a concern for him, but by selling to us now he will be able to do other things and also to make a better settlement for his divorce from Anni."

"Just Anni?" I asked. "Or is Elin included in the settlement as well?"

He played it straight-faced. "She is Anni's daughter, so of course. – I think they will move back to Denmark."

He waited for me to say something, but I didn't need to ask any more. It was a good deal all round. For the price of his selling his business, Kristian could buy Elin's silence and Magnus could protect the family name – as well as expanding his portfolio. It put me in mind of the way Signar had bought out Eric Beder's widow forty years ago and I wondered what sort of price Magnus had negotiated with Kristian. He was his father's son after all, and like Beder's widow, Kristian would have been in no position to haggle.

"So it's all sorted then," I said in the end. "Everyone's happy – except Nóa Lisberg and Tummas Gramm, of course."

Magnus gave me a stony look. "Maybe they should not have tried to make money by blackmail."

I considered a couple of responses to that, but in the end I didn't make either. Instead I said, "Just out of interest, did Kristian tell you what they had on him?"

He frowned. "I don't understand what that means."

"Did he tell you what proof they had that he was sleeping with Elin? They could only blackmail him if they had some kind of evidence."

"No." He shook his head. "He just said that they knew."

I wasn't sure I believed that any more than I'd believed it when Kristian had said the same thing last night, but there didn't seem any point in pursuing it.

And Magnus seemed to sense that I'd made that decision because he shifted and seemed to relax a little. He could afford to be magnanimous now that I knew everything was sewn up.

"I don't think it has been a good way to come home for you," he said. "I'm sorry for that." Then he gestured to the hospital. "Have you been to see our father again?"

Apart from shifting the subject I didn't get the feeling that there was any agenda behind the question. I shook my head. "No."

"The doctors say there has been some improvement. I think so, too. Perhaps you should see."

Like I said, he could afford to be magnanimous now.

"I'll see how things go," I told him.

Elin Langgaard sat in a high-backed chair beside the bed, with the plaster cast on her right foot supported by a low stool. Without make-up she was still slightly wan, and her clothes were practical and understated: a black rollneck sweater and a pair of grey sweatpants. Colours for mourning, Hentze thought, and wondered how much deliberation Anni Langgaard had put into this choice of clothes from her daughter's wardrobe. There was room for her to have sat beside Elin, but instead she'd chosen to sit on the far side of the bed.

Hentze had made a play of being slightly unfocused as he took off his coat, moved a chair, sat down, asked how Elin was feeling now. It was his way of saying *I am not a threat. There's no need to be guarded: I'm just muddling through.*

"Annika's told me what you've already said to her," he told Elin. "So we don't need to go through it again. I'm sure you don't need that. It must be an unpleasant memory."

"A bit," Elin acknowledged, dipping her head as if she was glad he understood. "I'd just like to go home and forget it."

"Sure, that's natural. Has anyone explained there are counsellors you can talk to? They can help a great deal."

"Yes, we—" She glanced briefly at her mother. "I want to see how I feel first."

"Of course." He eased himself slightly. "Well, I only have a few questions – just for clarification." He made it sound light, even inconsequential. "So, can you tell me, while you were with Nóa at the house, did you see a shotgun at all?"

Although it was a question with purpose it was also prosaic enough to test the water and allow him to gauge how she reacted. Some witnesses needed to be coaxed, others to be reined in and slowed down, but Elin Langgaard seemed remarkably measured. She considered for a few seconds, then nodded. "Yes. When we first— When he took me inside there was one beside the door."

"The front door?"

"Yes. But later it was gone. He must have moved it, but I don't know where."

"He didn't threaten you with it?"

Elin shook her head. "No. It was— He wasn't like that."

"But you were still afraid of him."

"Yes. He was— It was like he was so wound up – so sensitive – I didn't want to say or do anything to set him off. Do you know what I mean? I was afraid he could explode, lose his temper, like he did when he made me get in the car. I hadn't thought he was strong before, but he was."

"Yes, I see." Hentze nodded, let a little time spin out. "And while you were with him, did he ever seem frightened or afraid?"

"Frightened? Why would *he* be frightened?"

Hentze let the question slip past as if he hadn't noticed. "Annika said he talked about being safe – is that right?"

"Yeh, he— He kept asking if I felt safe."

"Did you?"

"No, of course not!" For a moment there was a touch of emotion, until she regained her calm. "But I didn't say that. I said yes – I played along."

"So he wouldn't lose his temper?"

"Yes."

Absently she toyed with a Faxe Kondi bottle. It was still nearly full, but Hentze noted that the label had been partially peeled away.

"Okay. I just need to ask about last night now," Hentze said then. "You told Annika that before you broke the window to escape, the light in the bedroom had gone off. Was it just that the bulb had blown?"

"No, it was the power – it had gone off. I knew there was a generator because Nóa had gone out to put fuel in, in the morning. I thought he'd just start it again but the light never came back on."

"How long did you wait?"

"I don't know. It seemed like a long time, but I couldn't see my watch. And then I started to get scared. I thought, if he doesn't come back and no one knows where I am…"

There was a slightly rising pitch in her voice as she said this, but then she seemed to recognise it and bring it down, flatter. "I knew I had to get out, so I broke the window."

Hentze nodded. "And during that time – before you got out – did you hear anything – any sudden or odd noise: a door slamming maybe? Anything like that?"

Elin's tone continued flat, matter-of-fact. "No. I didn't hear anything. There was rain on the roof."

"Ah. Yes, the tin roofs can be noisy."

Hentze lapsed into a thoughtful silence and after a few seconds Anni Langgaard grew restless.

"Is that all you needed to ask?" she said.

Hentze stirred himself. "Yes, almost. Perhaps I could have a word with Elin alone, if that's all right?"

It wasn't. Anni Langgaard's expression made that clear. "Why? Anything you need to ask— I think I should be here."

"In the circumstances it would help me. Of course, I can't insist, but…" He looked to Elin. "Would that be all right?"

There was just a brief hesitation and then, without

reference to her mother, Elin said, "Sure, if it helps."

When she heard this Anni Langgaard rose wordlessly from her place on the bed and crossed the room to the door. When she went out she left it open behind her, though; until Annika shifted and closed it with a soft *click*.

Still seated, Hentze studied Elin Langgaard for a moment, then seemed to make up his mind. "It's only one question," he said then. "But I need to know who else knew you were sleeping with Kristian Ravnsfjall."

"What?"

For a second or two the incredulous note hung in the air, as if she was waiting for him to signal that he wasn't serious. When he did not, she said, "That's crazy. You think— He's my *stepfather*." She gave a short laugh, meaning – defining – it as impossible, Hentze knew.

He held her eye, but she didn't flinch from the lie.

"You didn't tell anyone?"

"About something that didn't happen? How could I?" This time it was more definite. "Whoever said that— It's not true, okay? I like Kris, sure; he's always been nice to me. But anything else? No. No way."

Hentze gave it a moment, then dipped his head in a brief bow of acquiescence, if not acceptance. "Of course. You understand, it's my job to ask about these things."

"Yes. Sure. But—" She broke off, then clearly changed her mind about carrying on. "It's okay," she said.

"Then I'll leave you in peace," Hentze said, standing up. He gathered his coat from the back of the chair. "If you think you would like to talk to someone – about anything – I can give you the name of a counsellor here. She's very good and she would keep it in confidence, of course, unless you wish to tell us."

Elin took a moment, then shook her head. "No. Thanks."

"Okay," Hentze nodded. "Perhaps you will change your mind."

"Can I ask—" Elin hesitated, for the first time seeming unsure of what she was going to say. "Is Nóa here, in the hospital, too? I heard someone say he was hurt."

"Yes, I'm afraid so."

"Was it— How did it happen?"

"I'm sorry to tell you, he was injured by a shotgun. At the moment we don't know more than that."

"Oh. I see."

He waited for a moment to see if she would say more, but she had turned inward.

"Thank you for your help, Elin. I hope you feel better very quickly."

He was almost at the door when she said, "Will I be able to have my bag back? It has all my things in it."

"Of course. I'll have it brought to you as soon as I can arrange it."

Annika opened the door and Hentze followed her out into the corridor. Anni Langgaard was standing a few metres away, her arms folded, looking out of a window.

"Tell her we've finished, will you?" Hentze asked Annika, taking out his phone.

He moved along the corridor a little way as he picked out a number from his contacts list. A minute or so later he was put through to Elisabet Hovgaard.

"I retrieved your specimens and had a look at the scans," she said. "What can I tell you – if it's a suicide attempt?"

"Was it?"

"Did he leave a note?"

"No."

"Then it's fifty-fifty," Elisabet said. "I can't say yes or no. From the injuries the barrel of the gun was in his mouth when it went off, but it was a bad angle to kill himself: not typical. Perhaps he was just incompetent. Was he used to handling guns?"

"I don't know. Would it make a difference?"

"No, I guess not."

"Were you able to identify the shot?"

"Yeh, I've measured the ones which weren't too deformed. They're number seven shot, steel. I also have samples of wadding from the wound. The lab in Copenhagen may be able to match it to a specific brand of cartridge. You'd have to check with them."

At the end of the corridor Hentze saw Reyná range into view.

"Okay, I will. Thanks, Elisabet. Can you do me a favour and hold on to all the samples?"

"Sure, of course."

"Thanks. I have to go."

17

I COULD TELL HENTZE WAS ON TO SOMETHING AS HE CAME along the corridor: the brisk, fell-walking strides wasting no time.

"Anything useful?" I asked as he gestured us into the visitors' room.

He shook his head. "Elin says there was no sexual contact between her and Kristian, but I would like to have been listening twenty minutes ago when Magnus Ravnsfjall was in the room."

I nodded. "You'd have heard them doing a deal," I told him. "Kristian's selling his business to Magnus and the Four Fjords company. With the cash he can pay off Anni and Elin – a divorce settlement – and they can move back to Denmark."

"Magnus arranged this?"

"Yeah. Kristian came clean to him about the whole thing last night. This is Magnus's way of clearing up the mess and protecting the family name. If Elin and Kristian both say it didn't happen, end of story."

"*Ja*, I see that." He considered, then said, "It may not matter. I was just speaking to the pathologist. Nóa Lisberg's injuries were from number seven shot, made of steel, but his gun was loaded with number nine shot, the same as a box I found in the kitchen. They are old ones, made of lead."

There's a moment in any investigation when you *know* you've got the right line, even if you haven't tied all the threads together, even if some still need to be found. It's an instinct – sometimes that's *all* it is – but you know it's going to take you out of the maze and then it's a unique buzz. And Hentze had that buzz now, I could tell from the way his expression seemed to flick from one thought to another.

"So, you've proved your third man exists," I said. "If Nóa didn't shoot himself then someone else must have."

"*Ja*, without doubt."

"You think he found out where Nóa was hiding and waited around until the right moment to shoot him?"

Hentze shook his head. "I think maybe he *made* the right moment," he said, pinning it down. "Elin says the power went off, but this morning I looked at the generator. There was maybe half a tank of fuel, but the switch was to off. I think it was done on purpose, so that Nóa would come to see what had happened, and when he does it's a small space in the shed and easy to push a gun to his face, force it into his mouth maybe."

"Premeditated then."

"Yeh. You remember what you said about Tummas Gramm: that maybe he was suffocated so that after a few days in the water there would be no sign of murder? – So in the same way, I think the killer has planned all this to make it look like Nóa has committed suicide. And if we think that we won't look further: Nóa is crazy and he kills himself; that is the end of it. So, the killer uses one shot from his own gun to kill Nóa, then he takes Nóa's gun and fires into the air and leaves it with the body."

"Except Nóa wasn't dead."

"No. But maybe the attacker thought so – or maybe he thinks he will die soon from the injury so he leaves it like that."

"And Elin?" I asked. "If he knew she was there he was taking a risk. She could have heard more than one shot."

He shook his head. "With the storm I think it is a risk he could take. She says she heard nothing and I believe her."

He paced to the window as he considered this for a moment, then he turned back to me, a little flatter now. "But even with this, we don't know who he is. There are too many things – facts – where maybe it was one way or maybe it's another, you know what I mean?"

I nodded. "Rule a few out, then," I said. "Clear a way through."

"Is this what you do for a case like this?"

"Sometimes."

"Okay, go ahead then: pay for your breakfast."

I laughed, but he was serious so I said, "It starts with the blackmail. It has to, right?"

"Yeh, of course."

"Okay, so let's exclude Nóa from being involved with

CHRIS OULD

that because you don't think he was, except tangentially, as a threat to the plan."

"Okay," Hentze said, moving to plant himself on a chair.

"What's the most common man's name on the Faroes? First name."

He frowned but said, "Jákup or Jógvan, maybe."

"Okay, we'll call our third man Jákup. And with Tummas, Jákup sets out to blackmail Kristian about his affair... so, first question: how do they know about it? Kristian didn't tell anyone because he knew what was at stake. So, either Jákup or Tummas found out by accident, or from Elin."

I looked to see if he wanted to object to any of that, but he didn't. He was resting his elbows on his knees, hands cupped, staring at the floor in concentration.

I said, "I don't like the idea that they found out by accident. It's possible, but it needs too many coincidences. Also, Kristian said he and Elin were always careful about meeting. So that only leaves Elin as the source – directly or indirectly... Did you find any connection between her and Tummas Gramm?"

"No."

"Okay... So let's say he – Tummas – didn't set up the blackmail. That means it was Jákup, and therefore Jákup must have some connection to Elin."

"So Jákup is someone she knows. And if that is the case she won't tell us. It's a dead end."

"Maybe," I acknowledged. "But who *would* she tell something like that to? 'Hey, guess what – I'm sleeping with my stepfather.' It's not the sort of thing you tell to just anyone, is it? You'd only tell someone you trust; someone who'd give you an alibi when you went off to meet Kristian."

He straightened up. "You're talking about Silja Midjord. – You think she is the third person?"

"No," I shook my head. "But if Elin told Silja what she was doing and Silja then told somebody else…"

"Jákup."

"Yeah."

Annika was standing in the doorway now. I'd registered her presence a little while before but she'd had the sense not to interrupt us until there was a pause. Now she took a step inside.

"*Hjalti? Dánjal ringdi og segði, at Remi leitar eftir tær.*"

"*Ja, okay,*" he nodded, not entirely focused on what she'd said. He looked at me. "Silja will be at school, but I think we should talk to her now."

"Before she talks to Elin?"

"Yeh."

Then his phone rang. When he looked at the screen he seemed in two minds about answering it for a moment, then bit the bullet.

"*Hey, Remi… Nei, ikki enn.*" He listened for a few seconds longer, then said, "*Ja, okay. Bei.*"

He rang off and stood up. "Remi Syderbø, the chief inspector," he told me. "The fish leaped out of the net, so I have to see him now or Sophie Krogh will not come."

The demand for his presence clearly didn't sit well with

him, though, and after a second he turned to Annika. "Will you take Jan to the high school and talk to Silja Midjord?"

She frowned. "What do you want me to ask her?"

"Jan knows the details. He's talked to her before."

It was obvious that Annika still had reservations and when he saw it Hentze dropped into Faroese.

"*Tú gert bara tað, eg havi biðið teg um. Í lagi?* – Okay?"

Still a tad reluctant, Annika nodded. "Okay."

18

THE HIGH SCHOOL WAS A LONG, BLOCK-LIKE BUILDING; concrete and hard angles in an open landscape on the outskirts of Tórshavn. The corridors were quiet and empty and there was the same regimented, institutional feel that any school has.

I followed Annika and the school secretary, getting glimpses through classroom windows of pupils engaged in their own microcosms of facts and ideas, and I wondered how much direct meaning any of it seemed to have to life on the islands. At that age I couldn't see the relevance of Hooke's Law or *Jane Eyre*, but at least the subjects had been based in the culture I inhabited. If I'd been here, peering at the distant outside world through a telescope, watching it get on with its life, out of reach, I'd probably have hated it even more.

It was an uncharitably harsh view, though – of the attentive kids in the classrooms, and of myself to a degree – and I realised the black dog was sniffing around. I made a conscious effort to refocus and think about the best way to get Silja Midjord to betray her best friend.

The school principal was a guy in his mid-fifties called Hansen who looked as if he consciously dressed for the part, right down to the round glasses and the leather patches on the elbows of his jacket. His office was clearly designed to be welcoming and relaxed, with a couple of armchairs and a sofa occupying more space than the desk and business side of the room.

He spoke good English but even so I let Annika handle it in Faroese: she had the authority and I didn't want to get us tangled up in the whys and wherefores of my involvement. As it was, he clearly had some reservations, but in the end he left to find Silja.

"He would prefer if there is a teacher to sit with Silja," Annika told me when he'd gone. "But I've explained that this might make personal questions difficult, so he has agreed to let us talk to her here while he is outside. Is that okay with you?"

"Yeah, that's good. *Takk.*"

She gave me a frankly speculative look for a second, then said, "So, is there anything I should know before Silja gets here?"

"It's just one question: who did she tell about Elin's boyfriend?"

"Boyfriend? You mean her stepfather."

"Hjalti told you?"

She shook her head. "I was in the room when he asked Elin about it."

"Okay, well that makes it easier that you're here now then."

"You think? I'm not sure Hjalti was so keen. He thinks I should be worried about doing what he asks."

"But you're not?"

She shook her head. "*Nei*. He is the best cop I know."

Remi Syderbø wore rimless, almost invisible glasses, which enhanced the clarity of his impassive blue eyes. His grey hair was still thick, brush-cut, and he rested a hand lightly against his cheekbone as he listened to Hentze, who had not been invited to sit down as he explained his reasons for summoning a technical team back to the islands. Ári Niclasen *was* sitting, in the chair across the desk from Syderbø, studiously silent.

"I've only just had the confirmation from Elisabet Hovgaard," Hentze said, with just a shade of apology. "And of course, it isn't a full forensic analysis, but there's no reason to think that she's wrong. And if Lisberg wasn't shot with the gun from the scene…"

"It isn't a closed case after all," Remi Syderbø said.

He flicked a glance at Ári Niclasen, but directed his next question back to Hentze. "Which is why you want Technical to go over the house?"

"Yeh. I think we should treat it as a crime scene, not just for the abduction of Elin Langgaard, but for the shooting."

Remi Syderbø considered that, leaning back in his chair.

"Do we have anything else to go on regarding a suspect, or will we have to wait for Sophie Krogh's results?"

By now it was quite plain that he wasn't looking for

or expecting a definitive answer from Ári Niclasen and Hentze knew that wasn't a good sign. Generally speaking, the chief inspector wasn't inclined to get involved directly with cases unless his authority was requested or he had cause for concern. From the atmosphere in the office when he'd arrived, Hentze now suspected the latter.

"We do have a lead," Hentze said, deliberately using the plural. "She's a friend of Elin Langgaard. I asked Annika to go and speak to her while I came here. Depending on what she says we may get a name…"

"Someone responsible for the death of Tummas Gramm as well as shooting Lisberg?"

"It's possible, yes."

Remi Syderbø considered, but only briefly. "All right, then you'd better get to it," he said. "I don't want this stop-start business going on any longer than necessary. We're already in danger of looking as if we can't make up our minds what we're dealing with, so let's get it sorted out one way or the other, okay?"

"Sure. Okay," Hentze nodded, taking it as a dismissal.

"And keep me updated directly," Syderbø added as Hentze turned for the door. "If this current lead doesn't work out we'll have a conference to re-evaluate the case this afternoon."

"Right."

Hentze cast a look towards Ári Niclasen as he moved, but, as before, the man remained resolutely still.

* * *

Silja Midjord was dressed in jeans and a knitted waistcoat over a sweatshirt and she stood uneasily as Hansen spoke in Faroese. I guessed from his tone that he was explaining there was nothing to be concerned about, but even so Silja had the withdrawn, uncomfortable look that teenagers have when they know the odds are stacked against them by the sheer weight of adult attention. It was mirrored by her monosyllabic responses before she took up the invitation to sit, placing herself at one end of the sofa.

"Okay, so I will let you talk," Hansen said, moving to the door. "I'm just outside."

I waited until he'd left and then sat down at an angle on the free end of the sofa, as if I wanted to keep what was said on a personal level.

"I'm sorry to take you away from your lessons," I told Silja. "But I need to ask you about something. Is that okay?"

"Is it about Elin?" She risked a moment of engagement. "It was on the news that she was found and taken to the hospital, but that's all I know. Is she okay?"

"Yes, she'll be fine: nothing to worry about. I think they'll let her go home later today."

"Oh. Good."

She nodded, still not keen to look at me directly, and I gave it a second before changing the subject.

"You remember when I talked to you yesterday, you said that Elin sometimes told her mother that she was with you, but instead she went to see a boyfriend. You remember saying that?"

She nodded but didn't want to meet my eye.

"What can you tell me about him – Elin's boyfriend?"

"Nothing. I don't know anything."

I said nothing.

"I don't know," she repeated, glancing up briefly.

"Silja, this is important and I need you to be honest with me. I need to know what Elin told you about her boyfriend."

Head down, she kept silent. I glanced at Annika and she understood what I wanted, repeated what I'd said in Faroese until, halfway through, Silja cut her off.

"I understand. But I don't know anything."

I let a pause lengthen, and then I leaned forward a little, making my voice unequivocal, no room for doubt. "Silja, a man has been killed," I told her. "And Nóa Lisberg is in hospital. He was shot yesterday and he could still die. So you need to tell us the truth now – all of it. Because it's more important than promises about boyfriends and keeping secrets."

She'd raised her knuckles to her lips as I'd said this and now, after a beat, she looked to Annika and said something softly, almost muffled, which had the tone of asking if she would be in trouble. Annika shook her head, kept her voice serious and calm – reassuring. In the end she directed the girl back to me.

Silja hesitated, then bit the bullet.

"Elin told me she had a boyfriend," she said. "That was why she wanted to say she was with me – so she could spend the nights with him. I was— I didn't want to, but she said, 'Silja, please. Don't be— Don't spoil it for me. I will do the same for you…' At first it was one time in two weeks, then more in the summer. She liked to tell me about it, but it had to be a secret because he was married."

"That was what she told you?" I asked.

"Yes."

"Did she tell you his name?"

"*Nei*." She shook her head.

"Are you sure?"

"*Nei*," Silja repeated. Then earnestly: "I didn't *want* to know. I didn't— I didn't like to be part of the lie. I only did it because Elin pushes me to. You understand?"

She glanced at Annika and then back at me. I understood. I could guess how persuasive Elin might be. And I also believed Silja when she said she didn't know who Elin's lover had been. Which meant that she couldn't have passed that information to anyone else, either deliberately or by accident. My theory was busted.

As a last throw I said, "Do you – did you – know Tummas Gramm?"

Slightly to my surprise she nodded. "A little."

"In what way? I mean, how did you know him?"

"He worked at Elin's house in the summer, before she moved there with Anni. Elin and I sometimes went to see what was being done and we would talk to Tummas and the others. Elin liked to... to *tease* them. Is that the word? To pretend she is interested in them."

"To flirt?"

"*Ja*." Silja nodded. This was safer ground. "But Kristian didn't want her to stop them working, you know? So sometimes we went there when he wasn't around."

I could imagine. But that wasn't where my thoughts had jumped to.

I said, "So Kristian was there when Tummas Gramm was working at the house – he knew him?"

"*Ja*, sure. Kris would come to look at the work and see if it was okay."

"And he talked to Tummas about that?" I asked, wanting to be absolutely clear.

"Sure, or to Sámal."

"Who's Sámal?"

"Sámal Mohr. His father owns the building company. Most of the time it was only Sámal and Tummas working at the house."

I made another jump, uncertain where it would take me but trusting the intuition.

"Were Tummas and Sámal friends, do you know?" I asked. "I mean, outside work. Did they hang out together?"

"Sure. Yes. I think they know each other since school."

I thought about that for a couple of seconds, then nodded and stood up. "Okay. *Stora takk fyri, Silja*. Thank you for being honest. You've been a big help."

19

"SHE'S A STUPID GIRL," ANNIKA MORTENSEN SAID AS WE left the school.

It took me a moment to come out of my thoughts, but when I did her judgement surprised me because I thought she'd handled Silja well: the right amount of authority and understanding.

"Why?" I asked.

"Because she follows Elin Langgaard like a lamb. Whatever Elin wants to do she agrees."

"She's a teenager."

"Huh."

Annika turned aside for a moment to get shelter from the breeze as she lit a cigarette. When she'd done that she said, "Are you thinking something different for the case now? If Silja is not involved…"

I nodded. "Yeah, we were going in the wrong direction."

As I said it Hentze's car turned into the car park.

"We'd better tell Hjalti," I said. "If he's still got a job."

Hentze stopped the car across three vacant parking

slots and got out as we headed towards him.

"Is there anything?" he asked without preamble.

I looked to see if Annika wanted to answer, but she deferred to me with a nod.

I said, "Silja says she doesn't know who Elin's boyfriend was, so she couldn't have told anyone. I think that's the truth."

Hentze frowned. "So the blackmailers must have discovered it a different way."

"I don't think there *was* any blackmail," I said flatly, because by now I'd had chance to put things in place.

"What do you mean? We know that there was."

"No." I shook my head. "We took Kristian at his word – *I* took him at his word. He said he was being blackmailed, and there was no reason to disbelieve him, but if you stop thinking of him as a victim..."

"No, I don't understand," Hentze said. He looked as if I was trying to convince him that it never rained in the Faroes.

"Okay, look at it this way," I said. "Kristian's got money troubles. From what I've picked up, all his cash is tied up in his business. The other day he said something about trying to attract new investors for his company but I got the impression he hadn't been successful, and on top of that he also has to make a divorce settlement with Anni Langgaard. So what can he do? If he sells the business he's back to square one; if he doesn't, he can't pay his debts. So he's stuck."

"Then he could go to the bank."

"Yeah, maybe, but it depends how much he's already borrowed, doesn't it? If he's already up to his limit..."

"Then his father."

I shook my head. I was sure about this. "Kristian left Four Fjords because he couldn't work with Signar or Magnus any more. To ask them to buy into his business because it was struggling would have been humiliating for him. Besides, I think Signar might well have refused and told Kristian to stand on his own two feet."

"Then what are you suggesting?"

I shrugged my collar up against the breeze. "What if Kristian thought of a way to be *sure* he could get money from Signar by *pretending* he was being blackmailed?"

"Pretending?"

"Sure. But it had to be good: something he knew Signar wouldn't want to be made public; something that would blacken the family name. There was nothing that would do that better than sleeping with his own stepdaughter. So Kristian tells Signar he's being blackmailed over Elin and asks Signar for the cash. Signar is angry but to avoid a scandal he agrees and that would have been that if Signar had just given Kristian the money. But he didn't. Instead he insisted on taking the cash to the drop point himself. He wanted to confront the blackmailers and see their proof and that gave Kristian a real problem. There *wasn't* any proof, and even if there had been he couldn't go there to collect the money himself. So what does he do?"

Hentze had caught up with my thinking by now. "You think he hired Tummas Gramm to do it for him?"

"That's my bet," I said. "Kristian told me he didn't know Gramm, but that wasn't true. Silja Midjord just told us that Kristian talked to Tummas and a man called Sámal Mohr quite often at Anni Langgaard's new house. And Kristian could have known that Tummas wasn't averse to a bit of law-breaking, so he hires the two of them to go to Tjørnuvík and collect the cash. Two big young guys against Signar? They can just take the money from him if he won't hand it over. Except Signar's taken a shotgun and when they try to threaten him – *bang*: it all goes wrong."

Hentze drew a breath and chewed that over. "If this is correct then Sámal Mohr could be our third man, our Jákup."

"I'd say so, yes."

Hentze rubbed the stubble on his cheek, then nodded. "Okay. I think we're on the right line. Sámal Mohr has a criminal record for violence in Denmark two or three years ago. I know because I also know Sámal Mohr's father, Edvin. He's not an easy man to like but he will know where to find Sámal. Come. We'll start at his work place in Kollafjørður."

"All of us?" Annika asked, and for a moment I thought she was questioning my involvement, until I saw her gesture to her own car.

"You've had enough of CID work?" Hentze asked.

"*Nei*. Of course not."

"Okay then."

It was obvious that Hentze had had enough of pussyfooting around. As soon as we were on the main road he put his foot down, taking the car up past 100 kph on the long straights beside Kaldbaksfjørður where the water was running in sullen swells. Annika was behind us in the patrol car.

"You're still on the case then," I said, breaking the silence. He glanced at me, then nodded. "Yeh, for the moment."

"What did your boss say?"

"He wants to clear this up now."

"And Niclasen?"

Hentze pursed his lips for a second. "Yeh, him also," he said flatly.

I left it alone. Instead I said, "So what did you mean when you said Edvin Mohr wasn't easy to like?"

He considered, then said, "He's a person who thinks the rules are not made for him, only for others. Two years ago maybe we had to make a case against him for damage to another man's boat; before that for assault... Always he is the one who didn't start things – he is just protecting himself, you know?"

I nodded. "And Sámal? What's his record?"

"He stabbed a man in a fight outside a club. He was sentenced to only two years in prison because he claimed self-defence. When he got out he came back to the islands."

"He's not going to be pleased to see us then."

"No, I don't think so."

The builder's yard at Kollafjørður was on a waterside industrial development parallel with the main road. Between two commercial units it was bounded by a chain-link fence with a couple of freight containers and a Portakabin office inside the perimeter. There was only one vehicle – a Nissan hatchback – and no sign of life.

Hentze parked across the open gateway and went to the office. When he came out again a couple of minutes later he was walking briskly. "Only the secretary is here. They are all working at Hósvík – on new houses. It's not far, but by the time we get there Edvin will know we are coming."

He waved to Annika to follow and soon we were back on the main road. We drove east for a short distance, then north as the road made a right-angled turn, following the undulating coastline.

It was less than five miles to Hósvík, a collection of thinly scattered houses that sat back from the road in a flat-bottomed valley overlooking the sound. Hentze turned off at the first side road and then almost immediately again, up a slight rise which became an unmetalled road with a small housing plot at the end. It looked as if three houses were being built on the site, but they were all a long way from finished and the ground around them was mostly mud, cut by vehicle tracks.

Hentze slowed the car as he approached the first house – the one closest to completion – scanning the various workmen coming and going and eyeing the cars and vans on the side of the track.

"There is Edvin," he said then, stopping the car.

He'd been right that Edvin Mohr would know we were coming. Dressed in a plaid work shirt and a high-vis waterproof jacket, the man Hentze had indicated was in his early fifties, standing in the doorway of the house as if ready to bar entry. He had a mobile to his ear and only finished speaking as Hentze and I got out of the car. Annika pulled up behind us.

"I think we will make this official," Hentze said. "Will you keep a watch here?"

I knew he didn't need the complication of my presence so I nodded. "Sure."

"*Takk.*"

He looked towards Annika so she'd know to follow him, then started across the site to where Edvin Mohr was still watching impassively.

By now our arrival had attracted some attention from the mud-splattered builders, but none of them seemed inclined to do more than watch. I scanned a few faces, but apart from knowing Sámal Mohr's age there was no way I'd be able to recognise him unless he made himself obvious.

For want of anything better to do I leaned on the car and cultivated an inscrutable air. Hentze was talking to Edvin Mohr now, with Annika standing off a little to one side looking unimpressed but not without presence as Mohr made negative gestures. Even from that distance I could guess the tone of it: *don't know*; *haven't seen him*; *what's it about?*

It was probably the over-amped thud of the bass speakers that made me look first, but the fact that the pickup didn't slow down as it hit the gravel track was enough to keep my attention. The driver obviously intended to arrive with a flourish, but as soon as he spotted Annika's patrol car it changed things. He took his foot off the accelerator and slowed fast, skidding to a halt. Something in the bed of the truck clattered, loose and metallic.

Behind the windscreen I got a look at a guy in his mid-twenties, dark hair under a beanie hat, high cheekbones; not much more than that. He saw Annika, saw me, put two and two together and jammed the truck into reverse, wrenching the steering wheel round as he backed up fast. The pickup was twenty yards from me as it thudded over the newly laid kerb stones and went halfway on to the muddy grass beyond them.

I was already moving by then; as Sámal Mohr wrestled the gear lever into first and floored the accelerator again. It was too hard and too fast, though. The truck's rear wheels spun without traction on the wet ground, throwing up mud and steam and carving a rut.

As the engine over-revved and the truck dug itself deeper I saw Mohr look my way. I was three or four paces from him, maybe less in the number of seconds, and I'd got as far as aiming for the driver's door when there was a thud. He'd banged the truck into four-wheel drive and when he stamped the accelerator again the front tyres bit and shot gravel.

The pickup jumped forward just as I grabbed for the driver's door handle, too late to re-think. Deliberately or not, the truck swung towards me and my own momentum was added to that of the pickup, throwing me along the side of it. I felt a hard thump to my shoulder and had the shortest impression of something flying past or towards me, and then instant nothing.

* * *

Although he was running towards the truck, Hentze didn't see exactly what happened. His greatest impression was that of Reyná being flung backwards, perhaps side-swiped by the pickup, already rag-doll limp before he hit the ground amidst a number of scaffolding poles, thrown loose from the back.

Annika was some way ahead and when he saw her start to head towards Reyná instead of the patrol car, Hentze immediately shouted, "Annika! Go after Mohr!"

She glanced back, saw his gesture and ran on to her patrol car.

Hentze reached Reyná, closely followed by a couple of workmen, but they pulled up short and stood back as Hentze took the lead. He knelt down beside Reyná who was lying half on his side, unconscious. A bruised lump was already forming at the hair line on his forehead and the colour seemed to have been sucked from his face. Quickly, Hentze sought a pulse. It was there, although weak. Hentze tugged out his mobile and dialled 112. "Get a first-aid kit," he ordered the nearest workman. "Quickly."

Annika didn't try to turn the patrol car around, but instead reversed at increasing speed down the slope of the unmetalled road. Just before it hit the tarmac there was a hard, jarring clang under the engine somewhere, but by then she was already spinning the wheel in a sliding turn and seeking first gear.

Below and ahead she saw Sámal Mohr's pickup fishtail

as it pulled out on to the main road, turning right towards Kollafjørður, spray thrown up from the rear wheels. Annika changed gear and keyed her radio.

"Control from Unit 6. Urgent assistance needed to intercept a blue Toyota pickup, registration number Victor Bravo 932. Heading south on route 10 towards Kollafjørður. One male occupant."

"Received, Annika. What's the offence?"

"Hit and run." It was the first thing she thought of. "One person injured."

She made the turn on to the main road, momentarily catching a glimpse of the pickup before it disappeared round the curve of the road, maybe a kilometre ahead.

Over the radio other patrols were calling in. It wasn't an everyday incident and if there was to be a pursuit no one would want to miss out, but with only five or six patrols for the whole of Streymoy it would depend if there was anyone close enough to intervene quickly.

Anxious not to lose sight of the truck for longer than necessary, Annika picked up speed, although the patrol car seemed slightly sluggish and reluctant to respond. By the time she had reached the first bend the pickup was rounding the next, increasing its lead as she answered a request for her position from Tina in the control room.

"Still on route 10. Maybe three kilometres from Kjalnestangi."

"Okay. Heri and Hans David are on route 40, coming your way. They'll block the road at the turn for Signabøur."

"Okay, understood."

But the damned car was losing power; Annika could feel it on the incline and she remembered the clang under the engine block. She'd probably put a rock through the oil pan, she thought, cursing.

Changing down into third she pushed the revs higher, willing the car to crest the hill and make the downhill gradient on the far side, and it did. Over the top there was about a kilometre of straight road before the village and the right-angle bend. She strained to pick out the truck, to see how much of a lead it had gained, but it was almost too far ahead to be properly discernible. She knew she'd lose it now, but if Heri and Hans David could set up a road block...

Then, at the far end of the straight, Annika saw the flash of tail lights, followed almost immediately by another, brighter set. And then, not quite lost in spray and rain, there was a movement that wasn't natural for a vehicle on the road. It was too far away to see properly for several seconds, until she was closer, and then the scene gradually coalesced to make sense.

The pickup had flipped as it swerved around a bus, which had been pulling out from a stop. In four-wheel drive and at speed it was an easy thing to do. The wonder was that it hadn't rolled completely, but instead had gone across the carriageway on its side, coming to a halt at the far verge.

Annika let the patrol car slow as it approached the scene of the crash, then stopped on the white line in the centre of the road, leaving the blue lights flashing and adding the hazard lights before she got out. Behind her a couple of cars approached and she waved them to a halt as she grabbed the first-aid kit and jogged across to the pickup, calling the crash in on her radio as she went.

Even after nine years in the job, traffic accidents were still the incidents she liked the least, especially the moments before you knew how bad it was going to be. She already knew this one wasn't going to be good.

The truck was on its left-hand side and its slide across the road had left a scar in the tarmac. When she got closer, Annika saw that the truck had only been stopped from continuing on down the embankment by the first post of the roadside barrier. But that post had also demolished the truck's windscreen pillar, and the corrugated metal attached to it had all but decapitated Sámal Mohr, whose sideways face looked out at Annika through the spiderwebbed glass with a strange expression of calm.

When Heri Kalsø and Hans David Juul arrived less than three minutes later, Heri took one look at the cab of the truck and Annika's ashen face and then told her to go and sit in the patrol car and have a smoke: he and Hans David would deal with the traffic and the few onlookers who'd emerged from their houses.

Annika protested, but Heri told her "Go," so she went. She was finishing the cigarette as the ambulance sped past, weaving around the queuing cars, heading for Hósvík.

20

I DIDN'T REMEMBER ANYTHING MUCH ABOUT THE TWELVE hours after I came round. Apparently that's not unusual following a concussion.

I didn't remember agreeing that I should stay in Fríða's guest house either, but the following morning – Tuesday – that's where I was. Someone had collected my stuff from the hotel but when I pointed out that I'd hadn't checked out or paid for the room Fríða's response was a shrug: it was no problem. I could do all that when I was ready. The hotel staff knew the circumstances and they were cool about it. They knew more than I did for a while.

I spent the day balancing the pains in my ribs, shoulder and head with painkillers and doing a passable impression of Elizabeth Barrett Browning on the sofa. There was no word from Hentze, but I hadn't necessarily expected any. Apparently I'd talked to him while I was in the emergency department, but that was also something I'd failed to retain.

Fríða was solicitous without being fussy and allowed me one beer with dinner. Afterwards she fielded a phone call from Ketty, for which I was grateful. I didn't bother to ask how, six hundred miles away, Ketty had found out what had happened, but Fríða's reassurances to her were enough to give me some breathing space before I'd have to make them myself. By then the beer had kicked in on top of the painkillers and I took myself to bed.

"Can you tell me the nature of your relationship with Sámal Mohr?" Hentze said.

"I don't think I would say it was a relationship. I employed his father's firm to do some work on a house in Kvívík for my ex-wife. Sámal worked there."

Kristian Ravnsfjall was resting his forearms lightly on the table, fingers loosely knitted together. Beside him his lawyer was holding a pen ready to make notes but so far had not done so.

"So your contact with him was only to do with matters relating to the building work?"

"Yes, of course."

"And Tummas Gramm?" Hentze asked.

"The same. He worked with Sámal Mohr."

"I see." Hentze seemed to accept that. "Did you ever meet them socially, for a drink perhaps?"

"No, only at the house."

"Very well." Hentze shifted. "I believe you have said that over the last two weeks you have received blackmail demands. Is that true?"

"Yes."

"Could you tell me about it?"

Kristian Ravnsfjall looked to his lawyer, who now put down his pen and reached into a leather portfolio.

"*Harra* Ravnsfjall has a prepared statement he would like me to read with regard to that matter," the lawyer said. "With your agreement."

Hjalti Hentze drew a breath and sat back in his chair. "Sure. Go ahead."

Hentze turned up mid-morning on Wednesday with the look of a man who hadn't had enough coffee.

"Fríða says you are a good patient," he said, sounding vaguely disbelieving.

"You've been talking about me?"

"Sure. I asked her if I could come and see you. Yesterday she said no."

"Just as well. Yesterday I looked like *skít*."

He laughed. "You're learning Faroese?"

"Only the essential swear words."

"Who from?"

"Not Fríða. – Do you want coffee?"

Stupid question.

Once we were fixed with coffee we sat in the two wicker chairs by the French windows looking out over the deck.

"Anything you told me after I was knocked out on Monday I don't remember," I said. "Fríða said you were at the hospital, though."

"Yeh – until they knew you were okay."

In the circumstances I thought "okay" was a relative term, but it seemed churlish to say so. "*Takk fyri*," I said.

He shrugged it off. "You know what happened to Sámal Mohr?"

"Yeah. He crashed the truck?"

He nodded. "No one else was hurt. It could have been worse."

"Not for him."

"No."

For a few minutes he outlined what had happened afterwards. There was nothing I wouldn't have expected: interviews, searches, the tying together of timelines and evidence trails.

"So what's that leave?" I asked in the end. "Anything?"

"For the case? A lot of reports, but there is no doubt that Sámal Mohr was the third man. His print matches with the one at the boathouse, also other forensic traces, Sophie Krogh thinks. And in his house there was a shotgun with the right ammunition to have shot Nóa Lisberg."

"How is he – Nóa?"

"Still alive, but in a coma. It may be for good."

He clearly found it an unsatisfactory outcome but after a moment he put it aside. "Kristian Ravnsfjall has made a statement to us with his lawyer. He says that he received a blackmail attempt regarding confidential business matters he didn't wish to become public. He told his father about it and then things happened as we know."

I nodded. "Yeah, well, he had to say something."

"Yeh." Hentze sipped his coffee.

"You didn't find any way to connect him to Tummas Gramm or Sámal Mohr that couldn't be explained as related to the work on Anni's house?"

"No."

He paused to reflect on that and I waited for what I thought would come next. In the end he said, "The thing I cannot decide is whether Kristian Ravnsfjall was involved in the murder of Tummas Gramm and the shooting of Nóa Lisberg."

It had been occupying my thoughts as well, and I'd had plenty of time.

I said, "For what it's worth, I think Sámal shot Nóa out of self-preservation. Most likely Nóa had seen him kill Tummas, so Nóa had to be silenced."

Hentze didn't give much away, but I felt he was inclined to agree. "And Tummas?" he asked.

"You want me to play devil's advocate again?"

"I think you are good at it."

I didn't know how to take that so I let it go. I thought for a moment.

"It comes down to motivation, doesn't it?" I said in the end. "Sámal had a motive to kill Tummas because of what they'd done – or thought they'd done – to Signar. As long as no one could connect them to Signar they were safe. But if Sámal thought Tummas might blow the whole thing by seeking medical attention for the shotgun wound…"

"So you think Kristian has no part in this?"

"You mean would he ask Sámal Mohr to kill Tummas? Is that the question?"

Hentze nodded. "I think so."

"Then I'd say no. Kristian had nothing to gain from soliciting Tummas's death. Signar had had a stroke so there was no proof of anything Tummas and Sámal might say if they were caught. They might have *claimed* that Kristian had set it up, but he's a reputable businessman from a well-known family and they're two thugs with criminal records. It would be their word against his."

"This is what you called *plausible deniability* the other day." He clearly didn't like the phrase, or maybe just what it implied.

I nodded. "Even if a jury *did* believe that Kristian organised a fake blackmailing, what's the very worst he might face? A charge of fraud or deception? That's nothing compared with conspiracy to murder, which is what he'd be looking at if he told Sámal to kill Tummas. No, I can't see him taking the risk."

"As long as he had time to consider it all so carefully," Hentze said.

"He had long enough," I said flatly.

I shifted, put my coffee aside.

"I started off liking Kristian because he's smart and direct," I said. "Now I think he's probably manipulative and self-centred as well. But I don't think he's a murderer, directly or indirectly. That's just my opinion, though. What do other people think?"

"I still have to talk to the prosecutor, but I think it is over," Hentze said, matching my tone. "I expect so."

"And his relationship with Elin?"

"If no one will admit that it happened…" he said flatly, not happy. "You know the way. We must be realistic."

"I don't know; it never helped me."

He gave a dry laugh, but it seemed to be enough to put the subject away.

"So, Ári Niclasen must be pleased it's all wrapped up," I said then, just to see what that brought.

Despite everything else Hentze wasn't going to rise to that, though.

"Have you heard from your own boss?" he asked instead.

I had: another email – one I'd actually read this time – but I didn't feel like getting into that either, so I shook my head. "He can wait till I get back."

"Do you know when that will be?"

"Not yet. Fríða doesn't seem to be in any hurry to kick me out, so …" I shrugged.

"Ah. Okay."

He nodded and seemed to consider what he wanted to say next. "And your mother? Have you discovered what you wanted to know?"

That was the other thing I'd been brooding on a little over the past couple of days: how much more I could or should push it. Whether I should just box it up again, pack it away. It remained undecided, though.

"Not really," I said. "Not all of it, anyway."

"But you think there is more?"

"I don't know," I said, which was the truth. "It feels like there should be, but…" I shrugged. "Maybe I'm just making up stories because I don't have a theory, you know?"

He nodded, but didn't seem convinced. "Perhaps sometimes you need not to be so strict with a rule. Is there anything I can do?"

"No, I don't think so, but *takk*."

"Okay. Well… I should go back to the reports now I see you're okay."

We stood up and I walked him to the door. He held out his hand – not the natural thing for the Faroese to do, I'd learned by now. I shook it.

"Call me for a beer before you leave, yeh?"

I said I would.

I was dozing on the sofa when Fríða got back, mid-afternoon. She was still wearing her coat and when I'd come round enough and got myself upright she said it was good weather for a walk.

It was by then: a watery but persistent sunshine pearling the cloud cover; a chilly but inoffensive breeze. She helped me get my coat over my stiff arm and I was manly enough not to grunt too much at the effort.

We walked down a stone ramp to the black-sanded beach and then across it. A stroll. I told her that Hentze had paid a visit and asked how much she knew about the case. Enough, she said, which I took as both a statement of fact and an indication that she didn't want to know more.

"Are you okay about it?" she asked.

"I think so. Why wouldn't I be?"

She took a moment to consider an answer, but then simply said, "Okay."

A while later we stopped walking where a stream cut the sand. Fríða turned into the wind to push a strand of hair back from her face and tuck it behind her ear. When she saw me watching she made a faint smile, then let it wane naturally.

"I've found Lýdia's medical records," she said then. "Usually files are destroyed a few years after a person dies, but because the death wasn't registered here they are still in the system. Do you still want to see them?"

I thought about it, wondered if the black dog was around.

"Have you read them?" I asked.

"*Nei.*"

I still didn't know, but she didn't push me for an answer. Instead she moved closer, rested a hand in the crook of my arm – the good one – and then we started back across the black sand.

AUTHOR'S NOTE

BY AND LARGE THE GEOGRAPHY OF THE FAROES IS AS IT IS described in the book. However, I have used some licence with the descriptions of individual locations and buildings, some of which are transposed from other places.

The Faroe Islands are a small, close-knit community so I would like to emphasise that this is a work of fiction and that none of the characters or incidents portrayed here are based on real people or events.

ACKNOWLEDGEMENTS

I WOULD LIKE TO THANK DR NICK LEATHER FOR HIS MEDICAL advice while I was writing this book: needless to say, the responsibility for any factual errors is mine.

In the Faroe Islands a great many people contributed to my understanding of Faroese life and amongst these I must thank Svend Aage Ellefsen and Jens Tummas Næss, as well as Sóleyg and Hjalti for tending bar.

I am particularly indebted to the officers and staff of the Faroe Islands Police Department for their assistance, especially Per Skov Christensen, Jóannes Østerø, Katrin Poulsen and Hildur Hentze Sørensen. Above all, however, I must express my deep gratitude to Jens Jensen for his hospitality and unstintingly generous advice, not just on police matters, but on all aspects of Faroese life. His help has been invaluable.

ABOUT THE AUTHOR

CHRIS OULD IS A BAFTA AWARD-WINNING SCREENWRITER who has worked on many TV shows including *The Bill*, *Soldier Soldier*, *Casualty* and *Hornblower*. Chris has previously published two adult novels, and two Young Adult crime novels. He lives in Dorset.

THE KILLING BAY

A FAROES NOVEL

CHRIS OULD

When a group of international activists arrive on the Faroe Islands, intent on stopping the traditional whale hunts, tensions between islanders and protestors run high. And when a woman is found murdered only hours after a violent confrontation at a whale drive, the circumstances seem purposely designed to create even more animosity between the two sides. For Faroese detective Hjalti Hentze and DI Jan Reyna, it becomes increasingly clear that the murder has other, more sinister aspects to it. Knowing evidence is being hidden from them and faced with deception on all sides, neither Reyna or Hentze know who to trust, or how far some people might go to defend their beliefs.

PRAISE FOR THE AUTHOR

"Unmissable and thrilling fiction."
Lancashire Evening Post

TITANBOOKS.COM

THE FIRE PIT

A FAROES NOVEL

CHRIS OULD

When long-buried skeletal remains are unearthed at an
isolated farm on the island of Borðoy, Hjalti Hentze is charged
with investigating the death. But as Hentze's investigation
turns to the commune that occupied the farm in the 1970s,
Jan Reyna discovers a connection to the death of his mother
and to long-repressed memories from his childhood.
Increasingly driven to exorcise his personal demons, Reyna
pursues an ever-darker conspiracy of murder and abuse
spanning four decades, from the Faroes to Denmark and
back. However, as Hentze puts the same pieces together, he
has a growing realisation that Reyna may be about to follow
a course of action from which there can be no return.

PRAISE FOR THE AUTHOR
"Grittily realistic crime."
Independent

AVAILABLE FEBRUARY 2018

For more fantastic fiction, author events,
competitions, limited editions and more

VISIT OUR WEBSITE
titanbooks.com

LIKE US ON FACEBOOK
facebook.com/titanbooks

FOLLOW US ON TWITTER
@TitanBooks

EMAIL US
readerfeedback@titanemail.com